innocent

erin kinsley

HEADLINE

First published in 2020 by
HEADLINE PUBLISHING GROUP

1

Cataloguing in Publication Data is available from the British Library

ISBN 978 1 4722 7428 1

Typeset in Adobe Garamond by CC Book Production

Printed and bound in Great Britain by Clays Lrd, Elcograf S.p.A.

Headline's policy is to use papers that are natural, renewable and
recyclable products and made from wood grown in well-managed forests
and other controlled sources. The logging and manufacturing processes
are expected to conform to the environmental regulations
of the country of origin.

HEADLINE PUBLISHING GROUP
An Hachette UK Company
Carmelite House
50 Victoria Embankment
London EC4Y 0DZ

www.headline.co.uk
www.hachette.co.uk

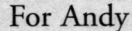

For Andy

'Life changes fast. Life changes in the instant. You sit down to dinner and life as you know it ends.'

Joan Didion, *The Year of Magical Thinking*

ONE

First times you can easily recall. First date, first kiss. First day at the job, your child's first birthday. Your first view of the house you fell in love with, the first time you held the keys to your own car.

But last times come and go, and you never notice. The last time you held his hand, the last time you saw her smile: you overlooked those moments, and they slipped by unremarked. Only in hindsight can you see them for what they were.

That hasty parting from an old friend, the visit to your mum that you cut short: if you realised they might be endings, mightn't you stay a little longer, take the time to say a heartfelt goodbye?

Be mindful of such moments with your loved ones. One of them, one day, will be the last.

Outside the window, a white butterfly settles on a tendril of spreading ivy.

Izzy doesn't see it. In front of the mirror, she's busy putting the final pins into her hair, adding a touch of pencil to her brows and pouting to slick soft pink on her lips. As she sprays

1

eau de parfum at her throat, Tristan walks up behind her in the glass.

He's so handsome in his suit.

'I brought you something.' He lays a few sprigs of forget-me-not on the dressing table, and she smiles her thanks.

'They're so pretty.'

He bends down and kisses the nape of her neck, exposed now her hair's in a chignon. At the brush of his lips, she shivers, and with a tantalising suggestion of wickedness, in the mirror his eyes meet hers.

'You look fabulous,' he murmurs, 'and you smell divine.' Hand beneath her chin, he tilts her head back and kisses her mouth. 'I love you so much, beautiful wife.'

Pouting, she picks up the lipstick. 'You kissed it all away.'

With the backs of his fingers he strokes her shoulder, naked below the strap of her chiffon dress, and talks into her ear. 'Let me do it again. Let's forget the wedding and stay here.'

She covers his hand with hers. 'We have to go. Flora's so excited. And what would people say?'

'Who cares what people say?'

'I'll make it up to you when we get home.'

'Now that I shall look forward to.'

He watches her slip on kitten heels and drop the lipstick in her clutch bag. 'Ready, Mrs Hart?'

In the mirror, she makes a final check, adjusting a hair-pin where a fair strand has broken loose from the chignon.

'Ready,' says Izzy, and as they leave the bedroom he slides his arm around her waist.

TWO

Absolute darling, perfect angel.

Flora, the youngest bridesmaid, runs gleefully across the lawns, trailing a pink balloon on a silk ribbon, not suspecting her pursuer can catch her whenever he wants. He's letting her believe she can win, but when she veers towards the high box hedge and the path leading to the swimming pool, he makes his move.

Three long strides, and the game's over. Tristan sweeps his giggling daughter up over his head, laughing as he spins her round in her taffeta dress, and carries her back to the marquee, where Izzy's watching, smiling, from their table.

Among the wedding guests, someone else is watching, thinking what a pretty picture father and daughter make.

Some people are just born lucky. Whether they deserve it, or whether they don't.

Little devil, wayward monster.

The circlet of blush rosebuds pinned over Flora's curls has come askew, and her satin slippers are ruined by grass stains. Aidan remembers how Gemma was at that age, mucky-faced

3

and grubby-kneed one minute, bubble-bath sweet the next. Those young years held Aidan's happiest summers: paddling pools and picnics, sandcastles and candyfloss, and her fast asleep on his shoulder as he carried her home from some windswept beach. Sometimes it feels like only yesterday, yet he can see her over there now, standing with her friends, fourteen going on twenty-five.

She's already a young woman. Where does the time go?

One of the girls Gemma's with spots Tristan coming their way and beckons him over, and Tristan appears happy to say hello. The girls try and make a fuss of Flora, but she's feeling shy and hides her face on her father's shoulder.

At the next table, Aidan notices big, bluff David Garner is watching too, stroking the side of his pint glass as his eyes run over the girls in turn. Dave's a local builder, with a reputation for spending as much time in bed with his clients' wives as he does working on their extensions, and he's currently involved – so Aidan's heard – with a part-time assistant at the high street pharmacy. Less than two months ago, he got punched in the mouth, explaining the loss of two teeth to his wife Karen with some cock-and-bull story about a fall from a ladder. For a builder, Dave's fallen off a lot of ladders in his time.

The girls gathered round Tristan laugh at something he's said. Gemma moves behind his back and puts her face up to Flora's, but whatever she says then makes Flora scowl. Tristan's apologising for his anti-social daughter, but the girls don't seem to mind. As he leaves them he encourages her to wave, but Flora doesn't comply.

Her cheeks are flushed from running in the heat. Yesterday was the hottest June day on record, and it's barely any cooler today. With the sides of the marquee pinned up to encourage a through-draught, the natural scents of the formal garden – lavender, roses and mown grass – waft in to compete with Jo Malone and Marc Jacobs, the yeastiness of barrelled beer and, increasingly, sweat.

The wedding's theme is swans, and every place setting has a glass swan filled with silvered dragées; the marquee roof is draped with garlands of white feathers, and alongside the cake – five tiers of sugarcraft, decorated with hearts formed from curved swans' necks – is a swan carved in ice, melting so fast in the heat, it will soon have to be wheeled away.

Tristan retakes his seat beside Izzy, lifting Flora on to his lap.

'Bit of a mad risk, ordering ice-sculpture in June,' he says. 'And what's with all the swans anyway?'

Flora leans across to Izzy, and Izzy reaches out to take her, not troubled by the dusty smears the soles of Flora's slippers leave on her dress. Izzy has a traffic-stopping beauty, a pale, willowy loveliness made unfashionable by the current fake-tanned, tattoo-browed ideals of reality TV. Compared to them, Izzy seems from another time, her looks as classically English as a Gainsborough portrait. Alongside Tristan in his vintage-cut linen suit and collarless shirt, with his blond hair falling across one eye, they resemble throwbacks to Sterndale Hall's heyday, before a receding financial tide left its titled owners high and dry and made conversion to a country house hotel the only possible alternative to slow decay and ruin.

As Izzy leans forward to take Flora, a curve of breast shows at the neck of her dress, and Aidan takes a sharp breath. He knows his lust for Izzy is predictable and clichéd, and he glances at Laura, afraid she might have noticed, but he's no cause for concern. Laura's happily chatting to Tristan, who's always fun to talk to with his anecdotes and wit.

Anyway, Aidan's very happy with Laura and isn't seriously looking to stray. She's attractive too, though in a different way, become what his mother would have called bonny since having two kids. Her fitted dress makes the most of her figure, and with her hair professionally done and careful make-up, he knows there are men in Sterndale who'd be keen to know her much better, given an opportunity. And if they were ever – God forbid – not together, Aidan would attract similar female attention. Even after his accident he's in good shape, but he'd need more than admirable biceps to compete with Tris. Tris is a celebrity, who gilds an occasion just by being there. If Tris snapped his fingers, women would be lining up, but none of them would hold a candle to Izzy.

Flora is reaching for a glass swan, or at least for the shiny sweets held in its back. Izzy grasps her hand and tells her no, which Flora accepts without argument. Putting her thumb in her mouth, she rests her head on Izzy's breast and closes her eyes.

'She's tired,' says Tristan, touching Flora's cheek. 'Aren't you, princess? I'll give Bridget a call in a few minutes and ask her to come and fetch her. Enough excitement for one day.'

'Swans are a symbol of fidelity,' says Izzy, beginning to unpin the rosebud circlet from Flora's hair. 'They mate for life, so I think they're a great choice for a wedding. And they're sacred to Aphrodite, Greek goddess of love and passion.'

'There you are, ladies and gentlemen,' says Tristan. 'That's the kind of useful knowledge you get from an expensive education.'

'I got a scholarship, actually,' objects Izzy.

'So much the cleverer, then,' says Tristan, as if he doesn't already know. 'An expensive education for free. Now, there are too many empty glasses on this table, and I believe it's my round. More bubbles, ladies? Aidan, mate, are you ready for another pint?'

Making his way towards the bar, Tristan knows that – as always – he is noticed. Sometimes, when he's being the star, it's the best feeling, an adrenaline high like no other.

But today he's trying to blend in. A ripple follows him, regardless – whispers and nudges – and the energy of people's interest creates an intangible shimmer, the aura of there being Someone in the room. There's a fine balance to be maintained between keeping his head down and attracting bad press if he offends anyone, so he gives the odd smile to be sure he's not coming over as arrogant or rude.

He's closing in on the bar when a young man stands up and blocks his way – gym-fit with a short, half-shaved haircut, looking uncomfortable in a fashionably over-tight suit. Holding out his hand to be shaken, plainly he's determined to have a word.

The people sharing his table have fallen silent.

Tristan has a practised strategy for these moments. He takes the offered hand, and the plan is that as he says, *Hello, nice to see you, are you having a good time?* a little backwards pressure from the forearm will knock the guy off-balance and out of his way, allowing him to escape without giving offence.

But the young man doesn't respond to the backwards pressure. Instead, he holds his ground, and keeps Tristan's hand in his.

7

'Tristan, mate,' he says.

'Good to see you,' says Tristan, trying to pull back his hand.

The young man's face is red with embarrassment, but at least he doesn't seem drunk.

'Sorry to bother you, but could I ask a favour?'

Favours Tristan is also prepared for, with a wad of cards with his agent's contact details always in his pocket.

'You can ask.'

More and more people are watching, but he's perfectly used to that; in Sterndale people frequently stand and stare at him, whether he's buying olives in the Italian deli or plant pots in Abbot's Hardware.

Finally, his hand is released.

'I'm on leave from the Duke of Lancaster's Regiment, based in Iraq,' says the young man. 'It gets tough out there some-times, and I was thinking it would be a real boost for the lads if you'd send them a video message. Just a hello, like. Anything really, just a few words.'

Do we still have soldiers in Iraq? Tristan doesn't know if we do or if we don't, but the young man seems in real earnest, and how can this be anything but a good thing?

'What's your name?'

'Simon, Simon Fisher. Lance Corporal.'

'Well, Corporal, where's your phone?' The soldier grins, and one of his companions hurries to pass over a mobile. As more and more guests wonder what's going on, an audible murmur is building across the marquee. 'You got any pictures of these guys?'

The soldier scrolls through his phone and shows Tristan a series of photos: groups of sunburnt men in desert fatigues and combat boots, posing in arid landscapes. Few of them are smiling. Some of them are close to Tristan's apparent age, late thirties or early forties, but their faces are more careworn, more adult than his own. Others are barely more than boys, but from the obvious juniors to the most senior their eyes are old, reflecting what they've seen that can't be unseen and their bafflement at life's cruelties, their optimism for the future having taken a fatal hit.

Tristan feels the awkwardness of inadequacy. While he has his enviable job and his beautiful wife and daughter, other people's children are out there facing landmines and hostile gunfire, taking the daily risk of being shot dead, blown up or maimed.

'That's my mate Steve,' says the soldier, pointing to one of the younger men. 'He's not with us any more. He lost a leg a few weeks ago.'

'So where is he now?'

'In hospital in Birmingham.'

Tristan's surprised to feel a tug of heartache. Since Flora was born, he's become an emotional weakling.

'I'm sorry to hear that. Send him my best wishes, won't you?'

He puts his arm around the soldier's shoulders, and the soldier holds up his phone.

'Let's do this,' says Tristan. 'Ready? Press that button, buddy.'

Tristan looks into the lens, and ad libs.

'Greetings to all of our friends out there in the Duke of Lancaster's Regiment. This is Tristan Hart here with your very own Lance Corporal Simon Fisher – give 'em a wave, Corporal – and we're here to let you know that all your families and friends are thinking of you, that they love and miss you very much, and that they can't wait to have you home. Meantime, keep your peckers up, guys – and girls. You're doing a great job most of us don't have the balls for, so stay strong, and most of all stay safe. This is Tristan Hart, over and out.'

The red light goes off, and there's low-key applause from around the marquee.

'That's brilliant,' says the soldier, grinning. 'Thanks so much.'

'It's a privilege,' says Tristan. 'I really mean that. And I meant what I said, you guys stay safe. You know what, Simon, I'm just on my way to the bar. Come on, let me buy you a drink.'

The delighted soldier follows him, turning back to give his mates an ebullient double thumbs up. His companions burst into excited chatter.

'I can't believe it,' the soldier's girlfriend is saying. 'Isn't he just the loveliest man? Just like he is on TV.'

Tristan finds a gap in the crush, and leans forward on the counter to try and get a bartender's attention. Down the bar, he hears the pop of a champagne cork, and the excited chatter of women ready to have fun.

'Simon, what are you having?'

The soldier is still beaming at his good fortune. 'Pint of Gold, please, Tristan.'

The customer to Tristan's left picks up his tray of drinks and moves away. Now Tristan can see he's standing next to Dave Garner.

Tristan takes one step to his left so no one can stand between them. 'All right there, Dave?'

Garner's focus is on the blonde barmaid. When he hears his name, he looks round and acknowledges Tristan with a nod.

'Listen, Dave.' Tristan matches Garner's pose, with both forearms on the bar. 'I'm glad I bumped into you. Your brother's still on the town council, isn't he?'

Garner turns to look at him. His breath is unpleasantly beery. 'Last I heard.'

The barmaid approaches and looks from one man to the other, not knowing who to serve first. When she recognises Tristan, she flushes in delighted discomposure and asks what she can get him.

Garner scowls.

'I think this gentleman was here before me,' says Tristan, and the barmaid looks indifferently at Garner, who orders a pint of IPA and an Aperol spritz.

As the barmaid turns away, Tristan says, 'The thing is, you guys might be able to help with a programme we're thinking of making.'

Garner shifts his position so he's looking straight at Tristan. Two of his front teeth are noticeably whiter than the rest. 'Oh yeah? What's that, then?'

'Didn't your company get involved last year in the refurb of the council chambers?'

'We did that, yeah. What about it?'

'And those repairs to the leisure centre roof, aren't you doing those as well?'

'Yes. A few more days and my boys will be done there.'

'And the library extension, when was that, two years ago, three?'

Garner's eyes narrow. 'What's this about?'

The barmaid brings his drinks. Garner pulls a roll of bank-notes from his trouser pocket and hands one over, gesturing to her to keep the change.

While she's at the till, Tristan says, 'A little bird told me your brother was active in pushing those council contracts in your direction. Pulling a few strings, you might say. That's a criminal offence, in public office. He could go to jail for that, if it turned out to be true.'

The barmaid returns, with a big smile for Tristan. Garner picks up his drinks, but he doesn't move away.

'What can I get you?' asks the barmaid.

'I've a long list.' Tristan turns round and touches the soldier on the shoulder. 'We'll start with a pint of Gold for my friend here, and a pint of Champion, please, my love.'

Pink-cheeked, the barmaid heads for the pumps.

'My viewers are interested in stories like that,' Tristan says to Garner. 'They're fed up with the creeping sickness of corruption in everyday life. They want to get back to the days when the people who are supposed to work for us, do work for us, and not for themselves. You understand what I'm saying?'

'Fuck you,' says Garner, as he walks away.

'Better mend your ways, or we'll be coming for you, Dave,' Tristan calls to his retreating back.

THREE

A blob of chocolate mousse Laura dropped during the meal has left a greasy mark. The designer label at the back of the neck was one of the reasons she chose the dress, and while she can't imagine she paid even a quarter of the original price tag, she still spent significantly more than she would ever normally consider for a dress, so it will be worth the cost of dry cleaning. For now, she has an easy solution to cover the mark with a quick switch of her brooch – a genuine piece of sixties vintage, once her mother's, whose pink glass gems are a perfect match for the fabric's showy peonies.

Laura sees no reason to worry about leaving Aidan talking to Izzy. Izzy has eyes only for Tris, and if she did ever think of straying, Laura imagines she'd choose an artist or a writer or an actor, not – poor Aidan – an ex-copper and committed sports fan whose favourite topic is how United performed in their last game.

As Laura reaches the powder room, she hears voices, and before she touches the door, it swings open.

Gemma was laughing at something her friend Hannah was saying, but seeing her mother, her laughter stops.

'Hi, sweetie! Are you girls having fun?'

There's a moment of silence, where Laura reflects that, for God's sake, the question wasn't difficult.

'Yes, thanks, Mum,' says Gemma, eventually.

'I think the dancing will be starting soon,' says Laura. 'I see Darren's here, Gemma. Might be your chance to kiss and make up.'

'For God's sake, Mum,' says Gemma, pushing past. 'You are *so* embarrassing! I've told you a million times, I don't even *like* him any more.'

As she goes by, Hannah raises her eyebrows in sympathy for Laura.

'Darren's going out with Rosie Stainforth,' she says. 'Anyway, Gemma says she likes someone else now.'

'Oh? Who?'

Hannah shrugs. 'I asked her but she won't say.'

'Well, it's news to me,' says Laura. 'By the way, I hope you two aren't drinking.'

Hannah shakes her head.

'Only Coke,' she says as she follows Gemma, but there's something about the careful way she's walking in her absurd heels which makes Laura doubt she's telling the truth.

In front of the powder room mirror, Laura switches the brooch from left side to right. It's hard to imagine her mother ever wearing such a frivolous thing; she never seemed the type for pink sparkles, and as she grew older, the only items of jewellery she wore were her wedding and engagement rings and the string of fresh-water pearls she kept for special occasions. But people change. Tell Gemma and Josh that their mum used to wear cowboy boots and bubble skirts, and they'd laugh in your face.

Thinking she'll touch up her lipstick, she searches for the gold case in her handbag. A toilet flushes in a cubicle behind her, the door opens, and in the mirror Laura sees a tall, thin woman, too old for the short, crushed-velvet dress she's wearing. Phyllida Gaze.

'Hi, Philly.'

Philly takes a few moments to focus, betraying the amount she's had to drink.

'Is that you, Laura? I didn't recognise you, all gussied up. Oh. You're wearing my dress.'

Laura glances down at her front, and a hot blush spreads across her face.

'Bang to rights,' she says. 'A second-hand bargain. Don't tell anyone.'

Philly crosses to the basins and begins to wash her hands.

'I wouldn't dream of it, darling. Between you and me, mine came from the same place.' Laura doubts Philly's telling the truth; she and Jerry are loaded, and Philly's always off to London for a spot of retail therapy, as she calls it. But bless her for trying to make Laura feel better. 'And I have to say it looks a million times better on you. You've got those fabulous boobs to show it off. It hung like a sack on old ironing-board me. Jerry's always admiring your boobs. If he could ever be bothered to get off his arse for a bit of extra-marital, you'd be his first port of call.'

Laura smiles.

'Good to know. I think Aidan's got a soft spot for Izzy.'

Philly waves a dismissive hand before presenting it to the hot air of the dryer.

'If he's not hiding it, then have no worries. Can I borrow a spot of lippy, by the way? Gorgeous colour, thanks. Anything they're doing in public has no serious intent. It's when they go underground you need to worry. Those deep, dark passions you know nothing about, that's where the danger lies. Sex has a lot to answer for in life. People say follow the money, but I say sex trumps money every time. Speaking of money, this little do will be costing Dennis an arm and a leg, but doesn't Suzie look fabulous in that gown? Makes me wish Jerry and I had had a proper wedding, instead of a registry office and fish and chips on Brighton beach. Didn't do us any harm in the long run, though – thirty-two years we've put up with each other. Maybe when it's Gemma's turn, you'd be better pushing her in the cheap-and-cheerful direction, save the money for a down payment on a starter home. Is she still seeing that Ferris boy, by the way, what's his name, Derren?'

'Darren. That seems to be well and truly over. I think she's taken it hard, to be honest.'

'Plenty more fish in the sea, though. I'm sure she's beating them off with a stick.'

More kindness from Philly. Gemma's still at the ugly duckling stage, and knowledge of the fact cripples her fledgling confidence.

'According to Hannah, Gemma's got a new one she's keeping under wraps.'

Philly pats Laura on the shoulder.

'Mums are always the last to know. If I were you, I'd grab a great big shovel and start digging him out. Young girls and secret boyfriends never end well. Anyway, I'm so glad to see that gorgeous dress found a good home. Time for another drink, I think, don't you?'

FOUR

When the cake's been cut, the bride and groom take the floor for their first dance, gazing into each other's eyes as they sway to Brad Paisley's *Then*. Ed and Suzie grew up at opposite ends of town, were a year apart at school, first held hands at the church hall youth club. When Suzie went away to university, Ed stuck with his electrician's apprenticeship, never looking at another girl, waiting for Suzie to come home, which she did after only a year away from him and Sterndale. They're true soulmates, faithful as swans. Izzy reaches under the table and squeezes Tristan's hand.

As the track comes to its end the DJ ups the tempo, and the dance floor starts to fill.

Flora is fast asleep on Izzy's chest.

'Bedtime,' says Tristan. 'Bridget will be here by now. Why don't you girls help get the party started?' Tenderly, he picks up his daughter, and holding her against his shoulder, carries her from the marquee.

With its grand Regency façade and Palladian columns, Sterndale Hall's architecture is too staid and uptight for Tristan's taste. His preference is for extravagant Victorian

Gothic, towers, turrets and arches, yet on this glorious summer's day, he'll admit the hall makes a fabulous backdrop for a flamboyant occasion. His wedding to Izzy was a small affair, trying to duck the press attention which Izzy's never welcomed. Now he's thinking it might be fun to hire this place and do it again much bigger and better, call it a renewal of vows. When his work commitments let up in the new year, he'll talk to her about it.

As distance grows between him and the marquee, the melody of the dance music fades, so only the pulsing club beat is audible, incongruous in the silent formal garden. The heat is finally losing its grip on the day, reduced to that delectable blood-heat warmth of Mediterranean August evenings. Midsummer is next week, so dusk is still an hour away, but the light is beginning to change. At intervals, the box hedge has been cut away into alcoves where marble nymphs stand on lichened plinths, their blank faces hidden in shadows. A blackbird flies up from a nearby tree, chattering its annoyance at being disturbed, and startled, Tristan pauses. Were those footsteps behind him on the gravel? When he turns around to see, no one is there.

Flora's growing impossibly heavy, and he's wishing he'd listened to Izzy when she suggested bringing a buggy. By the hotel's rear entrance, three men in morning coats – one of them the father of the bride – are smoking cigars and drinking whisky from crystal tumblers. Tristan has no appetite for either smoking or Scotch, so to avoid an invitation he'll have to decline, instead of going the quickest way to the car park – through the rear entrance, across the lobby and out of the main doors – he follows a path around the hotel side.

He finds himself in a gloomy shrubbery overcrowded with rhododendrons, where the air is clammily cool. The walls on this side of the building have the acid-green tint which comes from never seeing sunlight, but after the heat the dankness is welcome, and he pauses again to rest, listening for any repetition of the footsteps he thought he heard in the gardens. All he hears is the distant beat of music and the clatter of dishes from the kitchens.

He goes on, passing the foot of a rusting fire escape, looking in the windows of an empty ballroom where the unused chairs and tables are stacked away and the chandeliers are covered in dust-sheets.

The car park, when he reaches it, is full. Bridget has parked the tiny Fiat 500 – a car Izzy insisted they offer as part of the nanny's benefits, because it's unreasonable to expect someone to work unsociable hours at Foxcote Lodge without transport – in front of his Range Rover. She's sitting in the driver's seat, tapping the steering wheel to music only she can hear, but as he emerges from the shrubbery, she senses movement, glances in his direction and removes her earphones.

Bridget gets out of the car, smiling when she sees Flora blinking sleepily in her special dress and ruined slippers. Bridget's dressed as always in baggy black, making no concessions to the heat or the occasion, and brushes her dark hair off her face, still winter-pale at midsummer. Tristan's often wondered why she doesn't make more effort, leave the Goth look she's too old for behind, put on a dress, paint her nails red or pink or even yellow instead of that Bride of Dracula purple. And if she lost a couple of stone, she'd be a great-looking girl.

19

'Look who's here,' says Tristan to Flora. 'Someone's come to take you home.'

'Hey, poppet,' Bridget says quietly, holding out her arms to take the child, who goes to her willingly. 'She's exhausted.' Bridget's accent is southern Irish, though she was born in Liverpool, and she insists there's plenty of Scouse in there, if you know what you're listening for.

'Why don't you take the Range Rover?' suggests Tristan, handing her the fob. 'Her car seat's already in there.'

Eyebrows raised, Bridget gives him the keys to the Fiat. 'Wow. What did I do to deserve this?'

'I promise we won't be late. I know it's your day off tomorrow.'

'You go and have yourselves a good time, and don't worry about us,' says Bridget. 'We'll be just fine by our ownsomes, won't we, poppet?'

He watches her drive away, then decides while he's close by, he might as well pay a call to the gents.

As he walks down the aisle between the parked cars, a stone bench comes into sight, placed to give a view of the parkland which fronts the hotel. Sitting on the bench is a man, stout and balding, no suit jacket, his tie stuffed in his trouser pocket. Somehow, he looks familiar.

'Hello, Tris. Long time no see.'

Tristan recognises the voice before the face. The guy's put on a load of weight.

'Hello, Murray. What the hell are you doing here?'

Murray stands up and walks forward, proffering his hand, and Tristan looks at it, wondering how much offence he'll give if he doesn't take it. In the end, he decides he doesn't need the aggravation, and gives it a brief, loose shake.

'I knew it was you, soon as I saw you,' says Murray. 'I was watching you playing with that little girl. She your daughter, is she? And haven't you gone up in the world? We see you on the telly, from time to time. What's that programme you're doing now, *Take Hart*? Great title. You come up with that one, did you? Is that why you chose that name, so you could use all those lousy puns? *Take Hart*, *Hart of the Matter* – bit cheesy, aren't they?'

'It's just a stage name, Murray. That's what people in my line of work do, they use stage names.'

'Well, your real name wouldn't work half as well, would it? Though some people might say it's a much better fit.'

'Nice seeing you. Give my regards to Fiona.'

Tristan's ready to walk away, but Murray steps forward to block him.

'Give them to her yourself. She's over there, in the marquee. It's thanks to her we got the invite. The bride's mother's her second cousin or something. Not really my thing, weddings, but I'd heard you were living in Sterndale, and I didn't want to pass up the possibility of bumping into you. And here you are.'

'What do you want, exactly?'

Murray looks at him with malice in his eyes. 'There are wrongs still to be righted. I think you know that.'

'It was a clean break, Murray. I've got nothing to say to you.'

'It's not about me, though, is it? It's about other people. That woman you're with, she's a looker, isn't she? And what about your little girl? When she grows up, is she going to find out about her daddy's past life?'

'Get out of my way.' Tristan pushes past him, heading towards what he thinks will be the sanctuary of the hotel entrance, but Murray's so close behind he can smell his after-shave.

'All I'm asking is a few minutes of your valuable time, a private chat between you and me. What could be wrong with that? We'll go for a turn round the grounds, just two old friends, taking a walk together.'

Tristan stops and turns back to face him.

'You spend too much time watching those old films. What's that one from? Let me guess – *The Shawshank Redemption*.'

Murray laughs.

'You're still the sharp one, aren't you? Actually it's *Mystic River*, Kevin Bacon, Tim Robbins. It's in your best interests, Tris. If you won't talk to me, we'll have to think about going public.'

Tristan shakes his head.

'Don't threaten me, Murray. You don't have the chops to follow through. We went our separate ways, and that's how it's going to stay. It's nothing to do with you, and it never was. Now I'm going for a piss, and when I come out of there, don't you be here waiting.'

FIVE

An hour's passed since Tristan went to drop Flora off with Bridget. As the time slips by, at first Izzy's unconcerned, thinking he'll be caught in conversation, doing the rounds, spreading the love. She dances with Laura a couple of times and accepts another glass of prosecco, but she's had enough to drink and it's standing, untouched and fizzing, on the table.

Bending down to her handbag, she finds her phone, and presses the speed-dial button to call him. She hears his phone ringing out, but he doesn't answer.

Laura leans across the table.

'Where's Tris?' she asks, and Izzy shrugs.

'I don't know. Talking, probably. But I want to go soon. I tried to ring him but he didn't pick up.'

'He probably didn't hear his phone in this racket. Aidan will take a turn about the place and track him down, won't you, honey?' Aidan's only just sat down after visiting the gents. 'Sorry, we should have asked you while you were up.'

'I don't mind,' says Aidan, getting back to his feet. 'I'll have a see what Gemma's doing, while I'm about it.'

*   *   *

The music's getting louder; the dance floor is full.

Whoever did the seating plan, Aidan notices, has made a couple of gaffes, potential flashpoints as the evening progresses and alcohol removes inhibitions. Probably it seemed logical to seat the Proctor brothers and their wives together, but the brothers haven't spoken for three years after a row over their mother's will led them into a bitter court case. And they've put the farmer who shot an errant dog for sheep-worrying far too close to the dog's still-grieving owner. If the farmer has any sense and sensibilities, thinks Aidan, he'll be cutting his evening short.

Finally, he spots Gemma with Hannah and a few other friends. Most of the girls are laughing at something on a phone, but Gemma's not joining in and seems distracted, looking towards the marquee entrance as if she's waiting for someone to walk in. Is she still carrying a torch for Darren Ferris? If Darren's broken his little girl's heart, Aidan would love to get him in a dark alley and have a word, but that isn't how it goes. Life lessons are not to be interfered in, though it's incredible to him a toerag like Ferris could prefer another girl to his beautiful daughter. Maybe Gemma did the right thing and refused to go as far as Darren wanted. From what he's heard, Rosie Stainforth's boundaries are more flexible, but knowing Gemma's got some kind of moral code doesn't make it any easier to see her unhappy.

Someone touches his arm.

'Is that you, Mr Ridley?'

Aidan looks down on an elderly man sitting alone at an otherwise abandoned table, a half-empty half-pint glass in front of him. He's changed since Aidan last saw him, lost weight, gained years.

'Hello, Len, how's things?'

'I've been better, Mr Ridley, if I'm honest.'

Aidan glances round as he sits down. 'Where's Yvonne?'

Len looks away, tightening his jaw to stop it trembling. 'She passed, Mr Ridley. Six months ago now. All the stress over the years, in the end her heart gave way. Still, she's no more worries now. I got her a beautiful spot in the churchyard, not far from her mum and dad. The way I'm feeling, I shan't be far behind.'

'I'm very sorry to hear that. If I'd known, I'd have come to pay my respects.'

'Well, you can't be everywhere, can you? You lads have plenty on your plates, day to day.'

'I'm not in the force any more, actually,' says Aidan. 'I'm invalided out.'

'That's a shame. I always had you down for being one of the good ones. What are you doing now, then?'

'I've got a bike shop. It does all right, puts food on the table. What about Jason? How are things there?'

Aidan remembers Jason Tyndall too well – an addict with a ruthless streak when he needs cash to fund his habit, and a long-term, anti-social menace in Sterndale and beyond. In the White Lion, they still talk about the night Jason was refused service and threw a chair at the back of the bar, bringing down a Victorian mirror and several shelves of bottles in a catastrophic cascade of alcohol and glass. Sometimes, still, the regulars wind up the landlord by telling him Jason's been seen in town, and sometimes it's true, though Jason never stays long in one place, flitting between *Detained at Her Majesty's pleasure* and the ditches and squats which add up to *No fixed abode*. If

25

Len tells Aidan Jason is dead too, it will come as no surprise.

Len shakes his head. 'He's doing another stretch. They let him out early March, four weeks later he got recalled. I didn't even bother going to court, not this time. We've heard it all before, haven't we? All I know about it I read in the paper, that he robbed some poor bloke in a corner shop, threatened to cut his throat with a Stanley knife.'

'I heard about that case. Didn't they catch him on CCTV?'

'That was him. Too spaced out on his dirty damned drugs to cover his face, the silly fool.'

'Do you get to see him?'

Len shakes his head again. 'He's up in Durham at the moment. That's too far for me to go at my age, even if I could afford the train fare.' He musters a smile. 'You won't believe me when I tell you what a lovely lad he was growing up, the apple of our eyes. And he had a good heart, used to fetch a bit of shopping for old Billy Spence on Miller's Lane, until the day his daughter came knocking to say Billy's war medals had gone missing. Bit by bit he broke our hearts, and he wasn't even there at the end to lay a few flowers on his mother's grave. I made excuses for him many times – more than I ever should have, if the truth be told – but I'll never forgive him for that.'

The weight of Len's grief lies heavy between them.

'I know it hasn't been easy for you,' says Aidan.

Len picks up his glass. 'Here's to your kids, Mr Ridley. I hope you have better luck with yours than I did with mine.'

Amen to that, thinks Aidan, patting Len on the back as he moves on.

*   *   *

Darren Ferris and Rosie are sitting in the corner of the hotel lobby, holding hands. Rosie is uncharacteristically silent, and Darren thinks he might throw up, knowing he's overdone the illicit Jägermeister. When she notices Aidan, Rosie gives him an embarrassed smile which Aidan doesn't return. Darren puts his head in his hands, deciding to pretend he hasn't seen him.

A burst of laughter from a group of twenty-somethings in the bar draws Aidan's attention, and Rosie watches him cross to the open doorway and scan the room, where he seems not to find whoever he's looking for. Rosie assumes it's Gemma, and hopes he doesn't ask her where his daughter might be, guiltily realising she might have totally wrecked Gemma's day.

But Aidan ignores her and heads for the restaurant, which from what Rosie can see is deserted except for a sullen girl laying tables. Aidan's soon back in the lobby, where the harried-looking receptionist is speaking into a phone. When she finishes her call, she comes across to Darren and Rosie.

Aidan moves closer so he can hear what she says.

Darren's face has turned very pale, almost green.

The receptionist smiles. 'They want you to wait here. Some-one's on their way to get you.'

A man wearing a black suit appears at Aidan's side, his lapel badge announcing him as some kind of manager.

'May I help you, Sir?'

Rosie hears Aidan ask if something's going on.

'If you'd like a drink, we have full service in the bar,' says the manager.

Aidan says, 'I think I've had enough, mate,' and sits down in an armchair.

The manager leans over the desk to confer with the

receptionist. Another burst of laughter from the bar blurs what's being said, and Rosie only clearly hears one word: pool.

Aidan abandons his chair, heading out in the direction of the gardens.

Across the lawn, where the path leads between the box hedges, a sign reading *Pool closed* has been thrown aside. Aidan walks through the leafy archway and is confronted by a policeman in uniform.

'I'm sorry, Sir, this area's . . .' begins the policeman, but then he grins and says, 'Hello, Aidan mate, how're you doing?'

The cogs of Izzy's reality are slipping. She watches Aidan return, grave-faced, to the marquee table, sees his whispered exchange with Laura, and how she freezes for a moment, as if she were paused. Laura's face gives more away than Aidan's, so Izzy knows he's told her something bad, though she's already drawing her own conclusions, since Aidan's come back without any sign of Tris.

Laura gets up and stands next to her, and from her chair, Izzy looks up at her friend, who touches her shoulder in the universal gesture of comfort which means it's going to be something she really doesn't want to hear.

'What's going on? Tell me what's happened.'

There's a whoop from the crowd as the music segues into Flo Rida's *Low*.

'There's been an accident,' says Laura, speaking loudly so she can be heard over the voices singing along on the dance floor, and it's not her fault because she's trying to be sensitive and break it gently, but for God's sake, thinks Izzy, just spit it out.

'Who? What? Just tell me!'

'It's Tris. The police are asking for you and the ambulance is on its way. Aidan and I will take you over there.'

'What are you talking about? He just went to the car park to drop Flora off with Bridget. Has he been knocked down?' *Knocked down*. Such an oddly vintage expression, but if that's what's happened, surely it's not serious? Vehicles in car parks don't drive very fast. 'What about Flora? Is she OK?'

'It's nothing to do with Flora,' says Aidan. 'Tris is by the pool.'

'What pool?'

'Across the lawn, there's a swimming pool. We'd better hurry. The ambulance will be here any minute, and if you want to go with him . . .'

'Go with him where?'

'To the hospital,' says Laura. 'They'll want to have a look at him, I'm sure.'

'Did he fall in?' asks Izzy. 'But he's such a good swimmer.'

'Please, Izzy, let's hurry,' says Aidan. 'They can tell you everything when we get there.'

Blue lights strobe on the turquoise water. From a distance, they might be mistaken for a spin-off from the marquee dance floor, but there's no music here, just the splash of water in the pool drains and the murmur of voices. A police car's headlamps are trained on two kneeling paramedics, giving them light as they work under a sign saying *Hotel Guests Only*.

The dazzle behind the policeman obscures his face. He's asking Izzy's name and address and her relationship to the casualty, and when she doesn't answer him, he starts again, this time talking to her as if she were five years old. In fact she's already heard and understood him, but her focus is on the legs she can see in front of the female paramedic.

Izzy feels a lightness in her head, a strange, disorienting sensation as if she's split into two people, one trying to talk coherently to the policeman, the other a fearful observer, mentally distant. Who is that person on the ground? Surely it can't be Tris, and yet those are unmistakably his shoes. The male paramedic moves to take something from his bag, and Izzy sees a face made grey by the blue light, before the paramedic covers the nose and mouth with an oxygen mask. The mask gives her a measure of relief. If they're giving him oxygen, that must mean he isn't dead.

'Are you sure it's him?' she asks, and the policeman says, 'Yes, Madam,' before going back to his questions which, this time, Izzy answers.

'Can I go to him?'

'Better wait here until they get him stabilised.'

'What do you mean, stabilised?' asks Izzy, and immediately asks Laura the same, but Laura clutches Izzy's arm and doesn't answer.

'He's had a blow to the head,' says the policeman.

'You mean he fell?'

'It's too early to say.'

'But what was he doing here? Who found him? You have to let me go to him. He needs to know I'm here.'

A car arrives and pulls up behind the police patrol car. A man and a woman get out, and a policewoman steps forward to greet them, leading them forward, pointing at the ground.

Aidan speaks quietly into Laura's ear. 'CID.'

'We'll have answers to your questions down the line,' says the policeman, betraying no interest in the recent arrivals. 'I expect you'll be wanting to go with him in the ambulance?'

'Where will they take him?' asks Laura.

'An injury like that, I expect it would be Shrewsbury.'

'An injury like what? How bad is it?' demands Izzy.

'Shrewsbury's a long way,' says Laura, to deflect Izzy's attention on to domestic arrangements.

'What about Flora?' asks Izzy. 'Who'll look after her?'

'Bridget will, of course,' says Laura. 'That's where she is now, safe at home with Bridget.'

'But tomorrow's her day off.'

'You'll probably be home by then. I'll speak to Bridget. You just go with Tris, and do what you need to there.'

The policewoman joins them.

'They're ready to move him.' She looks from Izzy to Laura. 'Which of you is his partner?'

'I am,' says Izzy. 'I'm his wife.'

'You can go with them in the ambulance, but they've asked me to tell you he isn't conscious at the moment, just so you're aware. Can I ask when you last saw your husband?'

Izzy shakes her head. 'I don't know. An hour ago, maybe. Maybe a bit longer than that.'

'She was concerned about where he'd got to,' puts in Aidan. 'I offered to go and see if I could track him down.'

The policewoman peers through the growing darkness.

'Is that you, Aid?'

'Yeah, it's me.'

The paramedics are lifting their patient on to a gurney.

As they wheel him towards the ambulance, they leave dark liquid on the ground where he was lying, and the glint of broken glass.

'You'd better go,' says Laura, encouraging Izzy forward.

Before she follows, the policewoman turns smiling back to Aidan. 'Can't stay away from the drama, eh? When are you coming back? We miss you.'

'Sometime, never,' says Aidan. 'Other fish to fry, these days.'

Inside the ambulance, the paramedic tells Izzy to strap herself in, and as she does so, she sees the blood on Tris's jacket. It's one of his favourites, and she can't help thinking that it'll be ruined.

'Is he going to be OK?' she whispers.

'Hospital's the best place for him, at the moment,' says the paramedic non-committally, and his colleague closes the doors.

The ambulance begins to move and picks up speed. From where she's sitting, Izzy can reach Tris's hand, and she lifts it to her mouth to kiss it, telling him she loves him, not caring what the paramedic sees or hears. This is all her fault. Didn't he want to skip the wedding so they could be alone together at home? He'll remember those moments in the bedroom, probably never forget them.

But she can live with that. She can take a lifetime of ribbing and reminding, as long as he'll just – please, God, please – wake up.

At Foxcote Lodge, the night brings not the barking of foxes but the fluttering of bats.

Bridget puts Flora to bed without bath or stories, and

32

within moments, the child is sleeping. Downstairs, Bridget instructs the Alexa devices to monitor the nursery. She's already had dinner, but in the fridge there's caramel cheesecake left over from what Izzy calls a supper two nights ago. Both Izzy and Tris are too diet-conscious ever to eat dessert, and it's a shame to let it go to waste, so Bridget cuts herself a generous slice, pours on double cream and carries it into the lounge. As she's savouring the first spoonful, her phone buzzes with an incoming call from her boyfriend, Manzi, whose job as a mechanic lets him keep regular hours. When she can't be with him, sometimes he sulks. Saturday night, he'll have had a drink or two, so he could be upbeat, or on the way back down to maudlin.

'Hey.' She puts the phone on video call. 'How's it going?'

Looks like he's in the White Lion car park, smoking a cigarette on the bonnet of his crazy car, a slammed, souped-up Subaru. There's a loud crowd in the outdoor smoking area, making it hard to hear what he says.

'OK. I was missing you. Thought you might be done for the day, maybe you could come down for a drink.'

Bridget spoons in more cheesecake. 'No way. They're still dancing the light fantastic at that wedding to which I, of course, was not invited. Could be a late one.'

'Cinderella again.'

'You said it. We'll have all day tomorrow, though. He promised they wouldn't be late.'

'Heard that before. The guy's a prick. What are you doing?'

'Not much. I was thinking I might watch something on Netflix, that new . . .'

Bridget stops, listens. Through the window, the gravelled

drive and front gardens are lit up by the motion-sensitive security lights. 'Hold on. I think they might be here.'

Leaving her cheesecake on the sofa, she crosses to the window.

There's no sign of the Fiat. Everything is still.

Returning to the sofa, she picks up her phone. 'You still there, babe?'

Manzi grunts that he is, and she hears the crackle of burning paper as he draws on his cigarette. 'The security lights came on. Must have been a fox or a hedgehog. Izzy says there's a mum with babies in the garden, so me and Flora left out some cat food.'

'Probably a cat, then,' says Manzi. 'What do you want to do tomorrow?'

The doorbell rings.

It's late for callers. Bridget feels uneasy.

'There's someone at the door.'

'Don't answer it,' says Manzi. 'It's probably some drunk fan come for an autograph.'

'I'll have to answer it. They might have come home in a taxi and not got a key.'

'Check who it is before you open the door, then.'

'I'm not stupid,' says Bridget. 'Don't go away. I'll call you back as soon as I can.'

SIX

The male nurse who shows Izzy to the relatives' room is kind but sallow with weariness.

Izzy takes a seat in the windowless room and accepts the offer of tea.

'We'll come and get you when he's ready for visitors,' says the nurse.

'How long do you think it will be?'

'I expect one of the doctors will have a word with you,' he says obscurely, and closes the door very quietly behind him, as if she's a child asleep.

The claustrophobic room is plain grey: grey walls, grey furniture. A scattering of abandoned leaflets lies on the table, and as she reads the titles – *Children's Critical Care, Life After Discharge from Intensive Care, Bereavement Help and Support* – she begins to realise they're not just in the hospital, but in its place of last resort.

When their father was dying, Izzy and her sister went through many meetings in rooms just like this. They shared a macabre joke, that when their father's inevitable end was close, the news would be broken with tea in china cups, instead of the usual polystyrene. Relatives of other patients on the ward told them the gravity of news to come can be divined in this way, so she's praying her tea will be delivered in plastic.

Nothing feels quite real, and she knows she's not thinking straight. She wants to call Tris's parents – their company would be a comfort, and Eamon always knows the right thing to do – but what's the point in waking them now? It would be kinder to wait till a more reasonable hour, let them have a decent night's sleep.

She decides she'll wait until 6 a.m. before she makes the call.

Someone taps lightly at the door, and a woman in an orderly's uniform carries in a porcelain mug of tea.

When Bridget rings back, Manzi's already home, sipping a Jack Daniels nightcap as he flips channels on the TV.

'You took your time,' he says. 'Who was at the door?'

'Never mind that now,' says Bridget. 'You'll never guess what. Something's happened to Tristan.'

'What?'

'Some kind of accident. Laura Ridley just phoned me, asked if I could stay overnight.'

'I hope you said no.'

'Course I didn't. I can't leave the little one here by herself.'

'You're leaving me by myself.'

'Yes, but you're a big boy, aren't you? Laura says he's in hospital, that they took him off in an ambulance.'

'Maybe he got into a fight.'

'Doesn't sound like Tris to me.'

'Probably he got up someone's nose. That's not out of the question, is it?' Manzi switches from MTV Rocks to Kerrang,

36

where Behemoth are playing, and settles back on the sofa to watch. 'So you're not coming back tonight, then?'

'Doesn't look like it, no. If I can, I will, but don't wait up for me.'

'I wasn't planning on it,' says Manzi, draining his glass.

The last time Izzy and Tris were in a hospital was for Flora's birth, a day which bloomed from a blur of agony and fear into overwhelming love. All through that ordeal, Tris was there, holding her hand, wiping her brow, tears in his eyes because he couldn't stop her pain, and at the end, at Flora's first cry, he covered his face and wept. He is her rock and her best friend; he and Flora are the reasons for her being.

Now she sits beside her husband's body, wondering where he's gone. His lower half is cocooned in white sheets, and pouches of clear liquids are feeding through cannulas in the backs of his hands. The monitors show a regular heartbeat, his vital signs are in the normal ranges, and yet he's ominously absent, as if he's been unplugged. When the nurse comes to check his pupils, his eyes are glassy voids.

Watching, waiting, hoping. She's no idea how long she's been sitting when the nurse comes to let her know Tris's parents have arrived. Squeezing his lifeless hand, she kisses his forehead and strokes his hair, and tells him she won't be gone long.

In the relatives' room, someone has removed her porcelain mug. Steph, Tris's mother, is far from her usual chicly groomed self. Without make-up, she looks every one of her seventy-two years, and without heels, she's diminished from the stately woman Izzy's always taken her to be.

Izzy's expecting hugs and tears, but Steph's lips are thin and tight.

'You should have called us straight away.' She speaks without preamble – no *How is he?* or *How are you?* – and the admonishment is meant. Izzy's dismayed and hurt. She's always thought of her and Steph as being close, but in the light of this catastrophe, it seems that was mere illusion.

'I just thought . . .' she says, and begins to cry.

Eamon glares at Steph, and gives Izzy a fatherly hug. Dressed in his Higher Education standards of chinos, loafers and a short-sleeved shirt, at first glance he looks no different than usual, but a second look says he hasn't shaved, and the shadow on his jaw ages him, too.

Steph softens at Izzy's tears.

'Let's sit a minute,' she says, and Izzy does so with reluctance, anxious to get back to Tris, not wanting him to wake and find her not there. 'What have the doctors said?'

Izzy dabs at her eyes with a tissue. 'I don't think it's very good at the moment. He's got swelling on his brain. They're saying it's a case of watch and wait.'

Steph and Eamon are expecting her to go on, but in the haze of shock that's all she's taken in.

'Well,' says Steph eventually, 'the first thing is for Eamon to go and track down someone in charge and find out how they're going to treat him. And I can see we're going to be here for a while, so we'll be needing a hotel. While Eamon deals with all that, you and I will go and see him.'

'We've been wondering how this happened,' says Eamon. 'You weren't very specific on the phone.'

'The police said he'd been hit with something,' sniffs Izzy.

Steph's hand goes to her mouth.

'Someone hit him?' She's looking at Izzy as if she's withholding information. 'Who on earth would do such a thing?'

'I don't know,' says Izzy, beginning to cry again, upset to be feeling the need to defend herself. 'It wasn't me, if that's what you're thinking.'

'No one's accusing you of anything,' says Eamon. 'I expect the police will tell us more today.'

'On a Sunday?' asks Steph. 'I very much doubt it. That's not the priority, anyway. The first thing we need to do is to be sure he's getting the very best care.'

'They're keeping him comfortable,' says Izzy. 'I'm not sure they can do any more.'

'They can always do more, if they're pushed,' says Steph. 'Eamon, go and see who you can find.'

SEVEN

Laura's a firm believer in turning her phone off at night, but with Josh sleeping over at Ollie's and the previous evening's events, she left it on. When it rings she's already awake, feeling terrible and with serious regrets over that last glass of wine – it's hazy, but there might even have been two – after Tris was taken away.

The bed beside her is empty, and next to her phone is a cold cup of tea, its surface cloudy with fat from the milk. The thought of drinking it brings on a rush of nausea. Aidan must have brought it, but surely he hasn't gone out for his bike ride? He and his mates aim to do fifty miles on Sunday mornings, usually up to Shapston and back via Westley, but it's hard to imagine any of them have much enthusiasm for it this morning. No doubt, though, the male competitive spirit has done its work, since none of them will want to bear the dishonour of being called a lightweight. How lucky she is that women are so much kinder to their friends.

Aidan's police training still runs deep, and last night he was insistent she should keep quiet about what's happened to Tris. Out of loyalty to Izzy, Laura wouldn't say anything, but she knows as well as Aidan it'll need more than their silence to keep the incident under wraps. Tris will be a major story, and someone, somewhere, will leak the details the media need to fuel their headlines.

She picks up her ringing phone and sees Philly's name. Proof – if any were needed – that the gossip is on the fly.

'Hi, Philly.'

'Laura! How are you? No thick heads chez Ridley this morning, I hope?'

'A very thick head, thank you. I don't know about Aidan, but he seems to have made his bike club meeting. You sound chirpy, though. No hangover for you?'

'Oh, you know me, darling. I have to take it easy because of the bloody horses. It's no fun mucking out when all you want to do is throw up. I had a glass or two of fizz, which I didn't think was of the best quality, to be honest. If they'd asked Jerry, he'd have happily given them some pointers. You don't have to spend a fortune to get decent wine, but so much of it these days is just plain undrinkable. I had a glass or two, just to get in the spirit, and then I put myself on gin drowned in slimline tonic. That's pretty foul stuff too with that nasty aftertaste but it fills you up and voilà, no hangover. Oh dear, I hope I don't sound smug.'

'Maybe just a touch.'

'Jerry wasn't quite so clever. Rather unwisely he took it upon himself to join some of the gentlemen in their whisky sampling. He's lying on the sofa pretending to read the papers, though I don't see how you can read them when they're covering your face.' She gives a bark of laughter, and Laura smiles. 'Anyway, I was making him a cup of coffee when the radio news came on, and they gave it top billing.'

Laura sits up and dares to take a sip of the cold tea, which turns out to be balm to her dehydrated mouth.

'Did you hear it?'

'What?'

'About Tristan. I know you're such good friends with Izzy, so I thought you might know.'

'What?' asks Laura again.

'You're being so cagey, darling. I just can't believe you don't know. Apparently Tristan was taken away from the hotel in an ambulance. How did we miss that? Or maybe you didn't? They're saying he's in a coma, and doctors can't say how serious it is. What on earth happened, I wonder? A head injury, supposedly, but how would he come by that? Do you think someone bopped him on the head? It's got all the hallmarks of a jealous husband, if you ask me.'

Through the window, Laura sees a car pull up at the end of the drive. The rear door opens and Josh jumps out, reaching back inside for his backpack which looks to Laura's experienced eyes rather light, and despite her concern for Tris and Izzy, the mum in her hopes he's remembered to bring home everything he took with him to Ollie's.

'Why would husbands be jealous of Tristan?' she asks Philly. 'He and Izzy are devoted to each other. I don't believe he'd ever look at another woman.'

'Oh Laura, your faith in the opposite sex is so quaint. I suppose it comes from being married to steadfast and true Aidan. Even dear old Jerry wouldn't be immune to a fling if the right woman batted her eyelashes, and women must be lining up in droves to throw their knickers at Tristan. Mark me, there'll be another woman involved in this somewhere.'

Laura shakes her head.

'For God's sake, Philly, don't go spreading rumours like that! Poor Izzy has enough on her plate without the whole town thinking her husband's being unfaithful. Let's just wait for the facts, shall we?' Josh is saying his goodbyes, slamming the car door. 'I have to go.'

'Maybe I'll see you tomorrow. I might drop in the café for coffee.'

'I'll talk to you later.'

By the time Laura's climbed reluctantly from the bed and found her dressing gown, the doorbell's already chiming, and Josh impatiently rings it again when she hasn't reached the door within five seconds.

When she opens it, he rushes in, dropping his bag on the hall floor and heading for the kitchen, saying, 'Hi Mum,' in passing. By the time she's caught up with him, the fridge is open and he's already found a plate.

'Can I make a sandwich? I didn't have breakfast because I didn't want porridge. That's what Ollie always has for breakfast, every single day of every single year. His mum doesn't let them have normal stuff like cornflakes. I asked for toast but they only had that brown granary so I said I wasn't hungry. Have we got any Branston pickle?' He looks across at her from his scavenging of the fridge. 'How come you're not dressed yet? Have you got a hangover?'

Laura ducks the question by filling the kettle.

'Did you have a good time?'

'Yes, thanks. Ollie's got *Shenmue 3* so we played that until we were told to stop, then we watched a DVD. We got takeaway for dinner, pizza from that new place next to the Co-op.'

'Was it good?'

'It was OK. I asked for pepperoni but Ollie's family have all gone vegetarian so it wasn't allowed, only tuna and veggies. Isn't tuna a kind of meat? Hey, guess what, on the way over here we saw a BBC film crew.'

Laura turns round from the sink where she's rinsing a mug. 'A film crew? Where?'

'Outside Izzy's house. There was a man with one of those big shoulder cameras and another one with one of those fluffy things they use for sound. And a woman all dressed up Ollie's mum said is a BBC news reporter. And Ollie's dad says the police were called to the wedding last night. Did you and Dad see them? Has somebody been murdered?'

Laura pours hot water on to a tea bag and pokes it with a teaspoon. 'I don't think that's very likely, sweetie. Don't cut that cheese so thick, you can't possibly eat all that.'

'Where is Dad, anyway? When he comes back, we can ask him what's going on.'

'I don't see how Dad would know any better than you or I. You're putting two and two together and coming up with eight. I really don't think it's very likely to be murder. And sit down properly to eat your sandwich.'

'Can I have some crisps?'

'Just one packet. When you've finished, do me a favour, go up and ask your sister if she wants any breakfast.'

'It's way too late for breakfast, Mum. You have got a hangover, haven't you?'

'Maybe a little, tiny bit. I just need a few minutes to come round. I'll be absolutely fine when I've had this cup of tea.'

Josh chooses prawn cocktail crisps and climbs on to a stool

at the breakfast bar, making a case while he eats for why he should be allowed to have his own copy of *Shenmue 3* weeks before his birthday. Laura leans against the counter, cautiously sipping the sugary tea, thinking the glucose might give her a much-needed lift. As Josh goes into far too much detail on game strategy, Laura loses focus, and listens over his chatter for signs Gemma's surfacing, but upstairs remains silent.

Josh finishes what he wants of his sandwich, leaving the crusts parked at the side of the plate.

'I could do chores to pay for it,' he's saying. 'I could clean my room and take out the rubbish.'

'Those are things you ought to do anyway.'

'Please, Mum.'

'I'll think about it.' As soon as she's said the words, she knows they'll be taken as a promise, but that's a problem to be faced another day. 'Please, Josh, go and knock on Gemma's door and tell her to come and get something to eat.'

'OK.' He climbs down from his stool and almost skips, child-like, up the stairs, making Laura smile at his youthful vivacity. Not much in life troubles Josh; he was a carefree baby who's grown into a happy-go-lucky child. He and his sister have so little in common.

She hears him knocking at Gemma's door and calling her name, wincing at his over-enthusiasm which can only provoke a rebuke. There's a muffled reply from Gemma, and immediately Josh is running back down the stairs.

'Mum! She used the F-word! She told me to F-off!'

'Did she really?' Now Laura will have no choice but to discipline Gemma. If she did get hold of any alcohol last night, maybe she's feeling as bad as Laura.

45

'Boy trouble,' says Josh, heading for the lounge.

'What makes you say that?' Laura's hoping for insight, but Josh only replies it's what Laura herself says when Gemma's being moody, which recently seems so often to be the case.

Laura goes upstairs and knocks gently at Gemma's door.

'Gemma?' There's no reply. Inside the room she hears the bed move as though Gemma has turned over. 'Gemma, did you swear at Josh?'

'Leave me alone!'

'Don't speak to me like that. It's time you were getting up. You can't just lie in bed all day. And when you get up, you can apologise to your brother.'

Gemma doesn't reply, but Laura has no appetite for a serious fight. Aidan would tell her she's doing the wrong thing letting Gemma get away with it, but Laura needs paracetamol and a shower.

Just this once, Gemma can stay where she is.

EIGHT

'So you two have drawn the short straw on the Tristan Hart assault, have you?'

Brad Sherman is going into Burnt Common police station as DI Gavin Muir and DS Kirstie Weld are coming out. Sherman looks sharp, even though it's early Sunday morning. Being camera-ready 24/7 goes with his job.

'Not really a short straw,' says Muir. 'When we make the collar, we'll be covered in glory, free beer all round.' Muir looks pretty good himself, shaved, suited and booted, which isn't bad considering that an hour ago when he got the call, he was in his man-shed in a paint-spattered T-shirt and ripped shorts, looking for the tools to hang the kids a rope swing from the branches of an ash tree. When he had to leave, the kids were badly disappointed, but they know if Dad's been called out on a Sunday, something major's going on.

Sherman looks sceptical at his assessment of where it will end.

'A big wedding, people coming and going. You've a load of possibilities to sift through there, mate. What do we know about it so far?'

'All we've got is a short report from CID who attended last night,' says Weld. 'Apparently he was hit over the head with a champagne bottle. Forensics have recovered the fragments.'

'A champagne bottle? I suppose it makes a change from a glass in the face. Listen, no pressure, but with him being who he is, if you don't nail anyone for it in short order, the press will be all over us.'

'Always the optimist, eh, Brad? The way I see it, you're Head of PR, so if it comes to that, it'll be your problem, not ours. Which isn't to say that we have any intention whatsoever of dragging our feet, even though it's a Sunday and it was my day off. We always try to remain mindful we're on the same team. We do our bit, you do yours.'

Weld is inclined to be kinder to Sherman than Muir. The Press Office isn't somewhere she could ever see herself working; when balls get dropped anywhere in the force, or – worse – when people get hurt, they're the ones packaging the screw-ups in their best light, doing damage limitation for demanding senior ranks and fending off journalists who have got increasingly aggressive in recent years. Social media's made the PR job a nightmare. Even the smallest incident can get jumped on, ramped up and blown massively out of proportion with no one troubling to learn the actual circumstances or facts, like the recent three-hour stand-off with a guy holding his ex-partner and her kids hostage. When they finally talked him out and the woman and children were safe, he got a bump on the head getting in the van. Police brutality, hours later gone viral.

Sherman and his team have their hands permanently sewn into kid gloves, heart in mouth every time they press the

West Mercia Police Tweet button. Anyway, Weld likes Brad Sherman. He's too sensitive for the job in many ways, the kind of guy who gives a woman a compliment when she's had her hair done. Some would call that old-fashioned, even sexist, but Weld would call it human interaction, a brightener in what are often difficult days. Muir's at the other end of that spectrum. If she had a transplant and turned up with two heads, he'd never even notice.

'Don't worry, we won't drop you in it,' she says. 'Regular updates and a quick result, that's where we're aiming. We've got inside knowledge on the team. You used to live in Sterndale, didn't you, Gavin? The locals will open up to him and sing like bright yellow canaries.'

'I hope you're right,' says Sherman.

'In the meantime,' says Muir, 'while you're stuck in the sauna-like heat of your non-air-conditioned office, our only immediate problem is which is the best route to Sterndale, but since it's such a glorious day, I think we'll take the scenic option. What do you think, Kirstie? Lunch at the Star and Garter on the way back?'

'You'll never get in there on a Sunday, not unless you've got a reservation,' says Sherman. 'And you'd be far better on the bypass. The world and his wife will be heading out there today, so best of luck. No doubt there'll be news teams either already in situ or on their way there too, so please don't make any comment to the media without checking with me first.'

'We'll refer them all to you,' says Weld. 'Is anyone going to make a statement?'

'I'm going to give the Chief Super a call, organise a conference when she can get here.'

'Sounds like fun,' says Muir. 'Sorry we'll miss it. Better run up those stairs, Brad. I reckon I can hear your phone ringing from here.'

The car is already blazing hot, and the aircon's inefficient. Within a mile of the police station, Muir and Weld have both wound down their windows.

'Why do you always give Brad such a hard time?' asks Weld. The roads out of Ludlow are quiet, but predictably most of the lights they come up against are showing red. Muir cruises to a smooth halt and puts the car in first, ready for a quick getaway. It's in his nature; even when there's no competition, he likes to be first off the line. Keeping in fighting trim, is what he calls it.

'Do I give him a hard time?'

'You're always having a pop. He's a nice guy. You should be nice back. You know, karma and all that?'

The light is changing, and true to form, the car moves forward without the slightest delay.

'Nice is for family and friends,' says Muir, eyes fixed on the road.

Weld senses there's something she's not being told.

'Have you two got form?' she asks, but Muir's focus seems entirely on his driving. 'OK, be that way. Well, I like him anyway. I think he's a gentleman.'

Muir indicates a left turn, signposted for Sterndale.

'I really respect your brainpower, Kirstie, you know that,' he says. 'But sometimes I have my doubts as to whether you're a good judge of character.'

* / * *

The road to Sterndale leads out through the suburbs. As they reach open country, Muir takes the back lanes rather than the A-road, and before long they're climbing up into hills where the lowland meadows give way to moorland summits, letting in the scents of grass and bracken.

'That's the smell of my youth,' he says. 'Every opportunity I got, I used to be out here, biking or climbing. I was a lot fitter then than I am now.'

'You don't look so bad,' says Weld. 'And you can see why people come to live here, can't you? People like Tristan Hart, especially. You make your pile, buy yourself a nice place in the country. No wonder so many ordinary people round here can't afford a decent place to live.'

'What do you know about him, anyway?'

Weld shrugs.

'Same as everyone else, I suppose. Only what we've been told in the celebrity press. He started out on that game show, didn't he, what was it called?'

'*Find a Fortune*,' says Muir. 'My mum loved it.'

'After that he went quiet for a while. Now he's re-invented himself as a probing interviewer, amongst other things. I remember seeing a piece about him a while back in *Hello* magazine, him and his new wife. They made a lovely couple. She's a real stunner.'

'He's on his second marriage, then?'

'Aren't they all?'

'Some of them would be on number three or four by his age. He must be in his forties, isn't he?'

'If he's had work, he might be older than that. I guess we'll soon find out.'

They drive for a while in silence. Weld takes out her phone to check for messages, but the hills block any signal.

'How do people live out here?' she asks. 'It's like the Dark Ages.'

'Rural deprivation is what they call it,' says Muir. 'Only when you look at some of the villages, they don't look very deprived.'

As they reach the outskirts of Sterndale, Muir slows down and points to a cul-de-sac development of relatively new houses.

'That's where we used to live,' he says. 'Fifteen, Moor View Close. Sterndale was a great place when I was a kid – lots of freedom, dens in the woods and all that. A nightmare for teenagers, though. That great big world out there, and three buses a fortnight to the nearest decent-sized town. The arrival of a celebrity will have been a big thing for a small place like this, and with this assault, it's the gift that keeps on giving. They'll be talking about it well into the next century.'

'That's such a cliché,' objects Weld. 'Small town where nothing ever happens. I bet there was loads going on here you didn't even know about.'

'Oh yeah? Like what? In my day, the hot debate was where to site the new public toilets, and the biggest drama was the argument over who should get the lead roles in the Christmas pantomime. You have no idea.'

'I'd love to live in a place like this, with a sense of community and everyone looking out for everyone else.'

Muir gives her a look with full-on raised eyebrows.

'You've been watching too much *Doc Martin*. The hotel's on the far side of town. Just for interest, have you got an address for the Hart residence?'

Weld glances at her notebook.

'Foxcote Lodge. I assume that's a house name. On Jigger's Lane – do you know it?'

'I think it's out that way too.'

Muir drives them through Sterndale's centre, where the town's medieval roots show in the broad street still cobbled to both sides of the tarmac carriageway, and the timbered houses and shops are crookedly quaint. Weld notices some of the high street standards – Boots, Specsavers and a Co-op – but cheeringly, many of the retail businesses are small independents: the Blue Moon Café, Roberts and Sons High-Class Butchers, the Dreaming Hills Gallery, Copson's the Bakers.

'I love this place,' she says. 'It's got real character.'

'In spades,' says Muir. 'There's the butter cross.' He points to a stone stump set on a plinth of steps. 'Where the farmer's wives used to come and sell their butter on market days.'

'But there isn't a cross.'

'Sadly long gone.'

'What were the farmers doing while their wives were doing the selling?'

'Out toiling in the fields. Shearing the sheep.'

'Drinking the pubs dry, more likely, if it was market day.'

'You're such a cynic. There's the turn for the hotel, just past the White Lion.'

At Weld's request, Muir parks in the shade of a horse chestnut, so the car will be cool when they come out. A few spaces behind them, the Fiat Tristan was supposed to drive home is still where Bridget left it.

'This is lovely,' says Weld, as they head for the entrance. 'Elegant.'

With the hall's classical architecture she's expecting a traditional interior, so the lobby's contemporary décor is a surprise. The carpets are muted tartan, and generous sofas and chairs are grouped around low Swedish pine tables. The old family portraits are still here, but displayed on brilliant white walls, their beauty shines with no hint of fustiness. She smells freshly brewed coffee and sweet pastry, and begins to regret she didn't grab breakfast before she left home.

Muir shows his warrant card to the receptionist.

'DI Gavin Muir, DS Kirstie Weld, West Mercia Police. We're here in relation to the incident yesterday.'

The receptionist turns a little pink, and Weld knows she'll be storing this as a tea-break talking point.

'I'll just get Mr Dalton,' she says, and disappears into the back, returning moments later with a man in a navy-blue suit and polished black shoes.

He shakes both their hands. 'Craig Dalton. I'm the general manager. Can I ask you to come through to my office?'

'Why don't you just take us to where the incident took place?' suggests Muir. 'We can be getting a feel for it while we're talking.'

Dalton nods his agreement and leads them through the hotel, out the back doors and across the lawns, where a team of men – most working with their shirts off – are dismantling the wedding marquee. Weld notices that Craig Dalton walks straight-backed with his chin up, as if he might once have been someone's butler. He has an air of competent composure, suggesting he'd be good in a crisis – which considering what's happened, Weld thinks is just as well.

'We've tried to keep it under wraps as far as possible,'

he's saying, 'and although it's hardly appropriate to speak of luck under the circumstances, it was a blessing that it happened where it did. The pool complex, as you'll see, is set apart from the rest of the hotel. We couldn't get planning permission for it any closer to the main building, because of the façade being listed. But by and large, the guests don't seem to mind.'

They reach the gap in the box hedge, now blocked by a red-and-white barrier and a sign reading *Pool closed until further notice*.

Dalton moves the barrier aside to allow Muir and Weld to pass through.

The pool is before them, glinting in the sun. Blue and white police tape marks the place in front of the changing rooms where Tristan was found.

'Of course I understand that you have your job to do,' says Dalton, 'but the weather is very hot, and our guests are keen to use the pool. What I'm asking, really, is how long do you think we'll have to keep it closed? To be frank, there seems very little here to help you.'

Dalton's right. Muir and Weld look over the tape, where blood has dried in a dark stain on the paving stones. With the broken glass removed last night, nothing else remains.

'Do you have CCTV in this area?' asks Weld, and the manager shakes his head.

'I'm afraid not. The car park's about the only area that's covered.'

'We'd like a copy of yesterday's recording.'

Dalton reaches in his pocket, takes out a data stick and hands it to Weld.

'I rather thought you might.'

Weld gives him a smile. 'Thank you. If only everyone were as switched on as you.'

'Were you on duty last night?' asks Muir.

'I was. I took over from my colleague just before the wedding reception was due to begin, at about four p.m., for continuity. It wasn't long before my shift would normally have started anyway.'

'How did you become aware of what had happened?'

'One of the receptionists came to find me. Two young people had come running in saying they'd found a body. She didn't believe them at first, and to be honest neither did I. I thought it was a prank, so I asked them to show me where. Even as I was following them I expected them to go running off laughing at any moment, though on reflection they'd have been good actors to show the level of shock they did. As soon as I saw Mr Hart lying there, I called 999. One of your officers spoke to the teenagers last night and got their names and contact details.'

'You didn't see anyone else on your way here?'

The manager shakes his head.

'No. But it was getting dark, of course. Like I say, we're a fair distance from the house and where the reception was being held.' He gestures round at the garden. 'Plenty of places for someone to hide.'

'There wasn't any kind of trouble at the wedding? No fights or arguments?'

'Thankfully, no.'

'Were you aware of Mr Hart at all during the reception?'

'He did a short video for a soldier. The young man asked

him if he'd send a message to his friends in Iraq and Mr Hart made a good job of it. Quite touching, really.'

Muir and Weld look at each other, doubting the relevance of this.

'There'll be background, I suppose,' says Weld. 'Any idea of this soldier's name?'

The manager considers.

'Began with "S". Simon, I think. I can't remember his last name.'

'We can find him from the guest list,' says Muir. 'Speaking of which, do you have a copy?'

'I have a table seating plan. As I remember, all the guest names are on there. For contact details, you'll obviously have to speak to the bride's family. I believe the bride and groom have left the country for their honeymoon, but Mrs Clements, the bride's mother, was heavily involved in the arrangements. I have her address and phone numbers. She lives here in Sterndale. I'm sure she'd be able to help you.'

Muir does a three-sixty, looking round at the pool and the sunbeds arranged on the hardstanding.

'I don't see any reason why the pool shouldn't re-open,' he says. 'Can you find someone trustworthy to clean this discreetly? We don't want lurid pictures leaking to the press. You'd be amazed what they'll buy.'

'I'll do it myself,' says Dalton, and Weld looks at him admiringly. 'Then there's no risk. To be frank, wages here are not adequate to remove the temptation from any of my staff to cash in on Mr Hart's misfortune.'

'I'd be surprised if we don't see pictures of the hotel and

the wedding emerge online in the next few days anyway,' says Weld.

Dalton almost smiles.

'Without the blood, I have no problem with that. Don't they say there's no such thing as bad publicity?'

'What now?' asks Weld, as they pull out of the hotel's driveway.

Muir considers.

'We've got enough to make a start. First thing is to speak to Tristan's wife, see if she's any idea who might wish him harm. Then let's get in touch with the mother-of-the-bride for a guest list and have a look at the car park CCTV. And I'd like to get hold of that soldier's video. There's probably nothing on there, but you never know.'

Muir turns into the high street, which is already becoming busier with Sunday visitors. Looks like Sherman might be right about the Star and Garter.

'His wife might be a suspect, if she hasn't got a solid alibi,' says Weld. 'It could just be a straightforward domestic, transported to a romantic setting. They both have too much to drink, then a blazing row, she grabs the weapon to hand and knocks him on the head.'

Muir nods agreement. 'Could be. And we need to consider the celebrity factor. With someone in the public eye, you've always got the possibility of a complete wild card, the stalker fan scenario or the deluded and dangerous. Maybe he upset someone on Twitter or didn't reply to a letter twenty years ago, and now someone's tracked him down.'

'Possibly,' says Weld. 'But if it were a mad fan, I think they'd go after him in London. On the other hand, a small

58

town like this, people get upset over some offence or slight, and things fester. With the assault being here, I'm definitely thinking it's more likely to be someone local.'

As they reach a pedestrian crossing, the lights are red, and they wait while a couple with twin boys in a double buggy crosses in front of them.

'Do they have kids?' asks Muir. 'Tristan and his wife?'

'I don't know. If they do, they probably keep them away from the cameras. If they've any sense.'

At the moment the lights turn green, Muir moves efficiently on.

'I'll draw up a plan of attack for tomorrow,' he says. 'When Tristan comes round, he'll likely tell us who attacked him, so I'm reluctant to go all hands on deck for now. Interviewing a hundred and fifty wedding guests is a big ask on resources. But of course we have to make a start. Why don't you pay a visit to the hospital first thing, get a senior medic's opinion on how serious the injuries are and find out when we can expect to speak to the victim? And have a word with the family at the bedside, see if you can get a feel for how happy or otherwise the relationship is. We'll know better how to proceed after that. It makes a difference whether we're looking at attempted murder or common assault, after all.'

'Do you think I should go there today?'

'We need an expert opinion on Tristan's injuries, and I don't think we'll get to the right people over the weekend. We'll get better information tomorrow. But make first contact with the relatives, let them know our enquiries are underway and we'll be wanting to speak to them imminently. Sherman can put out a holding statement with the usual thoughts with the family and ongoing investigation, to keep the press and the top floor happy. As for me, it's still my day off, and my kids are waiting for me to get on with putting up their swing.'

NINE

Mid-afternoon, the storm breaks.

Laura doesn't realise she's been dozing until she's startled awake by thunder, and moments later rain hammering on the conservatory roof. Beyond that, the house is quiet.

She's stretched out on the sofa with cushions at her back. When she settled down to read, the sky outside was blue as yesterday, and the conservatory was so hot, she decamped to the lounge. Now the page of the book she was trying to read has disappeared from the blank screen of her tablet, and she's feeling chilly in her sleeveless top and skirt. But her headache has abated, and her stomach's settled enough that she's feeling hungry. What she needs is proper food, fat and carbs to soak up yesterday's excesses.

There's a chicken in the fridge Aidan wanted to barbecue, but the storm's put that out of the question. Maybe a proper Sunday dinner would be nice? They spend so little time together as a family; sometimes it feels as if they're living in the same house but leading separate lives. At this moment, Josh is no doubt on his PlayStation (she should tell him to get off it) and Gemma – who knows what Gemma's doing? As for Aidan, she's no idea where he actually is.

She finds a cardigan, drinks a glass of water and puts the chicken in the oven. As she's peeling the potatoes she thinks of Tristan, wonders how he's doing. Should she ring Izzy? She's reluctant to intrude, and yet shouldn't her friend know she's thinking of them?

By the time the potatoes are in the pan, she's made up her mind to call, but when she dials Izzy's mobile, it goes to answerphone. Leaving a message of best wishes, she finishes with *Call me when you can*. Then it occurs to her to try the house phone, thinking Bridget might answer and give her news, but the line sounds engaged. Instinct tells her the phone's been left off the hook – hardly surprising, given the interest there must be in Tris's accident.

As she makes a start on the carrots, Laura promises herself that if she's heard nothing by tomorrow morning, she'll walk round to Foxcote Lodge and speak to Bridget in person.

From a third-floor window, Izzy's watching the rain fall on the flat roof of the ugly hospital building opposite. People dressed in summery cottons are hurrying through the downpour.

Yesterday sunshine, today rain. The cliché's overused and trite, but the comparison to their situation makes her feel tearful again. Everything's falling apart. She wants to stay optimistic and believe a few days here will see Tris back to normal, but it's frightening to see him lying there still as death, and disturbing to hold those cold hands which refuse to respond to her touch.

Tiredness is undermining her resilience. She's dizzy with lack of food and sleep, and her legs are feeling wobbly, but the corridors are long, empty spaces with nowhere to sit down. Instead, she leans forward against the window, pressing her forehead to the cooling glass. At least it's less claustrophobic out here than it is in the ICU: the incessant beeping of the monitors, the unnerving stillness of the patients, the constant watching him for the first sign of improvement – the twitch of a finger or the flickering of an eyelid – creates unimaginable stress.

Someone touches Izzy's shoulder.

'Here you are,' says Steph. 'We were wondering where you'd got to.'

Izzy rubs away her tears.

'I was just getting some air.'

'There's no need to cry. He's going to be fine.'

Steph speaks firmly, determined to make it so, and in the face of her confidence, Izzy feels ashamed of the deep fear at her core, that she could lose him. Without Tris, the light will go out of her life. The tears begin again, and she turns her face away, embarrassed.

'I'm sorry,' she says. 'I just can't help it. In my mind I keep seeing him lying there, and there was nothing I could do. Do you really think he's going to be OK?'

'I know my son, and so should you. He's a fighter, and he'll be back with us before you know it. Look, you're over-tired, and it's been a shock. Eamon and I have been having a little discussion, and we think you should take a break. Why don't you go home for a while? Have a shower and something to eat, spend some time with Flora, try and get some sleep. I'm sorry to say I think we're in it for the long haul, and I can't believe anything's going to change in the next few hours. With all those drugs they're giving him to keep him sedated, there's no chance whatsoever he'll wake up and find you not there. What I'm saying is, let Eamon and I take this shift, and you come back and take over first thing in the morning. Both of you have suddenly vanished, and Flora will be wondering what on earth's going on. You have to think of her as well as Tris, and there's Bridget, too. Isn't she only supposed to work part-time?'

Izzy shakes her head.

'I can't leave him. Couldn't you and Eamon go and see Flora and let Bridget go home?'

'We're not Flora's mummy and daddy, Izzy. It's going to be hard enough for her not seeing him for a while, without you going missing in action too. And how are you going to take care of him if you don't eat and sleep? He's being fed by machine, but we can't say the same for you. Eamon will drive you. I'm more than competent to take care of Tris for a few hours, you know. I've had plenty of practice, over the years.'

Izzy feels a stab of guilt. Of course Steph is competent, and she deserves some time to care for her son, even if that care is no more than keeping the flame of the bedside vigil burning. This won't go on forever, and there's no need to shut Steph out.

She gives a wan smile. 'I know how capable you are, and I know you've always taken the best care of him, because he's told me so. You're right, I need to think of Flora too. And there's no one else I'd trust him with but you.'

*   *   *

Izzy's grateful for Eamon's silence as they drive back to Sterndale. The tail of the storm has left the sky grey and moody, and it's much cooler than yesterday. When Izzy shivers, Eamon turns on the heater, remarking on the absurdities of the British weather and the need for heating in June.

As they draw close to Foxcote Lodge, he clears his throat but still doesn't speak, though Izzy senses there's something he wants to say. They pass the hotel, and she sees their little Fiat in the car park, wondering why it's there when they arrived at the reception in the Range Rover.

Only yesterday, when life was normal.

There are strangers by the gate, and the gate is closed. It's another anomaly in this strange new world: Tris likes the convenience of driving unhindered in and out, and always prefers it to stay open.

'Press,' says Eamon. 'I'll sort this out.'

He stops the car a few metres up the road, and Izzy watches him speak to those waiting. He's smiling, charming, and when he's said his piece, he opens the gate and fastens it back. Tris has the same confidence and charm, and Izzy feels she could be looking at him, thirty years from now.

Will Tris still be here in thirty years? Will he be here in thirty days?

Eamon gets back in the car. 'If you don't want your picture taken, keep your head down. I've told them – very nicely – that if they come on the property, they'll be sued for trespass. It'll give them pause, at least.'

Izzy bends down to the dashboard with both hands over her face, and they drive into Foxcote Lodge through a whirring of cameras. Eamon pulls up by the front door, but leaves the engine running.

'I won't come in. Give Flora a kiss from us. Listen, Izzy, I know how you women are. You both love Tristan, and you both want to take care of him. I know Steph can be a little overbearing sometimes, but cut her some slack, won't you? In these early days, looking after him is a novelty – if that word doesn't sound too flippant – which I'm afraid will soon wear off. She means well. And she will take the best care of him, as I'm sure you know. She won't let those doctors get away with anything. Tiger mum, isn't that what it's called? What I'm saying is, we're all on the same team, on Tris's team, and we have to be prepared to rely on each other. It's the only way we're going get through this. Do I make sense?'

Izzy nods.

'What you need to do is get some rest and come back tomorrow fighting fit,' continues Eamonn. 'This is shift work, and you're back on duty first thing in the morning. OK?'

He has kind eyes. Tris's eyes are more intense than kind. Maybe Eamon is what he'll mellow into.

She leans across and kisses him on the cheek.

'Thanks for the lift,' she says.

'My pleasure,' says Eamon. 'See you tomorrow.'

Flora runs to Izzy as she walks into the hall, full of things she and Bridget have been doing and demands for Izzy to admire the egg-box caterpillar she's painted bright blue. There's a smudge of paint on her cheek, which Izzy kisses before she rubs it off.

Then Flora looks past Izzy to the closed door at the end of

the hall. The brightness in her face disappears, and the blue caterpillar she was so proud of is forgotten.

'Isn't Daddy here?'

Unsure of how much to say, Izzy glances towards Bridget, but her back's turned as she heads towards the kitchen.

So Izzy opts for a generous coat of whitewash.

'Daddy's going to be away for a few days.'

Flora pouts in disappointment. 'Why?'

Izzy hesitates. 'He isn't very well. The doctors and nurses are looking after him in the hospital.'

Flora brightens up. Hospital sounds interesting and exciting.

'Can I go and visit him?'

'Maybe. We'll have to see. But he'll be home before you know it, and then you can be the nurse.'

'But who's going to read my bedtime story?'

'Daddy gave special permission for me to do it,' says Izzy. 'He said I could read the squirrels one.'

Flora looks doubtful. 'I don't think you can do the voices properly.'

'Daddy gave me special training.'

Flora looks deep into Izzy's eyes, checking her sincerity.

'If Daddy said so, I think it would be all right,' she says. 'And if I'm going to be the nurse, I think I'll need an outfit.'

She seems content, then, to settle back down to her vet's surgery in the cupboard under the stairs, where she's treating Paddington Bear and a tiger cub with tissue-paper bandages. In the kitchen, Bridget holds up a glass of cold white wine.

'Thought you might appreciate one of these.'

'Oh God, yes.' Izzy takes the drink, feeling tearful all over again at Bridget's kindness. 'Wow, that's a large one.'

'You've had a shock.'

'Thank you so much for staying with Flora. It's all been so . . .' The tears are about to properly flow. 'I just can't believe it. I can't seem to take it in.'

'Come and sit yourself down,' says Bridget, in that same soothing lilt she uses when Flora's threatening to lose her temper. 'We've been doing a spot of baking. Things are always better with cake.'

In the kitchen, Izzy sits down at the scrubbed-pine table, where one of Bridget's chocolate fudge cakes – Tris's favourite – waits under a mesh dome embroidered with bees.

'Me and Flora already had ours,' says Bridget. She cuts a large piece, places it on a flowered side plate and hands it to Izzy with a fork. 'It took me an age to get the buttercream out of her hair. Come on, eat, drink. You've had the most terrible day.' Her face creases with concern. 'What the hell happened? How is he? When's he coming home?'

Izzy eats the sweet, soft sponge and drinks the wine, and as she tells Bridget about last night and this morning, a pleasant wooziness fills her head.

'So do they think somebody hit him?' asks Bridget, when Izzy's said all she has to say. 'But who on earth would do that? Do they have any idea? Do you?'

Izzy shakes her head. 'None at all. I don't understand it. Everyone loves Tris.'

'Of course they do,' agrees Bridget. 'Will you have some more cake? Or I could make you a salad. If you don't want it now, you could have it later. I've put a load of meals for Flora ready in the fridge there. You don't want to be worrying about what to feed her when you've not much appetite yourself.'

'Thank you so much, Bridget. You're such a rock. What on earth would we do without you?'

'Oh, anyone would do the same. When you're suffering a misfortune, of course I want to do all I can to help. But I really should get going now, if you think you'll cope. I need a change of clothes and a shower.'

'Yes, of course. It should have been your day off today. I'm sorry.'

'Oh, no worries. Do you want me to come tomorrow? You'll be wanting to go to the hospital again, won't you?'

'If you don't mind, I'd be really grateful.'

'I'll be happy to. I'll try and get here as early as I can. You might want to check the answering machine, by the way, the phone's been going mental. I had to take it off the hook in the end.'

The answering machine is showing eighteen messages. Izzy finds paper and a pen and makes notes as she listens to them all: her mother and her sister, Tristan's agent Duncan Painter, several people she's never heard of who identify themselves as press, some friends who don't live locally enough to get their updates from the Sterndale grapevine.

She calls her mother first, trying not to let Flora hear as she goes over events again, thankful for her mother's offer to come and help out if she's needed, though Izzy knows she'd much prefer not to make the lengthy journey.

Izzy's call to Duncan Painter is brief but necessary. After expressing his shock and concern, Duncan reverts to his usual efficient self, and says he will cancel all Tris's professional engagements, initially for the next month. He'll also put out a press release, and tells Izzy to direct any media to him.

All the other callers, Izzy decides, will have to wait.

The smell of roast chicken draws Aidan from his hiding place; he appears as Laura puts the carrots in to boil, telling her he's been upstairs going through the business accounts.

He asks if there's news of Tris, and she tells him no.

'Nothing so far. I'll try giving Izzy a call after we've eaten. Can you let the kids know dinner's ready? Only please don't shout. I'm still feeling too delicate for lots of yelling.'

Josh arrives as Laura's carrying the chicken to the table, and she asks him to bring the vegetables, knowing he'll pinch a couple of roast potatoes on the way. Aidan and Gemma come down together.

Gemma's looking pale, and Laura wonders again what she and Hannah were drinking last night. Without a word, Gemma sits down at the table and starts playing with her phone.

'Put that away, please,' says Laura. 'You can manage without it for mealtimes. Could you go and fetch the gravy for me, sweetheart?'

Gemma lays her phone down with the worst possible grace, muttering, 'I'm not even hungry,' as she goes into the kitchen.

Aidan takes his seat and begins to carve the chicken.

'This looks great,' he says. 'Good idea, proper dinner.'

Gemma returns, plonking the gravy boat on the table and herself in her chair. Josh has already sat down, placing himself as close as possible to the potatoes. Plates are filled and passed round, the gravy's poured. But one bite in, Laura hears her phone ring in the kitchen.

'Leave it,' says Aidan. 'Whoever it is will call back.'

'Yeah, leave it, Mum,' says Gemma. 'No phones at the table, remember?'

Laura does remember, and follows her own rule. There's plenty of chat from Josh, mostly about PlayStation games, a little about plans for the summer holidays, and too much information about life at Ollie's house, which makes Laura wonder if Karen and Dave Garner's marriage might be as bad as people say. While Josh chatters, Gemma pushes food around her plate, eating only a few mouthfuls of vegetables. Aidan asks if she wants to join him on a cycling challenge – fifty miles on Sterndale's hilliest routes – but elicits no more than a shrug in response.

As they carry the empty dishes back into the kitchen, Laura can't resist checking her phone.

'Damn,' she says. 'That was Izzy. I'd better call her back. Can one of you find some pudding bowls and the ice cream?'

'I don't want ice cream,' says Gemma, heading for the stairs.

'That's fine,' says Laura, 'but I want you to stay around and help clear up when we're done.'

Sighing, Gemma sits back down. Laura takes her phone into the lounge and dials Izzy's number.

Izzy answers on the second ring.

'How is he?' asks Laura, without preamble. In the background she can hear Flora singing.

'Not good.' There are tears in Izzy's voice. 'He has swelling of the brain. They're keeping him sedated until it goes down.'

'Where are you now?'

'I'm home. His mother insisted I spend some time with Flora, and poor Bridget had been here far too long. It was supposed to be her day off.'

'Do you want me to come round?'

'Thanks, but no. I'm going to try and get Flora to settle down early, then I'm going to have a bath and put myself to bed, though I don't know if I'll sleep.'

'We have sleeping pills, if you need one. I had them when my dad died and only ever took one.'

'I daren't. I need to keep a clear head for tomorrow. The police have been in touch so I'll be talking to them, and there are a load of questions I want to ask the consultant. Those things blunt your thinking.'

'If you change your mind, the offer stands. Josh says he saw a camera crew at your place.'

'They tried to ambush me when I got home. They got pictures, I think, but Eamon was fabulous. He drew himself up to his full height and shooed them off.'

'I'd have paid money to see that. Isn't there anything I can do?'

'Not at the moment.' There's a long silence. 'Laura, I'm scared.'

'What do you mean? What of?'

'I'm scared my Tris is never coming home. Or that he'll be some kind of vegetable. He wouldn't want that, I know. We've both said, if anything like this happens, we'd help each other – you know. Switzerland and all that.'

Laura feels a lump in her throat.

'Now you're being morbid. It's far too early to start talking about outcomes like that. When we're having a glass of wine at the kitchen table in a couple of weeks' time, I'll tell him you said that. Come on. Chin up. This is Tris we're talking about. He's no quitter, is he?'

'If you could see him, though,' says Izzy. 'He looks like he's already gone. Anyway.' She sniffs, and Laura knows she's wiping away snotty dribbles and tears. 'Flora wants her tea, so I'd better go. She's always so cheerful.'

'For the time being, she'll take your mind off things. Keep in touch, won't you?'

'I'll try,' says Izzy, and ends the call.

Back in the dining room, Josh is squirting chocolate sauce over a large helping of salted caramel ice cream and Aidan's digging into his. In Laura's place, a single scoop of vanilla is melting into a creamy soup. Gemma's bowl is empty.

'What's the news?' asks Aidan.

'Not good,' says Laura, settling into her seat. 'Apparently he's still in a coma.'

'I'm sorry to hear that,' says Aidan. 'I thought he would have come round by now.'

'Swelling of the brain, they say. I still can't quite believe it. I think I expected her to say he'd soon be coming home, but it sounds like he may be in there a little while.'

'Maybe he'll have to have brain surgery,' says Josh. 'They cut the top of your head off. They'll have to shave his hair.'

'Poor Tris,' says Laura. 'Such a lovely, lovely man. Who would do that to him?'

'People in that business, they make enemies sometimes,' says Aidan. 'Or maybe it's just some nutter.'

'I wonder if the police will want to talk to us,' muses Laura.

Gemma stands up from her chair, knocking the table as she does so.

'Everyone in Sterndale loves him just because he's on the telly,' she says. 'It's nothing to do with whether he's nice or not. I've got to do my homework.' And she's gone, disappearing upstairs.

'What's got into her?' asks Aidan.

'I keep telling her not to leave her schoolwork till the last minute,' says Laura. 'She puts herself under so much pressure.'

'That's not homework stress, it's boy trouble,' says Josh, knowingly. 'Since she didn't have any ice cream, any chance I can have hers?'

TEN

Bubbles and giggles invoke a welcome forgetting. At bathtime, Izzy and Flora have fun turning Flora's hair into Mohican spikes, but as Flora snuggles down in anticipation of her story, Izzy feels an undertow of guilt for the laughter which pushed Tris from her thoughts.

Flora is ready with *The Squirrels Who Squabbled,* which she and Tris bought from the bookshop in town. As Izzy begins to read, Flora becomes quiet and begins to suck her thumb – a habit Izzy thought she'd left far behind. When the story's finished, she doesn't demand another, but asks instead for Piglet, her favourite toy, cuddling him as she snuggles down.

'Will Daddy be here to read my story tomorrow?' she asks.

Izzy bends down to kiss the top of her head.

'It might be me again tomorrow, but he'll be home as soon as he can.'

'Shall we go and see him in the hospital?'

'We'll see.'

That isn't going to happen, so there will be disappointment. As she says a final goodnight, all Izzy can do is hope that sweet dreams and a new day will wipe the wanting from Flora's mind.

In the bedroom Izzy shares with Tristan, it's easy to believe that nothing's wrong. The dress she decided not to wear to the wedding is still lying on the bed, and the jeans and shirt Tristan changed out of are on the floor – despite her nagging, his terminal untidiness persists. On his bedside table, his glasses are in their case, and a yellowing second-hand copy of Isaac Asimov's *The Gods Themselves* lies waiting for its reader, who Izzy fears may be long absent before he opens it again. On the dressing table, the forget-me-nots he brought her have lost their freshness, though their intricate flowers are still blue.

Wandering into the en suite, she sees the last towel he used hanging over the shower door, and when she lifts it down, it still holds the residual dampness of the water from his skin, and very faintly, the musky, honey scent of Cartier.

Such a poor, poor substitute for the man she longs to be with.

Pressing her face into the folds so Flora won't hear, she weeps.

Philly can't bear David Attenborough – she finds him pompous and sanctimonious, and has doubted for years that he's physically fit enough to travel to those far-flung places where the films are made. All he does these days, she's sure, is to rake in an absolute fortune doing the voice-overs, which frankly are well within the capabilities of a ten-year-old. Crafty old beggar.

But Jerry's a huge fan, and he's sitting here now, gripped by the glowing images of sapphire seas and the bizarre and hideous creatures that live there. Philly's bored, but Jerry gets annoyed at interruptions, so Philly's dividing her time between a book of wordsearch puzzles and playing with the ears of the cocker spaniel lying beside her on the sofa. Around this time of the evening they usually have a gin, but Jerry doesn't want one with his hangover, and Philly always hates to drink alone.

'Jerry,' she says, and he grunts to signify he's heard her but isn't listening. 'Do you think the police will come and talk to us about this Tristan business?'

He glances across at her, and back to the screen.

'Why in God's name should they? It's nothing to do with us.'

'You're the only person I know who thinks that. Everybody else is talking about nothing else, and here you are, not even remotely curious. Aren't you interested to know who people think did it? And how can you say it's nothing to do with us? We were actually there, at the wedding. I should think they'll want to talk to the guests.'

'What, all those people? They haven't got the manpower to waste time doing that. I expect they've got their man by now anyway.'

'You think it was a man, then?'

'What?'

'You think it was a man who did it?'

'I haven't the slightest idea.'

'You just said so. Do you really not think they'll want to speak to us?'

'Not without good reason. How come you're so interested? Did you do it?'

'Of course not.'

77

'Well, it wasn't me either, so there's no need for us to think any more about it. Now please, for God's sake hush, and let me watch the end of my programme.'

Attenborough's solemnly pronouncing on the vastness of oceans and the negative impact of mankind.

Philly gets up from the sofa and pours herself a generous measure of gin.

Izzy must have slept because she has the sense something's woken her, but when she opens her eyes, time has barely moved on.

She can hear a vibration, an intermittent buzzing too sub-dued to be an alarm, like a phone on silent, but her own phone lies mute on the bedside table. Not Tris's iPhone, either; when she brought it home from the hospital, she put it in a drawer of the kitchen dresser.

The buzzing's on the floor, in the pile of Tris's clothes.

Climbing from the bed, she picks up the discarded jeans. The buzzing stops, but there's a weightiness in one of the pockets.

Izzy reaches in and finds a phone she hasn't seen before – a Chinese-sounding brand she's never heard of, plastic and cheap-looking, an object she can't imagine Tris would want to own. Why would he need a phone like this when he has his iPhone?

Odd that he hasn't mentioned it, or used it around her. Could it be for some business use? As she thinks about it, she recalls the *News of the World* phone-hacking scandal, and it becomes logical he'd have a second phone, a throwaway number to give to anyone he doesn't fully trust.

So if someone's calling it, could be it's some chancer from the press, or someone to offer him work. Easy enough to find out; if they've left a message, she can pass the details on to Duncan.

If circumstances were normal, going into his phone is not something she'd ever do, but this is an exceptional time. She finds the power button, and the screen lights up, inviting a fingerprint password.

There's no way she can bypass that. It's a problem she'll have to leave for tomorrow.

Climbing back into the empty bed, she hugs Tris's pillow against her body.

Sleep now comes quickly, pitching her headlong into ominous dreams.

ELEVEN

As she's promised, Bridget arrives early, letting herself in by the front door while Izzy's making Flora's pancake.

'Hi,' she says, dumping her black rucksack on the table. 'Wow, you look so tired. Sorry, but you do.'

Izzy's slipping Flora's pancake on to her favourite plate. 'I had a restless night.'

'Well, that's hardly surprising, is it? If you're going to go on like this, though, maybe you should get something from the doctor.'

'I'll be fine. It's just shock, isn't it? Can you take over here? I'd better get going.'

Bridget's already pouring Flora's milk. 'Of course.'

'And I hate to ask, but would you mind picking up the Fiat? It's still at the hotel. Oh.' Her hands go to her face. 'I'm so sorry, I never thought. How did you get home last night?'

Bridget shakes her head. 'Don't worry about it, honestly. I went to Manzi's. It's only a short walk.'

'He's at the other end of town. You should have said, I'd have run you over.'

'You were in no state to run anybody anywhere. And yes,

I'll pick up the car, but I don't have a key. I gave it to Tris when we swapped.'

'I brought his keys back with me,' says Izzy, opening the dresser drawer where she's put his phone. 'Here.'

'So go on, go,' says Bridget. 'And don't worry about us. We'll find plenty to do on a fine day like this, won't we, my poppet?'

At the hospital, Izzy finds Steph sipping coffee by the window where they talked yesterday, staring down on the world outside. An emergency ambulance is arriving at A&E, bringing in someone else's crisis, and Izzy feels a flash of sympathy for another family having a terrible day.

Steph looks drained, debilitated.

'Hello, Izzy. I'm just grabbing a breath of fresh air. Not that it's very fresh in here, is it? You look tired, my dear. Did you sleep at all?'

'Off and on. How is he?'

Steph shakes her head. 'Still the same. Go through and see. Now you're here, I think Eamon and I should head for the hotel and try and get some sleep ourselves.'

Eamon's already dozing in a chair at the bedside, and Izzy does her best not to wake him as she takes a seat opposite. In Tris she sees – as Steph has said – no discernible change, except that his pallor has increased, as if the essence of him has sunk deeper. When she squeezes his hand, there's no pressure in response.

She whispers, 'I'm here, my love,' in his ear, and glances at the monitors, hoping for some indication he might have heard, but the neon line is steady in its track, echoing a heartbeat that it's hard to believe is there.

After Steph and Eamon have left, the hours slide slowly by, one bleeding into another without waypoints or context. Wondering what the time is, Izzy hunts for her phone, and instead finds Tris's second.

Staring at its blank screen, she has a choice to make. The option to put it back where she found it is still there, but her curiosity is piqued.

She switches it on. Here's the difficult part, the part which last night seemed easy, but now feels both unethical and devious, a betrayal of the mutual trust he believes they have. She's going behind his back, prying into matters which if he were present and conscious he'd no doubt happily share.

Except he hasn't shared.

She lifts his hand, and speaks to him aloud. 'I'm so sorry to do this. When you wake up, I'll explain.'

Placing the phone under his index finger, with her own finger she presses down.

The screen unlocks. Replacing his hand where it will be most comfortable, she finds the phone's settings and adds herself as a second user.

Tom the nurse arrives to change an empty bag of intravenous fluid. As she talks to him, Izzy puts the phone away.

Out of sight, but not quite out of mind.

Laura's one of those lucky people who doesn't mind Mondays. Still in her dressing gown, she makes scrambled eggs and toast for Aidan, Josh and herself, though when she calls up to ask Gemma if she wants any, predictably Gemma declines.

Aidan drains his coffee, thanks Laura for breakfast and

kisses her on the cheek before taking down his cycling helmet from the hall coat-rack and heading out the door.

She calls after him to be careful, knowing it will make no difference; the carelessness around cyclists is mostly in the motorists who overtake too close or don't see them at all.

Josh eats his eggs at the breakfast bar, then asks if he can have cereal as well. He's starting to grow in a way Gemma never has, and his school trousers are too far above his ankles. Happily he's still at an age where he's not self-conscious about the way he looks, and those trousers will be fine for the last few weeks of term. Fingers crossed he stays relaxed about his appearance, not always obsessing like Gemma and her friends.

The kitchen TV's volume is turned down low, and Piers Morgan is interviewing an uncomfortable-looking woman in a suit which looks bought for this occasion. Laura can't hear what's being said but doesn't care; her priority is getting Gemma to eat something before school. Finding the last few pieces of a fresh pineapple in the fridge, she opens a zero-fat strawberry yoghurt and pours it over the fruit.

'Gemma! Hurry up! You'll miss the bus.'

She hears her daughter on the stairs, and when she comes into the kitchen, Laura's relieved to see she's looking fairly normal, without the vastly overdone make-up she sometimes tries to get away with.

Gemma drops her book-bag on the floor, and sits down on a bar stool as far away as possible from Josh.

Laura puts the pineapple and yoghurt in front of her, and though Gemma pulls a teenage face, she picks up a spoon and begins to eat.

'Have you got your homework?' asks Laura, and immediately regrets it.

'For God's sake, Mum. I'm not a child.'

Laura turns away so Gemma doesn't see her eyebrows lift. Piers Morgan's offering his disdainful thanks to the woman in the suit, and the next item begins.

A picture of Tristan's face fills the screen. Laura grabs the remote and turns up the volume.

'Police are no nearer to making an arrest . . .'

Both Gemma and Josh stop eating. Laura switches off the kettle, which is becoming noisy as it reaches a boil.

'. . . apparently motiveless attack on the forty-nine-year-old star, whose condition is given in a press release as serious but stable. I'm joined now by Dr Ahmed Khan, a specialist in head injuries from King's College Hospital here in London. Dr Khan, what can you tell us about the kind of treatment Tristan's likely to be receiving?'

Gemma finishes her breakfast and climbs down from her stool. As she goes to rinse her bowl at the sink, Laura asks, 'Shall I make you some toast? You'll be so hungry by lunchtime. There's peanut butter, or Marmite.'

Gemma picks up her bag. 'I'm fine. I might get something from the newsagent's.'

'. . . It's likely that his convalescence will be lengthy. In the worst-case scenarios, these patients . . .'

'Not . . .'

'I know, not chocolate or crisps.'

Laura touches her daughter on the shoulder and kisses her cheek, smelling the peach shampoo Gemma's loved since childhood. By her ear is a spot she's missed with her too-tan foundation, and Laura thinks how pale her skin is. As soon as the holidays start, they must get out more, get some fresh air.

'. . . and of course we all wish Tristan a speedy recovery. Get well soon, mate.'

'See you later,' says Laura. 'Have a good day.'

'Bye, Mum.'

Through the window, Laura watches her daughter walk away down the drive, head bowed as though the weight of the world is on her shoulders.

The pain of young love. She could murder Darren Ferris. What's Rosie Stainforth got that Gemma hasn't? If she's honest, the answer is big boobs.

She turns down the volume on the TV.

Josh has finished his cereal and is rinsing his bowl at the sink.

'Can I have toast?' he asks.

'Sorry, sweetie, no time.'

'Mum, is Tristan going to be OK?'

Laura realises she doesn't know.

'I hope so,' she says. 'I'll ask Izzy for an update later on.' A car horn sounds outside. 'Come on, get your shoes on, quick. That's Ollie's mum outside.'

TWELVE

The consultant is a stooping, slender giant whose wire-framed glasses make him reassuringly professorial, dressed in the trousers of a suit and a blue shirt with the sleeves rolled above the elbows, as if in readiness for any emergency. He picks up the chart from the end of Tris's bed, and frowns as he studies it.

'Not Tristan Hart after all,' he says, looking at Izzy for an explanation.

'His legal name is Tristan Savage. Hart's a professional name.'

'A stage name?'

'I don't think they call it that any more, and he's never been an actor. But yes, a stage name if you like.'

The consultant offers his hand.

'So you're his partner?'

'I'm his wife, Izzy.'

His hand is warm and he has long fingers, like a piano player. A craftsman's hand.

'Ian Talbot. I lead the head injuries unit here at the hospital. You know you hear people saying, it's not brain surgery? What I do, actually is.'

Mr Talbot seems nice, and Izzy smiles.

'I've never met a brain surgeon before.'

'I like to think you'd find me socially acceptable, but in a professional capacity, to be honest I'm not someone you want to have to deal with. No one wants to be under my care, but here we are. And I don't think I need to say we're doing all we can for Tristan. I wonder if you and I might take a little walk?'

The relatives' room is unchanged except for the pamphlets on the table. The one about bereavement is gone, replaced by a new one on tracheostomy.

'Have a seat,' says Mr Talbot. His legs are too long for the low chairs. He rests his elbows on his knees, touching his lips as he makes a steeple of his fingers.

'So.' His smile has a touch of sadness, and Izzy can't decide if it's for her personally or whether it's perpetual, brought on by being a specialist no one wants to see, or sorrow for all those he can't help. 'We've had a good look at Tristan's scans and, as we suspected, we're seeing some things we'd prefer, quite honestly, were not there.'

He pauses, waiting for Izzy to process this overture to what she's sensing is going to be bad news.

'You don't need me to tell you Tristan is in a coma. The scans show the blow to his head has caused his brain to swell, and in simple terms it's that pressure which has shut down his ability to function. As things stand, he's at what we would determine as the deepest level of coma, and in an ideal world as his brain heals and the swelling reduces, he'll travel back along the spectrum, gradually working towards regaining consciousness and waking up. That's what we're all hoping for.'

'How long will that take?'

A distant look comes into Mr Talbot's eyes, as if he's gazing into the future, though Izzy knows it's far more likely he's taking care to choose the right words.

'The thing is, Izzy, the prognosis for this kind of injury is highly variable. In some patients, we might see significant improvement in only a few days, or a couple of weeks. In others, the damage heals much more slowly, over a period as long as two or three months. I have to be honest with you, and say in a patient of Tristan's age, if we haven't seen major improvement within twelve weeks, the outlook is not awfully promising. We start to have issues with feeding and breathing tubes, and at that point we would need to consider our options. But for the time being, you should remain positive. Talking to him, playing him music, those kinds of things can all help.'

'Can he hear me, then?' asks Izzy. 'Does he understand what I say?'

Mr Talbot tries to smile.

'At the moment,' he says, 'Tristan's far away, and the truth is, I don't know.'

THIRTEEN

Twenty years ago, DS Nate Golding was on his way to the top, there when the arrest was made in the Dinah Steel murder, and a key member of the team responsible for the biggest drugs bust the force had ever made.

There were those who said he didn't fulfil his promise, and it's true he never passed his inspector's exams, nor did he find favour with the new management team when they came in – all young, fit men who couldn't hide their disdain for someone growing slow as he gained weight, who'd lost the necessary speed to make a collar.

Golding doesn't care too much that other members of the team moved on, and up. He still has his own set of talents which investigators value: a dogged attention to detail, an eye for anomalies and an encyclopaedic memory from which he can pluck out details of pretty much any case you'd care to mention since the day he put on his first uniform.

Anyone at Burnt Common police station needs quick answers on the who, when and where, Nate's the man to ask.

Officially, these days, he's on light duties. After his weight issue ballooned into obesity and his suit sizes went up – from a 44-inch to a 52-inch waist – he ignored warnings from his doctor that he was in the danger zone until a TIA – a mini-stroke – put him in A&E, with a lecture on discharge emphasising what the GP had already said.

He could have been invalided out, but his skillset saved him.

When Golding arrives on Monday morning, breathing heavily from having taken the stairs, Muir immediately calls him over.

'How's things?' asks Muir. 'How's Chrissie doing?'

Golding shrugs. 'She's up and down,' he says in his Welsh lilt. 'You know how it is. We had a bit of a ride out over the weekend, thought we might go and see the sea, but the weather was so fantastic you couldn't move for traffic. So we just found ourselves a pub in the end, had ourselves a bit of lunch. I think she enjoyed it, but she gets so tired.'

'You do a great job with her, Nate.'

'It's what you do, isn't it? She'd do the same for me if the tables were turned.'

'I've got something for you, anyway,' says Muir, and hands him the data stick he's got from Craig Dalton, the hotel manager. 'See if you can find any trace of Tristan Hart on there.'

'This the wedding, then?'

'Hotel front car park. That's all they've got. It's the only way in, so he must be on there somewhere, but the question is, beyond his arrival, does he show up again? It's a long shot, to be honest. Just for context, the call for assistance from the hotel came in at 21:38, so he was already injured by then. Which doesn't mean there isn't anything of interest beyond that point, only that it's not likely to be him in person.'

'How's he doing?' asks Golding. 'Is he still unconscious?'

'Kirstie's at the hospital finding out, but needless to say the press are all over it, so we're treating it as a serious assault until we find out otherwise. With him being who he is, if he'd broken a fingernail we'd be handling it as a priority. What it is to be in the spotlight, eh?'

Golding finds space on his desk for his pint mug of tea, hangs his suit jacket over the back of his oversized chair and plugs the data stick into his laptop. When the system locates it, he finds the video for the right day and presses play. Fast-forwarding to where the wedding guests begin to arrive, he uses an hour and a half before that as his start point, at 2.30 p.m. Folding his arms over his belly, he settles down to watch the show.

Golding's blessed with that rare and invaluable mindset which is fascinated by the mundane. He plays the video slowly as he sips his tea, watching the hotel car park slowly fill, freeze-framing to note down registration numbers when he has a clear view of them and noting too the type and colour of car they're on. Cars are one of Golding's specialist subjects, and he can tell a 2017 model from a 2019 by the tail-lights, a sport hatchback from a regular saloon by its alloy wheels. As the wedding guests leave their vehicles and head inside, as staff turn up for work and delivery drivers come and go, Golding's watching them for indicators of their moods and demeanours, noticing those who seem happy to be there, and especially those who don't.

He takes a break to make more tea, dropping in three Canderel sweeteners before he stirs it.

Back at his desk, the video runs on. A taxi arrives, drops passengers, leaves and arrives again twenty minutes later. A

Mini Cooper driven by a young girl puts a dent in a Toyota as she tries to park, then hurries away to a different area of the car park with no acknowledgement.

At 16:09, a metallic white Range Rover Sport pulls into one of the last available parking spaces. Golding admires the car, which is almost new and definitely expensive. Tristan Hart is in the driving seat. He and his gorgeous wife – lucky bastard – climb out, and Tristan helps a very pretty little girl in a bridesmaid's dress from the back. As they walk inside, the wife's holding the little girl's hand, and Tristan's affectionately touching his wife's shoulder.

They look very much in love.

But Golding knows looks can be deceiving.

FOURTEEN

Outside the closed gate at Foxcote Lodge a single reporter remains, a young man left behind on the off-chance he might get lucky with a photo or some unanticipated development in the Tristan Hart story.

He's sitting on a wall under a cherry tree, playing on his phone. Though Bridget doesn't mind him being there, it's her job to keep Flora out of the public eye, and the reporter's got a camera. If he sees her coming through the gate, chances are he'll try for a shot.

Bridget won't give him that opportunity. At the end of the garden where the vegetables used to grow is a place where it's easy to squeeze through the hedge, emerging on to a lane which leads eventually into Sterndale.

Flora's got over her upset at Izzy leaving her, and has enjoyed picking out her outfit for the day: a dress covered in sunflowers which Izzy bought at Harrods', yellow sandals and sunglasses with star-shaped frames, even though Bridget has pointed out the lack of sunshine. As for herself, Bridget never wears anything but black, but in deference to summer she's chosen a long skirt rather than jeans or jeggings, and a black T-shirt with a white slogan: *Even the genius asks questions*.

Flora's insisting she wants to walk, but that won't last as far as the hotel. Bridget's got firm hold of one of her hands, and with the other she's pushing the pink car Flora likes to ride in when her legs are tired.

By the time they reach the high street, Flora's installed in the little car, turning the steering wheel as if she has some control. Bridget's in no hurry. Except for collecting the Fiat, this is an entertainment mission, fresh air and exercise for them both, with no brief but to do what they fancy. Flora's been talking about ice cream, but Bridget's thinking of coffee somewhere with cheese-on-toast for Flora's early lunch.

It's market day, and the high street is busy. The annual carnival is only two weeks away, and Flora rides along with her head back, admiring the blue-and-white bunting stretched between the lamp posts. The livestock market is already over, and the slow-moving traffic is dominated by vehicles pulling trailers of traded cattle and sheep, the stink of the animals heavy in the warm air. As she steers Flora between the pedestrians, Bridget senses they're generating a frisson of interest, catching concerned glances in Flora's direction and heads bent to whisper about them as they go by. Passing the newsagent's, Bridget thinks she'll pick up a couple of magazines, but for Flora's sake changes her mind when she sees the newspapers' front pages. Almost every one of them features Tris's face.

Outside the baker's, the pavement narrows, and she manoeuvres the pink car close up to the wall to allow a young girl to pass.

But the girl stops, brushing back silky, blonde strands of

waist-length hair – exactly the hair Bridget's always wanted, but with her dark Irish curls could never have.

'Hello, Flora,' says the girl, and Flora shyly turns away. 'She doesn't remember me. I'm Debbie, from the hairdresser's. I do Izzy's hair. I just want to say how shocked I am – well, we all are – about Tristan. Is he OK?'

'I don't really know,' says Bridget. 'Apparently it's too early to say.'

'Oh my God.' A woman comes out of the baker's with a French stick under her arm, and Debbie steps into the gutter to let her go by. 'I thought you'd say he's already home and just nursing a headache. Is it serious, then?'

'Pretty serious.'

'Oh my God. We were there at the wedding, we didn't even know anything had happened until yesterday. I can't believe it! And him such a lovely guy. When Izzy was having her hair done last Christmas he came in with mulled wine and mince pies, and he stayed for ages talking to everybody in the salon. You should have seen the old ladies all over him! But who on earth would do that, you know, just bash him over the head? You just don't expect it, do you, in a place like this? Do they think maybe someone was trying to rob him? Listen, Izzy's got an appointment on Thursday, but tell her not to worry about it. If she comes in, great, if not, tell her she can re-book for another time. But send her and Tristan our love, won't you? Tell them we're all thinking about them.'

At the hospital's main reception, the woman's pinned-on tag gives her name as Peggy. It's an old-fashioned name, the same as Weld's maternal grandmother's, though Nanny Peg – unlike this plump Peggy – was a dour, scrawny woman without a maternal bone in her body, as far as Weld recalls. This Peggy is far more like Weld's own mother, who – in mitigation of her frugal childhood – devoted her life to the culinary arts, and put her skills towards what she saw as their best possible use by cooking at a care home for the elderly, where – as she said – the food she put on their plates gave them something to look forward to.

Unfortunately, the main reason for Nanny Peg's disinterest in food – apart from straightforward bitterness at the hand life had dealt her, and a malicious refusal to make it sweeter for her children – was the strength of her addiction to tobacco, and doctors declared passive smoking from Nanny Peg's forty-a-day habit to be the most likely cause of the tumour which took root in Weld's mother's lung. Once established, its growth was exponential, and at only forty-seven, her mother lost the fight. Through all that awfulness, Weld spent a lot of time in a place almost identical to this, first backwards and forwards for scans and tests, then holding Mum's hand through treatments which robbed her of her hair but not her humour. Before all that, Weld was indifferent to hospitals. Now, they have a tendency to make her feel sad.

This Peggy has a large packet of Walker's open under the ledge over her desk. Her smile is warm and genuine, and Weld wonders how she keeps it up, given the unrelenting stream of people lining up to ask questions. But when Weld asks where she'll find Tristan Hart the smile fades, and doesn't come back even when she produces her warrant card and refers to him by what she's recently learned is his legal surname. Peggy picks up a phone, and covers her mouth as she speaks to someone.

When she's put on hold, she takes the opportunity to eat a crisp, swallowing it quickly when she hears a voice responding. A few words are exchanged. Peggy hangs up, looks round to be sure no one is listening, and directs Weld to the ICU on the third floor.

One hospital is indeed very much alike another: the maze of corridors, the rumble of trolleys, the pensive looks on people's faces. And the absurdly long wait for the lifts. When one finally arrives it's the size of a freight elevator and shudders as if it's developed a terminal fault.

Regardless, Weld crams herself in with the other visitors and outpatients, alongside a female doctor in scrubs and white clogs, who glances impatiently up at the ceiling as if praying for people to hurry. Then, just as the doors are closing, a bony hand reaches in to stop them, and an emaciated woman in a dressing-gown shuffles in, pushing the drip feeding the cannula in the back of her hand ahead of her. Her face is creased and jaundiced from decades of smoking, and as she pushes her way into the crowded lift, the stink of fag smoke coming off her takes Weld back to the cheerless, sunless home of Nanny Peg.

At the door of the ICU, she presses the buzzer and waits. A couple of minutes pass before a nurse opens the door a crack, and asks if she can help.

Weld shows her warrant card.

'I'm part of the team looking into Tristan's assault,' she says, and the nurse appears interested. 'I need to speak to his wife – I think she's probably here – and if possible to one of the medical staff in charge of his care. We need to understand the severity of his injuries.'

'Can you hold on a second?' The nurse disappears behind the closing door, and Weld waits, but not for long. The nurse returns, and this time holds the door open, admitting Weld to the inner sanctum.

The unit hums and bleeps with machinery supporting the slow-beating hearts of patients unnaturally sleeping, suspended between life and death. Despite the warmth, Weld shivers.

'This way.' The nurse ushers her into a side-room – a kitchen with a table and four chairs, a microwave and a kettle, and a single porcelain mug on the draining board waiting to be put away. 'Have a seat. Mr Talbot will be in to see you in a moment.'

Weld sits, and tries not to listen to the uncanny silence swelling beneath the sounds of human activity. There are soft footsteps in the corridor, and a man appears in the doorway, looks questioningly at her, and when she stands to greet him, comes in and offers his hand.

'Ian Talbot. What can I do for you?'

Weld shows him her warrant card, and rather than take it at face value, Mr Talbot takes it from her and scrutinises it closely.

'Without wanting to be in any way offensive,' he says, 'I'll need to make a phone call to check your credentials. May I borrow this?'

Weld shrugs. 'Be my guest.'

He's gone for fifteen minutes. A woman who looks as if she hasn't slept for days comes in to make coffee; while the kettle boils, she helps herself to biscuits from a tin, offering it to Weld as an afterthought, though Weld declines. The woman eats her biscuits robotically, without pleasure, and Weld doubts she's tasting anything but sweetness as she stokes her system with calories, necessary but low-grade fuel. When the woman leaves with her coffee, Weld smiles, but the woman's outside the zone of social pleasantries and doesn't respond.

When Mr Talbot returns, his attitude is softened.

'Sorry about that.' He hands back Weld's warrant card and sits down. 'In cases like this, we exercise extreme caution. Members of the press can be totally unscrupulous, and a scoop on Tristan's condition – do they still use that word, or am I showing my age? – could be worth good money. Anyway, tell me what I can do to help.'

'It's straightforward, really,' says Weld. 'We just need an assessment of Tristan's condition, the severity of his injuries.'

'So you can grade the offence?'

Weld nods. 'To be honest, yes, that's about it. I know it sounds cold, but there's a significant difference in our world between a couple of stitches and home tomorrow and might never walk again. I need to know where we are on that scale. Approximately. I'm not asking you to sign your life away on your assessment.'

Mr Talbot smiles, summoning lines around his eyes which make her think he's older than she first thought.

'That's something, at least. I'm a neurologist, so my involvement in Tristan's care relates to his brain injury rather than keeping him hydrated and breathing, which is the work of our intensivists.'

Weld's eyebrows raise.

'Are you saying you're an actual brain surgeon?'

Mr Talbot smiles again, and Weld decides she likes him.

'I am.'

'Wow. That puts my job in perspective.'

'I need hardly say what I tell you now is in the strictest confidence. Tristan is very unwell. He has swelling on the brain which could lead to permanent impairment of day-to-day brain function, by which I mean could affect his speech or his ability to walk, or might render him blind. In short, this could be a life-changing injury for him. He is currently in a deep coma, which from Mother Nature's point of view is where he needs to be while the swelling reduces. It's at that point we'll know what the impact has been. There's not much else I can tell you, until he wakes up. If he wakes up.'

'If?' Weld is shocked. Tristan's a household name, and it seems impossible that for him, it might all be over.

'There are no certainties in the neurological world. Some patients in these situations do really well, others for no obvious reasons do not. We must hope Tristan falls into the first group.'

'Are the family aware of his situation? I'll be speaking to his wife and I don't want to put my foot in it.'

Mr Talbot hesitates.

'I have told them only what I believe is necessary at this stage.'

'So in your opinion, how should his injury be classified? How serious a blow was it, in medical terms? What I'm getting at is, has he just responded badly to an injury someone else might have walked away from?'

The surgeon shakes his head emphatically.

'Whoever hit him, hit him hard. What was the weapon used, by the way?'

'A champagne bottle. You think they meant him serious harm?'

'A champagne bottle is unlikely to deliver a mere tap on the head, so I would think so, yes. Wouldn't you?'

'So this could be attempted murder?'

'In my opinion, most definitely.'

FIFTEEN

As Debbie the hairdresser joins the queue in the baker's, Flora's eye has been caught by a market trader juggling fruit. Bridget's happy to stand and watch, and even happier when the trader presents beaming Flora with an apple.

As they're about to move on, a grey-haired man touches Bridget's shoulder.

'We haven't met,' he says, dithering over whether to offer a formal handshake, deciding in the end to put his hands in his suit trouser pockets. 'I'm sorry to intrude but someone pointed you out to me. I believe you work for Mr and Mrs Hart? I'm Roger Evison, vice-chair of the Town Council. I won't keep you, but I would like to pass on to the family – on behalf of the Council – our best wishes for Mr Hart's speedy recovery. We're most appreciative for all he does for the local community, most appreciative. If you could give them that message, I'd be much obliged.'

When Ian Talbot leaves Weld, he tells her he'll ask someone to find Tristan's wife. Weld asks one of the nurses if there's somewhere private where she can talk to Mrs Savage, and is pointed to the relatives' room.

She's not surprised to have a further wait. Talking to the police can hardly be a priority while her husband's so unwell.

She's checking messages on her phone when the door finally opens. Judging by what she's seen of Tristan on TV, the woman who comes in must be considerably younger than him, and despite the pallor of disturbed sleep is still hugely attractive, wearing this calamity with an enviable air of Gothic tragedy.

Weld gets to her feet and offers her hand, which the woman touches briefly.

'Isobel Savage.'

'DS Kirstie Weld, from West Mercia police. We spoke on the phone yesterday. I'm so sorry you're going through this. It's a shock to everyone that this could happen to someone like him. How's he doing?'

Izzy sits down on a chair that is becoming too familiar. 'Not good, obviously.'

'I'll try and keep my intrusion to the minimum, but there are questions we have to ask at this stage. If we could just go through those, then I'll let you get back to where you need to be. Some of it's basic background and the rest relates specifically to Saturday's events. Are you OK with that?'

Izzy looks at her with steady eyes and nods. Weld finds a clean page in her notebook, writes the date, location and time, and takes down Izzy's address and contact numbers.

'How long have you and Tristan been married?'

'Just over four years. Maybe nearer five.'

'Forgive my asking, but was he married before?'

'Yes. He'd been divorced a while when I met him. I don't

know anything about her, really. He doesn't like to talk about the past. He has a very positive outlook, always looking forwards. That's his life's mantra, forwards not back.'

Doesn't like to talk about the past, thinks Weld. Could mean there's stuff there he doesn't want this shiny new wife to know.

'Any children?'

'We have a daughter, Flora. She's three.'

'Does he have any children from his previous marriage?'

Izzy's face becomes stony.

'Is this relevant? Surely you should be restricting your questions to people who were at the wedding? I can assure you Tristan's son has absolutely nothing to do with this.'

Sore point. Weld makes a note.

'Why don't you just take me through what happened on Saturday? What time did you arrive at the hotel?'

Izzy looks doubtful.

'I don't really know. I don't wear a watch. If I want to know the time, I look at my phone, but it didn't seem to matter. We went to the ceremony at the church, which started at three, so probably about an hour after that.'

'We'll say four, then. What happened next?'

'We had the meal. That took forever. The food was good but the service was slow, I suppose because they had to get round so many people. Then they cut the cake, all the usual stuff. By that time Flora was getting tired and fractious, so Tris rang Bridget to come and collect her.'

'Bridget?'

'Bridget Feahny, our nanny.'

'I'll need her details.'

'You can find her at the house.'

'And what time did Bridget arrive?'

Izzy shakes her head.

'I don't know. Tris took Flora and he seemed to be gone ages.'

'When you say ages, how long do you mean?'

'I think it would have been over an hour. They started the music, and I danced a bit. When Flora wasn't there any more I had a couple of drinks, and time goes a bit fuzzy when you're drinking, doesn't it? When I started to get worried, I asked Aidan to go and look for him, and he was gone a long time, too. When he came back, he said you – the police, I mean – were looking for me, so I went with him and Laura to the pool, and there he was . . .'

'Aidan and Laura, who are they?'

'Laura's a friend, and Aidan's her husband. He has a bike shop just outside town, proper bikes, you know, racing bikes, mountain bikes. You might know him, actually. He used to be a policeman.'

'What's his last name?'

'Ridley. Aidan Ridley.'

Weld smiles.

'Oh yes, I know Aidan. A bike shop, is it? No surprise there. Do you have contact details for them?'

Izzy takes out her phone and reads them out.

'Just a few more questions,' says Weld. 'Was there anyone at the wedding Tristan had issues with or who might have had issues with him, anyone he wasn't very pleased to see?'

Izzy shakes her head vehemently.

'Everyone loves Tris. He's really popular in the town.'

'What about outside the town?'

'People approach him like he's a personal friend.' Unbidden, the memory of finding the second phone flashes into Izzy's mind, and Weld notices a nanosecond of hesitation before she goes on. 'How you see him on TV, that's just how he is in real life.'

Weld decides not to push it. 'Has he been bothered by anyone recently? Famous people sometimes attract the wrong kind of attention, stalkers, online trolls – anything like that?'

'Not that I'm aware of. He doesn't do social media. He says life's too short.'

'Had he been drinking? People can get themselves in trouble when they've had a couple of drinks.'

'Tris doesn't drink, he's teetotal.'

'So you're not aware of anyone who would wish him any harm?'

'No one. I just don't understand it. Who would do such a thing to him?'

'That's exactly what we're going to find out,' says Weld. 'We've recovered the weapon used . . .'

'Have you? What was it?'

'I'm sorry,' says Weld, 'I thought you would have been told at the scene. He was hit with a champagne bottle. Are you sure your husband wasn't drinking?'

'Positive. I've never known him drink in all the time I've known him. Have you found any fingerprints on the bottle, anything like that?'

'I believe the bottle itself was smashed, but forensics are looking at it. Another thing which could be helpful would be for us to have a look at his bank accounts, see if we can find anything there.'

Izzy frowns. 'That seems very intrusive. Why would you need to do that?'

'That kind of data often shows up useful leads. It's all in the strictest confidence.'

'I don't see why that's necessary when he's the victim. Tris is very protective of everything in his personal life. I'm sure you can understand that.'

'Of course.'

'The real problem for me,' says Izzy, 'is that I'd hate for him to wake up and be mad at me for giving permission he wouldn't have given himself.'

'It's certainly not our intention to put you in a difficult position with him. If you don't feel comfortable, we can apply to the courts for a production order, then it's not your fault if he doesn't like it. I know it might feel as if we're being pushy, but the faster we move, the quicker we'll get a result.'

Izzy sighs, seeming to breathe out all her self-assurance. 'Do whatever you need to do. I don't mean to be obstructive, but everything seems so surreal, talking to you, being in this place with Tris so unwell. It's like living in a bad dream I can't wake up from.'

'We appreciate what a difficult time this is for you,' says Weld. 'Here, let me give you my card. If you've any questions you've forgotten to ask, or if you think of anything you think we should know, even the smallest thing, please, call me. In an investigation like this, those tiny, seemingly irrelevant details can make all the difference.'

SIXTEEN

Bridget sees Philly before Philly sees her, and is almost quick enough to dive down the alley leading alongside the White Lion into Carter's Yard, where there's a chocolatier she'd usually avoid as Flora will get upset when she's refused one of their white chocolate rabbits. But the little pink car is awkward to turn round, and by the time she's pointing in the right direction, Philly is at her side.

'Hello, Bridget, how are you? How are you holding up? I just can't believe what's happened.' Philly's dressed as she always is, in effortless summer chic: chinos, Italian sandals, a plain but plainly expensive white T-shirt and a string of bright wooden beads which look like they came from a toyshop but probably cost more than Bridget earns in a week. She bends and chucks Flora under the chin, in the way Bridget's grandmother's friends always used to as they remarked how much she'd grown. 'Doesn't she look gorgeous? Such a pretty dress! Is it from Caramel? I'm sure it must be. Izzy always knows just where to shop. How's she doing? Is there any news?'

'Not in front of the children, Philly,' says Bridget, and

makes as if to head down the alley, since turning round again will only cause a delay she doesn't want.

'I'm just going for coffee.' Philly talks on as if Bridget hasn't spoken. 'The Blue Moon looks really busy, so I thought I'd try that place on Boongate, what do they call it, Darjeeling Unlimited? People say it's quite good but I'm not keen on the woman who owns it, I think her husband's something to do with the Lib Dems. Still, that shouldn't affect the coffee, should it? Will you join me? It'll just be a quick one. Jerry wants to run a couple of errands, but I asked him to wait in case the farrier arrives, and I told him I wouldn't be long. You'd like a drink, wouldn't you, sweetheart?' She bends down again to Flora. 'Or maybe Auntie Philly could buy you an ice cream.'

'No ice cream for us today, thanks,' says Bridget, but the damage is already done, and Flora's face is crumpling at the thought of being denied.

Bridget acts fast, producing a fruit roll-up from her pocket and handing it to Flora.

'I did try to ring,' Philly goes on. 'I didn't want to call Izzy's mobile – you just don't know what might be going on at the hospital, do you? – but I left a message on the house phone. I thought she might call me back when she was home, but I suppose she can't spend all her time talking to well-wishers.'

Bridget glances down at Flora, relieved to see she's occupied with unwrapping her fruit roll. 'If you ring, you'll get the answerphone, or me. Tris's agent's PA is responding to messages, so I'll let her know I've spoken to you and tell her to cross you off the list.'

'I only rang because we've been wondering what they've

said at the hospital, if they've said how long he's likely to be in there. We've been so worried, Jerry and I.'

Deciding that an argument over a white chocolate rabbit is preferable to Philly's insensitivity, Bridget's moving further towards the alley.

'I really don't think this is the time or the place for this kind of conversation,' she says. 'Like I say, I'll make sure Izzy knows you're thinking about them.'

'Have they any idea who did it?' Philly asks of her retreating back. 'I suppose when he comes round he'll be able to tell them. Do you think the police will be speaking to us?'

'Only if you're lucky, Philly,' says Bridget.

Laura makes virtuous use of some of her morning, ironing a whole basket of laundry while she watches *Homes Under the Hammer*, then cleaning the bathroom and vacuuming the stairs.

It's warm enough to enjoy a cup of coffee in the garden, and she takes a seat on the decking Aidan put together two summers ago when he was still recovering from his injury but felt well enough to do something outside. The decking's looking pretty; the fuchsias and trailing geraniums are all flourishing in their pots, though Gemma's been neglecting her organic vegetables – a sprawling courgette, tomato plants whose fruit may never ripen, and fledgling lettuces where slugs have been active. When she's finished her coffee, she fills the watering can and gives them all a drink.

The garden's always soothing. Over the roofs of the other houses in the cul-de-sac she can see the hills, and the faint smell of the bracken which covers them stirs thoughts of open country. Maybe this weekend they should all get out there, challenge themselves to a few miles' hiking.

And yet – with Tris so unwell, it feels disloyal to be planning things to enjoy. She wonders how Izzy is today, and thinks about trying to call, even picks up her phone to do so, but decides it might be inappropriate given Izzy's situation. Instead, she sends a text – *How's things? Thinking about you. Here if you need anything x* – and sits on a while, hoping for a reply, but her phone stays silent.

Maybe a wander round the market will take her mind off things. Picking up her coffee cup, she goes inside.

The pavements of Sterndale aren't the bracken-covered hills, but it still feels good to walk. The market's coming to its end, the stall-holders packing up vans with waste cardboard and unsold merchandise, and the greengrocer's calling knock-down prices on the last of his stock. The Herefordshire strawberries look fabulous, and she buys two punnets; Josh and Gemma will love those. Then she buys local farm cream from the butcher's, and a quiche to have with salad for this evening's dinner.

The chance to browse a while in the bookshop is too good to pass up. Fairey Tales is tucked away down a lane running off the high street, its curved Dickensian windows set in a frontage of old stone, its door so low, Aidan would have to duck as he went in.

But the lane's all but blocked by a blue transit van parked with its nearside wheels on the pavement, so Laura's forced into the road to get by. In a house opposite the bookshop, a circular saw whines.

Grace Fairey tells the story that she decided on her career as a child, when she realised her name was perfect for a bookseller. Laura thinks that's too twee to be true; in any case, she's heard the Sterndale rumour that Grace used to be a postmistress until she was prosecuted for embezzlement. That story doesn't ring true either, unless Grace managed to retain the misappropriated funds to set up the business.

Aidan doesn't like Grace. With what he calls his policeman's nose, he says there's something off about her. Laura's told him he's too suspicious, that his time on the force has made him see the worst in everyone.

As Laura goes in, the brass bell hanging over the door jangles. Tourists think it's part of the old-fashioned ambience, but Grace has admitted to Laura it alerts her when anyone comes in, making her less vulnerable to shoplifters.

Laura closes the door, shutting out the saw's whine. Grace is at the counter, unpacking a box of books which fill the air with the scent of ink and new paper. There's an elderly man reading in one of the comfortable chairs among the stacks, his walking stick leaning against the chair arm, and a weary-looking young woman with a sleeping newborn strapped to her chest, rocking from foot to foot as she studies the parenting section.

Grace removes the glasses she was using to read a packing slip.

'Hello, Laura. That damned racket from those builders! Every time anyone walks in the shop it sets my teeth on edge. I've asked him to keep the windows closed, but what does Dave Garner care about anyone else's livelihood but his own? I told them they shouldn't hire him – the man's an out-and-out crook – but they didn't listen, so let it be their funeral. Anyway, how are you?'

Laura nods non-committally. The truth is that Tris and Izzy are monopolising her thoughts, casting gloomy clouds over the day.

'I'm OK. I've come to pick up this month's book club choice, if you've got it.'

'I thought you'd be in, so I put one under the counter for you.' Grace reaches down and takes out a book. The cover is in blue pastels, the title silvery cursive. 'I think it was Karen's choice, wasn't it?'

Grace has a way of expressing her opinion of people's reading choices which Laura finds disconcerting. Plainly Grace doesn't think Ollie's mother Karen is any judge of literary worth.

Fearing she might be regarded the same way, Laura comes to Karen's defence. The last book she picked was a novel centred on gay relationships in the eighties, shocking, educational and funny in equal degree. All the group loved it, even elderly Miss Mason.

'If it's Karen's choice, you know the discussion's going to be lively,' she says, finding her purse to pay.

'Is there any news?' asks Grace lowering her voice, glancing across at the new mother and the old man. 'From Izzy?'

Laura hands over a ten-pound note and shakes her head.

'Not really, no. I spoke to Izzy yesterday but she didn't seem to know much. Weekend staff and all that. She said there should be more today, but I haven't heard anything yet.'

'It's been such a shock to us all. I find it incredible anyone could do that. Such a kind man, and so generous. I'm not supposed to say, but he made a big donation to the primary school, bought them several hundred pounds' worth of books, and all through me. So thoughtful. Small businesses like mine are so vulnerable, and he seemed to understand – not in a patronising way – that the little boost would do me good. Of course he's too modest to want it spread around, so I keep his confidences. And little Flora – he brings her in all the time, buying her books to read at bedtime. Such a gift to a child, isn't it, a father who reads? My own father was a very literate man – he'd read everything from Plato to Austen – and that rubbed off on me.'

She hands over change, and Laura puts the book in her bag. In the parenting section, the newborn is beginning to fuss, and the young woman makes her rocking more emphatic. The elderly man glances over at her sympathetically, and turns a page.

'Speaking of Flora, Bridget brought her in earlier,' Grace goes on. 'I'm always happy to have children in here, as long as they're not running round and causing chaos. But Flora's always so well-behaved, isn't she? Bridget bought her a couple of picture books – she was happy to take my recommendations, I'm flattered to say – and she bought a book for herself, too, a fantasy novel. Not a genre I know an awful lot about. I did wonder whether she ought to have put a personal purchase on the card Tristan gave her for household expenses, but it's not my place to say anything. A book is not a great extravagance, after all.'

'She's spending a lot of time at the lodge, with Izzy at the hospital. I suppose she needs something to pass her time while Flora's asleep.'

'Yes, I suppose so,' says Grace. 'Though you do wonder,

don't you, whether small acts of – well, it's not exactly dis-honesty, is it? Perhaps you might say taking advantage – but whether those small acts might be a slippery slope that lead to something more serious?'

The Blue Moon café is busy with an influx of out-of-town visitors, and all the outside tables are taken. Laura doesn't mind; she prefers to sit inside amongst Angie's regulars, and when she's ordered coffee and a slice of red velvet cake, finds a seat at a table where a couple are just leaving.

At the next table, Miss Mason is sitting with Professor Tarn. Miss Mason is wearing her sunhat, even though she's indoors, and despite the day's warmth, her home-knitted cardigan is buttoned up to the neck. Professor Tarn has removed his fedora and hung it on the back of his chair, along with his walking stick. The professor is eating a cherry scone, thickly spread with Angie's strawberry jam. Miss Mason doesn't eat in public, but is sipping tea from a pot of Earl Grey.

'Laura!' she says, as Laura sits down. 'How lovely to see you. We were just saying, weren't we, Professor, that we hadn't seen you for a while.'

'Busy, busy,' says Laura.

'Did you enjoy the wedding?' asks Miss Mason. 'I'm so sorry I wasn't invited. I do love a wedding, don't you? But what a drama there was, I gather. Did you see anything of it yourself?'

'Not really,' lies Laura. 'Too busy showing off my moves on the dance floor.'

Angie puts cake and coffee in front of Laura.

'It's all anybody's talking about in here, I'll tell you,' she says. 'Is it right somebody's whacked Tristan over the head?'

'I think that's a rather crude way of putting it,' says Miss Mason. 'Angela, would you put me a drop of hot water in this pot?'

'I believe he's sustained a head injury,' says Professor Tarn. 'That's what I read in the *Telegraph*.'

'National press, eh?' says Angie. 'Fame for Sterndale at last.'

'Not the kind of fame we want, really,' says Laura.

'Beats me who'd do something like that,' says Angie, picking up Miss Mason's teapot. 'It sends the shivers up me, thinking there's someone in this town capable of being so brutal. Makes you wonder who you've got living next door.'

'No doubt someone was inebriated,' says the professor, spreading butter on the second half of his scone. 'Alcohol and aggression go together, as often as not.'

'Maybe it was some crazed fan,' says Laura. 'A stalker who finally tracked him down.'

'If there was, it would be a female,' says Miss Mason. 'Mark me, there'll be a woman in it somewhere.'

'Do you really think so?' asks Angie, intrigued. 'What makes you say that?'

Miss Mason leans forward to press home her point. 'I think it's a crime of passion. A man like him draws women like moths to a flame. One of them will have had a hand in this. I can feel it in my bones.'

Back at home Laura finds the door is unlocked, and she wonders whether Aidan's come back for some reason, though there's no sign of his bike or helmet. Anyway, it's Maria's day off, so if Aidan left the shop he'd have to close it, and only a dire emergency would provoke him into that.

Gemma's schoolbag is on the kitchen floor.

Laura puts the quiche and the cream in the fridge, and the strawberries by the sink ready for washing. At the bottom of the stairs, she listens. Sounds like Gemma's on Netflix or YouTube, as usual.

Upstairs, as she stands outside Gemma's door she hears music that reminds her of a tune she can't quite recall. She taps at the door and walks in.

Gemma's sitting at her desk. As she hears the door open, she closes the lid of her laptop, a standard move for her these days. Laura's about to give her a telling-off – what does she think she's doing, playing truant? – but then stops. Gemma's been crying.

Disarmed, Laura goes to her and puts her arm around her shoulder, while Gemma wipes away tears.

'Sweetheart, what on earth's the matter? Why aren't you at school?'

'They sent me home. I wasn't feeling well.'

'What sort of not well?'

'I've got terrible period pains, Mum. Really, really bad.' She rubs her stomach to make the point.

'Poor old thing.' Laura strokes her daughter's hair. 'Why don't you jump into bed? I'll get you a hot water bottle and some paracetamol and you can have an hour's sleep. I thought you looked pale this morning. You should have said something. And why on earth didn't you ring me? I could have picked you up.'

Laura feels relieved. A case of PMS explains Gemma's mood over the weekend. Thank God for that: no anorexia.

In the kitchen, as she finds painkillers and fills a hot water bottle, she realises what the music on Gemma's laptop made her think of, proof – if it were needed – how much Tris and Izzy are on her mind. Upbeat and brass-heavy, the tune was reminiscent of the theme to an old show she used to watch before she was married with her own mum.

Find a Fortune, presented by an up-and-coming newcomer, Tristan Hart.

SEVENTEEN

Mid-afternoon, and the team is gathering in the first-floor conference room at Burnt Common. The air-conditioning's malfunctioned, and despite the cooler temperature outside, with so many bodies in there, the room's hot. Muir asks someone to open a window, but they're sealed shut. Weld has left her jacket at her desk, pleased she wore a short-sleeved blouse. Golding's really struggling, and his face is red. Taking a handkerchief from his pocket, he wipes away the sweat.

Muir's leading the meeting, standing up front alongside a pinboard holding a photo-portrait of Tristan and a map of Sterndale where the hotel's location is marked in red.

'OK, let's get started,' says Muir, and people settle into chairs and fall quiet. 'Thanks for coming. I think we all have the background to this case – if you don't, I suggest you get on iPlayer and take a look at the weekend's news bulletins. Basically this is a serious assault on Tristan Savage – known to most of you as Tristan Hart – which took place on Saturday evening during a wedding celebration at the Sterndale Hall Hotel. Kirstie's been to the hospital this morning, and the victim's condition is currently listed as stable with no firm prognosis as yet. In other words, he could make a full recovery, or he may have suffered life-changing injuries. Only time will tell. What we're all hoping is that he'll regain consciousness in the next few days and give us his account of what happened on Saturday, and that he'll name his assailant. That would make our job very much easier, but let's not be dragging our feet on the assumption that will happen. Most of us have dealt with cases where medically a victim did not get the outcome the family was hoping for.

'Obviously this case is very much in the public eye, which puts us under some pressure. Having said that, although the pool of suspects is potentially high – given there were a hundred and fifty guests at this event as well as hotel staff – the assailant is likely to be contained within that group, meaning it's on the right side of unlikely we'll be needing major resources from outside the area. That's the good news. The bad news is, we don't currently have much to go on. He was hit over the head with a champagne bottle, and I do mean champagne and not one of its cheaper cousins. Those bottles as you may know have some weight. He was hit from the side, which means he may or may not have been in dialogue with whoever struck him, and might or might not suggest it was someone he knew. Hardly conclusive, unfortunately. Anyone, even a perfect stranger, might have approached him. For someone like him, I'm sure it happens all the time. The big question for me is what he was doing in the pool area in the first place. It's a long way from the marquee where the reception was being held, so what prompted him to go there? I think there's the possibility of a pre-arranged meeting, but if that's the case, I don't think it's one the wife knew about. Is that right, Kirstie?'

Weld nods agreement. 'Mrs Hart, or Mrs Savage, says she noticed him missing and asked a friend to look for him, that friend being our old colleague Aidan Ridley, who some of you will know. If she knew where he was, she's lied about it to me.'

'As for the bottle, the weapon, that ended up in pieces,' continues Muir. 'Whether dropped after the assault or deliberately smashed is impossible to say at this stage. We've recovered prints, but they've been hard to isolate. A lot of people will have handled that bottle, from wine merchants to bartenders and waiters, before we even get to the wedding guests, and we don't yet know whether our attacker is among those people, or whether it's someone not yet on our radar. So the prints may prove useful, but there's a crowd of people who could have left prints without criminal intent who'll need to be eliminated.

'What we do have is CCTV of the car park area which Nate's been having a look at – how did you get on, Nate?'

Golding hauls himself out of his chair and lumbers to the front of the room where a laptop connected to a projector screen waits on a table.

'I may have got something,' he says, and the room shifts with anticipation.

Using a mouse, he opens a video file, and a blurry shot of the hotel appears on the screen. Golding fast-forwards to where the time on the screen shows 16:00.

'The victim appears twice in the time-frame I was looking at, between 14:30 on Saturday and the time the emergency call was made, which was around 21:30. He arrives with a woman I assume is his wife at around 16:10. Here they are.'

The team watch the screen closely as the white Range Rover

parks, and Tristan and Izzy climb out before Tristan goes to lift Flora from her car seat.

'The wife's Isobel, known as Izzy,' says Weld. 'The daughter's Flora.'

'And off they go inside,' continues Golding. He glances down at his notes. 'The next time we see him is at 20:21.' He moves the video on accordingly. 'Here he is, coming into shot from round the side of the hotel, carrying his daughter. You see him looking round, as if he's expecting to see someone.'

'He was supposed to be meeting up with the nanny,' puts in Weld.

'And here she is.' Golding runs the moments where Tristan hands Flora over to Bridget and watches her drive the Range Rover away.

'My kind of boss,' says Muir, 'giving her the keys to that beauty. If he'd given them to me, I'd have been inclined to take the long way home.'

'Maybe she did,' says Weld.

'Now this is the interesting part,' says Golding, letting the video move on at half-speed. 'Tristan's heading back inside, but he's intercepted, by this guy.'

He freezes on the clearest frame he can find: a balding, overweight man in shirt sleeves, no tie.

'So who the hell is that?' asks Muir.

'Looks to me like he was waiting for him,' says Weld. 'After an opportunity to speak to him away from the crowd.'

'What happens next?' asks Muir.

Golding lets the video run: the man rises from the bench where he's been sitting; the two men talk; Tristan goes into the hotel entrance; a few moments later, the man follows.

'Nothing after that?' asks Muir, and Golding shakes his head. 'Seems to me then this guy goes straight to the top of our list. First thing we need is to get an ID on him. He looks like a wedding guest, so Kirstie, why don't you make it a priority to pay a visit to the mother-of-the-bride and get hold of that guest list. Take Amber with you on that.' Weld turns round and smiles at Amber Gooch, the team's new transfer to CID, who gives her a thumbs up. 'Nate will print you a still from the video. Ask her if she knows who it is and we'll take it from there. When you've got the list, send it through pronto for distribution to the team. The rest of you, as soon as it arrives, divide it up between you and get talking to everyone who was there on Saturday, and that includes hotel staff and guests independent of the wedding. Excellent. What else have we got?'

'The video the soldier made,' says Weld. 'We could do with getting a look at that.'

'Nate, I'm putting you on that too,' says Muir. 'What else?'

'Just as background,' continues Weld, 'when I spoke to Isobel she mentioned a previous wife, and Tristan has an estranged son from that marriage, though she's insistent what's happened is nothing to do with them.'

'Noted.'

'And there's the nanny.'

'You and Amber can handle that too. OK? Everybody clear? We're looking for a fast result on this one. I know it's a lot of legwork, but the answer's there, somewhere. And whoever makes the breakthrough can have the pleasure of buying me a pint.'

As the team are leaving, press officer Brad Sherman approaches Muir.

'Just wondering what I should put out as an update,' says Sherman.

'You heard what I just said, Brad. We're doing the legwork, the nitty-gritty. You can say that we're making enquiries, how about that?'

'Not very sexy, though, is it?'

Muir regards him.

'You know what your trouble is, Brad? You want everything to be shiny baubles to bring the spotlight back to you. If you had any experience of policing more than just writing about what other people do, you'd know it's ninety-nine percent sweat and one percent sexy. The sexy part could be weeks away, maybe even months. So you'll just have to say, enquiries are continuing.'

'But you've got a suspect now.'

'No, we absolutely have not. We've got some bloke on a video who might be our victim's brother or his next-door neighbour or the husband of some woman he's been shagging. It might be the local publican come to claim an unpaid bar bill. I don't know who that guy is any more than you do, so don't you dare go saying there's a person of interest in this case until I tell you it's OK to say it. Do I make myself clear?'

'Perfectly clear, as always,' says Sherman, as he walks away.

EIGHTEEN

It's been a long day.

Izzy's amazed how exhausted she is, when she's done nothing but sit at his bedside, stroking his hand, talking nonsense to him, willing, hoping for there to be some flicker of a change. That hope won't switch off, won't let her focus on anything else – the book she's brought to read, a game on her phone, the tattered pages of a communal magazine.

There's been no change in him – no visible change, at least – but the waiting and watching take their toll, and it costs energy constantly to appear upbeat and optimistic in front of Eamon and Steph – and in front of Tris, because who knows what he can hear? – when all she wants to do is break down and cry.

And though they mean to be supportive and have every right to be there, Steph and Eamon don't help. Behind her crow's-feet smile, Steph's showing a tyrannical streak, inventing rotas for fetching the endless coffees and taking breaks, and having three of them there makes a drama of every decision: who should call the nurse to change his drip (Steph nominates Eamon), who should liaise with the neurosurgical team (Steph nominates herself), who should go and buy newspapers to see what's being said in the press (Steph nominates Izzy).

So it's good to be home, snuggled up with Flora, who seems happy enough to have spent another day with Bridget. Whether Bridget was happy, though, is another matter; she didn't hang around this evening, just said there was somewhere she had to be and called *See you tomorrow* as she hurried out the door. Izzy doesn't blame her for the quick getaway; caring alone for a small child will make anyone crave freedom, eventually. Doubtless Bridget's in the White Lion by now, drinking a pint of Timothy Taylor's and having a catch-up with Manzi.

Home's rhythms and routines are calming, borderline cheering, after the stresses of the day. There are some new books – obviously Bridget's been shopping – which Flora is desperate to read, and they turn the pages together, with Izzy enjoying almost as much as Flora the absurd tale of an elephant trying to get on a bus.

As Flora's settling down, she asks, 'Is Daddy coming home tomorrow?'

Izzy kisses her forehead.

'Not tomorrow, munchkin, no.'

'Shall we go and see him, then?'

'I think you might be too busy tomorrow.'

'I might,' agrees Flora. 'Bridget says we can bake cupcakes. We got unicorns to go on top of them.' She yawns. 'I think Daddy would like one, don't you?'

'I'm sure he'd love one. And he loves you, very much. Now, close those beautiful eyes. Sweet dreams, munchkin.'

When Izzy's sure Flora's sleeping, she runs a deep, warm

bath loaded with bluebell-scented oil and slips into the silky water. Tight muscles begin to loosen and her mind slows. Eyes closed, she begins to doze.

When her phone buzzes she's tempted to ignore it, but what if it's the hospital?

The bath water, anyway, is growing cold. Climbing out, she towels herself dry, finds clean pyjamas – a pair Tris picked out for her – and lies down on the bed to check who rang.

The missed call was from Laura, and Izzy decides to call her back. She needs to vent about Steph, and talk about her worries for Tris after what the doctor said. And maybe Laura can be persuaded to have Flora for a few hours, to give Bridget a break if she feels she needs it.

But the phone in her hand has reminded her about the one in her handbag, which she should check in case there's anything on it for Duncan. Digging it out of a side-pocket, she switches it on, presses her finger on the screen, and it opens up.

At the top of the screen, the Messages, Missed Calls and Voicemail icons are all lit. She goes to messages first and finds two unread, both from someone named Tina.

She frowns. Tina? Who is Tina?

One is dated Friday, the other Saturday, the day of the wedding. Both are short and give little away.

17th now no good, how about 18th x
Can meet on 21st if u prefer T x.

For a few moments she studies the texts, trying to remember anything he might have said about the 17th and where he's told her he will be, but his schedule's always busy and it's impossible to recall. A glance at the rest of the chat shows replies which are purely functional – arrangements to meet, nothing more – and typical of his style, without punctuation or niceties or emojis, reflecting his dislike of the technology. She wonders why they've been messaging when he'd usually prefer to call.

Does that mean he's been avoiding being overheard?

She feels a prickle of disquiet, and asks herself again, racking her brains – has he ever talked about a woman named Tina? No one comes to mind.

Don't get carried away. The obvious explanation is that Tina's someone of such little importance, he never mentioned her. She could be someone who cuts his hair – no, that's Beth – or does his facials – that's Rhianna – or looks after his nails. Didn't he find a new manicurist recently? Maybe it could be her.

There's still the voicemail, which she's somehow reluctant to hear.

Don't be absurd.

She presses play and listens, but there's no message. Whoever was calling hung up at the beep.

What does it matter? The whole country knows by now what's happened to Tris. No one's expecting him to call.

Why not leave it at that? But the disquiet is niggling, and she needs reassurance. She clicks on the Contacts file, thinking she'll see a random list of inconsequential people.

But the list contains only six names, and – she can't stop the thought – it reads like a list of hookers: Anna, Julie, Molly, Rowena, Sandi, Tina.

Too late to stop now. She opens up the text streams.

Apart from Tina, where the chat seems to have been going

on – for God's sake, it's been over a year – the messages are sparse, covering arrangements for a single meet-up, then nothing more.

If Izzy were the jealous type, she'd be thinking this is some kind of sleazy indulgence.

But she and Tris are in love, and he's always been faithful to her.

Hasn't he?

NINETEEN

Weld is pleased to have been teamed up with Amber Gooch for this trip. Gooch is bright and sunny-natured, happy to talk but not a chatterbox, keen to learn and prepared to take instruction without the kind of objections you sometimes get in male recruits, who tend to think that the moment they're in CID they've risen above the menial tasks of door-to-door enquiries and making tea.

Gooch is well turned out in a smart dress, and her hair is immaculate, as always. She specialises in vintage up-dos full of twists and knots, which she insists are easily accomplished, if your sister's a beautician and has taught you well. With her short, platinum bob, Weld could never dream of such a hairstyle, but she admires its feminine elegance, and so do the men in the office, if the attention Gooch gets is anything to go by.

The drive to Sterndale isn't the same summery outing as it was when Weld came up here with Muir on Sunday, but the heat and the traffic are both reduced, for which she's grateful. As they drive, Gooch points out a couple of hiking trails she's done with her boyfriend. Weld glances up the valley sides, thinking it looks too much like hard work.

'You'd get on well with DI Muir,' she says. 'He loves his hill walking. I prefer the flat. Give me a treadmill any day.'

'You should try it,' says Gooch. 'Fitness and fresh air, all for free.'

'Rain and wind,' counters Weld.

'And pubs.'

'There's a pub next door to the gym.'

The satnav takes them directly to the address provided by the hotel manager, on a prosperous-looking road leafy with mature sycamores whose roots are pushing up cracks in the pavements. The houses are oversized mid-twentieth-century semis which have been around long enough to have developed individual characters. Most of them look well cared for and cherished.

'I'd love to live in one of these,' says Gooch, 'but that's not happening unless we have a lottery win. We're saving up for a deposit to get out of our horrible flat, but I don't think we'll be moving to Sterndale any time soon.'

'Me neither,' says Weld. 'But you gotta dream big, girl. What number are we after, twenty-six? Looks like it's that white one.'

Weld parks the car, and leads Gooch up the drive towards a front door sheltered by the arched entrance of a porch. The front garden's tidy, the lawn cut and edged by weed-free beds planted with sapphire lobelia and white alyssum.

'Look on the bright side,' says Weld, ringing the doorbell. 'At least you don't have to do any gardening.'

But Gooch looks wistful.

'I'd love a garden,' she says. 'We've no room even for pot plants in our flat.'

The door is opened by a woman in late middle age, wearing

a heavily lipsticked smile and what Weld suspects would be called loungewear: pink joggers and a long-sleeved T-shirt to match. Her tan looks like it could be real, and her hair is freshly coloured; her toe- and fingernails are painted a beige shade of nude, though as she holds the door open, Weld sees one of the fingernails is chipped.

She holds up her warrant card, and behind her Gooch does the same.

'Mrs Clements? DS Kirstie Weld and DC Amber Gooch. I rang you earlier.'

'Yes, yes, come in, come in. You're very prompt. I've just boiled the kettle. Go through, we'll go in the lounge. Make yourselves comfortable. Will you both have tea?'

Gooch accepts for them both; it's a technique she's learned from Weld. Even if you don't drink it, while they're out making tea, it's an opportunity to have a look round.

The furnishings are tasteful but bland: cream sofa, cream curtains and a cream carpet that still has the smell of new wool. There's a blown-up black-and-white studio portrait on one wall – a boy and girl lying on the floor smiling together in an improbably harmonious sibling pose – and on another, facing the sofa, a huge TV. The whole room, thinks Weld, is a metaphor for modern life: lacking colour, too focused on the kids, too dominated by TV.

The most striking feature of the room is its partial transformation from a comfortable living room into something more like a warehouse. The sofa's been pulled away from the wall, and behind it are stacked masses of gifts wrapped in silver and white paper.

'Wow,' says Gooch. 'Christmas come early.'

'Wedding presents.' Mrs Clements is carrying in a tray of tea with, Gooch is pleased to see, a plate of biscuits. 'Excuse the mess. Suzie wanted to save them until they get back off honeymoon, something to look forward to. They've gone to Vietnam, of all places. It's such a long way – I couldn't face the flights myself – but Ed's always wanted to see it, and Suzie didn't mind where they went, as long as it was warm. Dennis and I thought we were being adventurous going to the south of France, but tastes change, don't they? Help yourselves to Hobnobs. I suppose you want to talk about what happened at the wedding. To be honest, Suzie and Ed don't know anything about it, unless they've seen it on the internet. Do they have the internet in Vietnam? I suppose it's everywhere, these days. We'd already seen them off before we knew anything was wrong, and you'll understand it didn't seem necessary to spoil what had been such a lovely day. They'll find out all about it soon enough, and obviously it's nothing to do with them.'

Seated on the sofa, Gooch has taken a biscuit and is nodding politely at Mrs Clements's monologue. Weld sees an opportunity to get a word in.

'You're quite right, Mrs Clements . . .'

'Gail, please.'

'Gail, we are here about the wedding. We got your details from the hotel manager, and he's suggested you could provide us with the guests' contact details.'

Mrs Clements pulls a face.

'I suppose I could. How is he, anyway, Tristan? Such an awful thing! You know, I shouldn't say it, but I regret inviting them now. It was Suzie's idea. We can't claim to be close friends – chance would be a fine thing – but Suzie knows

Izzy slightly through local events – they go to the local pub sometimes, attend fundraisers, they've been really good for Sterndale in that way – so she thought she'd like to ask them, and they accepted. Suzie was over the moon. Well, it adds a bit of sparkle, doesn't it, having a celebrity at your wedding? It was my idea little Flora might like to be a flower-girl to keep my granddaughter company, the other bridesmaids all being that much older. Of course, if we'd any idea of what was going to happen . . . Suzie will be so upset when she finds out.'

'So you could provide us with a list?'

'Yes, of course. Dennis was so organised, he put it all on a spreadsheet, names and addresses, whether they'd RSVP'd, where they were going to sit, any dietary requirements, vegetarians and gluten-free and even one or two vegans. Kept him quiet for hours, that did. I can print you a copy if you'd like.'

'If I give you my email, maybe you could send it to me before we go?' says Weld. 'And we have a couple of questions about people who were there. We're told Tristan made a video for some servicemen in Iraq at the request of a soldier. Can you tell us who that was?'

Mrs Clements's face softens.

'Ah, lovely Simon. One of Suzie's old school mates, such a likeable lad. Well, hardly a lad any more, is he? His mother worries herself sick about him when he's out there. Wasn't that a sweet thing for Tristan to do? It brought a tear to my eye, I'll tell you.'

'And his last name?'

'Fisher, Simon Fisher. His mum lives just round the corner from here. Pauline, I know her quite well. He lives with a local girl, and they've got a baby now, a little boy. It's a worry

134

for his girlfriend too, isn't it? His address will be on Dennis's spreadsheet, same as all the others.'

'One last question.' Weld hands Mrs Clements a video still of Tristan in the car park, talking to the man she's keen to identify. 'Can you tell me who this is?'

Mrs Clements looks around the room.

'I'll need my glasses.' She finds them in a case on the seat of an armchair, but the fashionable frames age her, and even wearing them she holds the picture far away from her face.

'Now who is that?' She squints, puzzled. 'There were so many people there, and some of them were Ed's friends and family I've never met before. Maybe he's from their side. No, wait a minute. I know who that is. Murray. Murray . . .' She looks out of the window for inspiration. 'Murray Roe. He married my cousin, Fiona. I hadn't seen either of them for years. Fiona and I are friends on Facebook, but that doesn't mean very much, does it? They live a long way from here, somewhere in the West Country, I think. Stroud, maybe? Is that the West Country? Anyway, after I put it on Facebook that Suzie and Ed were getting married, she messaged me and asked if they could come to the wedding. You could have knocked me over with a feather.'

'So you wouldn't have invited them as a matter of course?'

Mrs Clements shakes her head.

'No. Like I say, we hadn't seen them in years. But she said it would be lovely to see everyone and catch up, and it was difficult to say no, though to be honest we were trying to get the numbers down, not up. I wouldn't like to tell you how much it's all cost. So they got an invitation. That's him, anyway. That's Murray.'

'And his contact details will be on your spreadsheet.'

'Oh yes, Dennis put everyone on the spreadsheet. Except Tristan and his wife, of course. You can understand, people like that don't want to give out phone numbers and such. Suzie hand-delivered their invitation, and they posted back the RSVP. He's not lacking the money for a stamp, is he? Have you seen their house? It's gorgeous, just gorgeous. So much character.'

'So this Murray Roe,' says Weld. 'Can you think of any reason why he'd be talking to Tristan?'

Mrs Clements draws in her eyebrows, thinking, and is shaking her head to say no. But then light comes into her eyes.

'Yes, I can, as a matter of fact. I don't know why I didn't think of it before. There's a family connection there, or at least there used to be, years ago. Murray's step-sister was Tristan's first wife.'

Weld and Gooch leave with digital and paper copies of Dennis Clements's wedding guest spreadsheet file, and screenshots of the Messenger chat between Gail Clements and Fiona Roe. They've also copied Gail's excited Facebook announcement that the Harts would be attending her daughter's wedding.

In the car, the two women take a closer look.

'Look at the dates,' says Gooch. 'Fiona Roe makes first contact with Gail Clements less than twenty-four hours after she tells the world the Harts will be there. That's a coincidence.'

'But we don't like coincidences, do we?' says Weld. 'Maybe we'll be having a trip to the West Country. I'll forward this guest list through to Nate, then the rest of them can get going on working through it. Lucky them.'

'So is Stroud in the West Country?' asks Gooch.

'To be honest, I have absolutely no idea,' admits Weld.

TWENTY

The drive from the Clements house to Foxcote Lodge takes less than two minutes. The young reporter has disappeared; for the moment, Tristan Hart has slipped off the front pages.

Gooch jumps out to open the gate and Weld drives through. In an area which would hold at least six cars, only one space is taken, by a Fiat 500. Weld parks alongside it, nose-up to a lichen-covered sundial. As she climbs from the car, she reads the motto carved around its face: *Time brings all things to pass*.

Foxcote Lodge is made beautiful by its imperfections, by centuries of additions to the original manor house in a mismatch of architectural styles. The black-and-white geometry of half-timbering butts up against rough-cut, rustic stone; the intricately patterned chimneys are in terracotta brick. A white butterfly rests on the mauve wisteria shading the arched oak door.

'Wow,' says Gooch. 'This is what I'd buy if I won the lottery.'

Weld pulls a cast-iron handle, and somewhere in the house a bell jangles.

A young woman opens the door. She's wearing black, and

Weld wonders if that's what passes for a nanny's uniform these days.

Weld shows her warrant card.

'Bridget Feahny?'

'That's me.' Bridget holds the door open to let them in and leads them down a jute-carpeted hall. Inside, Weld's expecting dark wood and dimness, but instead the house is made bright by skylights and floor-to-ceiling windows, by maplewood floors and walls emulsioned in a shade of luxuriant cream suggesting Farrow and Ball. The lodge feels welcoming and calm, as if it's enjoyed centuries of happy occupation.

'That's a cool T-shirt,' says Gooch to Bridget. 'Nine Inch Nails, right? My boyfriend's a big fan.'

'Me and my boyfriend both,' says Bridget. 'We're saving up to go and see them in New York.'

She leads them to a beamed living room, where Flora is sitting on a soft rug which invites the burying of toes, surrounded by toys. Yellow roses in a Chinese vase are dropping petals on the windowsill. Flora looks up at Weld and Gooch with curiosity, then holds up a piece of a half-completed puzzle. Bridget crouches to help Flora put the final pieces in place.

'Done. You're a little star, aren't you? I think that deserves a treat. Shall you and I go and have a look in the biscuit tin, see if there's anything in there?' Flora nods, and Bridget takes her hand to encourage her to her feet. 'Have a seat,' says Bridget as she leaves.

Gooch is pleased to do so, stroking the silky sofa fabric and prodding a cushion to see what it's stuffed with. Weld wanders over to the window and looks out on the view of lawns and statuary, and a pergola cascading with mauve wisteria.

Gooch is smiling with delight.

'I'd so love a sofa like this,' she whispers. 'I can't wait to tell my mum what this place is like.'

'You've got a choice, sofa or deposit for a house,' says Weld. 'I'd go with the house.'

'I've given her a gingerbread man and set her up in the playroom with a few episodes of *Kipper*,' says Bridget as she returns, 'but don't for God's sake tell anyone. I'm supposed to limit her screen time to thirty minutes a day. But then I'm not supposed to be here full-time, so hey ho.'

Slipping off her shoes, she curls herself into an armchair. There's a paperback open face-down on an occasional table within easy reach, alongside an expensive-looking phone.

'So. What can I do for you?'

Gooch is hunting in her bag for a pen to take notes.

'We'd like to talk to you about what happened on Saturday,' says Weld.

'If you mean about the wedding, I wasn't there. I don't get invited places. I'm just the hired help.'

Weld checks Bridget's expression, trying to ascertain whether she's joking. The impression she's had from Izzy is of a woman kind and anxious to help, but there's an undeniable trace of sourness in Bridget's voice.

'This doesn't look a bad place to work, to be honest,' says Weld.

'No, you're right,' says Bridget. 'I've had worse. But my contract's part-time. I have a life outside, you know? I've been stuck here for days now and I'm ready for a break.'

Gooch has found a pen, and is also tuned in to the tone of what Bridget's saying. Taking a cue from a subtle nod of

139

Weld's head, she asks, 'How long have you worked for the family?'

Bridget shrugs. 'Since Flora was born, pretty much. Tris thought Izzy was too fragile to look after a baby by herself, so he found me. Don't get me wrong, I was only too happy about that, but nobody wants to be taken for granted, do they?'

'In what way, taken for granted?' asks Weld.

'Oh, you know. Coming home a couple of hours later than you said you would. Forgetting to pay me on a Friday and asking if I can wait till Monday. Well, no, I can't wait till Monday, because I haven't got tens of thousands in the bank like they have. It's just thoughtlessness. People like them forget how it feels to hurt for money. In her case, she's never known in the first place.'

There's a short silence. Weld's remembering what Gooch said earlier about trying to escape the grimness of their flat, and finds she has some empathy with Bridget. She gives Gooch the nod again. Let the girl get some practice.

'Could you run us through the events of Saturday?' asks Gooch.

'From my point of view?' asks Bridget. 'They all went off to the wedding, leaving me like Cinderella waiting to go and get Flora when they'd had enough of being parents and wanted to be free to enjoy themselves.'

'Where were you waiting?' asks Gooch. 'Were you here?'

'I drove over here about midday, got Flora ready in her bridesmaid's dress. After they left I didn't do much. I read a bit, watched TV, until Tristan rang.'

'What time was that?'

Bridget shrugs again.

'I dunno. About eight-thirty, maybe. Anyway, off I went and there he was, and he shocked me by giving me the keys to the big car, said they'd take the Fiat. You could have knocked me over with a feather. He's never done that before. I thought he must have been drinking.'

'How did he seem?'

'Tired. He'd been carrying Flora about. It's no picnic, carrying a child her age, take it from me.'

'Anything else you can remember about him?'

Bridget shakes her head.

'Not really, no.'

'Did you see anyone else in the car park while you were there?'

'I can't recall anyone, no. But as I was leaving, I was just concentrating on driving that great big tank, so I wasn't really noticing anything.'

'It's a Range Rover, isn't it?' asks Weld. 'Did you drive straight back here?'

Bridget looks at her.

'Yes, I did. You won't be finding me on any of your cameras, if that's what you're thinking. Flora was exhausted – too much heat and excitement – and she fell asleep as soon as I put her to bed.'

'And then?'

'And then they didn't come home. Laura Ridley rang me about half past ten, told me what was going on and asked if I could stay, which I did. Didn't have much choice really, did I? Laura sounded like she'd had a few so it wasn't an option for her to come and babysit Flora. So I said I'd stay until Izzy could get back here, which she did on Sunday afternoon. That's all I know.'

'And how was she when she got back?'

'How you'd expect. Exhausted. Upset. I gave her a big glass of wine which she looked like she needed.'

As Gooch is making notes, Weld asks, 'Would you say they have a happy marriage?'

'Perfect. Don't you read *Hello* magazine? Their wedding was all over that.'

'And in real life?'

'Yeah, I'd say they're happy. Far as I know, anyway.'

'No rows?'

'Not that I've heard. But you know what they say. Not in front of the help.'

'No money worries, as far as you're aware?'

Bridget gestures around the room. 'If they had, they could always sell something.'

'Are they popular in the village, as a family?' asks Gooch.

'They're celebrities. People can't get enough of them.'

'And do you like them?'

'She's not my taste, but she's OK. He's OK too, he's always been all right with me. But it's not me you want to be asking, is it? You want to be asking whoever it was who hit him.'

'And have you any idea who that might have been?'

'None at all. Well, not really. I've been thinking about it, because who wouldn't, and I wondered whether it might be some woman. You know, an affair that got out of hand.'

'But you just said they're happy in their marriage,' says Weld.

'I said they appear happy. The women round here treat Tris like George Clooney, and he's a man, isn't he? If someone were throwing themselves at him, would he say no? Mind you, it works both ways. He's irresistible to the women, she has the same effect on the men. Half the blokes in Sterndale have got the major hots for her, tongues dangling on the floor and drooling like idiots. Even my Manzi isn't immune, and he generally doesn't go for skinny bints. I don't know anything, mind. I'm only speculating.'

'Would you speculate about anyone in particular?'

Bridget considers. 'There's Philly. Phyllida Gaze. She seems very interested in what's going on and how Tris is doing. I mean, most people are interested, but she's way over the top. Made me wonder whether she has a bit of a crush on him, or whether there's something more.'

Gooch has made a note of the name. 'Can you give us an address for Phyllida?'

'You won't need one, their house is easy to find. If you turn right opposite the White Lion and go a mile or so down that lane, you'll find their place, a big, old stone house with horses in the field. Philly loves her horses almost as much as she loves her gin.'

'And you really think her interest in Tristan has been out of the ordinary?' asks Weld. 'You must have had plenty of people asking after him, surely?'

'Not to the extent she has. She even asked me if she should expect a visit from you guys.'

'Did she? Why would she be expecting us?'

Bridget shrugs. 'No idea, but then what would I know? I'm just the nanny, after all.'

'So what did you make of Bridget Feahny?' asks Weld, as she and Gooch get back in the car.

'Not exactly what I'd want in a nanny,' says Gooch, fastening her seat belt. 'I think I'd be looking for someone – well, fluffier. But listening to Nine Inch Nails would knock the fluffiness out of anybody.'

Weld starts the engine. 'Who the hell are the Nine Inch Nails, anyway?'

'An industrial rock band. Not my taste at all. But that T-shirt she was wearing, did you notice what it said across the front? *Grey would be the color if I had a heart.* That's a quote from one of their songs.'

'What song?'

'*Something I Can Never Have.*'

TWENTY-ONE

Gooch persuades Weld they should eat lunch before visiting Phyllida Gaze, and they're lucky to find a parking space right outside the Blue Moon café, which pleases Gooch because their lunchtime special sandwiches on the blackboard include local sausages with mustard and beef with horseradish and rocket.

They find a table outside, on a wide pavement with a view of the busy high street. When the waitress comes to take their order, Gooch goes with the beef, Weld with feta with roasted tomatoes and hummus.

When the food arrives, Gooch's bread roll is overflowing with slices of meat.

'You're such a carnivore,' says Weld. 'Don't you worry what it's doing to your arteries?'

'I'm too young to worry about stuff like that,' says Gooch. 'Besides, I need to keep my iron levels up.'

'You could take a supplement.' Weld bites into her salty cheese. 'A multivitamin.'

'That's not the same, though, is it?' suggests Gooch, chewing on a mouthful of her sandwich. 'Red meat builds your muscles, keeps me fighting fit.'

'Who are you planning on fighting? No one I know, I hope.'

'In this job, you never know, do you? Shall we split a pecan brownie before we get on?'

Bridget was right: the Gaze house is easy to find, standing in isolation on a lane which winds through Sterndale's outskirts and then into open country. Weld thinks it looks like an old vicarage - though there's no church anywhere near – and it's the kind of house that might feature in a period drama, with a drawing room and a wine cellar and a butler's pantry below stairs. Most of the outbuildings are still being used as stables, and a trio of handsome horses are grazing in a paddock, their tails flicking away flies in the shade of a spreading oak.

Gooch reads the brass nameplate as they drive between the stone gateposts: Beacon House.

'This isn't bad either,' she says. 'How many lottery wins for this?'

'Forget it,' says Weld. 'Would you really want to do all that cleaning?'

'I bet they have staff.'

'Exactly.'

There are two cars parked in front of the house, an old-fashioned silver Jaguar and a black Volvo estate. As Weld pulls up alongside the Jaguar, a liver-and-white spaniel trots towards them from round the side of the house, wagging her tail. Gooch gets out to stroke the dog, and Weld's taking a moment to check a message which has just pinged her phone, when a tall, thin woman appears.

'Can I help you?' The woman looks born and bred to this place – especially in her navy jodhpurs and riding boots – but

Weld knows that's by no means a given in this area which attracts the wealthy from across the whole country, especially the overpriced south-east. But her accent is as far back as minor royalty, suggesting she might be the real thing.

Weld shows her warrant card. 'West Mercia Police. We're looking for Phyllida Gaze.'

'Oh. That's me. I think you'd better come in.'

Philly leads the policewomen from the front door right through the house, checking behind herself as they go in case her boots are leaving marks on the carpets. Normally she'd never wear boots in the house, but she feels it would put her at a disadvantage to leave them at the door and be in stockinged feet while they're properly shod.

The study's not a room they normally use for visitors, but it's tucked away at the back of the house and not overlooked. Jerry's left it rather messy, with paperwork scattered haphazardly on the desk, and a heap of outdated newspapers on the floor beside the comfy armchair, but that can't be helped. In their line of work, she's sure these women have seen far worse than this.

'Please, sit down.' She watches Weld take the office chair while Gooch lowers herself into the armchair, and wonders if she should offer them tea. Far better not: tea will delay them too long. 'What can I do for you?'

'We're here to ask you some questions about the assault on Tristan Savage,' says Weld.

'Savage?'

'You probably know him as Tristan Hart.'

'Is that his real name, then, Savage? I didn't know that.'

'There's no reason why you should. Do you mind if I call you Phyllida?'

'Just Philly is fine.'

'Can you outline for me the nature of your relationship with Tristan, then, Philly?'

'Relationship? We don't have a relationship. Not beyond being casual friends, as a couple. Me and Jerry, him and Isabel. Izzy, she's known as, but I'm sure you knew that.' Philly senses Weld watching her and smiles to show she's relaxed. 'It's such a terrible business, isn't it? Do you have any idea yet who did it? Though I don't suppose you'd tell me if you had.'

Weld notes Philly's smile, which seems slightly off-key, given the seriousness of Tristan's condition. Beyond the study door, a floorboard creaks.

'I don't suppose I would,' says Weld. 'The thing is, your name has been mentioned to us as someone who may have been close to Tristan.'

'Close to him? Who on earth has said that? Close in what way?'

'Have you tried to make contact with Tristan's family since the assault?'

'Make contact? What do you mean? I've rung the house, of course. Hasn't everyone? I was hoping to get news of how he is, but no one answered. I'm sure they've much better things to do than answer the phone, though I don't imagine it would kill Bridget to pick up the receiver every now and again.'

'You mean Bridget Feahny?'

'Yes, Flora's nanny. She's in the house most of the time, and I suppose they're paying her plenty to be there, so you might think . . . Oh, wait a moment. She sent you here, didn't she? The little madam. What has she been saying, exactly?'

'So you have rung the house. How many times?'

'I might have rung twice, since no one answered the first time. It's not a crime, surely, to be concerned for one's friends?'

'No one's suggesting it is. Would you say the Savages are happily married?'

'How should I know? They certainly seem so.'

'And you, Philly – are you happily married?'

'Blissfully, thank you, for more years than I care to count. But what does the state of my marriage have to do with anything?'

'So just to be clear, you know Tristan only socially?'

'Yes.'

'And when he comes round from his coma, he'll confirm that, will he?'

'I should bloody well hope he will. It's the truth. What are you suggesting, exactly?'

Weld shakes her head. 'I'm suggesting nothing at all. We're just trying to establish the facts in the case.'

'Well, the facts are Tristan and I are friends, and not even close friends, to be frank.'

'And yet you phoned the house twice to have news of him? Most people would just have left a message or sent a card. Did you have a particular reason for being anxious about his condition?'

'I wasn't anxious, I was merely concerned.'

Weld leaves a silence, but Philly doesn't speak. Instead, she glances at her watch.

'I'm afraid I have to get on. My husband will be needing my help.'

'Of course,' says Weld, as she and Gooch stand. 'Let me give you my card. If you do think of anything, maybe you'd give me a call.'

Philly opens the door. A man is there, balding, fine-featured. If he weren't so scruffily dressed, Weld might take him for a lawyer.

'Jerry!' Philly puts her hand on her chest, as if calming her heart. 'For God's sake, you frightened me half to death. What on earth are you doing, standing there like some kind of wraith?'

Jerry looks at Weld and Gooch. 'Good afternoon. I came to see if you ladies might be wanting some tea.'

'Actually, they're just leaving,' says Philly, and she leads Weld and Gooch to the scullery door.

When they're gone, Jerry follows Philly into the kitchen.

'Shall we have some tea, then?' she asks, carrying the kettle to the tap. 'Since you mentioned it.'

Standing at the centre of the quarry-tiled floor, Jerry is clenching his fists. 'I presume that was the police. You did promise me, you know.'

Philly turns back from the sink. 'Promise you what?'

'That you wouldn't do this any more.'

Philly switches off the tap. 'Do what?'

'Is he something to you, Philly? Is that why they were here?'

Philly turns to face him.

'Don't be ridiculous, Jerry. I had a feeling you would think that. A man like him would never look at an old woman like me.'

150

Jerry's face falls into sadness. 'So you'll be faithful now, will you? Now that you're too old to have your pick?'

'I didn't mean it like that. For heaven's sake, Jerry. I gave you my word, didn't I?'

'You did, yes,' says Jerry. 'But I'm afraid when it comes to promises, your track record isn't too good, is it, old girl? Don't bother making tea for me. I've things to do outside in the yard.'

TWENTY-TWO

Muir is preparing to leave at a time which is early for him, though many in the office have already gone. Closing his office door, he walks towards the exit, raises a hand to Nate Golding, who's still at his desk.

''Night, Nate. Have a good one.''

'Do you have a moment, Boss?'

Really, Muir doesn't, but that's hard to say to a man putting in more hours than he is.

'If you can make it quick.'

'Very quick,' says Golding. 'But I think you'll find it interesting.'

As Muir crosses the office, Golding's lining up another piece of video footage.

'I've got a court booked in an hour,' says Muir. 'I haven't played this guy in a while, so I'm expecting a good thrashing. I'm hoping to get a few minutes' warm-up before he arrives. The last thing I need is to pull a hamstring.'

'It's a small thing, really,' concedes Golding. 'It could wait till tomorrow if you'd rather.'

'No, come on, let's see it. You've found it, least I can do is find a minute to look at it.'

'It's the video the soldier shot at the wedding,' says Golding. 'Kirstie sent me the guy's contact details and he was good as gold, emailed it through by return. It's only thirty seconds in total, but what you need to watch is who's in the background.'

He hits play, and there's Tristan reliving the moment, arm around Simon Fisher, giving what sounds like a sincere speech to Simon's mates in Iraq. But Golding freezes him mid-sentence, and points with a pencil at the screen. In the background, a man is moving closer to hear better what Tristan is saying. The look on his face is cynical malice, so pronounced he could be about to heckle or call bullshit.

'Recognise him?'

Muir peers at the screen.

'Is that the same guy?'

Golding nods.

'Same guy who was talking to him in the car park. No love lost there, is there?'

'There certainly isn't,' says Muir. He pats Golding on his bulky shoulder. 'Good work, Nate. Now pack up and be done for the day. That family of yours needs you every bit as much as we do.'

Izzy's home from the hospital earlier than she's been the last couple of nights. Steph is still keen to play nurse-in-charge, and if that's what she wants to do, Izzy's content to let her do so, knowing she has childcare responsibilities at home.

Flora's sitting at the kitchen table, colouring a picture of a fairy amongst what are now technicolour flowers. When Izzy kisses the top of her head, she looks up and smiles.

153

'Are you OK?' Bridget's gathering up her stuff, her phone and that book she's still reading. 'You look really peaky.'

Izzy pours herself a glass of iced water from the fridge door dispenser.

'I've got a headache. Dehydration, probably. There's nothing to do there but drink coffee. All that caffeine doesn't agree with me.'

'You're starting to look too thin. You should eat something. Sorry there's not much in the fridge. We didn't go shopping today. You could order in a pizza.'

The thought of melted cheese turns Izzy's stomach.

'I'll find something.'

'Do you want me to make you a drink? You know, a proper drink? There's lime if you want a vodka.'

'Really, I'm fine.'

'The police came to see me today,' says Bridget.

Izzy glances over to be sure Flora's focused on her colouring. 'Really? What did they say?'

Bridget shrugs. 'They just asked about the day of the wedding, what time you went out, stuff like that. It felt like they were ticking boxes, to be honest. I presume they've already spoken to you?'

'I didn't get a chance to tell you,' says Izzy. 'A detective came to see me at the hospital yesterday.'

'And?'

Izzy glances again at Flora, who's engrossed in choosing between a turquoise pen and magenta. 'She said someone hit him with a champagne bottle.'

'Oh my God. Who would do that?'

Izzy pours herself more water. 'They don't know.'

'What, no clues at all?'

'I think they have clues. They have the pieces of the bottle, at least, so I suppose they'll check those for fingerprints. She said she'd keep me updated.'

'And how's Tris doing? What are the doctors saying?'

Izzy shakes her head, grabs a tissue from the box and dabs at her eyes. 'Oh, Bridget. Sorry, look at me, I'm a mess. They say it's too early to know.'

'Too early to know what?'

'Whether he'll recover.'

Bridget's expression is of disbelief. Crossing to Izzy, she puts an arm around her shoulder. 'Ah, come on now, there's no need to be upset. If they think there's any doubt about him getting better, they just don't know our Tris, and that's a fact.'

The light midsummer evenings are long when you're spending them alone. Izzy does her best to be upbeat with Flora's bedtime routine, but Flora seems a little out of sorts herself, and falls asleep before her story's even halfway through.

Izzy spends a few minutes tidying the room, placing a teddy back on the armchair with Flora's soft toy menagerie, finding space for the book they've been reading on the bookshelves.

The Squirrels Who Squabbled, she notices, isn't there, and after a quick search, she decides to ask Bridget where it's gone.

But there's no need. As she bends to give Flora a last goodnight kiss, a corner of the book's cover shows under the pillow, and when Izzy gently pulls it out, it comes with Tris's reading glasses in their case.

She strokes Flora's head. Maybe she doesn't talk enough to Flora about how she's missing Daddy, and could she be

155

missing Mummy, too? A thought touches the back of Izzy's mind, that maybe Flora isn't happy with Bridget, but Flora's always loved Bridget, so why should that change now? This sudden and unwelcome upheaval is good for none of them. Flora will settle down again as soon as Daddy's home.

But when will that be?

There are hours of daylight still left. Downstairs in the lounge, she tries to relax, but the pages of her magazine don't hold her attention. She starts to watch a film – a romcom Tris would hate – but her focus comes and goes. Pausing the DVD to analyse why, she expects the answer simply to be her worry over Tris.

But that's not it.

What's needling her is what she's found on that damn phone.

TWENTY-THREE

When her phone rings, Weld's getting out of the shower. Wrapping her hair in a towel, she runs to the bedside table to answer it, and sees Muir's number in the display.

'Good morning.'

'Morning. Sorry to be so early.'

'No worries. What's up?'

'It's about this Murray Roe interview, the one in Stroud,' says Muir. 'I've decided I'll take that. Nate can go with me.'

'Nate?'

'He's been doing some great work lately, but he's becoming too office-bound. I think getting out and about would do him good. I don't want him thinking we're taking him for granted.'

'OK . . .' says Weld slowly.

'You were going down there with Gooch, weren't you?'

'That was the plan.'

'I'm reassigning you both for this morning. I want Gooch to go back to the hotel and talk to the staff there. Tell her to arrange for statements to be taken if she finds anyone with anything interesting to say.'

'By herself?'

'She'll be fine. Meantime, I want you to oversee the video interviews with the two youngsters who reported the assault, make sure it's all handled properly and that the right questions get asked. After that you'd better switch horses for a couple of hours and see how we're getting on with that post office robbery from last week. We're in danger of dropping the ball on that one. I'm calling a team meeting at four p.m. so you can give me an update then. All clear?'

'Absolutely clear.'

'Then I'll see you later.'

'See you this afternoon. Drive safely.'

There'll be no records broken, but the temperature for the next couple of days is forecast to be hot, just how Muir likes it. Golding, however, is struggling. Muir's got the air-con on full blast and Golding's removed his jacket and loosened his tie, but his face is still an alarming shade of red, and sheened with perspiration.

Ten minutes into the drive, Muir pulls into a service station and puts in an unneeded twenty pounds' worth of fuel. Inside the kiosk, he picks up two bottles of water.

'Here you go,' he says, as he gets back inside the car. He hands a bottle to Golding and takes a drink himself. 'We have to keep ourselves hydrated. I sweated buckets in my game last night, and I took a pasting so I can't even say it was worth it.'

Golding looks at the bottle as if he doesn't know what it is.

'I don't drink much of this stuff,' he says. 'I prefer something with some flavour, a Coke or a Pepsi.'

'That's better for you, in the long run.' Muir pulls back out into the traffic and is guided by the satnav on to the A49. Reluctantly, Golding drinks. 'How's everything at home, Nate?'

Golding fiddles with the air-con controls, trying to persuade more cold air out of it.

'Not so bad,' he says. 'Chrissie's all right, really. She gets a bit down sometimes, when she starts thinking why her, but that's just how things have turned out, isn't it? Easy for me to say, I know. She's at that age now where she should be starting to have boyfriends and be going out with her mates, but that doesn't seem to be happening for her.'

'But she does have friends?'

'Yes, she's got friends. But she feels self-conscious about the way she is. Peggy tells her she needs to find some uglier mates, make herself look good. I wish she wouldn't say it. I really don't think it helps.'

'Anything new on the medical front?'

Golding shakes his head.

'Not really. They keep talking about an operation to improve her hearing, but that's never come to pass. So we just soldier on. The thing with cerebral palsy is that it doesn't actually get worse, so that's a blessing.'

'She's not in any pain, though?'

Golding stares out of the window.

'She's always in pain, poor lamb. It's just that she's learned to deal with it.'

'But they can give her something for that, surely?'

'Up to a point. But most of the painkillers they prescribe have side effects and some of them are addictive. Besides, who wants to take painkillers for the rest of their life? Even if it's not a very long life.'

Muir's regretting now he raised the subject. They lapse into silence for a few minutes, during which Muir is pleased to see Golding sip his water.

As they join the A40, Muir asks, 'Any suggestions on how to tackle this guy?'

Golding shrugs. 'I'd ask him first if he spoke to Tristan, see if he volunteers it. If he lies about it, we'll know he's got something to hide. We can hit him with the video then.'

'Sounds good to me. Maybe he'll be upfront and say he was just being friendly.'

'Maybe he will, but I don't think Tristan was keen on being friendly in return.'

On the face of it, Murray Roe seems a nice enough bloke. He suggests they might sit outside – an idea Golding agrees to with alacrity, hoping for a breeze. Roe leads them to a table and chairs under a parasol which shades most of the mid-terraced house's small garden, which is what Muir, if he were being generous, would describe as minimalist – a stretch of block paving with high fences dividing them from neighbours on both sides.

Roe's wife – who Gail Clements named as Fiona – strikes Muir as dour and humourless, with deep lines at the bridge of her nose from years of frowning her discontent. Her long hair is dyed ash grey – a colour which does nothing to lift the sallowness of her skin – and the peppermint she's sucking might sweeten her breath, but it isn't dispelling the reek of cigarette smoke from her clothes.

160

She offers cold drinks, and Golding immediately asks for a Coke. Muir opts for water and Roe asks for a beer, which Muir thinks is an interesting choice before lunch. Plainly Fiona thinks so too, and she flashes him a look which urges caution. Is she thinking it will loosen his tongue, make him in some way indiscreet? If so, she heads it off at the pass; the bottle she brings him is well-chilled and tempting, but it contains alcohol-free beer.

As she goes back inside, she pulls the sliding French door to, though Muir notices there's a window open in the kitchen which means she'll hear everything that's being said, if she so chooses. Roe doesn't comment on the beer, but takes a long drink. He looks well-fed to the point of high blood pressure – a man on the same road as Golding, unless he takes care – and if you were judging by appearances, you'd take him for a stockbroker or banker. Yet this modest house on this down-at-heel street strongly suggests he's not, or at least not any more; the fact he's home during office hours implies he may not be anything at all, though he looks too young – just – to be retired.

Muir decides Roe's career or lack of one might be a good place to start.

'No work today?' he asks, lightly.

'I'm between jobs at the moment.'

'What line are you in, Mr Roe?' asks Golding, assuming the same tone of polite just-asking as Muir.

'By profession, I'm in marketing,' says Roe. 'But the company I was working for folded, showed us all the door. When you get to a certain age, it's not as easy as it used to be to get into something new.'

Muir wonders how long ago it was that Roe was laid off. No need to ask that question now, but they might come back to it.

'The reason we're here, as you probably know,' Golding is saying, 'is pretty much routine. We're talking to everyone who was at the wedding on Saturday where Tristan Hart was assaulted. We're trying to find anyone who saw anything, or who had contact with Mr Hart at that event.'

Roe drinks more beer. 'Mr Hart? Don't you mean Mr Savage?'

'I think Hart's the name most people would know him by,' says Golding.

'We've always known him as Savage, and we used to know him pretty well,' says Roe. 'He was married to my step-sister, Dolly. They got divorced, what, probably over a decade ago now. Anyway, what makes you so sure he was assaulted? Tris is a man who likes a drink. In fact, I'd go so far as to say Tris loves a drink. Quite possible, I'd have thought, he'd fall down and hurt himself. Wouldn't be the first time.'

Golding looks up from his notes. 'So did you speak to Mr Hart – Mr Savage – at the wedding?'

Roe leans back in his chair and gives a broad smile, not hurrying to answer, giving himself time, Muir thinks, to decide what he wants to say.

'As a matter of fact, I did. I spotted him outside, thought I'd go over and say hello for old times' sake.'

'Did you have the impression he'd been drinking at that point?'

'Hard to say with him. He's had years of practice at looking sober when he's not.'

'And what did you say to him, exactly?'

'I just asked him how life was treating him. Not that I didn't know. Plainly he's doing OK. He asked after Fiona and I invited him to join us for a drink, but he never did. That was it, really.'

Golding takes out his phone and finds the relevant video.

'This is you, then?'

Roe watches the clip to its end.

'That's me. I wondered whether there might be cameras. Surveillance everywhere in this country, these days.'

'You'll forgive me for saying,' says Muir, 'but Mr Savage doesn't look too pleased to see you. Can you explain why that might be?'

'A ghost from the past, intruding on his new life, I suppose. Maybe he didn't want wife number two to know about me. He didn't suggest introducing her, anyway.'

'So when Mr Savage recovers consciousness and we show him this video, is his account of the conversation going to match yours?'

For a moment, Roe looks uncertain, before shrugging a show of indifference.

'I don't see why not. Is he going to recover, then? There are hints in the press he might have permanent brain damage. Someone must have really meant to hurt him. Poor old Tris.'

'But that someone wasn't you?'

'Should I have a lawyer present? No, of course it wasn't me. I hadn't seen him in years. What possible reason could I have for hurting him? More to the point, how would I have been able to afford champagne to do it with?'

'We'd like a statement from you, if you wouldn't mind,' says Muir.

'Be glad to,' says Roe. 'Anything at all I can do to help. You can't help but feel sorry for that lovely wife of his, can you?'

'Maybe we could take your statement now,' says Golding. 'Or you're welcome to attend a police station, if you prefer.'

'I'm happy to do it now. Nothing else on, as you can see.'

Golding, as always, is painstaking in his statement-taking, insisting on writing down in his careful handwriting all the small details which made up Golding's meeting with Tristan. Beyond the fence, a lawnmower drones. Inside the house, a kitchen tap is running, the waste trickling into a drain overgrown with weeds.

Muir is happy to sit quietly, observing Roe, watching for any signs he's holding back or not telling the truth. From what he can see, his story stands up. The only question is, was there more to his involvement with Tristan that afternoon than the short meeting they have on video?

When the statement's finished, Golding reads it aloud for Roe's approval. The kitchen, Muir notices, is now silent. Roe shrugs his agreement to the account he's given and signs it with a flourish. His signature is elegant, the hand of an educated man, one used to dealing with significant documents.

As Muir and Golding stand up from the table, Fiona appears and offers to show them out, and Roe seems pleased to let her, settling back to finish the last of his beer.

Golding is already outside the front door and Muir is about to follow him when Fiona touches his arm. She's holding out a slip of paper.

'You need to talk to Dolly,' she whispers. 'She'll tell you how it was with Tristan.'

Muir takes the piece of paper and looks at her for an explanation.

But Fiona shakes her head and glances uneasily behind her. Muir takes the hint, and doesn't look back as he leaves.

Golding is waiting with his jacket slung over his shoulder, sweat stains marking the underarms of his shirt. Muir unlocks the car, and as they climb in, Golding lets out a sigh of relief to be sitting down again. A bulging vein is pulsing in his neck.

'This heat,' he says. 'It really does for me.'

Muir is reading the slip of paper Fiona's given him. 'Mrs Roe seemed very insistent we should talk to her sister-in-law, and rather anxious Mr Roe didn't know she was suggesting it. Tristan's ex-wife, Dolly Blythe. Sounds like someone from the good old days of musical theatre.'

'Might be another stage name,' suggests Golding. 'Birds of a feather.'

'Could be. But since this address isn't a major detour on our way back, I think we'll follow Mrs Roe's suggestion and pay her a visit.'

At a garage along the road, Muir pulls in for a comfort break and to buy more water. Golding takes advantage of the stop to buy a sandwich and crisps, which he eats as they begin the drive back.

'What did you make of Murray Roe?' asks Muir, as he makes the turn for Gloucester.

'He's not being straight with us,' says Golding. 'I think what he told us was the truth, as far as he went, but he was too careful in what he said, and a bit cocky, like he knew he was getting one over on us.'

'I think Fiona Roe's actions confirm the truth of that. She

thinks we should know something he wants kept quiet. The only problem is, how do we know what questions to ask Dolly Blythe?'

'We'll just keep it broad, see if she opens up. If you like, I'll have a look into Mr Roe's finances when we get back, see if there's anything there. He's plainly fallen on hard times, and he might easily have been asking Tristan for money. If he met with a refusal, maybe he took it hard.'

'Hard enough to be violent?'

'Possibly. He's a man who likes a beer before lunchtime, so there's no question he'd have been drinking at the wedding. A momentary loss of temper, maybe? And did you notice he knew about the weapon? I don't think we've released to the press that Tristan was hit with a champagne bottle.'

'We haven't,' confirms Muir. 'That was an error on his part. I agree there's more he could tell us.'

'Do you think he could be our man?'

'I certainly wouldn't rule it out,' says Muir.

TWENTY-FOUR

Contact lenses are the number one daily-use item Laura would hate to be without, and she doesn't mind the regular check-ups that go with a proper eye-health regime. But Russ, the optician, is too inclined to chat, and the overrun from the previous customer combined with his reluctance to let Laura leave without twice repeating the benefits of a new – more expensive – lens care product, has made her late for her appointment at the hairdresser's.

Still, as she – slightly breathless – pushes open the door, the hot, scented air announces sanctuary, the sacred space of women practising the rituals of beauty, and she feels herself relax.

Sophie, the pretty receptionist, gives her a vacuous smile, as if she's never seen Laura before.

'Can I help you?'

'I'm late for my appointment with Debbie.' She glances across the salon, to where Debbie is blow-drying a woman's freshly coloured hair.

'What name is it?'

'Laura, Laura Ridley.'

Sophie makes a show of scrolling through the screen listing the day's appointments, until finally she nods.

'Take a seat,' she says. 'Debbie will be with you in a moment.'

Laura's been so flustered at being late that she hasn't noticed a woman in the waiting area, flicking through a weeks-old copy of *Bella*. Only as she bends to choose a magazine for herself does she realise who it is.

'Is that you, Karen?'

Karen Garner looks up: tired eyes, dark roots on her honey hair.

'Oh, hi, Laura! How are you?' Karen puts the stress on the last word, almost an Americanism, though Sterndale's in her blood; her father still runs sheep up on the hills.

'I'm fine. How's Dave doing?'

'Oh, he's all right. Working, as always. They're still doing that job on the leisure centre. As a matter of fact, I was just talking about you. Well, texting.' She indicates a mobile on the magazine table. 'I was saying you would know, and here you are.'

Laura sits. 'Know what?'

'What the police are up to. My cousin works in the kitchens at the hotel, and he says the police are there again this morning. He's heard they're close to an arrest.'

'News to me.'

Across the salon, Debbie turns off the hairdryer, and the salon falls into the closest it gets to silence, Kiss FM in the background and the splash of water in a basin.

'Had you heard that, Debbie?' calls Karen.

Debbie and her client look across.

'That they're close to an arrest in the Tristan business. So my cousin says.'

Debbie shakes her beautifully groomed head. 'I didn't know that. I've heard they think it was a woman.'

'Who's told you that?' asks Laura.

'Angie in the café,' says Debbie.

'What woman?' asks Sophie, and Debbie shrugs.

'Pound to a penny he was shagging somebody,' says Karen. 'Wish it was me.' She catches Laura's look of disapproval. 'Sorry. But he is fit, though, isn't he?'

'Ah, don't,' says Debbie, going through her client's hair with a comb and scissors. 'Izzy's lovely, and I don't think he's the cheating kind.'

'They're all the cheating kind,' says Karen. 'Take it from me.'

'They've been to interview Philly,' says Debbie. She chooses a product from an array on a shelf, and sprays grapefruit-scented mist on her client's hair.

'How do you know that?' puts in Laura.

'Bit old for him, isn't she?' asks Karen.

'They're interviewing everyone who was at the wedding, surely?' says Laura. 'I expect that's what they were doing at the hotel.'

'They haven't interviewed me,' says Karen.

'Nor me,' says Debbie, leading her client to the reception desk to pay.

Nor me, thinks Laura, as Debbie helps her into a black gown.

Karen's stylist takes her to the basins at the back, and Laura sits down in Debbie's chair. For a few minutes they chat about Laura's hair, highlights and lowlights, how much to take off the ends. When Debbie disappears to mix the colour, Laura's left facing the mirror, looking into her own eyes.

Could it be true the police are looking for a woman? Is Tris's attacker among them here in Sterndale, maybe someone she knows, even one of her neighbours or friends?

The idea is ludicrous. As she crosses the salon to find herself the latest copy of *Grazia,* Laura puts it out of her mind.

Two hours later, she meets Karen again, waiting to book another appointment while Sophie takes an incoming call.

'You look great,' she says, and appears to mean it, though a compliment from Karen often carries a sting in the tail.

But there's no sting today.

'Is Aidan picking you up?' she asks.

'No,' says Laura, 'why would he be? He's at work, and I enjoy the walk.'

Karen lifts one eyebrow in that way she has, drawing attention to how much darker it is than her now uniformly coloured hair.

'I just saw him, that was all. Coming out of the bank.' She turns and points to Lloyds across the street.

'We don't bank at Lloyds,' says Laura.

Sophie's hanging up the phone.

'Oh,' says Karen. 'I would have sworn it was him. Imagine him having a doppelgänger in a tiny place like this. Can you book me in for the first week in August, please, Sophie, just before we go away?'

TWENTY-FIVE

The fastest route to the address Fiona Roe gave Muir is via Ross-on-Wye. Beyond that, they travel through countryside, to a village picturesque enough to have a coach park for visiting tourists.

There are coaches parked there now, from Birmingham and Kettering and one on tour from Germany. Muir finds a tight space in a crowded car park, and sends Golding to the machine for a ticket.

He comes back grumbling about the expense. 'At that price,' he complains, 'you'd think they'd be including a free car wash.'

They walk down the village's main street, passing buildings of mellow stone, roofed in terracotta pantiles, with Georgian shop fronts glazed in bottle-bottom glass. Beyond a gallery offering hand-thrown ceramics, Muir spots a sign hanging out over the pavement: *Nuance Dress Agency*.

'That's us.'

Both men stoop to pass under the low doorway. Inside, racks of second-hand women's clothes are artfully arranged by colour, blues, pinks, reds and greens shaded dark to light. Around the walls are shelves of handbags, shoes and scarves, and a sign offering a rental service for special occasion hats. The merchandise is attractive, but a background smell of mustiness isn't quite defeated by the strong vanilla scent of a reed diffuser. In the background, Eva Cassidy is singing quietly, but not quietly enough for Muir, whose taste is for Oasis and the Smiths.

At the back of the shop is a desk in polished walnut, where an antique cash register stands alongside a credit card processing machine and a vase of yellow dahlias.

The woman seated behind the desk gives them a welcoming smile.

'Can I help you?'

Muir and Golding show their warrant cards.

'We're looking for Dolly Blythe,' says Muir.

'That's me.' Dolly must once have been quite beautiful and is very attractive still: a natural-looking blonde, slender, elegantly dressed in cashmere and linen, no doubt cleverly chosen from her own stock. Muir has seen pictures of Izzy Savage, and decides Tristan has a type. Lucky man, that such women will entertain him. 'Can I ask what this is about?'

'Do you have somewhere private where we could talk?'

'We could go in the office.'

Dolly leads Muir and Golding up an awkward staircase to a low-ceilinged room above, where clothes are stacked in boxes and a large table holds a sewing machine and a scattering of needlework tools. By the window, facing out on to the busy street, are a Chesterfield sofa upholstered in poppy-red fabric, and a pair of Chippendale-style carver chairs in need of new varnish.

'Have a seat,' says Dolly. 'Enjoy our lovely view.'

She sits down in one of the armchairs, stretching out her bare legs and showing bony feet in pale suede ballet flats. Muir takes the second chair, and Golding's pleased to have the sofa. Finding his notebook, he writes the date and time at the top of a fresh page.

'So, enlighten me,' says Dolly. 'What business does the constabulary have with little old me?'

'You used to be married to Tristan Hart, or Tristan Savage.'

Her face falls, all its sunny animation gone. Muir wonders if he's misjudged her age; she looks older now than she did moments before.

'Ah. My past is here to haunt me. Is this about the attack on him? I can assure you it was nothing to do with me. Is he going to be OK?'

'I think at this stage there seems no reason he couldn't make a complete recovery,' says Muir. 'But I have to say we are treating the case as a serious assault.'

'Do you have any idea who attacked him?'

'Our enquiries are ongoing, which is why we've come to you. We're wondering if you can suggest anyone in Tristan's background who might wish him harm.'

'Apart from me?' The words slip from Dolly's mouth before she's considered them, and she blushes. 'I'm sorry, I didn't mean that. Of course I don't wish him harm. I haven't seen him in years. That chapter of my life is over, finished.'

Down on the street, a Japanese tourist is taking a photograph of the shop's frontage.

'Look,' says Golding, 'why don't you start from the beginning, tell us about your relationship with Tristan? This is all in strictest confidence. We're not asking you to make a statement at this stage, we're just trying to get a rounded picture of Tristan's life. Where did you and he meet?'

'A trip down memory lane, then?' Dolly sighs. 'We were both living in London, making our way in the world of entertainment. You'll think it a cliché, but we met in the BBC canteen. I was an actress at the time – sorry, we have to say actor now, don't we? I was doing all right, lots of little things and bit parts, kids' TV, the odd sitcom. I was in *Inspector Morse* a couple of times. I never got a speaking part, though they said I made a beautiful corpse. Basically I'd take anything I could get, always hoping for that big breakthrough that never came.'

'And was Tristan acting at that time?' asks Golding.

'No. Tris was never an actor. He wanted to be a journalist, and he was beginning to make a bit of a name for himself as a news reporter, someone they could send to the far-flung corners of the kingdom in a crisis, floods in Cornwall, that kind of thing. He was angling for a foreign posting – you know, our Washington correspondent, or Paris or Moscow – but it never came off. He didn't have the education for it, bluntly. For a job like that, they wouldn't look at anyone without a degree. That didn't matter, though, in the long run. He went in other directions, and it hasn't worked out so badly for him. Anyway, he was behind me in the lunch queue one day and we got talking. He asked me to go for a drink, and that was it.'

'What year was that?' asks Golding. 'Can you remember?'

Dolly shakes her head. 'I don't know. Bailey's twenty-two now, so it must be nearly twenty-five years. Gosh, is it really so long ago? I must be getting old.'

'Who's Bailey?' asks Muir.

'Sorry, I should have said. He's our son, mine and Tris's.

He doesn't have anything to do with Tris, though. He hasn't seen him or spoken to him since he was at primary school.'

'Are you sure about that?' asks Muir.

'Absolutely certain.'

'So your son is estranged from his father? Why is that?'

Dolly sighs. 'Do I have your word this is in confidence?'

'If it has no bearing on the case, there's no reason it would be made public,' says Muir.

'Tris wasn't the easiest person to live with,' says Dolly. 'To be frank, he had issues. The day came when I gave up trying to deal with his problems, and Bailey's never seen any good reason to reconnect with a man he believes failed him as a father.'

'What were these issues, Dolly?' asks Golding.

'Alcohol issues. I don't know whether you've ever experienced life with an alcoholic – I'm guessing probably not – but you can take it from me, it isn't easy. We were happy in the beginning, but after a while everything he wanted to do revolved around drinking, and that wasn't who I was. So he left me behind and went on benders, disappearing for days at a time. Of course I'd be out of my mind with worry, but as time went by, my attitude hardened. He spent time in rehab, more than once, and would come home promising he'd changed. And he did change, for a while, until the next time he didn't come home.'

Dolly lapses into reflective silence.

'We're sorry to put you through this,' says Golding. 'But this is important information, information we don't have.'

'A lot of care's been taken to keep it out of the press, a lot of care. You should talk to his agent, Duncan Painter. He's the mastermind who made sure Tris's reputation was never tarnished. And it was always Duncan who'd buy me expensive lunches and persuade me to stick by Tris whenever I was threatening to leave. Back then, a high-profile divorce would have done terminal damage to Tris's image, and the networks were far more particular than they are these days. If word had got out, his career would have been over.'

'But you left him in the end?' suggests Muir.

'In the end, yes. There was an accident, all Tris's fault. He'd been drinking, of course, but it had made him manic, and he was behaving like an idiot, trying to persuade poor Bailey to play indoor cricket with Tris's old school-team bat. As he was swinging the bat – warming up, he was calling it – I came through the door and he hit me in the face, broke some of the bones in my inner ear. I'm half-deaf to this day. Not to mention the mess he made of my face.

'Things almost got ugly for him then. The ambulancemen called the police to attend, and they didn't believe for a moment he hadn't hit me deliberately. It seemed an unlikely story, I have to admit, but with no complaint from me, they couldn't arrest him. When Duncan came to see me in hospital, he was truly shocked to see the state I was in. Tris paid for corrective surgery – Duncan got me the best surgeon in the business – and I was grateful for that.' She turns the left side of her face to each of them in turn. 'Look, no visible scars. But even Duncan knew the situation couldn't go on. He found me a place to go – a flat in Pimlico – and Tris paid decent maintenance for me and Bailey. That was the end of it, really. He went back into rehab for a while, again hushed up by Duncan. Over time, I rebuilt my life and then I met my current partner, Eileen. We take care of each other, and with her I don't have to worry where it will end if she has a glass of wine. I don't get any money from Tris these days. I have no reason to. When Bailey turned eighteen, I decided to cut the ties, sold the flat, and Eileen and I bought this place, which doesn't make us much, but it's enough to squeeze by. Bailey's working in the States and he sends me what he can. He's a good son. Teetotal, as am I.'

Muir nods in sympathy. 'Thank you for your honesty.'

'I don't think anything I've said will help you,' says Dolly. 'Tris and I are ancient history. Can I ask who suggested you speak to me?'

'It was your sister-in-law, Fiona Roe,' says Muir.

Dolly's eyebrows lift. 'Interesting.'

'Which prompts me to ask, can you think of any reason why your brother would want to make contact with Tristan?'

'Murray's not my brother, he's my step-brother. And no, I can't think of any reason whatsoever. Did he make contact?'

'It seems so. Were he and Tristan close while you and Tristan were married? Were they drinking buddies maybe, anything like that?'

'We saw him and Fiona at Christmas. That was about it.'

'So you'd think it unusual if Murray went out of his way to track Tristan down?'

'I'd think it a bit odd, yes.'

'Well, we'll leave you in peace,' says Muir. 'Before we go, can you give me contact details for Duncan Painter?'

'You can Google him. He's still one of the top agents in London.'

Golding hands her a card. 'If you think of anything else, please give us a call.'

'One other thing I have to ask,' says Muir, as he gets up from his chair, 'and I'm sorry, it's rather personal. Do you believe Tristan was faithful to you during your marriage?'

Dolly's laugh this time is filled with genuine amusement. 'Oh, God, no. I don't honestly think Tristan has it in him to be faithful. Women queued up to be with him, and while we were together, there weren't very many who went away disappointed.'

'Well, I wasn't expecting that,' says Muir, as he and Golding walk back to the car. 'Puts a different face on the investigation, wouldn't you say? Because it makes me wonder whether his past behaviour might have given someone a motive we know nothing about. Did you believe her about the accident with the cricket bat?'

'Not really,' says Golding, 'but I suppose it's possible that's how it was. And if she's been financially persuaded to keep quiet, what can you do?'

'Regardless of deliberate intent, sounds like there's plenty of dirt hidden in Tristan's past, and maybe Murray Roe's hard up enough to be thinking about blackmail,' says Muir. 'When we get back, put Roe's financial situation to the top of the priorities list. I'll ask Kirstie to make enquiries of Isobel Savage, see if she knows anything about Roe, and I'll get someone to have a closer look into Tristan Savage's past. If he's got an arrest record, it's time we knew about it, though it sounds like his agent probably kept the slate clean. Gooch can do that, under your supervision. You'd never know there was a problem, would you, when you see him on the telly?'

But Golding doesn't agree. 'Nothing would surprise me these days. Maybe it's just an act, playing the nice guy.'

'Maybe so,' says Muir. 'But wouldn't it be interesting if someone he's upset in the past just happened to be on the guest list of that wedding?'

TWENTY-SIX

In the Burnt Common conference room, the heat's intense. The fans someone's set running are doing no more than blowing hot air from one end of the room to the other.

'Sorry to do this to you,' says Muir. 'We'll be as quick as we can getting everyone up to speed with case developments so we can all get out of this hell-hole. Firstly, I'm sorry to report the news from the hospital is not the best on Tristan's condition, since there's been no change. Plainly this is bad news for us in terms of the investigation, because the sooner we're able to speak to him and get his version of events, the sooner we can clear this one up and move on to other things. I don't want anything regarding his condition to be shared at this stage, and it goes without saying that it's not for discussion or release to the press – understood, Brad?' He looks squarely at Brad Sherman, but Sherman appears to be busy with his phone. 'Any leaks will be dealt with as a disciplinary matter. So, where are we up to? Let me go first.

'Nate and I interviewed Murray Roe, the guy you'll remember from the car-park video where he was talking to Tristan. He turns out to be an ex-relative of Tristan's, in that

Tristan used to be married to his step-sister. They divorced some years ago. Roe claims he was having a friendly catch-up with Tristan and we have no evidence thus far to the contrary. We've taken a formal statement, and Nate and I are of the opinion that Roe has money issues, so it's possible he was hassling Tristan for money and didn't take it well when he was refused. Nate's going to be looking into Roe's financial situation. In the interests of thoroughness, let's also check with Tristan's phone records that he had no calls from Roe's number or the Stroud area in general during the weeks preceding the wedding. Roe says there's been no contact but I think it would be prudent to make sure that's true.' He looks across at a young detective constable. 'Sterling, I'm giving that to you. And one final thing of interest. Mr Roe knows that the weapon used in the assault was a champagne bottle, so he knows more than he should. He's definitely on our list.'

'Can I add something?' asks Weld.

'Go ahead.'

'When we interviewed Gail Clements, mother-of-the-bride, she told us Fiona Roe pretty much invited herself and Murray to the wedding after Fiona saw on Facebook Tristan was going to be there. Which seems to suggest a plan to bump into him. We got screenshots of the Messenger chat.'

'So certainly not the whole truth from Mr Roe,' says Muir. 'Sterling, make those phone records a priority, and Kirstie, can you make contact with Mrs Savage, ask her if she knows anything about him? I'm wondering whether Fiona Roe was coerced into asking for that invitation. On our way out, she gave me the address of Roe's step-sister, Tristan's ex-wife Dolly Blythe, and we made a detour to pay her a visit. She told a story which may be relevant, namely that Tristan has long-standing issues with alcohol, which was what ended the marriage. She also suggests he has form as a serial womaniser. I want to know if there's any record of arrests for Tristan, any incidents which might have been recorded while he was under the influence, anything of interest at all. Amber, can you look into that? Check with Nate on how to get started, and he'll keep you on track. Ms Blythe also suggested we speak to Tristan's agent regarding his past behaviour – apparently the guy is a master of keeping damaging news out of the press – so I'll make the trip to London to see him. Kirstie, why don't you join me for that?'

Weld nods her agreement. 'No problem. But what you've just said about Tristan's drink problem doesn't fit with what Isobel Savage told me at the hospital. She says she's never known him drink.'

'Interesting,' says Muir. 'Maybe he's a reformed character since Roe knew him. Has anyone got anything we haven't covered?'

'The interviews with the two teenagers who reported the assault – Darren Ferris and Rosie Stainforth – went off OK,' says Weld. 'Pretty straightforward, no bombshells. They were in the pool area thinking they'd go skinny-dipping, but that idea lost its appeal when they found Tristan. Rosie did say she felt there might be someone hiding behind the building, but she couldn't swear to it. Neither of them saw anyone or heard anything definite.'

'Amber?' Muir looks at Gooch, who blushes at being the centre of attention.

'I interviewed a number of staff at the hotel,' she says.

'I got the details of those who were on shift that day but not present this morning, and I've made arrangements to speak to them. None of the ones I've spoken to already came up with anything of interest. Nate suggested I take a photo of Murray Roe to see if anyone recognised him, but no one remembered seeing him, though the manager . . .' She glances down at her notes. 'Craig Dalton. He recalled a man acting oddly in the lobby, but definitely not Roe. The guy he noticed was younger, well built, very short hair. Not much to go on, sorry.'

'Good work,' says Muir. 'Make sure you follow up with the rest of the staff there, and find out if anyone else noticed Roe or this other guy.' He turns to Davis, who's heading up the guest list enquiries. 'How's it going, Andy?'

'Getting through them, Boss, but nothing to report so far.'

'Is that it?' asks Muir, looking round the room. 'Have we really come up all blanks?'

'Amber and I spoke to the nanny,' says Weld dispiritedly. 'Not much there, either.'

'Not much meaning . . .?'

'Just a gut feel the working relationship might not have been as rosy as it looked from the outside. Hard to pin down. I wouldn't go so far as to call it malice. Just that she didn't seem particularly enamoured of her boss.'

'Interesting. Anyone else? Don't be shy.'

'What about Tristan's bank records?' asks Weld. 'Mrs Savage wasn't keen to give the go-ahead on those without his permission, which plainly she isn't going to get any time soon, so we'll need a production order if we think there might be any value in looking at them.'

'I'm not sure,' says Muir. 'We'll probably just find out he's a wealthy man. It's a lot of hassle for that.'

'But if I'm already doing Roe's,' puts in Golding. 'Same case, I can get them both signed at the same time.'

'For thoroughness then, let's do it. Anything else? No? Looks like another slow news day for you then, Brad. OK, people, let's get back to it.'

Weld makes contacting Izzy her first priority, and puts in a call as soon as she returns to her desk. When Izzy answers, Weld can hear cars driving by in the background.

'Hi, Izzy, it's DS Weld from West Mercia CID.'

'Hi.' Izzy sounds listless, downbeat.

'Is now a good time to talk?'

Another car drives by.

'Yes, it's fine. I'm just outside getting some fresh air. Sitting in that hospital room all day makes me claustrophobic.'

'How's he doing? Has there been any change?'

There's a short pause where Weld suspects Izzy is shaking her head.

'We keep talking to him. I played him some music today but he didn't react.'

'You have to give it time.'

'That's what the doctors say.'

'Anyway, I won't keep you, but I have a question for you, regarding a man named Murray Roe. Does that name mean anything to you?'

Another pause while Izzy considers. 'I don't think so.'

'If I send you a photo of him, would you have a look and

see if he's at all familiar to you? We're wondering whether Tristan may have had any recent contact with him.'

'Of course.'

'I'll ping it through now. Have a good look at it and I'll call you back shortly.'

But a minute later, she receives a text from Izzy: *Don't know him.*

Weld texts back: *Thx. Will be in touch*, and ticks the task off her list.

When Izzy goes back to the ward, she mentions to Steph and Eamon that the police are asking about someone called Murray Roe.

'I've no idea who he is,' she says. 'Tris never mentioned him.'

She's busy then looking for lip-balm to put on Tris's dry lips, and doesn't notice the look that passes between her parents-in-law.

TWENTY-SEVEN

Somehow, days and nights go by. One week on from the wedding, Tris has shown no change, not a movement of a finger or the squeeze of a hand, just steady, automated breathing, rise and fall, rise and fall. Izzy's watched him, trapped within his coma, metamorphose from Tris indistinguishable from his normal sleeping self to Tris deep frozen yet not cold, waxen-faced and insensate, his mind alive but distant, maybe lost and drifting through the stars.

She misses him so badly. Everywhere's too quiet, even when she and Flora are at home together, as if the withdrawal of his crackling energy has put the house to sleep.

But a spore of mould can spoil a feast. That sliver of doubt about his phone and his fidelity is beginning to fester, and her love lacks the unshakeable confidence she felt before.

Please let him come home and make things right.

On this seventh day, she's forced to be away from his bedside.

Not unreasonably, Bridget wants a day off. Steph and Eamon are sympathetic, and Steph seems even to relish the prospect of being carer-in-chief, though in truth there's very little caring to be done. The major responsibility lies in the keeping of the vigil.

Izzy throws back the curtains on brilliant sunshine and the bluest of skies. If Tris were here, there'd be plans for the day, croissants and cherry jam for breakfast, rugs and deckchairs on the lawn, a long, languorous day of relaxing shut away from the world. Tris protects his Saturdays the way others guard their Sundays. Sundays to him should be sociable days, long lunches with friends, excursions to the coast or family teas.

What Flora would enjoy most would be to fill the paddling pool and have a morning splashing on the lawn. The thought of it is cheering, and while Flora's enjoying her egg and soldiers, Izzy makes an effort with her own breakfast, whizzing a strawberry and kefir smoothie in the blender, spreading a piece of toast with almond butter to enjoy with a cup of good coffee, the French roast Tris buys from Selfridge's. Bridget's right, she is looking too thin. She needs to take better care of herself. This could be a long, long haul.

As she clears away and loads the dishwasher, she suggests her plan to Flora, who squeals with delight. Upstairs they find Flora's favourite swimsuit, and – at her insistence – a bikini for Izzy too. While they're getting changed, the postman pulls up outside, and Izzy hears the letterbox clatter as the mail lands on the mat.

She and Tris have a simple system with the mail: whichever of them picks it up, scans and sorts it, his pile here, hers there. This morning the delivery's light, with nothing of much interest, except for a personal letter addressed to Tris, postmarked Oxford, franked by a firm of architects. Izzy studies it

187

with a growing feeling of excitement. If Tris has business with architects, it can only mean one thing. They've talked many times of a place by the sea, just something small for weekends away, and even got to drawing little sketches and discussing where it should be, Anglesey or Dorset, or – if Izzy has her way – deep into Cornwall. This letter can only mean Tris has been planning a surprise, working on their coastal hideaway. Now she feels bad for doubting his commitment.

The morning passes quickly, with Flora happily running in and out of the pool with her unicorn watering can sprinkling the buttercups on the lawn, and Izzy making daisy chains for Flora's head and wrists before retiring to a deckchair, closing her eyes to enjoy the healing warmth of the sun. By lunchtime, Flora's hungry enough to eat what she's given without any fuss, then settles down for a nap.

Izzy wanders into the kitchen to make iced tea. Tris's letter is still on the counter, and it occurs to her some reply may be required. That seems a good enough reason to satisfy her curiosity, and though she realises she may be ruining the surprise, she opens it. Maybe she can impress him, by moving the project forward while he convalesces. Isn't he always saying they're a team? When one member's down, the other must step up to the mark.

She draws a single sheet of paper from the envelope. The subject line reads, *Fairview, Upper Whiston, Oxon.* Izzy frowns. As far as she knows, no part of Oxfordshire is by the sea.

The letter is an invoice, for professional fees of almost £4,000.

Tris has been a very dark horse indeed. This project appears some way advanced, but she's confused. They have no plans to move – don't they both adore Foxcote Lodge? – and Oxford-shire has never been discussed. What on earth is going on?

Izzy immediately thinks of Rightmove; when they were looking for this house, she was on it daily. She pulls up the website on her iPad and puts in the postcode from the invoice, no restrictions on house price, no restrictions on when a property was sold. Nothing comes up, so she switches to Zoopla, thinking she can find out when Fairview changed hands. A couple of minutes, and there's an entry for it: sold just over a year ago for £124,000.

None of this makes any sense at all. She and Tris and Flora were living in this house then. There's no way Tris would spend that kind of money without talking to her.

Is there?

She thinks of the secret phone.

In Google Maps, the house's postcode shows her a remote rural area, and when she switches to Street View, a narrow country lane. Tracking along it with her cursor, she finds an isolated bungalow in considerable disrepair, standing among a tangle of overgrown shrubs and in the shadow of tall trees. On the dilapidated gate is a sign – *Fairview*.

This is no house for them, not somewhere she'd trade Foxcote Lodge for, not in a million years.

Maybe someone's sent Tris the wrong invoice? But that's hard to argue when his name's printed at the top.

There's one more place she can investigate – the Land Registry website, which she's visited to download the deeds to Foxcote Lodge. She opens the site in a new window and keys in the details from the invoice. Records are available for a fee of £3. She makes the payment, and up comes the result.

Fairview is registered in joint ownership, between Tristan Savage and Martina Stokes.

Her heart feels heavy as realisation dawns. Who else can Martina possibly be, but Tina from the contacts on his hidden phone?

TWENTY-EIGHT

On Sunday morning, eight days after the wedding, the pool area at the Sterndale Hall Hotel is busy.

Ten-year-old Danny has new goggles, a birthday present to replace the leaky ones he's had the last two years. Danny's a total water-baby, taught to swim by his mum at three years old, and a member of his local swimming club from age seven. When he grows up, he wants to be a professional diver.

Most of those here are adults, relaxing on sunbeds and enjoying coffee and pastries in the sun, or – in the case of the school reunion party from Bury St Edmunds – sleeping off hangovers in the shade. Danny's alone in the pool, and he's entertaining himself by dropping a pound coin his dad's given him into the water, watching it settle on the bottom before diving down to retrieve it.

The new goggles are brilliant, and his underwater view is crystal clear. He's quickly graduated to the deep end, treading water for a minute or two between dives to catch his breath. The water's beautiful, azure blue with crazy white patterns on the bottom where the sun reflects the ripples, and as he rests, Danny watches the honeycomb lattice as it twists and shifts.

Down near the filter, something's glittering as it catches the light.

Danny's heart lifts. This could be treasure, gold or silver, a dropped bracelet or ring. If it's something valuable, there might be a reward.

Tucking his pound coin in the net pocket of his waistband, he makes his dive, pulling down against the water's pressure. Close to the white tiled pool floor, he sees why what he's after can't be spotted from above; their transparency makes them all but invisible. They're not the prize he was hoping, but they're a discovery nonetheless: a discarded pair of champagne flutes, rolling back and forth in the filter vacuum's tug.

Danny's dad works in logistics at the most senior level, but despite his Hilfiger shorts, his ironic Hawaiian shirt and his Rick Owens sandals, he can't get past that stocky, bald, confrontational-looking exterior which makes him look like a Friday night bouncer. It doesn't help that, when he asks to see the manager, his accent is pure Walsall.

As he approaches the reception desk, Craig Dalton's smile is polite, as always. He introduces himself, and asks what he can do to help.

Danny's dad holds up the champagne flutes.

'Health and safety, mate,' he says, 'that's what that is. Glass in the pool? It's not on, is it? You want to be more careful. If someone had trod on one of them, you'd be getting yourself sued. Anyway, you can have them for nothing.'

Dalton puts his hand out to take the glasses.

'I'm sorry, Mr . . .'

'Needham.'

'I'm sorry, Mr Needham, but I'm not with you. Where did you find these?'

'My boy found 'em, in your swimming pool. Dived down and picked 'em up, right where it's deepest. In fairness to you, you couldn't spot 'em from above. It was only when he got down there he saw 'em. He was a bit cut up, actually. Reckoned he'd found some pirate's treasure or something, you know what kids are like. Anyway, like I say. I don't want to make a fuss. Only you want to be more careful. If they were in the shallow end, you'd have a problem, understand what I'm saying?'

Dalton takes the glasses by their stems and places them on the reception desk.

'I can't thank you enough, Mr Needham. As a thank you, may I offer you and your family something on the house? A drink from the bar? Does your son like ice cream?'

'That's very decent of you,' smiles Danny's dad. 'I'll have a pint of Oracle.'

Craig Dalton has seen on TV how the police bag up evidence, so he fetches a Ziploc bag from the kitchen and puts the glasses in it, being careful to touch them as little as possible. When he's sealed the bag, he searches his desk for the card Weld gave him, and dials the number for West Mercia CID. The phone goes to answer machine, so he leaves a message, that he's found something which may be of interest at the Sterndale Hall Hotel.

TWENTY-NINE

Izzy has slept poorly again, partly because of the sultry night temperatures, mainly because of the questions running through her head. But as her mind's been racing, she's come up with a plan.

She phones Bridget and tells her she won't be needed, then calls Steph to say she won't be coming to the hospital because Bridget isn't free to care for Flora. Bridget is pleased to have Sunday free, and Steph accepts Izzy's excuse without question, but as Izzy's about to hang up, Steph says, 'You haven't asked how he is.'

'Didn't I?' asks Izzy. 'Of course I meant to. I didn't sleep well last night, and my brain's all full of fog. Is there any news?'

She hears Steph take a breath and thinks maybe there is, but Steph lets the breath go in a sigh.

'I'm afraid not,' she says. 'Eamon's been reading to him – he's started on *Game of Thrones*, which will keep him going for a while. It's a bit graphic for me, but I think Tris will be enjoying it, don't you?'

'Yes. Yes, I do. That's a great idea. He's been meaning to read it.'

'I've been massaging his hands, trying to get them warm. I don't know why they feel so cold. And I trimmed his finger-nails yesterday. I know he's very particular about his hands, and I don't want him to wake up and think we haven't been taking care of him.' There's a short silence, and Izzy hears a catch in Steph's voice as she says, 'There seems so little we can do for him. Do you think he knows we're here?'

'I'm sure he does,' says Izzy, even though she isn't sure at all. 'He'll be loving every minute of the attention.'

'You'll be here tomorrow, won't you? I expect he misses you.'

'Yes, of course I will. Bridget said she'll come early, so I'll be there by breakfast time.'

'I'll ring you if there's news in the meantime.'

'Give him a kiss from me.'

'Of course, dear. See you in the morning.'

Izzy's mental fog was no lie. Tiredness slows her down, and she dresses Flora and makes her breakfast in a daze, barely speaking so Flora, sensing emotional withdrawal, becomes fractious. She wants another day in the paddling pool and becomes tearful when that's denied, and as Izzy straps her in the back of the Range Rover, she's still grizzling. Nerves on edge, with a long drive ahead, Izzy sets up a video on the iPad and hands it to Flora, who becomes quiet.

Izzy has researched the route, and promised gold at the end of the rainbow for Flora: a petting zoo just five miles from the address where they're heading.

As they draw close to the postcode, Izzy's more and more bemused. This area's no beauty spot; it's working countryside, with industrial-sized farms of featureless fields.

The satnav directs her to turn off the B-road on to a lane.

At the junction, there's an old farmhouse renovated into an attractive private residence. Beyond that, she sees nothing but a derelict barn, and straw bales blocking entry to the meadows, no doubt to deter travellers from setting up camp or grazing horses.

Alongside a field entrance, she stops.

She needs to be sure – absolutely sure – she wants to carry on. Her visit to this place could be life-changing, an irrevocable, no-going-back moment. If she finds Tina at this house and confronts her, at best the foundations of her marriage will be shaken. At worst, the future she imagined with Tris could be dust in the wind.

It isn't too late to turn back.

And yet, in truth, it is. If he wants to be with someone else, let her come and be his nurse. Izzy will take the money, bear the scandal and start a new life.

She drives on. As the satnav shows her closing on the chequered flag of her destination, behind her shoulder Flora is giggling at *Hey Duggee*. Izzy's looking for trees and the overgrown, dilapidated bungalow she's seen on Street View, but as she reaches the bend in the road where Fairview should be, she sees changes have been made.

The gate with the name, the trees and the bungalow are all gone. In their place is a building site of sun-baked clay, where a new house is rising, complete to the height of the ground-floor walls.

No one is here. Izzy feels immense relief that there'll be no confrontation, but the tension she lets go is replaced by anger at how he's fooled and deceived her. What other conclusion can be drawn, when she can see with her own eyes the tens of thousands of pounds that have already been spent on this site?

She parks the car, and opening the doors to let in air, leaves Flora in her seat. Flora asks if this is the zoo, clearly hoping from her dubious tone that it isn't.

'Just wait here a moment, munchkin,' says Izzy. 'The zoo isn't far away, but I have to look at something before we go there.'

She's glad the ground is dry. Anticipating a meeting with her husband's mistress, she dressed all in summery white, including open-toed sandals totally unsuitable for wandering among ditches where drains and cables will be laid, between piles of discarded part-bricks and the trip-hazard spills of dried concrete.

She finds a good vantage point and takes photos on her phone.

The step up to the threshold is high, with the path not yet built. Gripping the wall which will hold the front door, she pulls herself up, and stands in what will become the hallway of the resurgent Fairview. Skeleton walls of timber struts mark the layout of the rooms, and she wants to enter every one, get the measure of this house owned by her husband and another woman. Beyond doubt, Fairview will be bigger than Foxcote Lodge. While it's too early to say whether it will have beauty, what it will certainly lack are the history and character Tris insisted were important to him in a home.

What were his words? *I want a place where generations have been happy before us.*

And Izzy believed him, the same way she believed everything else he said: that she's the soulmate he'd searched for all his life; that he's never felt so happy as he is with her and Flora.

Words, it seems, are cheap.

When he wakes up, she swears she'll kill him.

THIRTY

On Monday morning, Muir's running late, and passes by the team already at their desks with only the most cursory of greetings.

Weld calls out to him.

'Can I have a quick word, Boss?'

Muir comes over, nodding a good morning to Golding as he does so. 'How's it going?'

'Yeah, good. Hope you don't mind me jumping in, but I sent Gooch back out to Sterndale. We had a call from the hotel over the weekend. They've found something they think might be of interest in the Tristan Savage case.'

'Go on.'

'A lad diving in the swimming pool found a couple of champagne flutes, from what I gather lying on the bottom.'

'Champagne flutes? Like the kind which might go with a champagne bottle?'

'Exactly.'

Muir looks like he finds the news vaguely cheering. 'Now that is interesting. What do you make of it?'

'It's hard not to jump to a conclusion which might be

entirely false,' says Weld, 'but I'm thinking firstly, there could be a connection to our case, and secondly, two glasses and a bottle of bubbly smack to me of a romantic assignation.'

'Could he have arranged to meet a woman?'

'If he did, it wasn't his wife. She never said anything to me about any poolside rendezvous. And remember she told me he's teetotal.'

'Which has never squared with Murray Roe and Dolly Blythe's views of him.'

'Secret drinker?'

Muir shrugs. 'Who knows? The bad news with the glasses is there'll be no fingerprints if they've been in water since last weekend. Why dump them in the pool, though?'

'Fear of fingerprints, maybe? Or just the easiest place to get rid of them?'

'Maybe the easiest, but not the smartest. If you took them back to the marquee, they'd be scooped up by a waiter, into the dishwasher and gone forever.'

'So they might easily be nothing whatever to do with the assault,' suggests Weld. 'They could easily have been dropped there by a loved-up couple later in the week.'

Muir shakes his head. 'Nothing's straightforward, is it? If we want to be bold, we might speculate they point to a pre-arranged liaison, but we need to be very careful not to rely on that as proven before it actually is.'

'But do you think it's enough to suggest we focus for a while on women rather than men?'

'With the progress we're not making on this one, I see no reason why not. Send them straight to Evidence for logging in when Gooch gets back. I can't see any point in putting them through forensics with the time they've been immersed. What time's our train?'

'I booked us on the nine thirty-three, so we should get going pretty soon. We'll probably hit traffic, this time of the morning.'

'Give me a few minutes to make a phone call and I'll be ready to go. And if I'm not mistaken, I think it's your turn to drive.'

At the hospital, Izzy feels a touch of coolness in the welcome she receives from Steph and Eamon. No doubt they're thinking she hasn't been in contact enough over the weekend.

At first glance, Tris seems the same, unearthly in his stillness. But there is change; in his face, the bones are more prominent, suggesting he's losing weight, and his skin is becoming smoother, waxier. Though she's angry enough to punch him, she leans down to kiss his cheek, and is taken aback by how cool it is.

Eamon offers her his chair, and she sits down at the bedside to take Tris's hand.

'Why don't you get us a coffee, Eamon?' suggests Steph, and he seems pleased at the suggestion, no doubt glad to escape for a few minutes the stifling atmosphere of the ICU.

'Are you all right?' asks Steph, when Eamon's gone. Steph herself doesn't look all right; she looks worn down with lack of sleep, and the make-up she's put on in what must have been bad light – too bright or too dark – is garish on her face, a sad attempt at a healthy glow from a woman dying inside.

'Are *you* all right?' asks Izzy, feeling emboldened – now she's no longer so in thrall to Tris – to be straightforward with this woman she's always been so wary of upsetting or offending.

To her surprise, Steph seems to sag in her seat, and Izzy sees that the effort of playing the competent matriarch is taking a heavy toll. Steph's head drops as she shakes with silent sobs, and Izzy finds Steph's tears provoke her own. She moves around the bed and, crouching beside Steph's chair, puts her arm around her mother-in-law's shoulders.

'I can't bear it,' Steph is saying. 'My baby, my baby! Why won't he wake up? I've begged him and begged him but he doesn't hear me.' Her face stricken, she looks up at Izzy. 'Please, you try. He might listen to you. Tell him to wake up. Tell him he mustn't leave us.'

'I've told him a thousand times,' says Izzy, brushing away her tears. 'You're his mother, Steph. He's always listened to you far more than me.'

Steph grasps Izzy's hand, squeezing it so tight that it hurts. 'He really loves you, Izzy, you and Flora. He'd never do anything to hurt you. You do know that, don't you?'

Too late for such reassurances: some damage is already done. Even so, Izzy wants to believe Steph is right, and that somehow, when Tris wakes up, everything that's happened, everything she's learned will be explained away, and their world will be reset, back to the days before she knew about Tina and Fairview.

But in the cold, white light of the ICU, she knows that's only wishful thinking.

Izzy hands Steph a tissue from a box on the bedside cabinet intended for the patient's belongings, but all Tris's needs are being met by tubes and pumps and machines. Life support, as Steph provided when she was carrying him, decades ago.

She dries her eyes and blows her nose. Izzy rises to her feet, touching Steph on the shoulder as she does so.

'I know it's hard,' says Izzy, 'but we have to stay strong.'

'I know,' says Steph, and she's grateful Izzy's there, especially when the black thought strikes her that what they're sharing is not an outpouring of love for Tristan, but a spilling over of grief.

Eamon's here with coffees in a cardboard carrying tray. As the door begins to close behind him, he looks back, and holds it open with his foot for the man following him: the consultant, Ian Talbot.

Eamon and Mr Talbot arrive at the bedside together. Steph feels the doctor's assessing eye pass over herself and Izzy, and sees he knows they've been crying. A week ago, she'd have been embarrassed. Now, she doesn't give a damn.

Mr Talbot addresses himself to Izzy as next-of-kin, but Steph appreciates that with his glances in her and Eamon's directions, he means to include them. He asks Izzy to join him for a chat, and Steph's heart hurts at the exclusion. How is it possible she isn't first in line for information where it's her son – her *son* – who's under discussion?

But even though Steph knows she probably doesn't deserve it after the way she spoke when Tris was first admitted, it seems Izzy is on her side.

'I think Steph and Eamon would like to join us,' she says, and Mr Talbot nods and says, 'By all means.'

God bless you, Izzy. God bless you.

As he leads them down the corridor, Mr Talbot keeps a businesslike silence, and Steph is afraid that doesn't bode well, that he'd be more chatty if there were something positive to say.

Always this same room, the family room, the room of revelations, hopes raised and dashed. As Mr Talbot points them to seats and sits down himself, Steph's heart gives a little fluttering palpitation, her personal measure of when she's too stressed. When Eamon squeezes her hand, she realises his interpretation of Mr Talbot's silence matches her own.

But nothing has been said. It's not yet too late for the news to be good.

And then it is.

Mr Talbot clears his throat, and Steph knows he's buying himself time, ordering his words.

'Sometimes in these cases, patients don't respond as well as we'd like,' he says. 'I'm afraid that's what's happening with Tristan. The scans we did this morning show the swelling around his brain has not yet significantly reduced, and obviously the longer that pressure is there, the higher the risk of permanent damage.'

The rest of what Mr Talbot says washes over Steph, except for one word which jumps out as if he's shouted it, though in reality he must have spoken it at the same volume as the rest. The word prods Eamon too; Steph feels the pressure on her hand increase.

Izzy's looking at the doctor as if she's understood nothing, but Steph knows it will soon sink in.

Eamon clears his throat in the same way as the doctor before he began, also being careful in his choice of words for her and Izzy's sake, and against the background of all that's happening Steph knows she doesn't appreciate him enough.

'What kind of disability?' asks Eamon. His voice sounds

almost normal, but the tension he's feeling lifts it a half-tone towards boyishness.

Mr Talbot looks round at all three of them, assessing what level of bad news they can handle. Usually Steph would say, *Don't patronise me, just tell me*, but she finds under these circumstances she wants the kid gloves approach. If she has to know the worst, let the blow fall softly.

'It's very hard to say at this stage,' says Mr Talbot. 'But you should be prepared for it to affect him physically, in the use of his limbs, or in his speech and his ability to talk. In some cases the senses are affected, especially sight.'

There's no colour left in Izzy's cheeks, and Steph knows she's seeing a glimpse of how she will age, of Izzy in her forties, going into her fifties.

Izzy says, 'You mean he could be blind.'

'It's too early to say,' says Mr Talbot, in a tempered voice Steph is sure he keeps for worst-case scenarios, which is where she's afraid they might be. 'It's a waiting game for the moment.'

'But those things can be fixed, can't they?' asks Eamon, playing the team optimist. 'You're a brain surgeon. You guys work miracles every day.'

'Some things can be fixed, yes,' says Mr Talbot. 'A great deal depends on the individual patient, how hard they're prepared to work at rehabilitation.'

There's a ringing in Steph's ears. She'd been thinking they'd be here a week at most, that Tris would be home and back at work before the month's end. Now there's talk of rehabilitation.

'But he will lead a normal life, won't he?' she hears herself ask, and immediately rebukes herself for the bluntness of the question.

Mr Talbot considers. 'Tristan is fit and strong. The best thing you can all do for the time being is to be with him, talk to him, call him back, if you will. When he wakes up, that will be the time to discuss next steps.'

'When will he wake up?' asks Izzy. 'What's taking so long?'

'I can't answer that,' says Mr Talbot. 'People heal at different rates. But as I say, Tristan has physical strength on his side. Let's continue to be patient, give him the time he needs. I'm sorry. I know it's hard. Is there anything else you want to ask me?'

Steph can't resist. 'He is going to wake up, isn't he? Surely you must at least be confident of that?'

'As confident as I can be,' says Mr Talbot. 'I think at this stage we may at least be cautiously hopeful.'

There's a silence which seems to be filled with many more questions that neither Steph, Eamon nor Izzy dare ask. Mr Talbot brings the meeting to a conclusion by slapping both his knees, saying, 'Of course we'll speak again soon. We're monitoring his condition very closely.'

As they stand, Eamon asks, 'What about the press? They'll be pushing for an update. What should we tell them?'

'I think you could say his condition is serious but stable. If you want to direct them to me, I'll say it on your behalf.' Mr Talbot's hand is on the door handle when he turns round to add, 'We should inform the police. They need to know his condition is – that he's suffered life-changing injuries. It may affect the way they decide to progress the case.'

'What do you mean?' asks Steph. 'I would hope they're doing their utmost for us, regardless of his expected outcome. My son has suffered a vicious assault.'

'Of course,' replies Mr Talbot. 'But it's a fact of modern life that the more serious the outcome, the higher priority the case will take. In the same way as we would treat someone with a broken hip more urgently than someone with a cut finger.'

'It makes sense, love,' says Eamon.

'I'll talk to the police as well.' Mr Talbot looks directly at Izzy. 'But when I've done that, don't be surprised if they want to talk to you again, Mrs Savage.'

THIRTY-ONE

Duncan Painter asked to meet Muir and Weld in a Soho pub, a Victorian place with flamboyant hanging baskets, leaded windows and well-heeled marketeers and media creatives drinking on the pavement outside.

Painter seems to know the place well and have some influence.

'Just come upstairs,' he said to Weld when she was making the appointment. 'There's a private room next to the gents. We can talk in there.'

Inside, the bar's a vast room of brass, mirrors and dark wood. The place is busy, especially for a Monday lunchtime; most of the pubs Muir frequents wouldn't expect a crowd this big even on a cup-final Saturday. Seems like the kitchen's doing good business too, and the smell of chips and sizzling beef reminds Muir that he's hungry. Maybe they'll have time to grab a bite before they catch the train home.

The journey has been long, the last leg on the underground particularly hot and miserable. Muir buys them both pints of lime and soda with extra ice, and, glass in hand, Weld leads the way up the red-carpeted stairs and knocks on a door next to the men's toilets.

A voice invites them in. Duncan Painter's seated at a long dining table, empty but for a large glass of red wine. He's in his sixties, sleek and well fed without being overweight, wearing a skilfully tailored wide-pinstripe suit and a made-to-measure shirt. His greying hair is longer than most men of his age would dare wear and brushed back off his forehead; his glasses are fashionable faux-wooden frames. He's relaxing in his chair, one foot resting on the other thigh, but when Muir and Weld walk in, he puts away his iPhone and stands up to offer his hand.

His handshake is firm and confident. Muir makes the introductions, and when Painter asks about their journey, Weld detects a touch of East London in his superficially well-bred accent, and wonders if he's from humbler roots than where he seems to have got to now.

'Glad you've got yourselves a drink,' he says, sitting back down and gesturing to nearby chairs. 'I didn't think you'd be joining me in the wine. Welcome to my unofficial office. I have a proper office in Putney, but you can't expect people to trek all the way out there for a short meeting like this, can you? So I have a little arrangement with the manager here which works pretty well. God knows I spend enough at the bar. Cheers.'

He holds up his glass before he drinks, and Muir and Weld are grateful for an opportunity to quench their thirsts. Weld takes a notebook and pen from her briefcase, and writes down the place and the time.

'As you know, Mr Painter,' begins Muir, 'we're here to talk about Tristan Hart, or Tristan Savage, who I believe is one of your clients.'

'My oldest and most profitable client,' confirms Painter. In his pocket, his iPhone buzzes. He glances at the screen and switches it off. 'Never a minute's peace these days, is there? I don't mean old in terms of age, of course, only that Tris and I go way back, over twenty years. How time flies. He came to me when he was just starting out. He was ambitious even then, and so was I. I suppose you might say we both made our names off each other's backs.'

'When was the last time you saw him?'

'Face to face?' Painter pulls a face as he considers. 'He and I had lunch just before Christmas. Since he left London and moved out to the sticks – sorry, I don't want to cast aspersions on the rural lifestyle – I see him far less often than I used to. When he was here, I probably saw him once a month or so, but since he met the lovely Izzy, those days are gone. It was a real shock when she called and told me what had happened. Of course I was happy to do everything I could to help, handling the press especially. They can be hugely intrusive, as I'm sure you know, and Izzy really has no experience of such situations.'

'When you first heard about the incident, what were your thoughts?' asks Weld. 'Did you have any ideas as to who might have done it?'

Painter shakes his head. 'Not really. No one specific sprang to mind. But when Izzy told me he'd been hit with a champagne bottle, I couldn't help thinking there might be a woman involved, maybe even Izzy herself.'

'Why do you say that?' asks Muir, and Painter sighs.

'I had to wonder – though I did hope it wasn't the case – whether Tris might have been up to his old tricks. He used to have a bit of a reputation, you know, one for the ladies. You could hardly blame him, could you? He's an attractive bloke, on the telly, and he only ever had to snap his fingers for the girls to come running, lucky bugger. So my first thought was that Izzy might have caught him *in flagrante* and lost her rag. She seems mild-mannered enough but hell hath no fury, does it?'

Painter drinks more wine. Weld looks up from her note-book.

'As far as you're aware, was the marriage happy?'

'Oh, blissful,' says Painter, throwing open his arms to illustrate his response. 'Absolutely blissful. Tris never stopped talking about her, Izzy this and Izzy that. I have to say, though, that she's been good for him. They're a much better match, I think, than him and his first wife.'

'Were there issues there, then?' asks Muir.

Painter regards him, considering whether to respond.

'We've already spoken to Ms Blythe,' Muir adds, and Painter gives a slow smile.

'Good work,' he says. 'And how is the lovely Dolly? I always liked her, but she was completely wrong for Tris. She let him walk all over her.'

'The way she tells it, she had a pretty rough time of it, living with his drink problem,' puts in Weld. 'Needless to say, we're very familiar with the fallout from those kind of relationships. She tells us you were responsible for handling matters so his misdemeanours and indiscretions never reached the press.'

Painter nods. 'Alcohol is Tris's Achilles heel, I don't know why. Some people are just wired that way, I suppose. The thing was with him, he was always professional enough to know when he could and when he couldn't. You'd never find him under the influence while he was in front of a camera. But when he wasn't working, all bets were off. I've no idea why Dolly put up with it as long as she did, actually.'

'She says you talked her into staying.'

'Fair comment. I suppose I did, once or twice. But then there was an incident which was the final straw, and she'd really had enough. I couldn't keep the press off it for much longer anyway – rumours spread like wildfire round the entertainment world – and I was getting phone calls almost daily from the tabloids. They were hearing things, and at some point, someone was bound to take their money. So I got her set up somewhere she could live without his antics, and I refused to tell him where she was. He hated me for it in the beginning, but he came to see sense in the end.'

'This incident which you describe as the final straw,' says Weld. 'Was it an accident?'

Painter looks at her, considering. 'That's a fair question, but I believe it was. I've never had cause to believe Tris is anything but the good-natured soul he appears to be.'

'He's not a mean drunk, then?'

'Exuberant, definitely. Mean, I wouldn't say so, no. But the accident was a game changer. If it had got out, it would certainly have looked bad. His career would have been finished, no question about it.'

'There wasn't anyone else, no accidents around any other women that you know about?' asks Weld.

Painter shakes his head. 'Not that I'm aware of. And I would be aware, I assure you.'

'The thing is,' says Muir, 'what we're short of is a motive, a solid motive. Assuming Tristan wasn't assaulted by his wife or another woman, can you think of anyone else at all who might have had a reason to wish him harm?'

'Did he owe money?' Painter asks.

'Why do you ask that? Surely he's very well off?' suggests Weld.

'There's no obvious reason he shouldn't be, I agree. Look, it isn't my place to say, and I don't want to overstep the mark. It's something you should talk to Izzy about, not me.'

'She hasn't said anything to us,' says Muir, 'so maybe she doesn't know. So why don't you tell us what you're thinking?'

'The thing is, Tris trusts me, as a business adviser and as a friend. When he's recovered, I don't want him thinking I've been telling tales out of school. That might terminally damage our relationship. He trusts me to be discreet.'

'I think your first duty to him at the moment is to help us find out who assaulted him.'

'Can my name be kept out of it?'

'We can do our best.'

Painter hesitates, then seems to make up his mind.

'The bottom line is, I have made him loans from time to time. Not recently, but in the past. He seemed to get through cash at an alarming rate. If he got himself into trouble, I helped him out. Advances on earnings, if you like.'

'How much cash?'

'I'd rather not say.'

'Hundreds? Thousands?'

'Ten thousand, maybe. Fifteen, once.'

'That's a lot of money to loan a friend. Was he gambling?'

'No. Not that. I'll tell you what I'll do. Just give me a minute.'

Painter stands, takes a long drink from his glass and leaves the room. Beyond the door, Muir and Weld can hear the murmur of his voice as he makes a phone call, while they sit silent, trying to hear what's being said. The call's short; when he returns, Painter drops a business card on the table in front of Muir. A name and a mobile number are written on the back.

'You'd be better off talking to this lady,' he says, sitting back down. 'Jackie Noble. She works at the BBC, and she produced *Hart of the Matter* for the three seasons it ran. It might have run longer, if Tris hadn't . . . Well, she'll tell it better than me. She says she'll speak to you, for Tris's sake, and she's in the office for a couple more hours. Call her mobile when you get there and she'll come down. You're on expenses, aren't you? It's too hot for the tube, so if I were you, I'd take a cab.'

They're in the taxi when Muir's phone rings. He glances at the screen and answers the call, mouthing *Golding* to Weld as he does so.

'Hey, Nate, how's things?'

'I thought you might be finished by now. I just want to pass on some information for you to be mulling over on the train.'

'Go for it.'

'Firstly, Amber's come back with the search results on Tristan's arrest record. Nothing there, really, a caution for disorderly conduct some years ago. If there's been anything else, we've no record of it.'

'Interesting. What else?'

'With regards to Murray Roe, his bank details show he's

213

completely on his uppers. Could be a motive for him pestering Tristan. He's a man very much in need of cash.'

'So he stays on the list.'

'For the time being, though he doesn't show up at all on Tristan's phone records. We've traced all his callers to that phone except for one, a pay-as-you-go which made several calls to his number over the last month, all from the Sterndale area.'

'Did he accept the calls?'

'Just the first one.'

'Someone he wasn't keen on talking to, then. A burner phone, maybe? Keep trying with that, see if you can track it down.'

'And last but not least, an interesting one from Tristan's bank account. A year or so ago, he made a significant payment to an account I haven't yet traced.'

'A UK account?'

'Yes.'

'How significant was the payment?'

'Twenty-five thousand.'

Muir's silent for a moment. 'That's a lot of cash to someone.'

'Tell me about it.'

'Great work, Nate. So your number one priority now is to trace that target account. I have to go, we're just pulling up outside the BBC.'

'All right for some.'

'We'll tell you all about it when we get back.'

THIRTY-TWO

Muir can't deny feeling a buzz as he and Weld climb out of the taxi near Portland Place.

'They'll love this, back at the nick,' says Weld, readying her phone to take pictures. 'I wonder if we'll see any celebrities? Who would be your top star spot?'

'Bear Grylls,' says Muir, as they walk the short distance from the taxi. 'Amy really fancies him. A life of jungles and helicopters, what's not to like?'

'Giant spiders and tropical diseases,' says Weld. 'I'd love to bump into Alexander Armstrong. Tall, handsome, intelligent, and he can sing. The perfect bloke.'

'My fingers are crossed for you, then. Here we are.'

The curved-fronted BBC building casts shade over the courtyard in front of it, cutting off the day's sunshine, though that doesn't seem to trouble the people there, chatting in small groups, talking into phones, drinking bottled water at outdoor cafés.

Muir and Weld head for the main doors, Weld snapping a couple of pictures of the BBC logo high over their heads and scanning everyone they pass for famous faces. Muir calls the number Duncan Painter gave them. It rings, then goes to answerphone. Muir leaves a message and hangs up.

'What now?' asks Weld.

'We'll give it ten minutes. If we haven't heard anything by then, I'll call again.'

'Time for more celeb spotting in the meantime.'

But only five minutes later, a woman appears at Weld's side and asks, 'Are you the police?' Muir takes her proffered hand; her handshake's soft and weak. 'I'm Jackie Noble.'

'How did you know it was us?' asks Muir after he's made the introductions, but Jackie just smiles and glances down at his suit and formal shoes. 'Are you saying we're overdressed for this location?'

'We're not big on formal wear here,' says Jackie, and Weld thinks that's certainly true of her. Jackie's petite, with very short black hair shot through with electric blue highlights which Weld admires, though she thinks the woman's pushing it age-wise for the short skirt she's wearing. Still, she has the legs for it. She's bare-faced and getting away with that too, thanks to a tan which suggests she's recently been somewhere properly, reliably hot.

'We could try and grab a table if you like,' suggests Jackie, nodding towards Caffè Nero, but the place is crowded and the tables close together.

'The questions we have to ask are of a confidential nature,' says Weld. 'Perhaps if we find somewhere we won't be overheard?'

Jackie looks dubious, but Muir leads them to a quiet spot in the courtyard, where they're largely hidden from view by a pillar.

'Ask away, then,' says Jackie. 'I heard about poor Tris. Is he going to be OK?'

'There's no reason at present to think otherwise,' says Muir, 'but he's suffered a serious assault, for which we're keen to make an arrest.'

'I'm sure you are, though to be honest when I heard, I assumed it was something to do with . . . Well, I assumed he'd had a fall or something. You know, had too much to drink.'

'Based on his behaviour when you were working together?'

'Partly that, yes. But in this business . . . Is this in confidence, by the way? I don't want him to wake up and think I've been blabbing his dirty little secrets.'

'We won't name our sources, no,' confirms Muir. 'Please, finish what you were saying.'

'Only that Tris has – or had – a reputation for being a pretty heavy boozer. I don't know if that's still the case, obviously. It's been a while since I worked with him.'

'Was it only alcohol?' asks Weld. 'When we spoke to Mr Painter, he suggested you might be able to tell us how come Tristan ended up needing to borrow significant sums of money on several occasions.'

Jackie glances round, as if to confirm there's no one within earshot.

'You absolutely didn't get this from me, and I would never put it in a formal statement, but he did use other – recreational drugs. Especially coke. I do remember a time he got a bit paranoid, using the side entrance, and he wouldn't leave the building alone. I assumed it was the drugs making him that way, but he insisted there were people out to get him, so maybe he'd overrun his credit limit with his dealer. But the thing was with Tris, he could always pull it together in front of the camera. When the lights went on, Tris lit up and played his part. If he hadn't been in current affairs and gameshows, I think he'd have been very successful on the stage.'

'He's quite an actor, then?'

'Very much so.'

'And the paranoia, what happened to that?'

'He came in one day and all his problems seemed to have disappeared. From what you just said, I assume that was courtesy of Duncan – acting in his own interests, of course. Tris has been his golden-egg-laying goose for many years. If Tris goes down, Duncan goes with him.'

'Doesn't he have other clients?'

'Not of Tris's stature. While he's got Tris, why does he need anyone else?'

'Can I ask you a personal question?' asks Weld. 'Do you like Tristan?'

Jackie looks doubtful.

'He's great at what he does, and he has real talent. And like I say, it's been a long while since I've seen him, so he might have got his act together by now. He's married again, hasn't he? Maybe his new wife has taken him in hand. When we were working together he was newly divorced, and people tend to go off the rails then anyway, don't they? But if you're asking me if I'd invite him round to my house for dinner, introduce him to my family and friends, the answer's no. He's way too unpredictable for my tastes. I prefer the company of people who are steady and reliable.'

THIRTY-THREE

Golding's been trying to put a name to the holder of the bank account where Tristan paid in twenty-five thousand pounds. Mid-afternoon, he receives an email with the result.

When he first reads the message, he does a double take.

It's a Lloyds account, belonging to Aidan Ridley.

Andy Davis drew the short straw of managing the guest list enquiries. He's a man after Golding's own heart and a lover of spreadsheets, and Golding knows he can be relied on to find the required information, no trouble at all.

Davis is so organised, there are rarely more than three pieces of paper on his desk. Two ballpoint pens lying perfectly parallel near his hand point to his OCD, but he has plenty of room for a small fan, blowing cool air into his face as he works. Put a fan on Golding's desk, it would cause a paper landslide.

'How's it going, Andy?'

Davis turns round and leans back in his chair, hands clasped behind his head. Golding can smell the antiseptic gel Davis rubs into his palms numerous times a day.

'All right, old fella,' says Davis. 'What can I do you for?'

'I need an address for one of the Savage case wedding guests, Aidan Ridley.'

'Our Aidan, as was?'

'The very one.'

'He'll be in the database.' Davis opens a new window on his screen and keys in a search term. 'How's the family doing?'

'Oh, they're all right, keeping busy. Chrissie's still waiting for the operation on her ears. It's been cancelled twice already, but that's the NHS for you.'

'Ain't that the truth. Here we go. Business or home?'

Golding glances at his watch, assessing the time it will take him to get to Sterndale.

'What's his business?'

'Looks like a bike shop.'

So it probably closes at 5 p.m. If he gets going now, he has time, but belt and braces are always better.

'I'll take both while I'm here, and phone numbers too, if you've got them.'

'I've always got them,' says Davis. 'Shall I print them for you?'

Golding holds up his notebook. 'I'll write them down, save the ink. And you can take him off your list of interviewees. I'm going over there to talk to him myself.'

Golding thinks Ridley's picked a good spot for the On Your Bike mountain bike shop – a converted barn right on the side of the A-road which bypasses Sterndale and eventually hits Shrewsbury, easy access, an attractive stone building full of character and plenty of parking outside. And the siting strategy seems to be paying off. There are a number of cars in the car park, making the place look reasonably busy for a weekday afternoon.

Inside, the barn lends itself perfectly to the business, with plenty of space to display all kinds of bikes, and a big area to one side where a few men – no women, Golding notices – are browsing the apparently necessary kit: Lycra shorts, helmets, water bottles, lights, bike parts, books and maps. And the bikes look complicated too. In Golding's day, if you had a bike with proper gears on it, you were the envy of the neighbourhood. Times change.

There's a woman at the counter folding some tight-looking jerseys, which Golding doubts would be available in anything close to his size. When she sees him approaching, she stops what she's doing and gives him a welcoming smile. There's a name tag on her blouse: Maria.

'Can I help you?' Her accent's like his own, central Swansea.

Golding returns her smile and produces his warrant card.

'I'm looking for Aidan Ridley, is he about? Nothing to worry about, just routine.'

'He's in the office,' says Maria. 'Give me a minute.'

She picks up an old-fashioned walkie-talkie and presses a button. In a moment a crackling voice answers, and Maria says, 'Someone here to see you.'

She puts the walkie-talkie back in its place. 'No reliable mobile signal up here, see. It's like living in the Stone Age.'

Glancing around at all the high-tech equipment for what used to be such a simple sport, Golding can't agree.

A man's walking towards them from the back of the store – tall, fit-looking but with a slight limp. Golding thought he might recognise him from Burnt Common, but he doesn't. The kind of work he does for CID doesn't bring him into contact with uniforms that often. When the man reaches Golding, he raises his eyebrows in polite enquiry.

'Can I help you?'

Golding introduces himself and flashes his warrant card again.

'Aidan Ridley?' Aidan nods. 'I wonder if I might have a word? Maybe in your office?'

Aidan leads the way to a room at the back of the barn. The usual paraphernalia of PCs and printers is there, but this office is a step beyond any other Golding's ever been in, with the rear wall entirely glass, making the place feel like an extension of the hills outside.

'This is quite a set-up,' says Golding.

Aidan takes a seat at his desk – facing the view, notices Golding, but then who wouldn't? – and gestures to Golding to sit too.

'Thanks,' he says. 'Most of it was paid for with compensation from my accident. Well, it was no accident, actually.'

'What happened? If you don't mind my asking.'

'I don't mind. I was on a shout, two blokes taking a car from a driveway. Nice car, actually, a Merc CLS. We were in the area, got there quickly enough for the scrotes to still be on the scene. One of them tried to take off, I grabbed him and got him on the ground, but he took me down with him. Unfortunately for me, his mate was determined to have that car and drove away over my leg, front wheel, then rear. Crush injuries. They did their best to pin it and rebuild it and I had months of physio, but it's never been good enough to go back on active duty. Happily I can still ride a bike. They offered me a desk job, but that's not me. I had a legacy coming to me, and putting that with the compensation, I took a chance on this place.'

'Good for you, mate,' says Golding. 'Glad to know some good came out of it. The money you had from Tristan Savage – Tristan Hart, you may know him as – what did you do with that?'

Aidan gives a slow smile. 'Is that what this is about?'

'All part of the enquiry. We've been looking into Tristan's bank account, and your name came up. Twenty-five grand, that's a significant sum.'

Aidan regards Golding before he answers, so Golding wonders if he's giving himself time to think.

'Tristan's a friend,' says Aidan eventually. 'He wanted to invest in this business, help me get it off the ground. It's an informal arrangement, just between him and me. At his request, I haven't told my wife and he hasn't told his, or at least he said he wasn't going to.'

'That's quite a secret you're keeping. Why did he ask you to keep it quiet?'

'He said money could ruin the balance of our friendship, maybe make things awkward between the women. I took his point. I think Izzy struggles to meet normal friends, you know, women who aren't after the glitz of showbiz connections.'

'And your wife isn't?'

'Laura's very down to earth. But I agreed with Tris, as it happens. I think she would feel awkward if she thought Izzy's husband was bankrolling our business.'

'So was it a loan, or a gift?'

Aidan shrugs. 'We didn't really discuss that.'

'You're a lucky man, Aidan. Lucky to have a friend who can lend you twenty-five grand and not worry about when he's going to get it back. He's certainly not worrying about it at the moment, is he?'

Aidan's eyes narrow. 'Are you trying to imply something?'

'Not at all. Should I be?'

Aidan gives him a much broader smile.

'You guys,' he says. 'What are you like? Take me off your list. It wasn't me.'

THIRTY-FOUR

When Laura's phone pings with an incoming text, she's in a queue at the Co-op checkouts. Glancing at the screen to check who the message is from, she sees it's from Izzy, and is tempted to read it there and then. But the customer ahead of her is moving on, and the young woman seated at the till is already smiling her welcome. Laura knows her, vaguely, from being a regular customer at the store. According to her name tag, she's called Kate.

'All right?' she asks, passing Laura's purchases – pasta, salad ingredients, minced beef for bolognaise sauce – past the scanner, and Laura smiles and nods.

'Any news about Tristan?' asks Kate, scanning the overpriced Häagen-Dazs Laura added to her basket at the last moment. Normally she wouldn't buy it unless it were on offer, but Gemma loves ice cream, and Laura's getting desperate to make her eat at least something. The more calories, the better.

Laura's stuffing the shopping into a bag, wondering what Izzy has to say, praying it's good news, not bad.

'I don't know,' she says. 'I haven't really heard anything.'

'That poor man,' says Kate, then reads off the total on the

screen. Laura readies her bank card for the contactless reader. 'He's always so lovely when he comes in here, always has time to say hello. Makes you wonder who'd do a thing like that, doesn't it? But we were saying in the staff room, people like that are never what they seem. Remember that Michael Barrymore? Look what he got mixed up in.'

'I don't think there's any similarity between Tristan and Michael Barrymore,' says Laura, but as she goes outside, she can't help asking herself how she knows that's true.

The message from Izzy is short: *Can you come over?* This is the first request for face-to-face contact since the day of the wedding. She'll have to take the ice cream home first, but that's only a short detour.

She types *Be there in 20 mins x*, and presses send.

At Foxcote Lodge, everything looks as it used to, in that long-ago-seeming time when life was day-to-day. The Range Rover and the Fiat are in the driveway, and Laura parks so as not to block the Fiat, thinking if Izzy's home, Bridget will soon be leaving. As she climbs from the car, the beauty of the place strikes her afresh: the house's old-world imperfections, the hum of bees on lavender and the scents of an English garden in full summer. As she walks towards the door, she catches sight of Bridget looking out of an upstairs window and raises a hand to wave; but Flora must have demanded Bridget's attention, since she turns away from the window without responding.

She rings the bell, and Izzy opens the door promptly, as if she was already on her way to open it. She looks older, washed out, unhappy; her light-up-the-room beauty has faded, like a butterfly with the powder knocked from its wings. Laura steps across the threshold and wraps Izzy in a hug. There seems to be nothing of her but skin and bone.

Izzy allows herself to be held for a few moments before breaking away, laughing at herself as she brushes away a tear.

'Tired and emotional,' she says, leading the way to the kitchen. One of Tris's favourite songs – Sarah Vaughan's *Once in a While* – is playing in the background, the piano softly melodic, Sarah's voice filled with heartbreak, but Izzy cuts the music off by telling Alexa to stop. Laura notices Izzy makes sure the kitchen door is closed.

'Tea? Or something stronger?'

'Tea's fine,' says Laura, and Izzy switches on the kettle. 'Where's Flora?'

'Upstairs playing with her fairy castle. I asked Bridget to stay on for a little while so we can talk.' Izzy takes mugs from the dishwasher, dropping in organic Ceylon teabags from a Fortnum & Mason caddy. 'She's been a rock. Though I've been giving her a bit extra so I suppose that doesn't hurt.' She rips open a packet of chocolate biscuits, pours them on to a plate and takes one for herself. 'Sugar's all that's keeping me going. Sugar and a glass or two of rosé. I can open a bottle, if you like.'

Laura shakes her head. 'I've got the car, and dinner to make when the kids get home. But I'm so glad to see you. How is he? What's the news?'

The kettle boils, but Izzy's gazing out on the garden and seems to have forgotten about tea. Overhead, they hear Flora running from one room to another.

Laura pours hot water into the mugs, adding milk to her own and a slice of lemon to Izzy's. She carries both cups to the scrubbed pine table, sets them down and takes a chair.

'Come and tell me everything.'

When she turns back from the window, Laura sees Izzy is silently crying, betraying what she's truly feeling inside. Blowing her nose and wiping her eyes, she brings a box of tissues as she joins Laura at the table.

'How he is, is one thing,' says Izzy. 'How he and I are, is another.'

Laura frowns, not understanding. She waits for Izzy to go on.

'I spoke to the police. They say someone hit him with a champagne bottle. Which is an interesting choice of weapon, don't you think? As to what they say at the hospital, I don't know what to make of it, whether they're being optimistic or pessimistic or if they just don't know. He's still in a coma, and that's not good. You don't need to be a rocket scientist or a neurosurgeon to know that. But they're talking about permanent disability.'

Laura covers Izzy's hand with her own.

'I'm so sorry.'

Izzy shrugs.

'That needn't be the end of the world, for two people who love each other. But I'm damned if I'm going to play nurse to someone who doesn't give a shit about me.'

'Izzy! What are you talking about? Tris is devoted to you, absolutely devoted, to you and Flora!'

Izzy gives her an odd look, somewhere between coldness and despair.

'Let me show you something, and you can see for yourself how devoted to me and Flora that bastard is.'

She stands up and crosses to the worktop, where she rummages in the handbag Laura's always coveted before drawing out the architect's letter and handing it over.

'Read that, and then I'll tell you what it's all about.'

Laura reads, uncomprehending as to what the problem might be.

'Is this to Tris? This says to Mr T. Savage.'

Izzy looks contrite. 'That's his real name.'

'So you're not Izzy Hart?'

'Sorry, no. I'm Izzy Savage.'

'And I didn't know you were building another house.' Laura feels hurt. 'You didn't tell me that, either.'

'How could I tell you if I didn't know? And *we* aren't building another house. Tris is building it with someone else, some woman called Tina. If he hadn't had his accident, I don't know when he'd have let me in on the secret. Maybe the day he moved out to be with her.'

Laura shakes her head in disbelief.

'But you and Tris . . . You've always been so solid. He worships the ground you walk on, Izzy. There has to be some kind of mistake.'

Izzy picks up her phone, flips through her photos to find the pictures of the building site and passes the phone to Laura.

'See for yourself. He's building the house on land he co-owns with this woman. I checked on the Land Registry website.'

'But who is she?'

Izzy sits back down at the table and buries her face in her hands.

'I have no idea! I suppose I shouldn't be surprised. It was all too good to be true. In his line of work, it's just commonplace, isn't it? A merry-go-round of relationships – marry, divorce, marry, divorce. How could I have been so stupid as to fall for it?'

Laura says the right thing – 'You weren't stupid, Izzy,' – but is beginning to feel she's been naive herself. Have they all been taken in by a slick veneer, all been fooled by the acting of a very accomplished player?

Then she asks, 'Have you told the police?'

Izzy shakes her head.

'But you have to,' says Laura. 'This might have some connection to the assault. There was no accident, Izzy. Someone was angry enough to mean Tris real harm. What if it was this woman?'

Izzy gives a great sigh.

'Can I trust you? Absolutely trust you?'

'You know you can.'

'Because if I tell you something, you must swear you won't repeat it to a living soul.'

'I swear.'

'There's more. I found a phone, one I didn't know he had. It's full of phone numbers, only women's numbers. A few texts, a few missed calls. Looks like my wonderful husband had quite a harem.'

'Izzy.' Laura looks disbelieving. 'It can't be. There must be another explanation. I can't believe Tris would do that to you. To Flora.'

'Perfect father, perfect husband, perfect life. That's what can't be. It was only ever a lie.'

'Oh, Izzy, no. He loves you.'

'Does he?'

'There's bound to be some logical explanation,' says Laura, but her voice lacks conviction. 'You mustn't jump to conclusions. When he wakes up, you can talk to him, let him explain.'

'There is a logical explanation,' says Izzy, bitterly. 'My husband's

230

a lying, cheating shit, and I'm just another idiot who's been taken in. It's a story older than time.'

The silent tears begin again, but Izzy barely seems to notice, only wiping them away as if they're some irritant.

'You have to take all this to the police,' insists Laura. 'It might easily have some bearing.'

'You mean one of his other women might have done it?'

That is what Laura means, but she chooses her words to make them more palatable.

'I mean if there are things going on in his life you weren't aware of, they need to know. If you want justice for Tris.'

Izzy wipes her eyes.

'You know what? I don't want justice for Tris, not after what I've found. What I want is justice for me and Flora, and that's for me not to be made a complete fool, and for Flora never to know the kind of man her father actually is. If the press get hold of any of this, if it all comes out, our lives will be ruined. I'll be another ex-wife in a sea of celebrity divorcees. So I don't care if they never find out who did it. I'll just assume some other woman got pissed off with him the same way I am now and saved me doing the job myself. In other words, he got what was coming to him.'

'You can't possibly mean that, Izzy.'

'Can't I? If Aidan had done this to you, how would you feel? Wouldn't you feel the same? And if you're any kind of friend to me, you won't say anything to anyone about this. No one at all, not even Aidan. Promise?'

'I promise,' says Laura, and she sincerely means it, at the time.

THIRTY-FIVE

It's another warm evening, and windows are open to allow a through-draft to cool the overheated rooms. Aidan slides open the glass doors at the back of the house so they can eat on the deck. Gemma's coaxed reluctantly from her room, but only plays with her pasta, picking at a few slices of tomato and cucumber from the salad. Josh, as always, wolfs his food, and offers to eat Gemma's if she doesn't want it, but Laura carries the plate back inside, telling Gemma she can eat it later if she'd like. The ice cream is a hit all round, and Gemma eats a bowlful while Laura tries not to watch every spoon she puts in her mouth. The nutritional content might be poor, but the calorie content is high, so Laura considers it a win.

When they're finished, Aidan asks Gemma and Josh to clear the table before they do their homework. As the kids go upstairs, he says, 'Fancy a glass of something cold?'

Laura nods. 'A rosé would be great. There's beer in the fridge if you want one.'

While Aidan's inside, Laura looks out across their small garden. Josh's slowly deflating football lies on the bald patch of grass in front of his five-a-side goal, the borders need tidying, and she thinks how badly it compares to the beautiful gardens at Foxcote Lodge. She's always seen Izzy's life as so idyllic, unashamedly envying her, believing her good fortune is fair reward for her natural gifts. Izzy herself seems so flawless. What kind of a man would feel the need to cheat on her?

Aidan places a glass of blush wine on the table.

'You look thoughtful.' He sits down across from her and gives her one of those smiles she loves, charged with affection and concern. At least, that's how she's always read it in the past. Now she knows she's been wrong about Tris and Izzy, how can she be sure her own husband isn't faking it too?

Laura tastes her wine. 'I'm having a *What would Dad do?* moment.'

Aidan's smile disappears.

'Uh-oh. That's not good. Tell me.'

Laura sighs. 'To be honest, it's the telling that's the problem. I promised Izzy I wouldn't say anything, not even to you. But I think she should be talking to the police.'

'I'm intrigued.'

'But I said I wouldn't tell you.'

'So what would your dad do? While remembering he was a decorated senior police officer who left the job with very few friends, thanks to his determination always to do the right thing. And you've told me that story more than once, about how you snitched on your ex-best friend at school in a *Who's been smoking behind the bike sheds?* kind of enquiry.'

'It was nothing to do with smoking. It was about nicking lunch money.'

'But the outcome was the same. One seriously pissed-off friend who never spoke to you again. There is such a thing as being too principled, Laura. We all have to get along in life. Sometimes you have to put your faith in karma, and let others dole out the punishments and rewards.'

'I won't tell you, then.'

'Then again, if you can't trust me, who can you trust?'

Laura sips again at her wine. 'I think that's exactly the question. About trust. Whether you can trust the people closest to you.'

'So come on, what would your dad do?'

'He'd march down the road first thing in the morning and demand to speak to the officer in charge and tell him – or her – everything he knew.'

'Consequences and fallout be damned.'

'Consequences and fallout be damned. Exactly.'

A couple of gardens away, they hear the shouts of children playing.

Aidan looks serious. 'Policing's not black and white, you know. It's awash with shades of grey. And I should know. Can I tell you something?'

'Always.'

Laura looks across at her husband, at his still-handsome face, and watches him take a long pull at his beer bottle, knowing him well enough to see he's weighing something up.

'Once or twice,' he says, 'while I was still in the job, I didn't make an arrest I probably should have. One or two people, I let walk away. People I knew had just got themselves in too deep in a bad situation, who wouldn't be doing it again. People whose lives would be ruined by a criminal conviction or even an arrest record. I made a judgement which wasn't really mine to make. Your dad would have made those arrests, but I don't think the world would have been any better for it. So what I'm saying is, sometimes in life you should pay more attention to the possible consequences than to playing by the rules. That's my take on it.'

'So you think I should tell you.'

'You know I'm discreet. And I can give you sensible advice about whether your dad would have been right in this case, or wrong.'

'You never liked my dad,' says Laura, teasing.

'I was terrified of your dad. He was like the force beacon, a shining example to flat-footed rookies like me.'

'He liked you.'

'I suppose he must have, or he wouldn't have let you marry me, would he? So come on, what's on your mind?'

'OK. But you mustn't tell a soul.'

'What soul would I tell?'

'The first bad news is the update from the hospital. They've been told today Tris is unlikely to make a full recovery, that he'll suffer some permanent disability.'

'What? Permanent as in . . . Wow.' Aidan shakes his head. 'That's horrendous. Did they say what kind of disability?'

Laura shakes her head. 'No. Izzy didn't seem to know whether they meant physical or – God forbid – whether they were talking about some kind of brain damage. But life-changing.'

'Brain damage? Tris? I can't even begin to imagine how that would be for him, not when he's such a livewire. Surely there's something they can do? These days they seem to be able to fix everything. Poor Tris.'

'Poor all of them.'

'So the police investigation will be cranking up a notch.'

'Presumably. I suppose they were already doing plenty, given how high-profile he is.'

'That's always the way of it. PR will be looking for a quick win, to make everyone look good. Have they anyone in mind for it yet?'

'Izzy didn't say so. But what she did say I think opens up a whole new list of potential suspects.' She gives Aidan the details: the hidden phone, the architect's letter, the half-built house. 'Shall I tell you the worst thing, the thing that's been preying on my mind? What if Izzy wasn't telling the truth about when she knew all this? What if she's known for a while that he's been playing away? Doesn't that give her a motive for the attack? If she was seriously, murderously mad at him before that day, what if she was just biding her time for an occasion like the wedding to muddy the waters? If she'd confronted him and stabbed him out of jealousy in their kitchen, it would have been pretty obvious who'd done it, wouldn't it?'

Aidan considers.

'Would it? What about Bridget?'

'Bridget?'

'If Tris has been putting it about, what're the chances he's overlooked the nanny? Don't they all get caught out that way?'

'Tris wouldn't look twice at Bridget. Would he?'

Aidan shrugs. 'You ask me, it could happen.'

'But do you see what I mean about opening up the list of suspects? One of these women he's been – well, at least talking to on that secret phone – one of them might have a reason for wishing him harm, but the police don't even know they're out there.'

Aidan stands up. 'I'm having another beer. You want a top-up?'

'Two beers on a weekday? What's going on? I will if you will.'

Aidan takes her glass, and Laura hears the fridge door open and close, the spin of a bottle cap, wine burbling into her glass.

When he sits back down, his face is serious. 'There's something I have to tell you too.'

Laura feels the stirrings of disquiet.

'Don't tell me you . . .'

Aidan interrupts with a shake of his head. 'It's nothing like that. You should know me better than that.'

'I suppose that's what Izzy thought about Tris.'

'Don't you dare, Laura. One man's infidelities don't make all men guilty. Besides, you've no proof that Tris has been unfaithful. Izzy might be jumping to conclusions.'

'What other conclusion could there be?'

'Listen. I know Tris is someone who likes to keep stuff to himself. That's why I didn't tell you about our arrangement.'

Laura's disquiet is growing to alarm. 'Arrangement? What arrangement?'

'I know I should have told you, but he persuaded me not to. He said he wouldn't tell Izzy and I shouldn't say anything to you. He said it would unbalance your friendship if you knew, maybe make things awkward.'

'What things?'

'When I was setting up the business, Tris offered me a loan, a long-term loan as a sleeping partner. He said I could repay it when I was ready, and it seemed like a much better idea than borrowing more from the bank. It meant I could buy more stock, ramp up the online business.'

'How much?'

'It doesn't matter how much. Enough to make a difference at the time. I was glad to take it and to be honest I didn't think much more about it. Tris seemed relaxed and I assumed he wasn't hurting for cash. Then three or four weeks ago, he rang me and asked if he could have the money back. I was shocked. If I'm honest I was hoping he might not ever ask for it, and I certainly never expected a request for immediate repayment. You know we don't have a lot of cash on hand, and I told him so. He was sympathetic but he said he really needed the money himself, and that I should approach the bank to fill the gap if that's what I needed to do. Since you've told me what Izzy said, it all makes sense. I suppose he wants funds for this house he's building. But the point is, with him laid up, it's given me breathing space I really, really need. The bank said no, so I was looking at drastic action. Remortgaging, anything I could think of.'

Laura's not sure if she feels more hurt, or angry. 'Without telling me?'

'I'm sorry. I should have told you in the beginning.'

'Damn right you should. What were you thinking?'

'Tris persuaded me. He was so insistent that we should keep it between ourselves. And I understood his reasoning. It might have changed how you felt about Izzy, and he wanted her to have a friend on equal terms. To be honest . . .'

'A bit late for that, maybe.'

'To be honest, I never thought it would be an issue. He told me over and over I could repay him in my own good time, whenever, *mañana*. Then he changed his mind.'

238

'Which actually gives weight to Izzy's suspicions he's thinking of leaving her.'

'I suppose it does, yes. Anyway, it's not mine and Tris's secret any more. Someone from CID came to see me at work today. They've found the payment to me from Tris's bank account. They wanted to know what was going on.'

'You had a visit from CID? Is that something else you weren't going to mention?'

'I wasn't sure how to frame it.'

'So if they came to see you, it really was significant money, wasn't it?'

'Depends on your point of view. To Tris, probably not.'

'How much was it, Aidan?'

'Twenty-five thousand.'

In the depths of her stomach, Laura's indignation burns. 'Are you serious? A twenty-five thousand pound debt you never mentioned?'

'I'm sorry.'

'You should be bloody sorry. And you've got yourself in a bit of a mess, haven't you? What did you tell the police?'

'What I just told you.'

'So would you have mentioned that they'd spoken to you if I hadn't just told you what Izzy said?'

Aidan looks a little sad. 'Honestly, probably not.'

'That's really hurtful.'

'I just want to protect you from worry.'

'I don't need protecting.'

'Sometimes you do, Laura. It's not a bad thing, is it? The real question is, what would your dad do now? Because if you come at this with a CID hat on, not only does Izzy have a possible motive for a row with Tris, they might say that I do too.'

'Oh my God.'

'I hope you're not going to ask me if I did it.'

'Did you?'

'Don't be ridiculous.'

'But it seemed ridiculous before this afternoon to think that Izzy would want to hurt him.'

'New information shifts the picture.'

'Which is why I should tell the police.'

'Which is why you should keep quiet and let them do their job their way. If there's anything to find out, they'll get to it in the end.'

'And what about your arrangement with him?'

'They've asked their questions, and I answered them honestly. I saw no reason to disclose that he'd asked for the money back. That was in a personal phone call, no record of what was said.'

'You're starting to talk like a guilty man.'

'I'm guilty of nothing. You can trust me on that. The attack on Tris is one hundred percent nothing to do with me. I swear on our kids' lives.'

'How come I never saw anything of this money?'

Aidan bows his head. 'I opened a new account.'

'You have a bank account I don't know about? Are you serious? Is it with Lloyds, by any chance?'

'How did you know that?'

Laura stands and picks up what's left of her wine.

'Thanks for making a complete fool of me. Karen Garner saw you coming out of there and I told her we don't bank with them. So it'll be all round town you've been keeping secrets.'

'Ah, come on, love,' says Aidan, trying to catch her hand.

Laura's eyes are stinging with tears. 'I thought we didn't have secrets.'

'We don't. But I thought it was for the best. For your friendship with Izzy.'

'You patronising prick,' says Laura, and leaves him at the table, alone.

THIRTY-SIX

In truth, Laura's more troubled than angry. The conversation she had with Aidan has put a distance between them, turning out to be one of those moments in a long relationship where you realise you don't know the person you're sharing your life with anything like as well as you thought.

And Izzy's revelations have left her rattled, shaken her confidence. She's not naive enough to think people don't have secrets. Over the years, there have been things – small things – she hasn't shared. But now it turns out some people go one step further, and make a life of lies. Which side of that divide is Aidan on?

Might a man keeping one secret not easily have more?

The evening grows cooler. From the lounge, she hears Aidan go upstairs to the spare room he uses as his office. Any other night, she wouldn't have thought about it twice. Now she can't help wondering what he's doing behind that closed door.

Finding the TV remote, her tablet and her phone, she settles down on the sofa. Her nail polish has lost its gloss, and she thinks about giving herself a manicure. Or maybe she should call Izzy. She's feeling guilty for having left her in that big house, all alone, but Flora will be asleep by now, and Izzy might be too. Heaven knows she looked in need of rest.

Hoping for diversion, she switches on her tablet and scrolls through the latest posts on her Facebook and Instagram feeds. Nothing grabs her.

She puts the tablet aside and casts her mind back to the wedding. If Izzy already had suspicions about Tris, did she have any opportunity to assault him? Did she leave the party for any length of time?

Aidan did. He went to the gents before he went looking for Tris. Aidan was gone a long time, but Tris had already been missing a while before that.

The exercise is pointless. Her memories are blurred by the alcohol she drank, and what she remembers is a kaleidoscope of people coming and going, so she really can't recall who was where, when. As a witness to that evening she'd be useless, but the fact remains, Aidan and Izzy have motives for a falling-out with Tris. If she were her father's daughter, she'd report them both, but that wouldn't be the right thing for a loyal friend – or wife – to do.

The book club choice is still waiting to be read. Opening her copy, she reads a page, then reads it again because the words have made no sense. Giving up, she decides to do her nails after all, but as she's about to go and fetch her kit, her phone rings.

Mandy, Hannah's mum, no doubt wanting a catch-up. Well, what the hell. A round-up of Sterndale gossip is as good a way as any to pass the time.

'Hiya.'

Mandy sounds breathless, intense, but that's not unusual.

Mandy likes everything to be a crisis, and can make a drama out of a trip to the garden centre.

'Laura, thank God I've caught you.'

'What's up?'

'Laura, is Gemma OK?'

Laura bristles. The last thing she wants is for Gemma's current moodiness to be the subject of local speculation.

'As far as I'm aware, she's fine.'

'When did you last see her?'

'What's this about, Mandy?'

'Hannah says Gemma's texting some really odd stuff, weird enough for her to come and tell me about it, and you know how secretive they are. I just thought you might like to, you know, make sure she's OK.'

There's a prickling at the back of Laura's neck. What Mandy's saying, she realises, is hooking into a fear that's been prowling her subconscious for the last few days, that Gemma's mood might be running deeper and darker than the usual teenage angst.

'What kind of weird?'

Mandy hesitates. 'I don't want to speak out of turn. It's really not my business, but if it was Hannah, I know I'd want . . .'

'What kind of weird?'

'Self-harming weird.'

Laura ends the call without the nicety of a goodbye, figuring she'll apologise to Mandy later. Knowing if there's nothing in it, Gemma will never forgive her – and there isn't going to be anything in it, is there? – she doesn't quite run upstairs, but she's moving much more quickly than normal.

She knocks on Gemma's door. There's no answer.

'Gemma.' She turns the handle, but the door's locked. 'Gemma, open the door, sweetie. I just need to have a word with you.' She puts her ear close to the wood, but hears nothing inside. Nothing is unusual. Gemma's never without music or Netflix, but all she's hearing is silence. 'Gemma, open the door.'

Aidan appears from his office.

'What's going on?'

She tells him what Mandy's said. Immediately he switches, from family-man Aidan to policeman in crisis-handling mode.

He knocks on Gemma's door, much harder than she'd dare. She's always fearful of Gemma's fallout, whereas Aidan's hardened to all kinds of abuse and doesn't care.

'Gemma, open the door now.'

No response. Aidan and Laura look at each other.

'I'll break the lock,' he says.

'Really? We'll look a bit stupid if she just can't hear us because she's got her headphones on.'

'We'll look really stupid if what Hannah says is right and we do nothing.'

There's a moment of indecision. Then Aidan steps back and kicks hard at the lock.

The door flies open, and he steps into the room.

If he's honest, he's expecting blood, so his first reaction is relief when there is none. But relief turns to concern, and concern to near panic, held in check only because ingrained training stops it from taking over. Calm, calm, calm, and do what's necessary. Behind him, Laura's shouting Gemma's name, and

Josh is running down the landing to find out what's going on. Laura grabs Josh by the shoulder to stop him going into the room, and for his sake stops her own shouting by biting her knuckles.

The sudden quiet is a relief, giving Aidan a moment to decide what he needs to do first – because there in the teenage detritus of her bedroom, among the scattered clothes and make-up, among the posters and the schoolbooks and the outgrown, still-loved toys, Gemma's lying on the pink carpet she chose when she was nine, ghastly pale and showing no sign of life.

As she and Aidan wait for an update on Gemma's condition, the thought occurs to Laura that somewhere in this hospital, in another department, on another floor, lies Tris.

They've found seats in a busy corridor, near a pair of vending machines. Aidan seems calm, holding her hand when she needs it, telling her not to worry when she asks him how long they've been waiting, trying to reassure her this is routine to the medical staff, that they're all too familiar with overdoses and that Gemma will be fine.

Anyone who doesn't know him would take him to be relaxed and in control, but to Laura, the constant jigging of his knee gives him away.

Aidan is seriously worried.

'What I don't understand,' says Laura, 'is where she got those pills. We've never had anything like that in the house.'

'Stuff like that's easy enough to come by. She probably got it at school.'

'At school? You have to be joking!'

But Aidan shakes his head. 'Diazepam, Valium, you name

246

it. Kids nick it from the bathroom cabinet at home and sell it in the playground.'

'But why do they want it?'

'Same reason adults do. It makes them feel good, or better, at least. And you know what kids are. They like to experiment.'

'Do you think that's what Gemma was doing?'

Aidan looks away, as if taking an interest in a young woman battling the coffee machine for her change.

'You think she meant to overdose. Oh my God, what if she'd taken them all?'

Aidan squeezes her hand. 'But she didn't, did she? And we found her pretty quickly. It's nothing like as bad as it might have been.'

He looks away again, and Laura knows he's remembering other nights in hospital corridors, waiting for news of other people's kids, knocking on doors after midnight to break hearts with the worst of all news. Maybe he misses those days, but she's glad he doesn't have to be that unwelcome messenger any more. Even if he wasn't aware of it, those harrowing visits made him moody, pushing him into dark places where he was impossible to reach.

'Maybe it was a cry for help rather than a serious attempt to . . .' She can't say the words, articulate the idea that her daughter, her precious girl, might have wanted to end what Laura has spent fourteen years trying to make a wonderful life. The knowledge that she has somehow failed is crushing. She must be to blame. Something she has – or hasn't – done is what's brought them to this pass.

'I should have spent more time with her. I should have found out what was on her mind.'

Aidan looks sceptical.

'You think nagging her would have made her come clean? It wouldn't, Laura. She was in a low place, OK, but there could be any number of reasons for that, none of which a girl of her age would go confiding in her mum.' His words strike a broadside to her cherished illusion that she and Gemma are close, and Laura's face shows her pain. 'Sorry. But she's not our baby girl any more. We have to accept that. She just isn't.'

A nurse is walking towards them. 'Are you Gemma's mum and dad?'

Laura gets to her feet. 'Yes.'

'You can come and see her now.'

Without saying anything else, the nurse walks back the way she's come.

Laura keeps pace with her. 'Is she OK?'

'She'll be staying with us overnight. We're trying to find a bed for her now. She'll be having a psychiatric evaluation before she's discharged.'

Gemma is lying in a side-room, ashen-faced, eyes closed. Laura rushes to take her hand, and when she squeezes it, Gemma opens her eyes. Her focus wavers; then her eyes fill with tears.

'I'm sorry, Mum.'

Laura bends down to kiss her cheek. 'I'm sorry too. I didn't know things had got so bad. Just try and sleep now, sleep it off. I'll stay here with you. I love you, sweetheart.'

'I love you too,' says Gemma, and she closes her eyes.

There's no space for Gemma in the Paediatric Unit. Somewhere in the small hours, as she drifts in and out of sleep and Laura strokes her hand, a nurse disconnects the drip of benzodiazepine antidote which probably saved Gemma's life. A while later – Laura has been dozing, and doesn't know how long it's been – a taciturn porter releases the brake on Gemma's bed, and with Laura following close behind, pushes her through the glare of white-lit corridors, the only sounds a squeaky wheel and Laura's hard-soled shoes on polished tiles. Beyond the windows, the world is dark.

Even on the far side of midnight, the general admission ward is noisy and unsettling. Gemma is wheeled into a corner bay, watched by the wakeful eyes of those who should be sleeping. A woman with wild hair and a drooping breast exposed at the front of an open nightgown is watching a live casino on TV. In a bed diagonally opposite, an elderly woman's repeated cries – *Mary! Where are you, Mary?* – go ignored.

'Don't leave me here, Mum,' begs Gemma.

Laura doesn't want to lie.

'I don't think they'll let me stay with you much longer, sweetie. This is an adult ward.'

'That woman's mad,' says Gemma, and her eyelids slide closed.

'If I have to go, I'll come back straight after breakfast.' Laura brushes a lock of hair off Gemma's forehead. 'Just sleep, my darling. Get some rest.'

But Gemma is already sleeping – sleeping normally, not hovering, as she was earlier, on the borders of deep-space coma. Laura shudders at the way this night might have gone, without Mandy's phone call. How could she have borne it, if Gemma had been lost?

Her thoughts go again to Tristan, floating alone in his own inky black hole, physically close, his consciousness adrift.

Gemma set out on that same journey, but they managed to bring her back.

Please God they can find a way to do the same for Tristan.

THIRTY-SEVEN

There are hours of waiting in getting Gemma discharged. When Laura arrives on the ward – still the crazy place it was last night, still next to impossible to find anyone who knows what should happen next – Gemma is already dressed, sitting on her bed and desperate to go home. After a long time, a nurse arrives to take Gemma to the psychiatric unit, and she returns not long afterwards with a prescription for antidepressants.

She hands the paper to her mother.

'I'm so not taking those. So many people at school are on them. They just make you into a zombie.'

'Maybe you should think about it, sweetie. Under the circumstances, I mean.'

'Mum. No.'

Laura's unable to resist asking the question, even though she knows Gemma won't answer. As she's learned, the two of them aren't close.

'So what did they ask you?'

'Just stuff. She talked about the importance of mental health and dealing with stress, like I don't know already. Can we go now?'

As they walk across the car park, Laura sees Gemma sniff the air, as if she might, on some level at least, be grateful she's here to see this new day. In the car, she's quiet, until they're approaching a McDonald's, where she asks Laura to pull in.

'I'm starving. The food they were handing out at the hospital was rank.'

Fast food in the Ridley household is normally reserved for special occasions, but if Gemma still being with them isn't a special occasion, then what is? In the drive-through, she orders a Big Mac, fries and a chocolate milkshake, and wolfs them as if she hasn't eaten for a week. Which, on reflection, she hasn't.

Could it be that this episode marks a turning point, a low spot from which the only way is up? Is it possible she's given herself a wake-up call, and whatever it was that was getting her down, she'll start to get over it?

Laura's fingers are firmly crossed.

At home, Laura expects Gemma to disappear upstairs and close her bedroom door, but something's different. The sun is shining, and the garden looks, if not pretty, inviting. When Laura puts the kettle on to make coffee, Gemma finds juice in the fridge, pours herself a glass over ice, and heading out on to the deck, takes a seat at the table.

As Laura's pouring milk into her mug, her phone rings. Mandy, no doubt wanting chapter and verse on Gemma's drama. Not happening. Laura bounces the call and joins Gemma outside.

The breeze is off the hills, and there's that heady scent of heather and bracken, of rocky streams and weathered stone. Gemma's taking deeper breaths than normal, breathing it in, and Laura wonders again if she's thanking her lucky stars for her narrow escape. Too narrow, by far.

'Do I have to go to school tomorrow?' she asks.

'I don't think so,' says Laura. She can imagine the difficulties Gemma will face if Hannah hasn't kept her mouth shut (and when has Hannah ever kept her mouth shut?) – stares, nudges, maybe even taunting and teasing. That can't be helped; it's a crucial life lesson, learning to rise above it all when you've done something gossip-worthy, but a couple of days in the sanctuary of home will make Gemma much better prepared.

Gemma leans her head back and watches the clouds move slowly across the sky.

'Penny for them?' asks Laura.

'What does that mean?' Gemma looks smilingly baffled, and Laura smiles too.

'Haven't I ever said that to you before? It was one of Grandma's favourite expressions. Penny for your thoughts, it means. From the days when a penny had some value. Do you remember Grandpa telling tales of the penny chews he used to buy with his pocket money?'

'Old people live in the past.'

'They have a long past to live in.'

'Do you miss Grandma and Grandpa, Mum?'

The question takes Laura aback. Gemma never asks personal questions, not since she hit the self-obsession of her teens and lost interest in almost everything but herself. As she considers how to answer, she feels the pricking of tears. Delayed shock, no doubt, from last night.

'Yes, I do. Every day.'

'I miss them too.'

'I would have missed you far, far more if we hadn't found you in time.'

Immediately Laura's said the words, she wishes she hadn't. They're far too intimate for their present relationship, way too exposing. She expects Gemma to leave her, and will be sorry if she does, but Gemma's focus seems to be back on the clouds passing overhead.

'Do you think that's where people go when they die, up there behind the clouds?'

Laura lightens her tone. 'I like to think so. I like to think Grandma and Grandpa are up there somewhere, looking down on us all, keeping us safe, being our guardian angels.'

'If that's true, they'd see everything we do. Good and bad.'

'So you'd better not do anything bad.'

Gemma falls silent again and Laura sips her coffee, hardly daring to move, not wanting to startle her daughter away. But still Gemma remains, and Laura begins to realise she has something to say, if she can find the right words.

The doorbell rings: the postman, needing a signature for one of Aidan's internet orders. By the time Laura returns to the garden, Gemma has disappeared.

Late that afternoon, Aidan texts and asks if he should bring a takeaway, for which Laura is grateful. Having had almost no sleep the previous night, the fog of fatigue has taken over, and the thought of cooking is too much. She suggests pizza, and asks him to bring a side salad for her and Gemma, and plenty of chips for Josh, otherwise he'll bolt a whole pizza to himself and everyone else will go hungry.

Even though it's takeaway, they eat at the outside table.

Gemma is quiet, but manages two slices with tuna and peppers. As predicted, Josh takes far more than his share, chattering about a dramatic experiment in the chemistry lab as he dives into the chips. When there's nothing left but greasy boxes, Gemma slips away upstairs. As she carries the plates into the kitchen, Laura's eyes follow her anxiously.

Aidan's about to leave the table too when Josh says, 'Fancy a game of footie, Dad?'

Aidan has invoices to produce and orders to submit, but it's been a difficult twenty-four hours. Recalling how he felt seeing Gemma lying on the floor, he reckons he can spare some time for his son.

'Think you're up to it? I'm in goal.'

They play for about half an hour, Aidan letting in a few balls he could have saved, then finding when Josh is in goal he cuts his father no slack. Josh makes a great save, and Aidan calls time.

'I'm about done, buddy. Shall we go and get a drink?' Walking back towards the house, he puts his arm around his son's shoulders. As he does so, Josh stops.

'Dad, can I ask you something?'

'Ask away.'

'What's wrong with Gemma?'

Aidan hesitates. Stupid to think Josh wouldn't be upset by what had happened. He should have been proactive, talked about it this morning before school.

'She's just having a difficult time at the moment, son. Sometimes things affect us more than they might at other times – all those things like hormones play a part. And when the world looks dark, people do mad things, like taking too

255

many tablets they think are going to make them feel better, and they end up feeling worse.'

'She took an overdose.'

Aidan sighs. 'Yes, she did. She took an overdose.'

'Doesn't she love us any more?'

Aidan squeezes Josh's shoulder. 'Of course she loves us. But do you know why she got in that mess? Because she didn't trust any of us – me, or your mum, or you – enough to tell us how she was feeling. She kept it all bottled up inside, so it all went rotten.'

'Like brain rot?'

'Well, not exactly like that, but brain rot if you like.'

'What if you hadn't found her? Would she have died?'

Aidan doesn't want to answer that question, so he says, 'What you always have to remember is that we're your family, and you can always come to us with any problem, any problem at all, and we'll listen and we'll stand by you. That's what families do. Never bottle things up, Josh. There's never anything so bad you can't tell me or your mum. Nothing. I used to be a policeman, remember? There's nothing you can tell me I haven't heard before. We have to trust each other. Promise?'

Josh nods, and glances up at the bedroom window where he hopes Gemma is listening.

'Ice cream?' asks Aidan, and he and Josh go inside.

THIRTY-EIGHT

Izzy's at the wrong end of another lonely evening, standing with the fridge door open, hesitating between a Chablis and a Rosé d'Anjou. The house is full of that disturbing silence which gets inside your head, the kind where you hear dust-motes falling and every drip of a leaky tap, the kind where every empty second lets you know you're all alone.

She isn't alone, in truth. Flora's asleep upstairs, and if it gets too much, Izzy will take a glass of wine and go and sit in the nursing chair at the corner of her daughter's room, sipping while she watches Flora's breathing, comforted by the knowledge that even though she has no one to talk to, another living soul is here. Yet sole care of Flora is a weighty responsibility, one which she feels she's failing. What kind of woman drinks in her child's bedroom? The answer is simple: the kind of woman who's been betrayed by the man she thought was in love with her. The kind of woman whose faith in everything she knows lies like rubble around her feet.

She stands indecisive before the fridge until the sensor starts to bleep because it's getting too warm, and pressed into a decision by the noise, chooses the rosé because of its attractive hawthorn colour. When she tastes it, the wine has some of hawthorn's sharpness too, but Izzy doesn't mind. Sweet or sour, the effect's the same, though with Flora in her care, she really ought to eat something to stop it going straight to her head. Bridget has bought eggs from Taylor's farm; Flora loves to go and see the chickens strut and peck about. An omelette, then, and maybe a slice of toast.

She's heating olive oil in a pan when the house phone rings. Immediately, she's tense. Every call might be the hospital. Then she thinks it might be Laura, and if it is, she'll be pleased. Turning off the gas, she looks at the phone display before she answers.

A London number.

'Hello?'

'Izzy, my dear, it's Duncan. How are you?'

'I'm all right. Just getting something to eat.'

'That's the ticket. Got to keep your strength up. Listen, before we go any further, have you got that machine switched on, that robot house controller?'

'Do you mean Alexa?' She glances over at the machine, and sees a light come on as it hears its name.

'Exactly so. Could you turn it off? I mean right off, unplug it or switch it off at the wall.'

'Is that necessary?'

'I really think it is.'

Izzy lays down the phone and tracks the wire connecting the device along the countertop to a power point near the floor. She turns off the switch, then decides to go one better and pulls the plug from its socket.

'Done.'

'And are you alone this evening?'

'Flora's asleep upstairs.'

'But your nanny's not there?'

'She's been gone a couple of hours. What's this about?'

She hears him take a swallow of what will certainly be wine.

'Well, it's not good,' says Duncan. 'And I really don't want to put you under any more stress, especially with the way things are. How is Tris doing today, by the way? Has there been any change?'

'No, no change. I thought it might be the hospital when you rang. I get jumpy, you know.'

'Of course you do, of course you do.' His tone is always soothing; he's competent and capable, always to be relied on, like a favourite uncle with unlimited resources of whatever you need – advice, sympathy, cash – always at his disposal. 'The thing is this, Izzy. I'm afraid you have a spy in the camp, my dear.'

Izzy feels a coldness in her stomach.

'A spy? What on earth are you talking about?'

'Let me tell you from the beginning. I had a phone call from someone you don't know, a woman called Dolly Blythe. Does that name ring any bells?'

The coldness mutates into the beginnings of nausea.

'Dolly? Isn't that what Tris's first wife was called?'

'That's her. Quite a blast from the past, I can tell you. I haven't spoken to her in many, many years, so you can imagine how surprised I was to hear from her. Anyway, we went through the usual pleasantries, until she finally got round to telling me why she'd called. She herself had been contacted by her half-brother or step-brother or whatever relation to her he is, a chap called Murray Roe. You don't know that name, I'm sure.'

'No.' A thought strikes her. 'Wait a minute.' She finds her mobile and scrolls through her messages to find the photo sent by DS Weld: a face she didn't recognise, captioned *Murray Roe*. She goes back to the house phone. 'I don't know him, but the police asked me about him the other day. I think he was at the wedding.'

'So they're already aware of him, are they? Interesting. Let's park the wedding, just for a moment. Back in the mists of time, while Dolly and Tristan were married, Murray was Tristan's brother-in-law. From what Dolly says, they were never close, but he was a relative nonetheless.'

'Where's all this going?'

'Where it's going, I'm sorry to say, is that Murray thinks he's got a story about Tris he's going to sell to the papers.'

'What story?'

There's a slight hesitation before Duncan replies.

'Look, I don't want you to worry about that. It's all cobblers, of course – these things very rarely have any substance to them, but the newspapers have become less and less careful about what they print. Let me worry about that part of it. I'll make a few phone calls, call in a few favours. It might cost me a couple of lunches, but I think I can persuade the right people that going to print with anything Mr Roe tries to sell them could turn out to be very costly indeed. When they know I'm on the case, they'll soon leave it alone. Without Dolly, they don't have a story anyway, and she's most emphatic she doesn't want to see anything in the media. She's dead against the whole thing. But happily for

260

us, Dolly was a very clever girl. She played along a bit with Murray, suggested she might be interested in making a few quid – who isn't, after all? – and so she got the full story from him, what he was planning. Turns out he's turned your nanny – what's her name, by the way?'

'Bridget,' says Izzy quietly.

'Bridget, that's the one. Sounds like he's turned her into a mole. She's been recording your conversations through that Alexa thing. I do hope you haven't been too indiscreet?'

'Why shouldn't I be indiscreet in my own home?'

'Does that mean you have?'

Izzy immediately thinks of her conversation with Laura, where everything – everything – spilled out.

'Oh my God.'

'I'm guessing that's not so good. But not to worry, not to worry. We'll get this all sorted. There's no harm done. Yet.'

'But how's he got in touch with her? And how can she be recording? It isn't possible.'

'As to the first question, you're right that Mr Roe was a wedding guest. When your nanny picked up little Flora, he followed her home. Straightforward, really.'

'But she'd never have spoken about us to some stranger, I know she wouldn't. I trust her.'

'Maybe that isn't wise. Do you have CCTV?'

'Yes.'

'Why don't you check it for the day of the wedding, see what you can find? Secondly, I've consulted my nephew – he's a bit of a whizz in the technology department – and he's told me how to check your Alexa machine and see what's been recorded. Apparently there's an app you can download to your phone – here it is, Voicegram – which connects to Alexa and sends sound files to wherever, via email, I suppose. I'm going to send you his instructions to look inside your machine and see exactly what's there. Do you think you can do that?'

'Yes.'

'And if you find conversations recorded, and you didn't record them, Tris certainly didn't, which only leaves your nanny. So you have your proof.'

'Then what?'

'Then you fire her without references.'

'She'll be angry. She'll tell everyone what she's heard.'

'Not if you warn her I'll come after her for breach of her non-disclosure agreement. I'm sure you can persuade her it would be far better for her if she doesn't mess with me.'

Duncan's words have made another hole in Izzy's heart. Tristan *and* Bridget? Bridget's the woman she trusts with her daughter's care.

She wanders into the room they call the study, a room they rarely use; being at the back of the house, it's gloomy even during summer, and over time it's become the place for sorting household finances, paying bills, dealing with dull correspondence. There's a laptop on the desk, a joint one they use for only those purposes, and bookshelves loaded with Tris's prized collection of boyhood annuals, alongside his books on planes and cars and architecture.

At the far end of the bookshelves is the unit which controls the CCTV camera, set up to monitor callers at the front door. Tris had it installed when they first moved in, but Izzy had all but forgotten about it. She can't remember an occasion when they've needed the recordings. Sterndale has always been a safe place for them. Until now.

The camera is well hidden by the wisteria trailing down from the wall. Bridget probably doesn't even know it's there.

She brushes dust from the lid of the laptop, opens it up and signs in. This has always been Tris's thing, but she can easily learn. The app's easy to spot on the welcome screen; she clicks on it, and goes to the View History tab. The video from the day of the wedding is in the archive. She pulls it up and skims through it.

The quality isn't great; a frond of wisteria splits the frame in two, and the lens needs a clean. But here they are, the three of them, Flora so pretty in her bridesmaid's dress, herself and Tris seeming so happy together. How could she have got it so wrong? Sipping on her wine, she fast-forwards through more of that day. Here's Bridget leaving in the Fiat to come and collect Flora from the hotel; not long after, here she is returning in the Range Rover.

What happened next?

She runs through the next half-hour at double speed, but that's too fast, because she almost misses him. She's looking for a car, but there is no car, just a man on foot, in formal trousers, a shirt and a loosened tie, wandering down the drive with his hands in his pockets, looking behind him to make sure he isn't seen. He rings the doorbell, and he waits.

She rewinds the video a few seconds, to a place where the man's face is most clearly visible, and freezes it to compare it with the photo DS Weld sent to her phone.

Same guy. No doubt about it. That's Murray Roe.

Bridget opens the door to him; it must be Bridget, though

263

she's standing inside the doorway and can't be seen. They have a conversation, though it seems Roe is doing most of the talking, his animated body language suggesting he's putting plenty of energy into his spiel so she doesn't slam the door in his face.

And she doesn't slam the door. She invites him in.

He's in the house for twenty minutes. Then the video shows him walking away up the drive. Hands in pockets. Smiling.

Her mobile pings with an incoming message: Duncan's instructions on how to get inside Alexa. Izzy doesn't even have the Alexa app on her phone – that was another of Tris's toys. She downloads it now, and while she's in the online store, confirms the existence of the app Duncan's nephew mentioned, Voicegram. There are so many technical tricks out there she's unaware of or doesn't understand.

It's easy to connect the Alexa unit to her phone, and she's no doubt Bridget could have done it too. Duncan's nephew's sent clear instructions on how to get to the stored recordings, and she follows the steps one by one, until she finds a list of files ordered by date. Prior to Tris's assault, there were almost none, just a couple of her and Flora chatting she's prepared to accept might have been accidentally triggered.

After that date, it's a different story.

There are over twenty recordings, and a few samples tell her it's mostly her talking on the phone.

The largest file is dated a couple of nights ago, when she and Laura had that long heart-to-heart. That was the evening she asked Bridget to stay late, and Bridget seemed pleased enough to do so, saying she could do with the overtime. Was there an ulterior motive?

Still disbelieving, she clicks on the file, and hears her own and Laura's voices grow louder as they walk into the kitchen from the hall, the gush of water into the kettle, and the beginning of that conversation, when Izzy told Laura everything.

Duncan must be told, so he can properly stamp on it.

But not the police. Murray Roe may not be the only one who'd like to cash in on a gutter-press story, and an anonymous source from inside the police would make Duncan's efforts all in vain. For Flora's sake, Tris's reputation must be protected.

One problem remains outstanding, though: how best to deal with treacherous Bridget.

THIRTY-NINE

The house phone is ringing. Izzy's lost in the realms of sleep, dreaming she's hunting some lost object, her path blocked by undergrowth whose thorns snag her dress and draw blood from her hands. Her subconscious weaves the ringing phone into the dream's irrational plot, and by the time she's awake and realising the sound is real, whoever's calling will be close to hanging up.

But she's prepared for a call like this, and left a handset on the bedside table just in case. As she grabs it and presses the answer button, she notices the time: 4:18 a.m.

'Mrs Savage, Isobel Savage?' A voice she doesn't know, a woman's voice. In the background, another phone is ringing.

'Yes.'

'Are you next of kin to Tristan Savage?'

Izzy's mouth goes dry.

'Yes.'

'I'm calling from the ICU on behalf of the medical team. There's been a change in your husband's condition, and they're asking that you come in as soon as possible.'

Izzy's still confused by the abrupt awakening.

'Now?'

The voice sounds firm, insistent.

'We suggest so, Mrs Savage. As soon as you can get here.'

'There's my daughter. I'll have to find someone . . .'

'I'll tell them you're on your way. Just come straight to ICU, someone will let you in.'

Lying back on the pillows, she tries to make herself believe it could be good news, that Tris has woken up or shown some improvement, until the implication of the timing crushes that hope. No one phones at 4 a.m. with good news.

She reaches out to touch Tris's side of the bed.

As soon as you can get here.

Whatever he's done, whoever he really is, she can't help but still love him. Love doesn't fade that fast; her anger at his betrayal is only on the surface, masking the true emotion in her heart. If he will only get better, they can work it out, stay together, have the life they always planned.

And if she gets there quickly, maybe she can persuade him not to go.

Laura's mobile is on the dressing table, a feeble nod to keeping it some distance from her brain so it won't be irradiated during the night.

Like Izzy, she's blurry with sleep, disorientated, heart pumping. As she stumbles from the bed, Aidan mumbles something she doesn't hear over the ringtone – the fun one she chose for Izzy's calls, so she knows who it is before she answers.

'Izzy? Are you OK?'

Izzy's voice is not quite normal, and Laura knows she's holding back tears.

'I have to go to the hospital. They just rang.'

'What did they say?'

'Just that I need to go there now. The thing is, can you come and stay with Flora?'

'Of course I will. I'll come straight away. Oh, Izzy.'

'I'll see you in a few.'

'I'm on my way.'

Fumbling in the dark, Laura pulls on yesterday's clothes, not turning on the light so as to give Aidan a chance to go back to sleep.

But he's wide awake. 'Where are you going?'

'To Izzy's. They've called her into the hospital. I said I'll go and be with Flora.'

She's fastening the buckles on her sandals when he says, 'That won't be good news, then.'

'It doesn't sound good, does it? Poor Izzy. Poor Flora.'

When she's ready, she crosses to the bed and leans down to kiss his cheek. 'I'll give you a ring, let you know what's going on.'

As she stands up, he grasps her hand.

'Tell Izzy I really hope he's OK.'

'I will. Go back to sleep. I'll call you in a while.'

While she waits for Laura, Izzy calls Eamon, who sounds so alert when he answers, Izzy wonders whether he has some inkling, some blood-borne awareness telling him his son's in trouble, a kind of parental instinct she briefly hopes she'd have with Flora, before praying she'll never have to find out.

When she tells him the hospital have called, his response is brusque – *OK, thanks, we'll see you there* – as if he's been on standby, so ready to go Izzy pictures him lying fully clothed in the dark while Steph sleeps, prepared to answer an inevitable call. Maybe he's suspected for some time this moment might come; maybe his unflappable optimism has always been no more than a mask concealing a foreboding he was hiding inside.

Laura arrives. Izzy is waiting on the doorstep, and accepts a hug and promises to call before driving along the empty roads as fast as she dare. In the hospital car park there's a space next to Steph and Eamon's car. Since they're still living out of suitcases at the Premier Inn, of course they're there before her.

The sky is growing lighter, a line of pink splitting the purples and storm greys. Running to the ticket machine, she fumbles with coins, thinking how ironic it will be if anything (an anything she daren't name) happens in this couple of minutes she's wasting being a law-abiding citizen. Before she met Tris she would have skipped the ticket and paid the fine, but he's always encouraged her to be more mindful with money, to think of it as Flora's future and take more care.

She runs to put the ticket on the dashboard, then from the car park to the main building. Only A&E is open, and she doesn't know the way from there to the ICU. An impassive security guard points the way, and she hurries down a silent, empty corridor which brings her, at last, to a bank of lifts she recognises. At the press of the call button, she hears the hefty machinery clunk into life, and tracks its crawling descent as the floors change on the indicator: 3, 2, 1, G.

The doors slide open. Stepping inside, she presses for the third floor, and the steel doors seal her in. Only then, in this slowest part of her journey and almost at its end, does the thought occur to her: if this is bad news, she could be coming here for the very last time.

No need to give up yet. She fights the swelling in her throat and the pricking in her eyes, determined she will not cry.

Behind ICU's locked door, the corridor is dark, lit only by a single light burning at the reception desk, where a female nurse bends over paperwork. Izzy presses the buzzer and the nurse looks up, recognises her and walks briskly to let her in. As she holds the door for Izzy to pass through, the nurse gives her an enigmatic smile which might be sympathy for the craziness of the hour, or for what she's about to find.

'How is he?'

'Your mother-in-law's already here,' says the nurse, and as they round the corner, she points to Tris's bed, concealed by curtains, which Izzy passes through.

Steph is sitting on one side of the bed, dabbing her eyes; on the other, Eamon is holding his son's hand. Izzy has never seen him do that before, and she finds it both touching and disturbing.

Steph shakes her head at Izzy, and Izzy finds herself mimicking the gesture, only then asking what it means.

'What's going on? Why have they called us?'

But one look at Tris, and she can see the change. Behind his oxygen mask, red spots of fever have bloomed on his cheeks. His breathing, too, is changed, no longer a silent, rhythmic rising and falling of his chest, but a rattling, faltering labour.

Izzy shakes her head again, and Eamon says, 'Pneumonia.'

'I'll get a chair,' says Izzy, but she doesn't move, and Eamon – who normally would fetch her one – stays where he is, keeping hold of his son's hand.

'I don't want him to know we're upset,' says Steph, and laughs at her own absurdity as she wipes her nose. 'I don't want him to think we've given up on him.'

Izzy looks around for the drip stands which have been keeping Tris alive.

'Aren't they giving him antibiotics? Where are his fluids?'

Steph shakes her head again.

'What exactly have they said?' asks Izzy, dry-mouthed, not really wanting to know.

'They said they'd wait until you got here before they took his oxygen away,' says Eamon. 'I'm afraid it's hopeless, Izzy. We have to . . .' Eamon's last words are lost in a sob, and he lifts Tris's hand to his lips and kisses it. 'My boy. My dearest boy.'

They hear footsteps, and a doctor draws back the curtain. He looks round at them all.

'I am so very sorry, but there's nothing more we can do. If you're ready I'll remove his oxygen, and then I'll leave him with you.'

Eamon sobs again. Steph's face is ghastly with grief.

She asks if he'll be in pain, and the doctor shakes his head.

'No, there'll be no pain. His body is so weakened, once the oxygen is removed he'll just slip away.'

'No,' says Izzy. She moves forward to the bed, and leaning in front of Steph, kisses Tris's forehead. 'He isn't going to leave me. He doesn't want to go.'

'Izzy,' says Eamon. 'Come and sit here, be with him.'

With a final kiss, he relinquishes Tris's hand and goes to stand at the foot of the bed, allowing Izzy to sit down, and she picks up her husband's hand and kisses it as his father has been doing.

She leans down to Tris's ear. 'Stay with me. Flora and I need you. We all need you. Please don't go.'

The doctor gives a sigh, and steps forward to take the mask from Tris's face.

'He's still so handsome,' says Steph, stroking Tris's cheek. 'Still my handsome boy.'

The doctor leaves them.

In silence, they watch and wait. Moments pass, and minutes, until they no longer hear the crackle in Tris's chest, and the red spots on his cheeks both melt away.

FORTY

Golding knocks at Muir's office door just as Muir's hanging up the phone. Muir beckons him in, then leans back in his chair with his hands behind his head. His expression is sombre.

'Morning, Nate. What can I do for you?'

'I need to get a production order approved and forwarded to the court,' says Nate. 'I've emailed it to you but I just wanted to explain what it's about. Is everything all right?'

Muir leans forward on to his desk. 'Bad news. Is Kirstie in yet?'

'About ten minutes ago.'

'Do me a favour, ask her to come in, will you? I'll update you both together.'

Golding beckons Weld over. She brings a large mug of coffee and when Muir gestures towards the chair next to Golding's, sits down.

'I just had a call,' says Muir. 'Tristan Savage died during the night.'

'Oh no,' says Weld. 'I thought he was going to pull through.'

'I'll make a team announcement shortly,' says Muir, 'but the obvious change this means for us is that we're now treating this case as murder. Brad Sherman will be putting out a statement later this morning, and no doubt there'll be a press conference so someone can say all the right things about priorities and lines of enquiry. Meanwhile, I've been invited upstairs to brief the upper ranks on where we're at, so I think it would be useful for us to have a quick catch-up on where we're going next.'

'Maybe I can start that ball rolling,' says Golding. 'The production orders I've emailed you relate to the account Tristan paid the twenty-five thousand into. It belongs to Aidan Ridley.'

Muir and Weld look at him in surprise.

'Really?' asks Weld.

'Yeah, I know, who would have thought?' says Golding. 'I would have told you last night but I thought it would wait. I went to see him yesterday, as soon as I found out, because what I thought was interesting was that the account Tristan paid into is with Lloyds, and all Aidan's other accounts are with NatWest. That struck me as unusual.'

'It strikes me that way, too,' says Muir. 'How did he explain it?'

'He says he had some secret arrangement with Tristan, a business loan they were keeping from their respective wives.'

'Why?' asks Weld.

Golding shrugs. 'To maintain the integrity of their friendship. Apparently Tristan didn't want Aidan's wife to feel beholden.'

Muir looks doubtful. 'Did you believe him?'

'Depends what those production orders show up,' says Golding.

'I'll get them processed ASAP,' says Muir, opening up his

emails. 'Could Ridley really be involved? What would be the motive?'

'Maybe it wasn't a business loan,' says Weld. 'Someone like Tristan, could be some kind of extortion.'

'Especially given the fact he was a serving officer in the Sterndale district,' says Golding. 'He might have come across information he was holding over Tristan's head.'

Muir raises his hands. 'Hold on, hold on. It's a long jump from Ridley's story to police corruption and blackmail. Let's not get carried away. His story's plausible.'

'But not provable,' says Weld. 'Not now Tristan's dead.'

'It might be provable, with those orders,' says Muir. 'And I'm going to hope so, because the last thing we need is the kind of scandal West Mercia will face if it turns out he is somehow involved. What's the situation with Tristan's financial records?'

'The requests went to the banks last week,' says Weld. 'They should be back with us anytime.'

'In the meantime, what else do we have?' asks Muir. 'I'd hate to go upstairs and tell them the only whisper of a suspect we have is one of our own.'

'There's Murray Roe,' says Weld. 'Surely he's still on our radar?'

'And the pay-as-you-go phone we haven't identified,' says Golding, 'the number which called Tristan. We still need to find out who that belongs to.'

'I've had an idea which could rule Aidan out, or move him down our list,' says Weld. 'Though worst-case scenario, it could rule him further in. Remember Amber saying the hotel manager recalled someone behaving oddly on the night of the wedding? We must have a photo of Aidan somewhere on file – she could take a copy over there, see what he has to say. At the very least, she can try and get a better description from him.'

'Maybe we can get the manager to do a Photofit,' suggests Golding.

'That's a good idea,' says Muir.

'Something Gail Clements could have a look at,' says Weld. 'And her daughter must be back from honeymoon by now. We could ask her and her husband too.'

'So we still have leads to follow,' says Muir. 'Fingers crossed they don't take us in a direction we really don't want to go.'

FORTY-ONE

Two days since Tristan's death.

From the kitchen, Izzy hears the key in the door, the turn of the latch, and a light tread on the hall carpet before the front door is gently closed.

Izzy's sitting at the pine table, an untouched mug of coffee to her left, an open laptop to her right. The shell of Flora's breakfast egg is still in its Peter Rabbit eggcup, and honey-sticky crusts of toast lie on a matching plate.

In the kitchen doorway, Bridget stops. Izzy looks utterly wretched, sallow and skeletal, her hands bony and repugnant. It's almost nine but she's still in her robe, her usually glossy hair pulled back in a rough ponytail which shows oily roots at her scalp.

'Come in, Bridget,' she says.

Bridget has been crying. She drops her black bag on the floor and was thinking she'd give Izzy a hug, but Izzy steers her away by pointing to a chair on the opposite side of the table.

Today the slogan on Bridget's black T-shirt reads, *Go Ask Alice*. She fumbles in her skirt pocket for a tissue, and as she sits, says, 'I'm so, so sorry. I just never thought we'd lose him.

Are you OK? I don't know what to say.' She dabs her eyes and looks round. 'Where's Flora?'

'She's with my mother in the lounge,' says Izzy, in a voice with no emotion. 'Thanks for coming over. I just wanted to have a chat about where we go from here.'

Bridget sniffs, and wipes her nose. 'You know I'm always here for you. For Flora. Whatever I can do.'

Izzy pulls the laptop towards her and brings it out of sleep mode. The screen fills with a black-and-white video still. She presses the Play arrow, and feeling a tug of sadness at the coming ending, turns it round to face Bridget.

'What can you tell me about this?'

Bridget watches the footage: the evening of the wedding, Murray Roe walking up the drive of Foxcote Lodge, Bridget letting him into the house. She watches the whole thing before she speaks, giving herself time, Izzy assumes, to come up with a plausible response.

'It's just a friend of mine,' she says at last, and Izzy knows she's weighed up the odds of her not knowing who Murray is and decided to gamble. 'He was in the area and wanted to see me. He wasn't here very long, and I really didn't think you'd mind. You guys were all out enjoying yourselves.'

The note of petulance in Bridget's voice is plainly intended to make Izzy feel unreasonably restrictive on her life, but all it does is stoke her anger. As this man was sauntering up the drive, Tris had probably already been attacked and left in a pool of his own blood.

'I know who that man is, Bridget, but I don't believe that you did.'

'So why did you ask me if you knew who he was?' That

petulance again. 'Are you trying to catch me out or something? What's going on?'

'Why did you let him into our house? We made the rules very clear, but you still let someone in without knowing who he was.'

'He said he was family. What was I supposed to do?'

'So why did you say he was your friend?'

'Did I say that? Please, Izzy, don't be like this. If I'd known you'd be so upset, of course I wouldn't have let him in. He said he was family, and I didn't know what to do. It would have been rude just to send him away.'

'Why have you been recording my private conversations?'

Bridget shakes her head in apparent confusion.

'What conversations? Why would I do that?'

'You've been recording my conversations, and you've been sending them to Murray Roe to support the story he wants to sell to the media.' A subtle change in Bridget's expression shows Izzy she's hit home, and the knowledge is painful. 'What was your cut going to be, Bridget, for dishing the dirt on my family?'

'I would never do that. You know I wouldn't. You must know I wouldn't.'

'You signed a confidentiality agreement and a non-disclosure agreement which clearly you've now broken. If anything goes into print, I'll sue you, and every single penny you make for years to come will come straight back to me. Duncan will be writing to you formally warning you of that fact, and if there's the slightest whiff in the press, he'll serve you with an injunction.'

Bridget begins to cry again. 'I'm so sorry. I didn't mean any harm by it, only money's tight, you know, and Manzi doesn't make that much either. I don't expect you to understand, but it's hard when you're hurting for cash. Please, Izzy, we can sort this out. I love you guys, I love Flora, I love this job more than anything. OK, I fucked up, but please, give me another chance.'

'What you did was despicably underhand. I'm only glad Tris never knew about it. We trusted you with our daughter's care, and you betrayed us.'

'I didn't betray you, Izzy. We needed money, and he said . . .'

'If you needed money, you could have asked for a loan. Or an advance. Knowing Tris, he would have given it to you.'

'Listen, Izzy, please give me another chance. I'll work for free. Whatever you say. Please.'

'If you've left anything in the house, I'll send it on. You can drop your keys on the side there, and you know the way out. I'll tell Flora you said goodbye.'

Izzy hears the front door slam. Flora will miss Bridget, and once her mother's left, Izzy will miss having someone around the house, which is much too big for a family of only two.

Tomorrow, she'll ring the estate agents, and make arrangements for Foxcote Lodge to be sold.

Amber Gooch has been on temporary loan to a team working another case, but as soon as they can spare her, she makes the journey back to Sterndale.

Pre-lunch, the hotel car park is all but empty. Inside at reception, she asks if she can speak to Craig Dalton, and settles into an armchair with a view of the gardens to wait.

Dalton soon appears. When he sees Gooch, he smiles

warmly. He has the beginnings of a carefully trimmed beard, and Gooch thinks how well it suits him.

She stands to shake his hand. 'Me again. I'm like a bad penny.'

Dalton shakes his head. 'Not at all. Can I offer you some coffee?'

Gooch smiles. 'Thanks. That'd be great.'

Dalton gives an instruction at reception and takes a seat across from Gooch, leaning forward in expectation.

'So how's it going?' he asks. 'I was really sorry to hear about Tristan's death. A guy like him, you can't quite believe it, can you? And I keep thinking, it happened here. This place will be forever famous. Can you believe his official fan club have been in touch, asking if they can put up a shrine or a plaque?'

'Are you serious? Sounds a bit morbid.'

'I thought so too. Happily it's not my decision. I've passed the buck to someone more senior than me.'

A waitress brings a tray holding a cafetiere and a trio of mini-croissants, which she unloads on to the table in front of Gooch.

'I thought maybe you hadn't had breakfast,' says Dalton.

'That's very kind,' says Gooch. 'In fact, I haven't.'

'And I'm glad you're here. You've saved me a phone call. A relatively small thing, but I want to report a theft. I'm not expecting you to put the full force into action on it, but if I could have a crime number, we can put in an insurance claim.'

'Actually, I can't give you a crime number,' says Gooch. 'Sorry. You'd have to phone it in through 101. Can I ask what's been taken?'

'A couple of watercolour miniatures from one of the

bedrooms. Not hugely valuable – obviously we'd never put anything high-value in public areas – two or three hundred pounds at most. Just about enough to make it worth the claim.'

Gooch cuts a piece off an almond croissant. 'Any idea who took them?'

'Almost certainly one of the guests,' says Dalton. 'The staff who service those rooms have been with us a while, and I believe they're trustworthy. The problem is, we're not sure how long the miniatures have been gone, and the occupants of our rooms change almost daily.'

'What about SmartWater? I saw the sign in the doorway.'

'Well spotted.'

'A trained eye. Were the paintings marked?'

'I believe so, yes.'

'Maybe not gone forever, then. But call it in to 101. Anyway, I know you're busy, so let me tell you why I'm here. Firstly, I'm hoping to have a chat to the staff I didn't get to talk to before. These four.'

She slides a piece of paper with their names on across the table, and Dalton reads it.

'You're in luck. They're all here but one. If you stay where you are and enjoy your coffee, I can send them through.'

'Great. And the other thing is, going back to the last time we talked. You told me you remember on the night of the incident seeing a man sitting here in the lobby area for a while, looking what you described at the time as . . .' She glances at a page in her notebook. 'Somewhat on edge. He's someone we'd like to speak to, to rule him in or out of our enquiry, and we'd like to ask your help in making an identification.

To that end, I've brought a photo to show you, but if it's not him, can I ask if you'd be prepared to work with us on an identikit picture? You could either come to Burnt Common, or we could send someone here. Whatever suits you.'

Dalton nods. 'Absolutely. Anything I can do to help.'

'OK.' From her shoulder bag, Gooch pulls out a photograph, a head and shoulders shot blown up to A4 size. 'I'm afraid the quality's not great, but could this be the man you saw that evening?'

Dalton takes the picture and studies it very briefly.

'That's him,' he says. 'Who is it?'

'I'm not at liberty to say,' says Gooch.

But Dalton's made a positive ID on ex-PC Aidan Ridley.

FORTY-TWO

Through the bedroom window, Izzy can see police cars and a crowd of strangers gathered behind the closed gate. Some of them are media, reporters and paparazzi, come to Sterndale for the chance to snap celebrity funeral attendees. Most of the others are women, who began to gather almost as soon as news of Tris's death emerged, a sisterhood of superfans Izzy never knew existed, who hug each other, lay offerings on a growing mound of bouquets, cards and soft toys, light tea-lights and candles, creating a shrine at the end of the drive to a man most of them probably never even met.

Seven days since his death, Izzy's holding it together enough to have put on make-up and a plain black dress she's wearing with modest heels and a black-veiled hat to hide her face. Her jewellery, too, is simple: only her platinum wedding band, and the pearl earrings he bought her on their Seychelles honeymoon. She believed then that they were happy, but now she's racked with doubts. How can she ever know whether any of it was real?

Behind the hedge, the hearse and limousines are approaching, and her mother calls to her to come down.

Izzy picks up her hat. On the dressing table, the forget-me-nots Tris brought her are no longer blue, but faded to powdery grey.

It's not a day to be wearing black. Weld's driving herself and Gooch to Tristan's funeral along roads lit by bright sunshine, past meadows where buttercups are blooming and cows graze the lush grass.

When they reach Sterndale, the bustle about the town seems upbeat, more excitement than deference. Weld finds a spot in the public car park behind the Co-op, and sends Gooch to the machine to pay for the maximum allowed stay. She hopes they won't be here that long, but there's a full hour to wait before the service begins. They're early, knowing the church will be full, and that there's no point in their being here if they have to stand outside.

The walk to the church is a pleasant one, past shops and busy cafés. Gooch pauses outside the Blue Moon to read the specials board, already thinking of lunch and hoping to see roast beef is still on the menu. Looming over the rooftops, the church tower shows their route, across the marketplace and down a cobbled side street, where the churchyard lies behind a railing-topped wall.

A crowd has already gathered, held back on the pavements by traffic police trying to keep the road clear for vehicles. Many of those waiting are Tristan's fans, older women holding up homemade placards: *We love you Tristan* and *Tristan RIP*. Some are wearing black, but more are colourful in the don't-give-a-damn style of the contemporary post-menopausal, and there are some interesting-looking women amongst them.

285

Weld spots what must be grey hair tinted blue, purple and pink. Led by a woman with a short crop dyed vibrant red, a few of them are singing a recognisable version of *You'll Never Walk Alone*, and the red-haired leader waves her arms above her head, showing a red dragon tattooed down the length of an arm exposed by an orange vest top.

Space for the cortège has been coned off directly outside the church gate. Beyond there the press are gathered among the lopsided gravestones.

A wiry man in an oversized black suit steps in front of Weld to block their way. Scanning his clipboard, he asks if they're on the list.

'Doubtful,' says Weld, 'but we're going in anyway.' She shows her warrant card and he waves them through, telling them to sit at the back.

'This is how I want my funeral to be,' says Gooch, as they approach the church porch. 'If your name's not on the list, you don't get in.'

'Have you been to many funerals?'

'Not really,' admits Gooch. 'I went to my grandma's, about five years ago.'

'Well, let me tell you,' says Weld, 'you'll probably never go to another one like this, and I've been to too many where it's pretty much just us and the vicar. If you want this kind of send-off, you'd better start being nice to people and making friends from this moment on, build yourself some credit.'

'I am nice to people,' objects Gooch. 'Well, mostly, anyway.'

'In the meantime, I'm happy to share with you my number one tip for blending into the background during funeral surveillance. Make sure your phone is turned off.'

Even on this balmy day, the church has a musty under-tone of damp, but it's almost overwhelmed by the scent of flowers: white roses and freesia interwoven with ivy, in stately arrangements beneath every window and at the altar, where two empty trestles wait. An organ is quietly playing. As they take seats in a rear pew – where Weld would sit regardless of instruction, since that location gives the best view of arrivals – a sidesman hands each of them an order of service. On its cover is a photo of Tristan – not a posed publicity still, but a natural shot of him smiling over his shoulder at whoever's behind the camera – probably his wife, thinks Weld – relaxed, tanned, with a stretch of blue sea and sky as background.

Gooch seems quite touched. 'Such a waste. Wasn't he handsome?'

'I suppose he was,' concedes Weld, 'but we're not here as mourners. Our job is to maintain a discreet watch, notice who's here and any behaviour which strikes you as out of the ordinary. In these kind of situations, people sometimes give things away, especially at the wake when they've had a couple of drinks.'

'Are we going to that?'

'We certainly are. There might even be lunch.'

A single bell begins its melancholy tolling. Gooch is watching everyone who arrives, nudging Weld at every famous face.

Weld sees Aidan Ridley and his wife, and watches them take seats in a pew three rows in front. The organ playing stops, and the hum of conversation falls silent. Through speakers, a familiar tune strikes up, bringing back memories of Saturday nights years ago, settling in with Mum and Grandma to watch *Find a Fortune*, which always began with this famous theme, and Tristan bursting on to the stage, basking in the audience's adoration, revelling in the applause.

Maybe it's the memory of those lost days – Mum and Grandma are long gone – or maybe it's the sight of Izzy walking in behind Tristan's coffin, dignified and tragic as she leads their little daughter by the hand; but as the organ strikes up and the congregation stands for the first hymn, something brings an ache into Weld's heart.

When the service is over, Weld and Gooch keep their seats until almost everyone else is gone. Walking out among the stragglers, they pause on the porch steps. Down by the gate, the hearse is pulling away, leading the family cars to the burial site. Across the street, many of the fans are weeping. Among the gravestones, a man in a pale linen suit is chatting to one of the news teams gathering up their kit.

Something about the man is familiar.

'Wait here a moment,' Weld says to Gooch.

Approaching the man, Weld stands so close to him, he has no choice but to break off from his conversation and give her his attention, though he looks annoyed at the interruption.

'Mr Roe?' asks Weld. 'Murray Roe?'

Roe scowls. 'Who wants to know?'

Weld flashes her warrant card. 'DS Weld, West Mercia CID. Can I have a private word, Mr Roe?'

Roe gives the news team an apologetic shrug and promises to be back. Weld leads him away to the shade of a yew tree overhanging an ivy-covered tomb.

'I'm wondering what brings you here today,' says Weld. 'It's our understanding you and Tristan Savage weren't the best of friends, so it seems odd to me you'd travel all this way for his funeral. For which, I have to say, you don't appear appropriately dressed.'

'As far as I'm aware, I'm as entitled to be in this town as the next man.' Weld smells alcohol on Roe's breath. 'I was just passing through Sterndale by chance.'

'No one passes through Sterndale by chance. What exactly are you doing here?'

'Since I happen to have hit on the day of Tris's funeral – by chance, as I say – I thought I'd take the opportunity to drink a toast to him at the wake. I doubt he'd begrudge me that. How is your investigation going, by the way? I gave my statement to your colleagues when they came to visit, and I don't have anything to add to what I've already said.'

'I hope you're not here to cause trouble.'

'Trouble? Why should I cause trouble? One drink and I shall be on my way. Scout's honour.'

'Your presence here has been noted, Mr Roe.'

'From the eagle eyes of the constabulary I should expect nothing less,' says Roe. 'Now, do you mind if I resume my conversation?'

FORTY-THREE

The wake at the White Lion is too well attended, a crowded, noisy affair where the tension and tears of the funeral evolve into cheerful reminiscence, and as the alcohol kicks in, bursts of raucous laughter sound loud in the low-ceilinged bar. The buffet food goes quickly, and Izzy watches her mother – why does black make people look so old? – catch the ear of the manageress, and smilingly ask if there might be more sandwiches. Izzy plays her part, accepting condolences, declining drinks. This is not an occasion for her to be anything but sober.

Eamon and Steph are with Flora at a corner table, sipping their drinks while Flora colours a basket of puppies in her farmyard activity book. Both of them look dreadful, aged by years, but they're gamely encouraging Flora as she picks each fresh colour from her wallet of pens. It's unfortunate Bridget couldn't care for Flora today; Flora talks about her often, asking when she's coming back, and Izzy hasn't had the heart yet to say *Never*.

They're joined by Izzy's mother, so Izzy makes her way there too.

'There you are, dear,' says her mother. 'I've asked them

to put out more food. I don't think Tris would have wanted people to go hungry, would he, Steph?'

Steph seems tuned out, as if she hasn't heard the question, and replies with only an uncertain smile. The large glass of white wine she's holding is close to empty.

'Definitely not,' says Eamon, careful and dependable with his Appletiser, ready even at this early stage of his loss to supply the right social response.

'I think I need some air,' says Izzy. 'Are you all right looking after Flora a few more minutes?'

'Of course we are,' says her mother. 'We'll be a little grand-parents' convention. Won't we, Steph?'

Steph drains her glass and holds it out to Eamon for a refill.

The beer garden's in a derelict orchard, with picnic tables and benches around an old apple tree carrying a crop of fledgling fruits among its leaves.

Izzy sits on one of the benches, looking back at the pub. A breeze runs through the tree's branches, tickling her arms into goose-bumps, making the solitude she was seeking feel too much like loneliness.

So when Aidan comes out of the tap room and walks towards her, she's pleased to see him.

He's carrying two glasses of sparkling wine.

'How are you doing?' he asks. He doesn't sit, but sets both glasses down on the rustic table beside her.

She smiles up at him. 'Getting through it. I think that's the best I can hope for. Where's Laura?'

'On her way. She saw you heading outside and thought you two could share a glass of bubbles to toast the old man, only she got waylaid by Karen. Careless on her part, especially as she's got my pint. I'm sorry, I don't suppose the White Lion's fizz is up to much, compared to what you're used to.'

'It's the thought that counts.'

Aidan looks back, to see if there's any sign of his wife. 'Poor Laura, looks like she's got well and truly stuck. I'll stay with you till she gets here. We don't want you drinking alone on a day like today.'

Izzy reaches out and touches his hand, and Aidan's heart leaps. 'You're a good friend, Aidan. Thank you.'

'We're always here for you, you know that. Anything at all. Don't you forget it.'

'I won't.'

Across the car park, Weld and Gooch are heading for their car. When she notices Aidan and Izzy, Weld stops, watching the intimacy of their conversation, seeing the two glasses of sparkling wine.

'What's going on there?' she asks, pressing the key fob to unlock the car. 'That's Aidan Ridley with Isobel Savage, and don't they look cosy together?'

As Weld's driving out of the car park, Izzy jumps up from where she's sitting and moves to where she can intercept them as they leave.

Weld pulls up alongside Izzy and winds down the window.

'We're on our way,' she says. 'How are you feeling?'

'Glad it's all over. Listen, there's something I'd like to talk to you about. Can you come to the house, maybe tomorrow afternoon?'

'We'll be glad to,' says Weld. 'I'll check my diary when we

get back to the office and I'll text you what time is good for us.'

'Thanks,' says Izzy. 'And thank you for coming today. Flora and I both appreciate it.'

'Wouldn't have missed it,' says Weld.

FORTY-FOUR

Weld can tell Gooch is glad to be returning to Foxcote Lodge, pleased to have something to tell the boyfriend and her mum. No doubt she's hoping for another seat on that fabulous couch, but Weld herself isn't feeling it. Tristan's dead, and Foxcote Lodge isn't a celebrity's house any more, only a place he used to live.

The white Range Rover and the Fiat are in the drive, alongside a red Mazda which looks brand new. When they ring the doorbell, Izzy herself answers. Yesterday, she was looking elegant in widow's black. Today, she could be a model for heroin chic, unattractively thin but – even without make-up and her hair pinned up in the messiest of knots – still the kind of woman all other women think they want to be, like Marianne Faithfull in the sixties or Courtney Love back in her Kurt Cobain days. And she has the spaced-out look to fit that bill, making Weld wonder if she's been taking tranquillizers or sleeping pills, or maybe drinking. Weld wouldn't blame her if she was comforting herself with drugs – what else is she to do in this situation? – but there's a lack of focus in her eyes which suggests she's not one hundred percent present. Which could mean, if Weld's being brutal, that this is a good time to ask a few searching questions, there being no better time than when your witness's guard is down.

'Come in,' says Izzy, and leaving Gooch to close the door as they enter, she leads them down the hall away from the lounge and towards the kitchen. Weld glances round at Gooch, who pulls a face of disappointment.

But the kitchen is as luxurious in its own way as the lounge, and there'll be plenty for Gooch to tell her mum. The décor's the same inspired mix of contemporary and traditional, wall-to-ceiling white units, a scrubbed pine table that would seat twelve, copper pans hanging from meat hooks on the old beams, an Italian coffee machine which surely needs a trained barista. Gooch thinks she's seen something similar in a magazine, possibly this very kitchen in *Hello*.

Somewhere, super-calming music is playing, the kind you'd hear while you're getting a massage. Izzy tells Alexa to be quiet, and the music stops.

'I want one of those,' says Weld, as a conversation starter. 'Clever things, aren't they?'

'That's Tris's,' says Izzy, maybe not realising she's used the present tense, or maybe she does, because then she says, 'He always loved his gadgets. I'm sorry we have to be in here, but my mother's looking after Flora in the living room. Coffee? It'll have to be instant. I was never trained to use that monster.'

Gooch looks disappointed again, but Weld accepts for both of them. Izzy fills an expensive-looking kettle and finds a pair of Habitat mugs.

'It's good your mum's come to be with you,' says Weld. She's expecting Nescafé, but Izzy's idea of instant coffee involves proper ground stuff in bags like teabags. 'What's happened to your nanny – what was her name, Bridget?'

'Sugar?' asks Izzy, and Weld and Gooch both shake their heads. 'Milk? We have cow's milk, I think, Mum always buys some. I only drink goat's milk but I know some people don't like the taste. And Tris just took everything black. Sometimes a slice of lemon in his tea.'

'So isn't Bridget with you any more?'

'I let her go. It was very sad and she was quite upset, but there you are. Things will be different now. I'm going to sell this house.'

'That's a shame,' says Gooch, and means it.

As she hands them both coffee, Izzy says, 'I know you're busy, so I'll get to the point. There are two things I need to tell you. The first is, I found something which might be of interest. I was going through the archives of our CCTV, looking for the day of the wedding – just being sentimental, you know? It occurred to me we'd all be on it, leaving the house, the last day we were all together. When I found it, I let the video run, and there's something else on there. A man came to the house, the same man you sent me a photo of – what was his name, Murray Roe?'

Weld is startled. 'Murray Roe was here, at the house?'

'Yes. I can send you the clip if you'd like.'

'Yes, please. Did you know he was in Sterndale yesterday?'

'No. Was he at the funeral?'

'Not exactly. We saw him outside the church, and he said it was a coincidence he was in town. Not very plausible to me.'

'I didn't see him,' says Izzy. 'Duncan's got everything under control, so I might as well tell you the reason he came here.

He was enrolling Bridget in his scheme to spy on us, to sell stories about us to the press.'

'Ah,' says Weld. 'That would be why he was talking to a TV crew.'

'What stories?' puts in Gooch. 'If you don't mind me asking.'

Izzy shrugs. 'Anything she could pick up through Alexa.'

'And did she pick anything up?' asks Weld.

Izzy gives a wan smile. 'The thing is, I have to make a confession, about something I didn't tell you. At the time it didn't seem important and I didn't think it would have any bearing, but now Tris is . . . Well, it's a different story, isn't it, now you're treating it as . . . You know, somehow I can't bring myself to say the M-word. Now that he's been unlawfully killed.'

'You've been withholding information?'

'I suppose I have, yes. I had my reasons. I thought if it leaked out, it might damage his reputation, which I could stand for myself – I wouldn't like it, but I could stand it – but I was thinking of Flora. I just didn't want her to grow up thinking her father was anything but the lovely daddy she'll remember. But now it's going to be a massive thing anyway, isn't it? There'll be a trial eventually when you get your man – or woman – and the whiff of scandal will be unavoidable. So I thought, what the hell, you might as well know what I know.'

She opens a drawer, takes out Tris's second phone and hands it to Weld.

'What's this?'

Izzy's trying to be matter-of-fact, but her face shows her vulnerability.

'It's a little surprise he left for me to find.'

'When did you find it?'

'The day after the wedding.'

Weld looks disapproving. 'You should have handed it over straight away.'

'Probably. I was just trying to spare us the embarrassment.'

'Embarrassment? What are we going to find on here?'

'Contact details for his little harem. And the woman he was going to leave me for.'

'He was leaving you?' asks Weld, incredulous. 'Why didn't you tell us? When did you know?'

Izzy reaches out to a box of pale blue tissues and dabs away tears. 'Don't mind me, I just weep all the time at the moment. I didn't know, not even when I found that phone. I could see there were women's names on it, and that's a bit of a giveaway in the infidelity game, isn't it? But I still thought it might be, you know, casual.' She wipes her eyes again. 'If adultery is ever casual. It seems it was with Tris. Anyway, I didn't realise how serious it was until I opened the architect's letter.'

'What architect?' asks Weld, and Izzy gives a small, sad laugh.

'That's what I thought. What architect? Turns out Tris and Tina – catchy pair of names, aren't they? – are building a house together. Out in rural Oxfordshire. I went and had a look. I even took pictures. I can send them to you as well if you like. Anyway, I don't know who she is. Her name's Martina Stokes, according to the Land Registry. I haven't tried to contact her. I wouldn't lower myself to calling his whores. What would I say, anyway? Hands off, he's mine? I expect you can find out who she is for yourselves. I suppose she watches the news like everyone else, so she'll know what's happened. No doubt that house will belong just to her now.'

Weld puts up her hands. 'Wait a minute. This is all new information. You're saying that on this phone are the contact details of women Tristan knew, but you didn't tell us? Were any of these women at the wedding?'

'How should I know?' sniffs Izzy. 'I've never met them. At least, not as far as I know.'

'So these are all potential new suspects?'

'Yes, I suppose they are. One of them might have wanted to kill him. Believe me, I know how that feels.'

'That's understandable,' says Weld, 'but I have to caution you, that kind of statement is very unwise.'

'It's a figure of speech, not a confession. I'm sorry. It's a very difficult time.'

'I understand that too, but you haven't made our job any easier by withholding what might be crucial evidence in Tris's case. If any of the contacts on this phone are of interest to us, they've got a huge head start. Plenty of time to conceal evidence and fabricate alibis, even leave the country if they're minded to do so. Is there anything else you haven't told us?'

Izzy shakes her head.

'Good,' says Weld. 'Well, before we head back and get started on this line of enquiry, we have a couple of questions we need to ask, beginning with your husband's relationship with Aidan Ridley.'

'Aidan?' Izzy looks baffled. 'What do you mean, relationship? I told you before, Laura's a close friend of mine, and sometimes we get – got together as a foursome. You know, drinks or supper, stuff like that.'

'They weren't business partners?'

'No. How could they be? They're in completely different lines of work.'

'So you're not aware of Tristan making Aidan Ridley a significant loan for his bike business?'

'A loan? I don't think so, no. Though if Aidan had asked him for money, I expect Tris would have given it to him. He was generous like that.'

'Generous to the tune of twenty-five thousand pounds?'

Izzy's eyes widen. 'How much?'

'Twenty-five thousand.'

'Well, I seriously doubt that. I mean, a couple of thousand, yes, but what you're talking about, that's the kind of sum you borrow from a bank. Isn't it? No, I don't think he would give him that much. Not without asking me first.'

'But he did, Izzy,' says Weld gently. 'The transaction's recorded in his bank account.'

Izzy frowns. 'I don't understand. I'm sure he would have told me.'

'Like he told you about his phone?'

Izzy's head drops. She grabs herself a tissue.

'I just didn't know him, did I? I've been such a fool. There were so many lies.'

'What about your relationship with Aidan?'

'My relationship? What are you asking?'

'Whether there was anything between you and Aidan which made you more than friends.'

Izzy looks up slowly. A blush of anger is brightening her cheeks.

'That's outrageous.'

'We have to ask, I'm afraid.'

'The suggestion's disgusting. Whatever he was, I loved my husband, I certainly never cheated on him, and Laura is my very good friend. So you can make a note that I'm stating categorically there's never, ever been anything between me and Aidan Ridley. What kind of person do you think I am? Jesus.'

'I don't mean to insult you,' says Weld. 'But this is a murder investigation, and that means if we have to offend people's sensibilities, that's what we'll do. We have to dig in the dark places. Most often, that's where we find our answers.'

'I'm sorry,' says Izzy. 'I'm a bit of a wreck at the moment, and being in Sterndale isn't helping. Every time I go out, I feel people watching me and whispering, and there's still the odd reporter hiding in the bushes.' She gives a small laugh. 'That sounds so paranoid.'

'Not to me,' says Weld.

'Mum thinks we should get away, take Flora to the seaside, the whole walks on the beach, fresh air and sandcastles thing. She's booked us a cottage for a few days. Is that OK?'

'I think it sounds like a great idea. Take some time for yourself, gather your thoughts, process what's happened. Eat properly and recharge your batteries. You're going to need to be resilient as the investigation moves along. We'll try not to disturb you, but if there's anything you really need to know, don't worry, we'll be in touch.'

'Can I ask you a question before you go?'

'Ask away.'

'You mentioned Aidan and this money – he's not a suspect, is he?'

'If you don't mind,' says Weld, 'I'd rather not comment on that until more enquiries have been made.'

'There's another public reputation potentially in tatters,' says Weld, as they get into the car. 'I feel really sorry for her. But why the hell didn't she tell us about this phone from the start?'

'Desperate to keep the lid on it,' says Gooch. 'For the reason you just said, that his reputation is about to get shredded. But doesn't it really open up our investigation? What if one of these women was at the wedding? Tristan might have used it to arrange a rendezvous. But what I don't get is why he was wanting to leave his wife. She's gorgeous, the house is fabulous. She has my perfect life.'

'Begs the question, doesn't it, how happy the marriage was. And if she knew he was going to dump her, might that not be a motive for her to get mad at him? I mean really mad?'

'Easily. At least I know that's how I'd feel.'

'You know what else?' says Weld, starting the engine. 'If he had inside info from the nanny, that could explain how Murray Roe knew the weapon was a champagne bottle.'

'So you don't think it was him who actually assaulted Tristan?'

'I don't think we can rule that out yet, but what she's just told us suggests another possible reason for him being front and centre in all this, namely his trying to sell an exclusive to the media. I think we need to talk to him again, ask him if he wants to change his statement.'

'This is exciting.'

'It's not exciting, Amber, it's possible new evidence in a murder enquiry. And it's one thing telling your mum about the kitchen gadgets, but don't for God's sake be telling her about the phone. This is confidential information, and we don't need any leaks tipping anyone off.'

'As if I would,' says Gooch. 'But I am going to tell her about the coffee machine. Fancy stopping somewhere for a sandwich on the way back?'

FORTY-FIVE

Weld finds Muir in the canteen, finishing a mug of tea and a chocolate muffin. She gets herself a coffee and joins him at his table.

'Don't tell Amy,' he says, wiping cake crumbs from his fingers. 'We're supposed to be doing this low-carb diet together. Thing is, I've lost pounds and she's lost next to nothing. I'm trying to put a bit back on so she doesn't get disheartened.'

'Best excuse for breaking a diet I ever heard,' says Weld. 'Why do you need to diet, anyway? If you get any thinner, we won't see you when you turn sideways.'

'Moral support. I know it's harder for women. How did you get on with Mrs Savage?'

'Very interesting.' Weld tries her coffee. 'This stuff never improves, does it? If it didn't look so nerdy I'd bring a flask. Anyway, are you ready for this? Isobel Savage has been withholding possible evidence, in the form of a phone Tristan was using apparently to call a number of women.'

Muir raises his eyebrows. 'Are you serious? Do you mean a burner phone?'

'Essentially. She found it soon after he was taken to hospital.

Meanwhile she's been sitting on it out of fear – she says – of the media getting hold of the story and trashing Tristan's carefully curated public image, which she's understandably very keen to protect for the daughter's sake.'

'Wow.'

'There's more. By doing her own detective work, she's also discovered Tristan was in the process of building a house with one of the women who features on the new phone. Looks like he was thinking of leaving her.'

'And she's kept all this quiet until now?'

'I suppose now he's gone, she knows there's no way of keeping his reputation intact indefinitely. Don't they say you can't libel the dead? No more hiding behind threats of injunctions or damages.'

'I need to think for a moment,' says Muir. 'More tea.'

He goes to join the short queue at the service counter. Weld sips her coffee, wishing she'd had water instead.

When Muir returns, he's brought a slice of fruit cake to go with his drink.

'Brain food,' he says, as he sits down. 'This could be a real game changer. Doesn't it give Isobel an excellent motive to assault Tristan herself?'

'I've been thinking about that,' says Weld. 'It might and it might not. If it's true she didn't find the phone until after he was hospitalised, the motive goes away, and we can check that by looking at the phone's recent usage. But she's by no means stupid. If she thought the phone was going to incriminate her in any way, why even tell us about it? Wouldn't she just quietly dispose of it, drop it down a drain? We'd never be any the wiser.'

'Good point,' says Muir, picking up his cake.

'Anyway, it's in our hands now and loaded with a list of contacts which should be straightforward enough to trace, given we can start the easy way and ring them. Especially someone called Tina. She's the one Tristan's building a house with.'

'Maybe Tina's got a jealous partner who didn't care for Tristan's interest.'

'Maybe she has.'

'Well, it's good to have a new avenue to explore, but we'd be in a much better place if we'd known about it from the beginning.'

'And speaking of avenues, I don't think we're in any way done yet with Murray Roe or Aidan Ridley.'

'Tell me more,' says Muir.

'Izzy's also found out – via CCTV we didn't know she had – that there was a visitor to the house on the night of the wedding. None other than Murray Roe.'

'You're kidding. Well, he didn't mention that when Golding and I spoke to him. I knew we weren't getting the full story there. What was he doing?'

'By her account, recruiting the nanny, Bridget Feahny, into a scheme to sell some kind of Tristan exclusive to the press.'

'What kind of exclusive?'

'Good question. He might just have been casting a net to see what swam in. Or he might have had knowledge or expectation that something big was going to break around the family.'

'What does the nanny say?'

'We haven't asked her, not yet, anyway. Unsurprisingly, she's been let go.'

'So you're right about Roe. He's still on our list. What about Aidan Ridley?'

'Izzy Savage confirmed she had no idea about Tristan's loan to him, and she didn't take the news too well. More proof, as she said, that Tristan's been less than honest – to put it mildly – throughout their marriage. When I asked about her personal relationship with Ridley, she became very defensive, and I can't help wondering if she was protesting too much. On the way back here, I remembered something Bridget Feahny said to me when we interviewed her. She talked about Tristan being irresistible to women, but she said Izzy has the same effect on men.'

'I could see that,' says Muir, with a smile.

'Well, at the funeral wake, Gooch and I saw Izzy and Aidan Ridley looking very cosy together. Which makes me wonder whether there's something going on there we should know about.'

'A large sum of money and a possible interest in the dead man's wife,' muses Muir.

'Not forgetting the hotel manager's identification of him behaving oddly in the lobby that evening. I know that's not hard evidence, but it could be evidence of an agitated state of mind.'

'So Aidan Ridley definitely has the makings of a person of interest. Where do you reckon we should go next?'

'I think we start with the phone, see who we're dealing with there.'

Muir nods. 'I agree. We need to understand what's been going on, so make that your number one priority. For the time being we'll put Murray Roe and Aidan Ridley on the back burner, but let's be sure we don't leave them there too long.'

FORTY-SIX

Gooch is disappointed to find the house on the Oxford outskirts is several notches downmarket from Foxcote Lodge. In a long street of nondescript sixties semis, at number 85 someone is at least making an effort, with pots of flowering plants in the tiny front garden, and the place overall looking tidy and clean. There's no car in the driveway, only a moped tucked in close to the house, a heavy lock on the front wheel to deter thieves.

Weld turns off the engine.

'This doesn't look like somewhere Tristan Hart would stash his mistress,' says Gooch, and Weld agrees.

When the doorbell sounds, the seventies reggae playing inside is turned down. The woman who opens the door is in her late fifties, overweight and dressed in cut-off denims and a bright pink T-shirt. Her hair is dyed vibrant crimson, and on her right arm is a tattoo of a writhing red dragon. She's a distinctive-looking woman, and Weld has seen her before.

'Martina Stokes? DS Weld, DC Gooch from West Mercia Police. We spoke on the phone.'

'Yes, we did. Come in.' Martina's accent is more Basildon than Oxford, but her welcome seems warm.

'You were at Tristan's funeral,' says Weld, as they step into the hallway.

'I wouldn't have missed it,' says Martina. 'Sobbed my eyes out, I did. He was one in a million, he was, a diamond, an absolute prince. I still can't believe he's gone. Takes a while for it to sink in, don't it? Do you want a cuppa?'

'Yes, please,' says Weld. 'We're looking forward to hearing how you know Tristan.'

'Long story,' says Martina, 'and to be honest, he's left me in a bit of a hole. Go through, make yourselves comfortable. If the cat's on the sofa, shove her off. Don't let that little madam be taking any liberties.'

While Weld's driving them back to Burnt Common, she asks Gooch to call Izzy Savage and arrange for them to meet, but Izzy's phone goes straight to voicemail.

'She'll be on a beach somewhere,' says Weld. 'Leave her a message, tell her we need to talk.'

At Weld's request, Gooch then puts in a call to Muir.

'It's Amber, Sir, on behalf of DS Weld,' she says, when he answers. 'She'd like to respectfully suggest it's time we started talking to Aidan Ridley.'

'Thanks for coming in, Aidan. I appreciate this may be difficult for you.'

From across the table, Aidan eyes Muir and Golding. He looks relaxed and he's declined a legal representative, which Muir knows is supposed to signal his innocence, but those tactics don't work on Muir. In Aidan's position, he'd have a lawyer here, no question about it.

'No worries,' says Aidan. 'You've got your job to do. I just want to get this straightened out, so you can focus resources in the right direction.'

The implication that they're getting it wrong nettles Muir. It's a cocky attitude from an ex-beat officer, but if Ridley's not their man, then he's quite right – this will be a waste of valuable time.

Better get on with it.

'You'll know why we want to talk to you today,' Muir begins. Beside him, Golding's taking his usual careful notes, even though the interview's being video-recorded. Golding always maintains that when you need to refer back to what's been said, it's easier to find what you're looking for in a few pages of handwriting than in hours of digital media. 'This is in relation to a sum of money paid to you by Tristan Savage, also known as Tristan Hart. Do you want to tell us how that came about?'

'Like I told DS Golding before,' says Aidan, nodding in Golding's direction, 'it was Tristan's idea.'

'Why did he suggest giving you money?'

'He wasn't giving it. It was a loan.'

'For what purpose?'

'I needed more investment for the business. I was complaining that the bank was dragging its feet on a decision, and he said, "Screw them, I'll lend it to you."'

'And you didn't question whether such an arrangement would be wise?'

'Why should I?'

'Money and friendship aren't always a good mix.'

'Fair comment. But I knew he could afford it. Most of my

mates have mortgages to pay. I wouldn't be borrowing off one of them.'

'How did you know he could afford it?'

Aidan shrugs. 'He said he could easily spare it, and I took him at his word. Anyway, you've only to see their house to know they weren't hurting for money.'

'Still, it was a sizeable sum.'

'Maybe to a lowly policeman. Not so much to him.'

'And how long had you known Tristan?'

Aidan considers. 'A couple of years. Laura – my wife – met Izzy soon after they moved to Sterndale, and they really hit it off. I think Izzy appreciates having a friend who's down-to-earth and normal. She invited us both over for drinks, and Tris and I got along well too. I liked him. He had an energy about him. There was never a dull moment when he was around.'

'When you say you went for drinks, was Tristan a heavy drinker?'

Aidan smiles, shaking his head. 'Never. The job kept him on the straight and narrow. He drank a lot of those daft-expensive posh juices and scented waters, but never alcohol. He said it was dehydrating for the skin, and that HD showed every wrinkle. You might say he was vain, but actually I think he was terrified he'd get picked on in the press, you know, end up in one of those "Look how shit Tristan Hart looks on a Sunday morning" photos in the *Daily Mail*.'

Muir pauses before his next question, putting his thoughts in order.

'So, going back to this loan. Despite the fact it was supposedly all above board, you didn't tell your wife anything about it, and Tristan didn't tell his wife, either. You even went to the lengths of using a bank where you've never been a customer before. Can you explain why that was?'

'Explain again for the recording, you mean? Because I've already said this.' Aidan nods again towards Golding. 'Tris insisted it be a condition of the loan that they should be kept out of it, for Izzy's sake. He didn't want to upset the balance of her friendship with my wife, and to be fair, I could see where he was coming from. They were already very generous to us, paying for meals, entertaining at home in a way we could never match. I saw no need to make Laura feel any more beholden to them than she already did.'

'Was there interest to be paid on this loan?'

'That was never discussed.'

'So what did you think was in it for Tristan?'

Aidan frowns. 'What do you mean?'

'I mean,' says Muir, 'did you take this large, interest-free loan to be a simple act of generosity? The kind act of one friend to another?'

'Yes. Why shouldn't I?'

'You never asked yourself why he might want to park that money – without making any interest on it, as you say, and without his wife's knowledge – in a place where no one was likely to find it?'

'I don't understand what you're getting at.'

But Aidan's face suggests light is beginning to dawn.

'Do you expect us to believe that, Aidan?' says Muir. 'As an ex-copper, you're surely more aware than most of the kind of tricks people pull. Tax dodging, money laundering. Which of those do you think this was?'

'Neither. He did it as a favour.'

'And was that purely as a favour to you, or were there benefits for himself?'

'I never thought about that.'

'Well, you'd better think about it now. Aiding and abetting in tax evasion is a criminal offence.'

FORTY-SEVEN

With no explanation, Laura's received a text from Aidan saying he'll be late home. She tries calling him to ask why, but his phone goes to voicemail; when she rings the shop, Maria only knows he said he had to go out and left her in charge.

It's after 7 p.m. when she hears his car in the drive. Laura and the kids have already eaten, and Aidan's share of a chicken risotto is cold in the pan.

As soon as he comes into the kitchen, she knows something is wrong. Aidan goes straight to the fridge, finds a Budweiser, pops the cap and drinks down half.

Josh comes in from the lounge carrying his PlayStation handsets.

'Hi, Dad. You want to give me a game of *FIFA*?'

'Not now, Josh, OK?'

It's not like Aidan to snap, and his response stings. Josh's bright smile disappears, and Laura hears his quick feet on the stairs, the click of his bedroom door closing.

Aidan takes another pull on his beer.

Out of hurt for Josh, Laura's cross.

'What did you speak to him like that for? He only asked if you wanted a game.'

'I don't want a game, all right?'

'What's going on? What's the matter with you? Where have you been?'

Aidan drains the beer bottle, opens the fridge and takes the cap off a second.

Laura is filled with misgiving.

'Aidan, talk to me. What's wrong?'

'I've just spent the last three hours at Burnt Common police station,' he says. 'Apparently I'm a suspect in Tristan's murder investigation.'

'You? Why?'

'Because of that money Tris gave me, lent me, whatever he did. First they tried to say I was aiding him in tax evasion. When I persuaded them there was nothing in that – not deliberately, anyway – they moved on to coercion, and suggested I was blackmailing him or something.'

'Blackmail? What would you blackmail him over?'

'Exactly.'

'Could it have been tax evasion, do you think? He wouldn't have used you like that, surely?'

'How the hell should I know? Maybe he would. Thick ex-copper in need of cash, maybe he scented opportunity. I'm not ruling it out. Seems to me none of us knew him as well as we thought.'

'Look, let me get your dinner. We can talk while you eat.'

'I'm not hungry.'

'What's going on?' Gemma is standing in the doorway,

looking from her mother to her father. 'Are you OK, Dad? You look really stressed.'

'Everything's fine, sweetie,' says Laura. 'Your dad and I are just having a chat.'

'I wanted to get some ice cream.'

'Well, get some, then, and take it upstairs.'

Gemma looks at Aidan. 'I heard you mention the police. Are you in some kind of trouble, Dad?'

Aidan's face softens. 'Not really, honey. There's been a bit of a mix-up, that's all. Nothing for you to worry about. How was school?'

'The usual.' Gemma's walking away, towards the stairs.

'What about your ice cream?' Laura calls after her.

'It's OK, thanks,' says Gemma. 'I've changed my mind.'

Aidan's news has left Laura's shoulder muscles so tight with stress, she's poised on the cusp of a migraine she knows will kick in if she dares have a glass of wine. Instead, she runs a deep, warm bath, and adds a double measure of the camomile foam Josh gave her for her birthday.

As she slides her shoulders under the water and closes her eyes, she hears the *Top Gear* theme tune, confirming Aidan has made his apology to Josh and they'll be settled in front of the TV for a while. Of course things will get sorted, when Tris's attacker is finally found; it just might be an uncomfortable ride until then.

When the water becomes chilly, she dries herself before putting on pyjamas and a cotton robe. With the house quiet, there's time for a few chapters of the book club choice.

Borrowing Aidan's pillows to make a backrest, she begins to read.

'Mum?' Gemma appears in the bedroom doorway. 'Can I talk to you?'

'Of course you can, sweetie.' Laura pats Aidan's side of the bed. 'Come in, snuggle up.'

In truth, she's expecting no snuggling – the expression is a hangover from the days of young childhood – but Gemma climbs under the lightweight duvet and presses herself up against Laura, laying her head on Laura's shoulder.

Though she tries not to show it, Laura's taken aback. Resisting the temptation to ask what's brought about the display of affection, she puts her arm around her daughter, grateful – whatever the reason – for this rare opportunity to do so.

'How are you feeling?' she asks.

Gemma lets out a long breath, as if relaxing after a period of tension. 'I'm tired.'

Laura kisses the top of her daughter's head, and smells the familiar peach shampoo.

'Have an early night tonight, then. No Netflix till the wee small hours.'

Gemma doesn't immediately reply, and Laura's thinking she may be falling asleep.

But then she asks, 'Mum, what's it like in prison?'

The question is a surprise.

'Well, happily I can't speak from personal experience, but I imagine it's pretty grim. I suppose the biggest thing is loss of freedom, so you can't go anywhere, you can't see your family or friends, you can't wear your own clothes or have a shower when you like, or chat on the phone. Or even have a phone. And I can't imagine the food's very good. No Häagen Dazs in there. Why are you asking? I hope you're not worrying about Dad?'

She feels Gemma nod.

'Oh, sweetie, Dad's not going to prison. It's just that the police are trying to narrow down their list of suspects in Tristan's case, and he and your dad had a business connection they need to ask about. That's all that's going on, I promise.'

Gemma wipes the back of her hand across her eyes, and Laura realises she's crying.

'Gemma! What on earth's the matter?'

'I've been thinking how bad it would be if our family got split up.'

Laura passes Gemma a tissue, and Gemma blows her nose.

'You sound like you're still a bit down to me,' says Laura. 'Do you want me to see if I can find someone for you to talk to, in private? Someone you can tell all your worries? I know you don't want to confide everything that's happening in your life to me.'

'I don't need counselling, Mum.'

'Are you sure, Gemma? Because I could easily ask . . .'

'Mum. No. Do you really promise me Dad's not in any trouble?'

Laura holds three fingers in the air. 'Guide's honour.'

'You say some funny things.'

'You mean I say some old-fashioned things. We just have to trust the police. Mostly they get things right.'

'Mostly isn't always, though, is it?'

'It's often enough for you not to worry about it, and your

dad can take care of himself. Trust me. You know what I think you need? Hot chocolate.'

'Mum. It's the middle of summer.'

'I think we have marshmallows.'

Gemma shakes her head and sits up. 'No, thanks. I'm going to bed.'

'If you're going to bed, turn your phone off. Don't be texting for the next three hours.'

'I won't.'

'Sleep tight. And don't lie awake worrying, either. Everything's getting straightened out, and Dad's going to be just fine.'

FORTY-EIGHT

People think they've got it all worked out.

Proof of that came yesterday evening with four heavy thuds, as if a quartet of disoriented birds had hit the lounge window. Laura was working through a basket of ironing, wishing she could smooth away her anxieties as easily as the creases in the pillowcases. Aidan was in his office, but ran down to find a slimy mess running down the double glazing, and smashed eggshells all over the gravel path.

The culprits were nowhere in sight.

'Youngsters, to be that quick,' he said.

Josh stood silently by him as he fetched a bucket of water and a cloth, and did his best to wash the insult away.

'Why did they do that?' asks Josh.

'Because people are idiots,' says Aidan, pouring the cloudy water down the kitchen drain.

'They think you had something to do with what happened to Tristan, don't they?'

'Well, they didn't leave a note, but I'm guessing it has to do with that, yes.'

'But you didn't do it, did you, Dad?'

320

Josh looks close to tears. Aidan puts down the bucket, beckons him closer and stands facing him, hands on his son's shoulders.

'Who's said I did?' he asks, and Josh shrugs. 'Who?'

'People at school.'

Aidan squeezes Josh's shoulders. 'Listen to me. You tell anyone who says anything against anyone in this family they can come and talk to me. Let them come and say it to my face. Tris and I were friends, we were mates, and people don't do things to hurt their mates. Am I right?'

Unconvincingly, Josh nods.

'Fancy a game of *FIFA*?'

'Not really,' says Josh.

'Afraid you'll lose?'

'No way.'

Aidan ruffles his son's hair. 'Put your money where your mouth is, then. First to five goals wins, and you can have first pick of teams.'

The next morning, as therapy to cut down on worrying about Aidan, Laura walks into town. In the Co-op, she adds two bottles of wine to the basket of necessities, and a bar of dark chocolate, which is always good for a low mood. She thinks half an hour among Fairey Tales's bookshelves would help tune out the world, but if Grace isn't busy she'll have time to probe, and Laura's not feeling up to close interrogation. The Blue Moon, though, is late-morning busy, so she hopes she can find a corner to hide in and drink a coffee undisturbed.

Ready with her order pad behind the counter, Angie seems

almost her usual bubbly self, but Laura senses an untypical coolness in her manner.

'Hi, Laura. What'll it be?'

Now she's here, the smell of food is turning Laura's stomach. 'Just a latte, please.'

Always the saleswoman, Angie runs through the specials.

'I've a red velvet cake, fresh this morning, or I've got local bacon if you want a BLT.'

'Not for me, thanks.'

'Not like you to turn down red velvet cake,' says Angie, with a slight lift of one eyebrow, and realisation hits Laura that Angie's playing to the floor. 'I hope you're not sickening for something. Don't you go giving it to me if you are.'

Laura hands over money to pay for her coffee, and Angie finds her change from the till.

'Heard anything from Izzy, have you?' she asks, placing coins in Laura's hand.

'Not for a little while, no.'

'Thought you might not have, somehow. I've heard she's gone away for a few days, having a break from all the drama. Can't blame her for that, can you? Mind you, I've been hearing you're having a bit of drama yourself. I'll bring your coffee over, shall I, if you can find somewhere to sit.'

The café is fuller than Laura thought, but there's a seat near the window table where Hannah's mum Mandy is finishing a sandwich. Pleased to see a friendly face, Laura makes her way to the table.

'Hi, Mandy. Mind if I join you?'

There's a blob of mayonnaise at the corner of Mandy's mouth, which isn't smiling. She puts the remains of her sandwich back on the plate and picks up a napkin to wipe her hands and dab at her mouth.

'Oh, hi, Laura. Yes, of course, sit, but actually I'm just leaving. I've got a dentist's appointment, and I'm already running late.'

Mandy's picking up her phone, ready to drop it in her bag. A sudden lull in conversation brings the soft background music to the fore. Laura hears the sizzle of frying bacon, and a ringing in her ears.

She raises her hand. 'No, please, Mandy, stay where you are. Don't be leaving on my account.'

As she's heading for the exit, Laura meets Angie bringing her coffee.

There's a smirk on Angie's face. 'You two had a falling-out, have you?'

'Seems so,' Laura calls over her shoulder as she walks out of the café.

'What on earth was that about?' Miss Mason asks the room.

'I thought you would have heard,' says Mandy. 'Aidan's been arrested in connection with Tristan's death.'

'I didn't know that,' says Professor Tarn, digging his spoon into damson jam. 'I thought he was supposed to be some kind of policeman.'

'Well, I must say you surprise me,' says Miss Mason, refilling her cup with Earl Grey. 'I always thought from the very beginning it would turn out to be a woman.'

Laura's only gone a few paces along the high street when someone touches her arm.

'Mrs Ridley?' The man's a stranger to her, short and

323

bent-backed, as if he's carried too much weight for too many years. Beneath the peak of his cap, he has an outdoorsman's face, wind-burned and lined. 'You don't know me, but I saw you with Mr Ridley at the funeral, last week. My Yvonne has a place in the churchyard there, and I was sat with her, watching the comings and goings.' He holds out a grimy hand, thinks better of it and lets it fall. 'Len Tyndall. Mr Ridley was always a help to me where my Jason was concerned. He wasn't always a bad lad, but he took a wrong turn. Sometimes they do that, and you struggle to get them back on the right path, but if they're set on going their own way, there's not much you can do about it, take it from me.'

'I'm sorry to hear that,' says Laura, keen to get away.

'Anyway, I'm sorry to hold you up, but I've heard Mr Ridley's got problems of his own. Of course it's not my business, and I don't believe a word of what they say, knowing him as I have in the past. They talk some rubbish in this place and they always have done, three parts invention and the rest all lies, as my mother used to say. But I wonder if you'd pass on a message, just in case? Tell Mr Ridley if he needs a character witness to stand for him, old Len is here. He did all he could for my family, and it seems only right that I should do the same for him.' He looks at Laura with rheumy eyes. 'Will you do that?'

'Of course.'

'Mr Ridley tells me you've children yourself.'

'We have.'

'I hope they're a joy to you, a pleasure and a joy.' Len looks down at his feet, and there's a moment's silence before he carries on. 'Well, I'd better let you get on, I've kept you long enough. You've other things to do than listen to a yabbering old fool like me. But you'll give Mr Ridley that message, won't you? Tell him he can always rely on me.'

Gooch's phone rings as she's heading for a lunchtime workout at the gym.

She doesn't recognise the number, but it's a Sterndale area code.

'DC Gooch.'

'Yes, hi, Detective Constable. This is Craig Dalton here, at Sterndale Hall.'

'Oh, hi, how are you doing?'

'I'm good. Listen, I'm getting in touch because I've been contacted by Gloucestershire police, which I know is way off your patch. But they've found those miniatures I told you about, the ones which went missing from one of the bedrooms. I got a crime number for them, by the way, so thanks for your advice on that.'

Gooch looks at her watch and keeps walking, wondering where this is going. 'No problem.'

'It was the SmartWater which caught him,' says Dalton. 'First time we've had any success with it. The items were taken to a pawnshop in Gloucester, and the owner had the sense to scan them. When he found out they were marked, he handed them in for forensic examination, and now we have them back.'

'That's great. I'm glad you got it sorted.'

'This might be the interesting part for you.'

Gooch stops, ready to pay full attention.

'The pawnshop owner had CCTV, so the police asked if

I could identify the guy who brought the paintings in. As it turns out I couldn't – we have dozens of guests every week, and I can't remember them all – but it occurred to me it might possibly be someone you know, if they were from this area.'

'It's a long shot,' says Gooch, 'but if you send it through to my email, it couldn't hurt to take a look.'

'I can do that.'

'And if you can send a photo of the miniatures too? Just in case we get an ID. But if I'm being honest, don't hold your breath.'

'I won't,' says Dalton.

The email arrives after lunch, when Gooch is back at her desk.

She opens the attachment, and a familiar face fills her screen.

FORTY-NINE

Golding catches Muir's eye as he comes into the office from an upstairs meeting. Golding's grinning, so Muir hopes there's positive news.

'What's up, Nate?'

'I may have got something,' says Golding, 'but before I show you, I want to clarify we've already seen the records of Aidan Ridley's calls to Tristan through his contract phone, to which he's openly admitted.'

'That's right. He says those calls were made when they were talking about the alleged loan.'

Golding nods. 'But what's still outstanding is the pay-as-you-go phone which was trying to make contact with Tristan, the one he answered once and from then onwards he bumped. We've still to identify who owns that phone.'

'Yes.'

'Have a look at this.' Golding points to a line of data on his screen. 'This is a copy of transactions on one of Ridley's credit cards. See here, two months ago. A charge of £34.99 at Carphone Warehouse.'

Muir bends down to study the screen.

'Does that mean anything, though? Maybe he bought head-phones or an SD card.'

'Except he didn't.' Golding opens a new window, displaying a Carphone Warehouse receipt. 'Voilà. He bought a cheap, SIM-free phone.'

'Son of a gun,' says Muir. He looks around the office. 'Kirstie, come over here.'

Weld joins them, and Golding shows her what he's found.

'Great work, Nate,' she says, and gives him a high five.

'Just hold on, though,' says Muir. 'If Ridley's already calling Tristan, why does he need a second phone?'

'Legitimate and non-legitimate business,' says Weld. 'He's an ex-copper. He knows how things work.'

'But the calls only connected once,' says Muir. 'It looks like they never really spoke on that number.'

'Could have been a signal,' says Golding. 'A "meet me in the usual place" kind of a thing.'

'They could have been texting,' suggests Weld. 'Maybe Tristan deleted the text stream because he didn't want Izzy to see it.'

'The big question is, if it's Ridley's, does he still have the phone or has he dumped it? How can we find out without spooking him more than we already have?'

'We could ring it,' says Weld. 'While we're in close prox-imity, at his home, or at his office.'

'It's a hell of a long shot,' says Muir, 'and it won't work if it's not switched on. We'd better go armed with a couple of warrants, one for the house, one for the office. Nate, can you organise that?'

'And if we don't find it in either place?' asks Weld.

'Let's stay optimistic,' says Muir, 'and cross that bridge if and when we get there.'

Aidan's going to work as normal, deciding he might as well; his premises are off the beat of normal Sterndale foot traffic, and the majority of his customers are from outside town. At the shop, he can focus – at least some of the time – on something other than their troubling situation.

Laura spends the day alone, passing the hours as best she can until the children are back from school. She's pleased to see them, and Josh is hungry, as always.

When the doorbell rings, she's watching him slather Nutella on a thick slice of toast.

Laura answers the door to a man and a woman.

Laura's only too familiar with the type, and she knows who they are even before the man holds up a warrant card and says, 'DI Muir, West Mercia police. This is my colleague, DS Weld. We're looking for Aidan Ridley.'

Laura feels disturbed that they're here. Apart from upsetting the children, the neighbours miss nothing, and the last thing they need is this kind of fuel stoking the fires of local gossip. Why can't they leave Aidan alone?

'He's at work,' she says. 'I expect you've got the address.'

'Is it Mrs Ridley?' asks Muir. 'Do you mind if we come in?'

He takes a step forward into Laura's personal space, and without even thinking she moves back.

'I've told you, he isn't here,' she says, as they pass her going into the hall.

Muir notices a photograph on the wall. 'Is that the old Chief Super I see there?'

'My dad,' says Laura. 'He died last year.'

'I'm sorry to hear that,' says Muir. 'Gavin Barton was one of the best, climbed the ranks the hard way and was one of the most respected men I knew. I didn't realise you were a relation. Through here, is it?'

He's leading the way into the lounge.

'You'll find Aidan at the shop,' says Laura, following him and Weld. 'He won't be home until this evening.'

'It's just a couple of questions, following up on our interview with him regarding the murder of Tristan Hart,' says Weld, as she sits down on the sofa.

Laura feels a cold trickle down her spine.

'We're trying to trace a mobile which made a number of calls to Tristan's iPhone. This is the number, here.'

From his suit pocket, Muir produces a piece of paper with a mobile number scribbled in red ink. When he shows it to Laura, she frowns. The digit sequence is vaguely familiar.

'Do you know that number, Mrs Ridley?'

Laura's answer lacks conviction. 'I don't think so.'

'I'll tell you what, why don't we try calling it?'

Weld has the number already programmed into her phone. She presses the call button, and seconds later, a jangling ringtone sounds upstairs.

'Whose phone is that?' asks Muir.

And then the call is answered, and Gemma says, 'Hello?'

FIFTY

Josh has tight hold of Laura's hand, tighter than she can remember him holding it even as a much smaller child, as tight as he used to squeeze her finger when he was a baby six months old. He's silent and very pale, standing stiffly beside her on the lawn as the men and women in white suits go in and out of their house, the house they're barred from entering. In other circumstances, Josh would be thrilled at all the excitement, but there's no excitement in watching your family fall apart.

How can this be happening?

Aidan has been picked up from the shop and is on his way here. Laura keeps looking over to one of the police cars parked at the kerb. Gemma's sitting alone in the back, with a policewoman standing guard, and Laura's desperate to catch her daughter's eye, but Gemma's head stays bowed, her face covered by the curtain of her hair. And if she catches her eye, how would that help? What Laura wants more than anything is to be with Gemma and hold her hand, but they've been separated to prevent them collaborating, and contact's not allowed.

Keeping an eye on Laura and Josh is a second policewoman, older and jaded with eyes which show no empathy.

Laura asks if she can borrow a phone, and the policewoman, says, 'I'm sorry?' as if the request is so outrageous, she thinks she's misheard.

'I need to call my mother-in-law,' pleads Laura. 'I need to ask her to come and take my son.'

The policewoman says nothing, but wanders across Laura's lawn to the front of the house, where Muir is conferring with one of the SOCOs. The policewoman interrupts him, and points at Gemma as she speaks. Muir glances in their direction.

'Will they let Grandma come?' asks Josh, in a voice so quiet Laura can barely hear him. Is he afraid he'll be swept along in all this, taken into custody too? How frightening a prospect must that be to a boy of his age?

Laura strokes his hair. 'Of course they will, sweetie. She'll take good care of you until Dad and I get home.'

She sees him look over at Gemma, and his eyes fill with tears.

'What will they do to her?' he asks, in that same quiet voice. 'Is she going to prison?'

Laura doesn't know, and doesn't know what to say, so she's grateful for the return of the policewoman, who's taking out her mobile phone.

'The inspector says under the circumstances I can call on your behalf. What's the number?'

'I can't remember,' says Laura. 'I've got her landline written down somewhere, if I could just go in the house.'

The policewoman raises her eyebrows a fraction. Request denied.

'I know Grandma's number,' says Josh uncertainly, and he recites it for the policewoman to key in. As it rings out, Laura's surprised to see her give Josh an approving smile.

Aidan's mum Jeannie answers, and the policewoman says, 'This is West Mercia police, everyone is safe, no one is hurt. There's a situation at your daughter-in-law's home in Sterndale, and she's asking if you could come and take care of . . .' She looks at Laura. 'What's your son's name?'

'Josh.'

'If you can come and take care of Josh.'

Inevitably, Jeannie starts asking questions, but the policewoman shuts her down.

'It's a matter of some urgency, Madam. When shall I tell her you'll be here . . .? OK, thanks.'

She ends the call and re-pockets her phone. 'She's on her way.'

A SOCO in a white suit has Gemma's pink laptop in a plastic bag, and is taking it to a van. Laura glances across at the police car, but Gemma hasn't noticed. She hasn't moved.

'Shall I get my stuff?' asks Josh, and he looks up at Laura as if the decision is hers.

'Yes, can he get his things? He'll need a change of clothes at least, and his pyjamas.'

'And my football.'

The policewoman shakes her head.

'Sorry, young man. Not today. You can't touch anything until the search is complete.'

Josh is still holding tightly on to Laura's hand, being her brave little soldier, and Laura knows what it's costing him not to cry, because she's feeling the same way.

She hears a car turning the corner into their cul-de-sac, and prays it's Aidan, come to make everything fine. But the vehicle is a taxi, which pulls up at the end of the driveway. The passenger pays the driver and climbs out: a middle-aged woman in a fashionable dress and bright lipstick, who reminds Laura of one of Josh's teachers a couple of years back, a teacher he didn't much like.

The woman glances round, spots Gemma in the back of the police car and speaks to the policewoman standing guard over Gemma as if she's some kind of threat. The policewoman nods, and the new arrival gets in beside Gemma. Laura sees her daughter turn towards this stranger, can see her listening to what she has to say.

The policewoman watching Laura and Josh takes out her phone again and dials a number. When she gets an answer, she turns her back, but Laura hears clearly what she says.

'Your appropriate adult is here.'

Two policemen appear from round the back of the house. From a distance, one of them looks like Aidan in his uniformed days; as they draw closer, the resemblance fades, but she recognises Danny, one of his old colleagues. As they head towards their car, he glances covertly at Laura and she knows he's recognised her, though he gives her no acknowledgement.

She's on the wrong team now.

Danny gets in the driver's seat, his passenger beside him. The engine starts.

This is actually going to happen. They're going to take Gemma away.

Laura starts to run forward, pulling Josh with her, but the policewoman blocks her way.

'Gemma!'

Gemma's terrified face is at the window. Laura sees her lips mouth *Mum!*, and she bangs on the glass, trying to get out. Then the police car turns the corner, out of sight.

FIFTY-ONE

On a hard seat inside the main entrance of Burnt Common police station, Laura endures a seemingly endless wait, wishing every moment that Aidan were here. This used to be his place, his comfort zone, and he's well versed in procedures and rights in custody, whereas Laura finds it intimidating, disempowering, and doesn't even know where to get a cup of tea. Not that she wants tea; what she wants is to be reunited with Gemma, and for both of them to go home.

But Aidan's still officially a suspect in the case, and not allowed to speak to his daughter, which leaves Laura to sort out this mess.

What would her dad say now?

Two hours pass before a young woman comes to fetch her, leading her without pleasantries to a room designated *Interview 3*.

The young woman allows her to enter, and closes the door to leave Laura and Gemma alone.

Gemma's sitting on the far side of a table, already different to the girl she was when they took her away. Something in her face is closed, guarded, hardened by the instinct of self-preservation, but when she sees her mother, she jumps up and rushes to her, clinging to her as she begins to cry.

'Mum, help me!'

And Laura cries too, because what help can she offer?

But plainly they don't have unlimited time. As Gemma becomes calmer, she wipes away her tears and goes back to her seat. Laura places a second chair next to her.

'You have to tell me what's been going on,' she says. 'I need to know everything so we can get this sorted out.'

Gemma hides her face in her hands.

'Look at me,' insists Laura. 'You've got to be honest now. Me and Dad can't help you unless we know the truth. Tell me what happened.'

Gemma looks up and shakes her head.

'It can't be sorted, Mum. I've done something so bad, and they know it was me. Please don't let them put me in prison! If they do that, I really will kill myself!'

There's fear in Gemma's eyes, desperation as she peers into the abyss.

Laura squeezes her hand. 'Don't say that. Never, ever say that.'

Then, the blow falls.

'I did it,' says Gemma. 'I hit him. It was me.'

Oh. My. God.

Laura softens her voice, suppressing the panic inside. 'What are you saying, Gemma? I don't understand.'

Gemma's crying again.

'It was my fault,' she sobs. 'He asked me to meet him by the pool and I shouldn't have gone.'

'Of course you shouldn't,' says Laura, and immediately

regrets how judgemental she sounds. 'Why on earth did he ask you to meet him?'

'Oh, come on, Mum, it's obvious. Only I didn't think it would be like that. I thought he was someone I could trust. I thought maybe he was planning some surprise for Izzy, or you. I never thought he'd do what he did.'

Laura feels sick. 'I'm so, so sorry. Is that why you've been so unhappy? Tell me exactly what he said, what you did. If it was an accident, the police will understand.'

But common sense prevails over wishful thinking, and Laura immediately sees the unlikelihood of that being the case. Whoever hit Tris hit him hard, according to Izzy.

She doesn't want to think about what this will do to Izzy.

Gemma brushes away tears. 'I don't want to tell you.'

'Sweetie, I can't help you if I don't have the facts. What happened when you got to the pool?'

'He was waiting with a bottle of champagne. I was so stupid, I still didn't get it. He gave me a glass and I drank it. I'm sorry, Mum. I know you said no alcohol.'

The least of our worries, thinks Laura. 'Never mind about that. Just tell me what he did.'

'He tried to kiss me. He told me I was beautiful and tried to touch my boobs, but when I said no he kind of changed and got really angry. He grabbed my wrists and it hurt. Then he said he'd always wanted me, how an older man would be good for me. He pushed me up against the wall, and I said no again and I tried to scream, but he covered my mouth with his hand. He was trying to pull my dress up and undo his trousers but his zip got stuck, so I saw my

338

chance and picked up the bottle and I just hit him with it. I thought he was going to rape me, Mum. I didn't know what else to do, but I hit him too hard. Now he's dead and it's all my fault.'

Gemma drops her head, and Laura puts her arm across her back, remembering other times she's comforted Gemma, in infancy and beyond.

And as she soothes with maternal comfort, her rage against Tristan ignites, and the flames begin to grow.

'Will I go to prison, Mum?'

'Over my dead body.'

'How do you know?'

'You won't go to prison if it was self-defence, sweetie. If he was going to rape you, you have the right to protect yourself.'

Gemma sniffs. 'I didn't want to tell anyone. How could I prove I'm telling the truth? But they think Dad did it and it wasn't him. I don't want him to be in trouble instead of me.'

A thought strikes Laura.

'Is this why you took those tablets?'

Gemma nods. 'I overheard what you and Dad were saying about Tristan being disabled, and I felt so bad. I thought it was the only way. I knew how mad you'd be, how everyone's going to hate me.'

'I'm not mad at you, I'm mad at Tristan. No one's going to hate you when they know what happened. And don't worry about your dad, either. He'll know what we need to do. Sometimes it's useful having a policeman in the family.'

'But he's not a policeman any more.'

'He still knows how things work, and he'll know what to do for the best. Anyway, Izzy's told me some things which will make your story more likely to be believed. Or did you hear all about that too?'

'It's not a story, Mum, it's what actually, really happened. And if you mean about those other women, yes, I did hear that. He was just an old pervert.'

'What's going to happen next?' asks Laura. 'Have they told you?'

'They're going to interview me. They're waiting for a lawyer because that woman who was in the police car with me told me to say I wanted one.'

My daughter needs a lawyer, thinks Laura. *How did none of us see through him, when Tristan was such a complete and utter bastard?*

'All you need to do is tell the truth,' she says. 'When they know how it was, they'll let you go.'

'Really?'

'Guaranteed. The police know what they're doing, and they're not going to put someone in prison who doesn't deserve to be there.'

Time spent in the sea air has been good for Izzy, improving her appetite, helping her sleep better than she's done in a while. A smuggler's cottage with no Wi-Fi and hopeless mobile signal has cut out the stress of calls and texts, and a place where no one knows her has provided freedom to relax and think things over.

But almost as soon as they drive out of the seaside village, her phone begins to ping with messages, streaming in from the ether where they've been awaiting her return.

She's not ready yet to face the world. Paused at traffic lights, she switches the phone off.

What difference could a couple of hours make?

FIFTY-TWO

The video's been recorded in a bleak, white room, hard fluorescent light, no windows. Gemma looks unwell, her lips dry.

Muir's team are gathered round a monitor to watch. The voice asking the questions is Weld's, and she's taking it slowly, not applying any pressure. Out of shot, the appropriate adult and Gemma's lawyer are making sure of that.

Weld pushes a cheap phone in a clear evidence bag across the table.

'Is this your phone, Gemma?'

Gemma glances at it and nods.

'Your dad bought it for you, is that right?'

She nods again.

'And that was recently?'

'I had a decent phone on contract, but Dad said my bills were way too high. He got me that instead and made me pay my own top-ups.'

'Did you use this phone to call Tristan?'

Gemma gives no answer. Weld leaves plenty of time for her to speak, then moves on.

'Can you tell us what happened between you and Tristan at the wedding?'

On the screen, Gemma looks down at her hands, and starts to pick at a hangnail. Her fingernails are bitten down to the quick. Weld's assuming she's going to maintain her silence – no doubt she's had the lawyer's standard *No comment* advice – but then Gemma looks up and says, 'He asked me to meet him by the pool.'

Calmly, Weld asks, 'When did he ask you to do that?'

Gemma mumbles her reply. Muir rewinds a few seconds and turns up the volume.

'At the wedding, after we ate. He came over to talk to me and my friends and he asked me then.'

'How did he manage to do that?' asks Weld's voice. 'With all those people around that must have been quite difficult.'

'I was in a group, and he bent down and said it in my ear. I suppose he thought in that situation he could speak to me without Izzy noticing.'

'Izzy being Isobel, his wife?'

'Yes.'

'So he suggested you should meet him in secret – is that what you're saying?'

'Yes.'

'And you were compliant?'

'I don't know what that means.'

'I'm asking if you wanted to meet up with him as much as he wanted to meet up with you.'

Gemma lapses back into silence, folding her arms and staring directly at the wall behind Weld's head, as if there's something fascinating there.

An unseen woman's voice – the lawyer's – says, 'You can say *No comment* to any question you don't want to answer, Gemma.'

'Why did you go to meet him, Gemma?' persists Weld. 'What were you expecting to happen?'

Gemma's cheeks flush pink, a blush of embarrassment.

'Did you think he was attractive?'

She shrugs. 'Not really.'

'A bit old for you, maybe?'

Gemma nods.

'But you still went. Did you tell anyone you were going?'

'No.'

'You didn't tell any of your friends?'

No response.

'Was that because you thought what you were doing was wrong?'

'I didn't think it was wrong,' objects Gemma. 'Our families are friends. Izzy and my mum are good mates.'

'So with him being a family friend, you thought you would be safe?'

'Yes.'

'But you still didn't tell anyone?'

'I thought it would be a laugh. I thought he might buy me a drink. My mum wouldn't have liked that.'

'Obtaining alcohol for you would be against the law. Did he do that?'

'Kind of. He brought a bottle of champagne with him.'

'Just a bottle? No glasses?'

'Two glasses.'

'What kind of glasses?'

344

'Wine glasses.'

'Round ones, tall ones, big ones – what kind of wine glasses?'

'The tall, thin kind.'

'So there you were, you two alone by the pool. What happened next?'

A short silence.

'I can't remember.'

'We need you to remember, Gemma. This is terribly important. What I don't want you to worry about is being embarrassed. Whatever you say we don't have to share with anyone you don't want us to. OK? We just need to get to the truth. So please, do your very best to remember. Did you drink any champagne?'

'Yes. He opened it and we both drank some.'

Weld senses Gooch shift in her chair.

'And while you were drinking, what else were you doing? What were you talking about?'

'About the wedding, mostly. About whether I was having a good time. Just chat.'

'Just friendly chat?'

'Yes.'

'He didn't say anything to you of a sexual nature?'

Gemma blushes deeply. 'He said I was beautiful.'

'That's all?'

'Yes.'

Weld waits, but there's nothing more.

She continues probing. 'Did you mind him saying that?'

'Why should I?'

'Well, you have to think about Tristan's age, don't you? How old would you say he is? As old as your dad, maybe?'

'About that.'

'Who's your best friend at school, Gemma?'

Gemma frowns at the change of tack. 'Hannah, I suppose. What's she got to do with it?'

'If you found out your dad was telling Hannah she was beautiful and getting her to drink champagne, would you think that was an OK thing to do? Or would you think it was creepy?'

'I'd think it was disgusting.'

'Don't you think people might think the same about Tristan doing that with you? That his behaviour was inappropriate?'

'Not really.'

'Did you think it was OK because of who he was? On TV, I mean. I suppose it must have felt glamorous, drinking champagne with a TV star.'

No response.

'So what happened next?'

Gemma starts to look upset.

'Everything turned bad. He tried to kiss me but I didn't want him to. He grabbed my wrists and started pushing me up against the wall. I asked him to stop but he didn't, so I hit him to get him off me. I was frightened. I thought he was going to rape me.'

'If he had hold of your wrists, how did you pick up the bottle?' asks Weld.

Gemma looks tearful and bewildered.

'I don't know. It all happened so fast. I wanted to get him off me. I was frightened, and I didn't want to get raped. Can we have a break, please?' She turns her head to ask this last question of someone sitting beside her.

'All right, Gemma,' says Weld. 'I think that's enough for this evening.'

When Flora's asleep and her mother's settled down in front of the TV, Izzy sits down at the kitchen table and turns on her phone.

She's missed a lot of messages and calls. Most can wait till morning, but there's a recent voicemail from Weld which she thinks she should listen to.

'Hi Izzy, this is Kirstie Weld from West Mercia CID. I'm calling to let you know we've made an arrest in Tristan's case. Can you call me as soon as you get this, please, and I'll update you.'

An arrest can only mean one thing.

Izzy sees red.

FIFTY-THREE

Aidan's sitting in the near-dark.

Along the cul-de-sac, someone's having a party, and the thump of upbeat, bright music only blackens his mood.

Laura lets herself in the front door, drops her handbag on the stairs and goes to him on the sofa, letting herself be folded into his arms. A moment passes where neither of them speak, not wanting to break the sanctuary spell of silence. Once they begin to talk, their catastrophe will become overwhelmingly real.

Aidan says, 'Tell me,' and Laura shakes her head, not knowing where to begin.

'She did it, didn't she?'

Laura sits up. 'I need to get something for my headache.'

In the kitchen, she takes two paracetamol. Finding vodka at the back of the fridge, she pours two long measures into tumblers and tops them off with orange juice.

Back in the lounge, she hands a glass to Aidan and they both drink.

Now they sit side by side but with space between them.

'They let me speak to her, like you said,' says Laura. 'Yes, she did it.'

Aidan bows his head. 'For Christ's sake. Why?'

'It wasn't her fault. He tried to seduce her, and when she said no, he was going to force her. It was self-defence.'

'She hit him with the bottle?'

'Yes.'

'Why did she hit him so hard?'

'She must have been so scared, Aidan. It kills me to think about her being in that situation. Why weren't we there to help?'

'Why were they together?'

'He asked her to meet him. She thought he was planning some kind of surprise for Izzy.'

'And the champagne? Where did that come from?'

'She says he brought it with him. A tool of seduction, I suppose.'

Aidan shakes his head. 'I can't believe I've been such a mug. When I think how we've been taken in.'

'She won't go to prison, will she? Not if it's self-defence.'

Aidan swallows what remains of his drink. 'Not if I have anything to do with it. But our little girl against one of the darlings of the entertainment world? I think we're going to have a fight on our hands.'

'Then we'll fight with everything we've got.'

Aidan reaches out and touches her face.

'What have we got, Laura? Not money, that's for sure.'

'We'll sell the house. We won't be staying in Sterndale anyway, not after this. And he isn't the first. There are plenty like him locked away for doing the same thing. We'll get her the best lawyers. They'll make sure she doesn't pay for what he tried to do.'

'I hope so.'

'Please, we have to be positive. Why wouldn't people be on her side?'

'Because,' says Aidan, 'Tristan isn't like those others. Even when you were telling me what Izzy had found out about him, with his other women and his burner phone, I didn't quite believe it. It just didn't seem like the Tris we think we know. He's plausible, people like him. Didn't I fall for his bullshit, and let him recruit me in his tax evasion scam?'

'You don't know that was bullshit.'

'No, I don't know for sure. But when the police were grilling me and laid out the possibility, I felt such an idiot for not thinking of it myself. I mean, who actually does that, just gives someone money because they need it? But he always seemed so genuine. What if a jury feels the same, buys into the image and thinks it's impossible for him to have done wrong? Gemma could end up with a criminal record and a life in ruins, and I would take that very, very hard, because the thought of him touching our daughter makes me want to throw up.'

'You're thinking about that girl, aren't you?'

Aidan nods. 'Faith Ogden. Raped by a taxi driver with form as long as your arm, none of it admissible in court. What did CID tell her? All you have to do is tell the truth, and you'll be fine. But that toe-rag was likeable and not bad-looking, she'd been drinking, so when he claimed it was consensual, the jury believed him. By the time she reported it, any bruises or other injuries were gone. She had no evidence to support her case, and he walked free.'

'We won't let it be like that for Gemma. Will we?'

The doorbell rings.

Aidan goes to answer the door. The pulsing party music down the street has been turned down, and a few people are beginning to leave, calling to each other as they head for their cars.

In the fading light, for a moment he isn't sure it's her. The Izzy in his mind is a slender, elegant beauty, wholly unlike this haggard, emaciated creature on the doorstep. A part of him is pleased to see her, but only until he remembers Gemma. Then he doesn't know what to say to her, so he says simply, 'Izzy.'

And loud enough to catch the ears of the party guests, she says, 'What the fuck are you doing here?'

Laura comes to stand at Aidan's shoulder.

He decides he's going to keep his cool.

'I live here,' he says. 'What are you doing here?'

'I came for a word with my so-called friend there,' says Izzy, waving a contemptuous hand at Laura. 'I got a message to say you'd been arrested. For my husband's murder.'

Sensing an escalating drama, the party guests are slowing their departures.

'You've been misinformed, then,' says Aidan. 'See, here I am, still at liberty.'

'I don't understand,' says Izzy, beginning to blush, realising Weld's message said only that an arrest had been made. Unaware of anyone apart from Aidan being under suspicion, plainly she's made a dreadful mistake.

But as she's about to apologise, Laura steps forward, right in Izzy's face.

'I'll tell you who's been arrested, lady,' she spits. 'Our

daughter, that's who. And since you seem to be out of the loop, let me fill you in. Your husband tried to take advantage of her. He tried to rape her. You and your perfect marriage, your perfect bloody everything, when he was nothing but a dirty, disgusting pervert. That's who your wonderful husband was, another monster hiding in plain sight.'

The slap Izzy lands on Laura's cheek is hard. The sound of it echoes between the houses, and the party guests fall into astonished silence, watching to see what will happen next.

Laura puts her hand up to her face and covers her stinging cheek.

Aidan looks at Izzy.

'I think you need to go now,' he says.

Watching her walk back to the Range Rover, he feels both anger and regret.

He doesn't wait for her to start the engine before he closes the door.

He goes to comfort Laura, while the party guests are already busy on their phones.

Izzy doesn't drive far before she pulls over. Not giving a damn about the time, she finds her phone and dials Weld's number.

Weld answers on the fifth ring, sounding drowsy, as if she might have been asleep.

'Izzy. Hi.'

'Who have you arrested?' demands Izzy.

Weld doesn't immediately answer, and Izzy knows she's deciding how much to say.

'We've been trying to get in touch with you,' says Weld eventually. 'I left you a couple of messages.'

'I've only just picked them up,' says Izzy. 'Where we've been, the signal was terrible. Could you please tell me what's been going on?'

'This is a conversation I'd far rather have in person, but since you're asking, we're currently talking to Gemma Ridley, who was brought in this afternoon. We've spoken to her at some length, and we'll be interviewing her again tomorrow.'

'Did she do it?'

'It's far too early to say.'

'But you must have your reasons.'

'We have our suspicions. But I promise we'll keep you updated, if you make sure I can get in touch.'

After the call's ended, Izzy sits a while, taking in what Weld has said.

Not Aidan, but sweet, gentle Gemma.

Sounds like Laura was right.

She's been deluded and hoodwinked, trapped into playing the gullible wife to an absolute master of deceit.

FIFTY-FOUR

As Weld prepares for Gemma's second interview, Gooch brings her coffee, a dull latte from the first-floor machine.

Weld takes a sip and pulls a face. 'At least it's reliably bad. I've spoken to Nate about the outcome of yesterday's search, and he's confirmed via Facebook photos that the dress and shoes they found hidden at the back of Gemma's wardrobe are the ones she was wearing at the wedding. They've sent them to forensics as a rush job, but there's no way we'll have the results today.'

'Do you think there'll be enough to send her to trial?' asks Gooch.

'If she hit him with that bottle, they'll find blood spatter, and with a match to Tristan, we won't need too much else. What did you make of yesterday's interview?'

Afraid of calling it wrong, Gooch is reluctant to offer an opinion.

'Something's off to me,' she says, in the end. 'I don't think she was telling the truth.'

'That's very astute of you,' says Weld. 'As a matter of fact,

I didn't think she was, either. So let's see if she's reconsidered, now she's had chance to reflect overnight.'

'The thing is, Gemma, there are one or two things we already know which don't quite fit with what you've told us so far,' says Weld. 'For example, Tristan's wife Izzy – you know Izzy, don't you? She's told us Tristan didn't drink alcohol. Never. Which leads us to wonder how come he was drinking with you.'

'I don't know. I suppose he was trying to get me drunk.'

'So you'd be less likely to object when he touched you? Is that what you mean?'

A shrug. 'Suppose.'

'And can you just clarify for us how this meeting came to be arranged. You said . . .' Weld appears to be reading from her notes. 'Here we are. You said that he asked you to meet him, but we're wondering whether it might have been the other way around. That maybe you asked him to meet you.'

A short silence.

'Why would I do that?'

'Did you have a crush on him?'

'No.'

'You deny that you had any interest in Tristan?'

'Why would I be interested in him?'

'Lots of women are. People think of him as an attractive man, and here you are with easy access to him.'

'That's nuts.'

'Is it? I don't know whether you're aware, but we can do an awful lot with people's phones, these days. We can tell what numbers you've been calling and when, even where you were when you made the calls, where the person you were calling was when they answered. Even when you're not making a call, if your phone's switched on, we can look at data on it to find out where you've been. Did you know that?'

'No.'

'The reason I'm mentioning that now is that we've tracked several phone calls from your phone to Tristan's. Do you remember making those calls?'

Silence.

'Most of them Tristan didn't answer. Why do you think that was?'

'I expect he was busy. Or with Izzy.'

'Over a period of five weeks before the wedding, you called him rather a lot, but apart from one call – the very first you made to him – it appears he never answered those calls, nor did he ever call you. Can you tell us why that was?'

Silence.

'Where did you get his number, Gemma? Did Tristan give it to you himself?'

Silence.

'Gemma? Where did you get his number?'

She gives a small smile, as if pleased at her ingenuity.

'From my dad's phone.'

'So when you rang him, was he surprised to hear from you?'

Silence.

'Here's the thing, Gemma. Whatever happened between you and Tristan that night, he's no longer with us. He had a lot of fans and they all feel his loss, but the biggest tragedy is for his wife who's now a widow, and especially his daughter, little Flora, who's going to grow up without a dad. Whichever way you look at it, life going forward is going to be difficult for them. But you know what would make it a hundred times more difficult? If they believed – if the whole world believed – that Tristan was a bad person, that he attacked you, and that it wasn't true.'

'It is true!'

'The facts say otherwise, Gemma. The facts suggest you were pursuing him, probably making life difficult for him. If that's how it was, given the tragic outcome of that night, don't you think you owe it to his family to tell the truth?'

'I am telling the truth.'

'You could wreck his reputation forever. Do you think that's fair? Does he deserve that?'

Silence. Gemma appears to be thinking about nothing in particular, gazing around the room as though interested in where she finds herself, her eyes everywhere but on the person in front of her: a classic stress behaviour.

Weld lets the seconds tick by, until Gemma straightens up in her chair and says, 'Can I talk to my lawyer for a minute?'

'Be my guest,' says Weld, and she leaves the room.

'I don't think I used enough pressure,' says Weld to Gooch, as she waits to be called back in. 'You have to be so careful in these situations. People jump in and shut you down if they think you're pushing too hard.'

'Do you think she'll tell the truth?'

Weld shrugs. 'Hard to say. I hope so. If not, I'll have to lean on her a bit harder, and I don't want to do that. She looks like such an innocent.'

'Not that innocent,' says Gooch.

*   *   *

Back in the room, Weld asks, 'Are you OK to go on?'

Gemma nods.

'Let's talk again about the phone, then,' says Weld. 'You're saying Tristan never called you?'

Gemma glances at someone out of sight. 'I don't want to hurt Izzy and Flora.'

'Then you must tell the truth, or they might be hurt. Did he ask you to meet him by the pool?'

Gemma starts picking again at the hangnail.

'I asked him. I told him if he didn't meet me, I'd tell Izzy we were having an affair.'

There's an audible sigh from Weld before she says, 'So you blackmailed him into meeting you. Did you take the bottle with you?'

'There was a bottle on the next table to ours. I took that.'

'And the glasses?'

Gemma nods.

'And when you found him there, what did he say?'

Gemma's expression becomes hard to read, but there's petulance, and anger.

'He said I had to stop contacting him, that I was putting his career in danger if anyone found out. He said he loved Izzy and that I should find someone my own age. But I already had, and he'd gone off with my so-called friend.'

'So what did you say?'

Silence. Weld is about to go on, but Gemma begins to speak, falteringly.

'I told him I was in love with him, that it could be a secret. I showed him the champagne and I was going to pour a glass, but he told me he doesn't drink. I felt really stupid. He made me look a total idiot, you know? So . . .'

'So what, Gemma?' asks Weld quietly. 'What did you do?'

'I didn't mean it to be hard. I was having a really shit evening, first Darren and then him. I felt like no one wanted me. I was angry, so I hit him, and he fell down.'

'You hit him with the bottle?'

'Yes.'

'What did you do next?'

Gemma shakes her head. 'I didn't know what to do. I thought he'd just get up. I dropped the bottle and it smashed everywhere and I thought the noise of it would bring people, so I left him. I thought someone would come and help him, but I didn't want them to find me.'

'You knew it was wrong?'

'I was angry. I told him I loved him, and he just didn't care.'

'What did you do with the glasses?'

'I dropped them in the pool.'

'Just to be clear, then,' says Weld, 'when you hit Tristan, you didn't feel under any threat from him, he hadn't tried to touch you against your will or made any kind of unwelcome suggestions to you?'

Now Gemma's face is sad. 'No, he didn't do any of that. I told my mum that's what had happened, but it wasn't true. I loved him and he didn't want me. That was it, really.' She turns to the side, towards her lawyer and the appropriate adult.

'Can we stop this now? I don't want to say any more.'

FIFTY-FIVE

At Weld's suggestion, Izzy's meeting her at the Quiet Woman, which Weld judges to be about the halfway point between Sterndale and Burnt Common police station.

Izzy and Tris used to visit the Quiet Woman in the early days of their romance, beguiled by its idyllic location, alongside a packhorse bridge crossing a river renowned for its trout fishing. The pub itself is charming too, a low, whitewashed building roofed in thatch, with tables spread over the river's grassy banks.

They sat, once, at one of the riverside tables, talking over a lunch which lasted well into the afternoon, until Tris excused himself and went inside. When he came out, he was holding a key, and took her hand to lead her upstairs to a misshapen, sloping-floored room with a leaded-glass hobbit window over-looking the river, and beams so low, he could only walk round with his head bent. They spent many hours in the four-poster bed, leaving it only to go down to eat the chocolatey desserts they were too full to eat at lunch, and long after that, to a breakfast with home-made marmalade and pots of strong Indian tea.

As she leaves the car, she looks up at that window, wondering whether the shade of their time there might somehow be locked behind it, whether if she asked to go up and see the room, she might catch a gossamer breath of how they were that day. The memory of it provokes a pulse of pain, like the soreness of a splinter.

Izzy is a few minutes late, and Weld is already seated at one of the wooden tables – by chance, the same table where she and Tris ate that day – close to where a weeping willow spreads its rustling branches over the water. Weld is alone, but there are two full glasses on the table.

As Izzy approaches, Weld smiles. 'Hi, Izzy. Good to see you. I gambled that you'd like a sparkling water. If you'd prefer something else, I'll get it for you.'

'No, that's great, thanks. Sorry I'm late.' Izzy brushes a few willow leaves from her chair seat, and folds the skirt of her white dress under her before she sits down. When she takes off her sunglasses, Weld thinks how different she looks to when they first met: rundown, unwell. Trauma and stress will do that, no exceptions.

'So.' Weld leans forward on to her elbows. 'How are you?'

Izzy's eyes go to the water and its steady flow. Some things, at least, are constant. 'As well as may be expected, I suppose. One day at a time, you know? There's so much to sort out, all the legal processes. He didn't leave a will, or at least nobody's found one. With us only being married a short time, it could get complicated. His ex-wife might be making a claim on the estate, on behalf of her son. Flora and I will be OK, but I really could do without it.'

'How's Flora coping?'

Izzy taps her glass but doesn't drink from it.

'She's confused, she doesn't understand where Daddy's gone. That's not a surprise, at her age, and to be honest sometimes I feel the same way. One minute he was there, the next he vanished. She's become very clingy, holding on to my clothes all the time, not wanting to be in different rooms. You can almost see the emotional damage happening, but what can I do? I'm staying with her as much as I can, but sometimes I need a break to deal with my own feelings. So I'm glad you suggested we meet here. Sterndale's so claustrophobic.'

'I know it's hard,' says Weld. 'You have to give it time. Meanwhile, I have news for you. We've concluded our interviews with Gemma Ridley, and we're waiting on a decision from the CPS. Our expectation is that they'll tell us to go ahead and charge her with Tristan's murder.'

Izzy's hands go to her face, and her mouth falls open. 'Gemma? But isn't she claiming self-defence?'

Weld shakes her head. 'We're not aware of any such claim at the moment, at least. Her barrister may want to try that route, of course, but she's already told us that she struck him in anger because he rejected her.'

'He rejected her,' whispers Izzy. 'He didn't – try and have sex with her?'

'No.'

'So he was innocent.'

'Yes.'

A swallow flies low over the river, almost skimming the water with its breast.

'I'm going to get myself a proper drink,' says Izzy.

When she returns with a large glass of rosé, Weld says, 'I

362

wasn't sure whether you'd regard Gemma being charged as good news.'

'Honestly? I think it's another tragedy,' says Izzy. 'She's so young. And poor Laura. Poor Aidan and Josh. Are they OK?'

'They will be, in time. People adapt, they cope. But for now, why don't we focus on some undeniably good news. We've spoken to Martina Stokes. Amber and I went to Oxford, and I'm going to be honest with you, she wasn't at all what we expected.'

Izzy takes a long swallow of her wine. 'What were you expecting? I'll tell you what I'm expecting: blonde, early twenties, big boobs. Am I right?'

'If I'm being frank, we were on the same page, but Martina's nothing like that. How about mid-fifties, razor cut and tattoos? She's had a tough life, tougher than most, but she's come through it.'

'So how did Tris know her?'

'These days, Tina's involved with a network of havens for women trying to escape domestic abuse. Tristan found her via the internet, and said he wanted to help make things better for those women, but in a low-key, no publicity way. That house they were building together is a safe house, a women's refuge.'

Izzy frowns. 'You're kidding. That makes no sense. Why wouldn't he tell me about it? Why the secrecy?'

Weld's unsure of how much she should say. 'It's a sensitive issue, Izzy, especially since Tristan chose not to involve you in what he was doing. If I play by the rules, I shouldn't tell you any more than what's relevant to our investigation, and should only say that Martina Stokes and the other women whose contact details you found on Tristan's second phone are not people of interest to us and have been eliminated from our enquiries.'

'In police speak.'

'In police speak. Off the record and woman to woman, there are some aspects of Tristan's past of which you're plainly unaware, and I'm concerned it's not my place to fill you in. But now we've ruled her out as a suspect, I can put you in touch with Martina. If you'd like to speak to her, she's very keen to talk to you. She wants to tell you what a wonderful man your husband was.'

'So he definitely wasn't having an affair with her?'

Weld emphatically shakes her head. 'Absolutely not. She states there was never any question of any kind of intimate relationship between them and I believe her. The other contacts in his phone all say the same.'

'Then I've misjudged him on everything.'

'That's understandable.'

'He never had the chance to defend himself. I came to think the very worst of him, and I was wrong.'

'Martina can help you. Talk to her, because I think you need to know the truth. I'll send you her details and you can get in touch. And I think you should speak to his family. I don't believe they've been entirely straight with you.'

A breeze rustles through the willow tree, and Izzy shivers. Glancing up at the window of that bedroom, she almost thinks she sees a face there, her own face from those happier times.

'I will,' she says. 'And thank you for everything you've done.'

'We meet again,' says Muir, as he and Golding take their seats in the interview room. 'Thanks for making the journey.'

Murray Roe is dressed for the office where he no longer works, pinstripe suit, white shirt, garish tie. The shirtsleeve cuffs, Muir notices, are beginning to fray, and there's a stain – tea or coffee – on his tie.

'As it happens, I had nothing else on,' says Roe. 'But I don't want to hang about. I only put an hour on the meter.'

Golding opens a folder, takes out several stapled sheets of paper and pushes them to Roe across the table.

'You do not have to say anything,' says Muir. 'But it may harm your defence if you do not mention when questioned something which you later rely on in court. Anything you do say may be given in evidence. Is that clear?'

'All a bit formal,' says Roe.

'Do you wish to have a legal representative present?'

'Should I?'

'It's your right. Do you wish to exercise it?'

'I don't think so, no.'

'Let's press on, then,' says Muir, 'since you're on a meter. When we met before, you made that statement regarding the day of the assault on Tristan Savage.'

Roe glances down. 'I did.'

'Is there anything you'd like to add to it?'

'No.' Roe looks from Muir to Golding, and seems less certain. 'Like what?'

'Like the visit you made that evening to Tristan's house. I think you'll find you forgot to mention it.'

Roe smiles. 'Did I? I suppose it slipped my mind.'

'You don't deny, then, that you were there?'

'Why should I? I committed no crime.'

'You conspired with Bridget Feahny to gather personal

information for the purposes of making a profit. I think there might be something there that we could use.'

'Hardly worth your time, though, is it? Anyway, I thought the case was closed. I heard on the news that you've made an arrest.'

'So we have,' says Muir. 'But for completeness, we'd like to invite you to amend your statement, so we have a true record of your movements that evening. Just to keep things nice and tidy. And as we prepare the case for court, it's possible your testimony may be pertinent.'

'Pertinent in what way?'

'You may have been the last person to speak to Tristan before he died. With the exception of his killer, of course.'

'Really? Well, actually I find that rather chilling.'

'I should tell you we do have CCTV of you at Tristan's home.'

'In that case, I see no reason to refuse.'

'There is another matter.' Muir pauses as Golding takes more papers from his file and pushes the first sheet across to Roe. 'I wonder if you can tell me what you know about these?'

The paper is a photograph of two small but pretty water-colours in gilded frames. Roe studies them and pulls a face.

'Never seen them before,' he says. 'Not my kind of thing. I'm more of a French impressionist man myself.'

Golding offers Roe another photograph.

'Is that you?' asks Muir.

He watches Roe carefully. The photo's a CCTV still, and now Roe has to gamble. Is it from Tristan's house – where Roe's already admitted he's been – or could it be from elsewhere?

'Hard to say,' says Roe. 'Those things are never very clear, are they?'

'I think it's you,' says Muir. 'It's from a pawnbroker's in Gloucester. Do me a favour, will you, and hold out your hands.'

'What for?'

Golding produces a torch.

'Nothing to worry about, Murray,' says Muir. 'Standard procedure.'

Roe offers the palms of his hands, and Golding shines the torch's ultraviolet beam on to the skin.

Roe's hands light up with splashes of neon-green.

'SmartWater,' says Muir. 'Sticks around for weeks. We can still call a lawyer for you, if you've changed your mind.'

FIFTY-SIX

'I've been hearing things about Tris,' says Izzy. 'Things I didn't know.'

Steph is standing by the window, watching Eamon laughing with Flora as she's picking daisies on the lawn. Flora's wearing a bikini, and a pink cowgirl hat with a sheriff's badge embroidered on the crown.

Steph looks as though she hasn't heard, so Izzy says, 'He was building a women's refuge. Trying to make amends, is what they said.'

When Steph turns round, she's close to tears again. Her son's death has been too hard on her, and Izzy wonders how she goes on, whether in her place, at her age, she'd think it was worthwhile. The thought must surely cross any mother's mind. If she lost Flora, what would be the point?

Steph crosses the room and sits down on the sofa, perching on its edge, facing Izzy. There's a depth of sadness in her eyes which matches the pain in Izzy's heart, now she's learning the truth about the man she married, and still loves.

'I'm sorry, my dear,' says Steph. 'There's so much you didn't know, so much he didn't want you to know, and I'm sure he'd be mortified that it's all going to come out now. I understood his reasons, but I didn't like the idea of his keeping so much from you, and I always thought he should tell you, because secrets are so very hard to keep, especially with someone in his position. People are always digging for dirt, and the sad fact is that with him, it was there to find if they came searching. I loved my son very, very much, but for a long time he was really quite hard to like.'

'You shouldn't talk about him that way,' says Izzy.

'We should talk about him honestly,' insists Steph. 'You mustn't put him on a pedestal. You need to know the truth. For many years he had problems which got progressively worse. A taste for alcohol became a drink problem, and as he became better paid, he added drugs to the mix. When he was drunk, he was unpredictable and sometimes downright unpleasant.' She looks down at her hands. 'Duncan saved his reputation, of course, knowing the right people and pulling strings. We all paid for his drinking. It cost us our grandson, Bailey – we haven't seen him in years. He might have children himself now, for all I know, and we might be great-grandparents. Nothing would give me greater pleasure than to see him again, or just to know how he's doing, what path he chose in life, whether he's happy. When Tris's first wife, Dolly, left him, she took Bailey too. We tried to make contact with him – Duncan knew where they were – but all we heard from Dolly was that Bailey wanted nothing to do with us, because we'd be on his dad's side. We weren't on anybody's side. We were just stuck right in the middle.'

'I don't understand,' says Izzy. 'It's as if you're talking about a different person. This isn't the man I knew.'

'Ah, but it is, my dear, and you need to hear the whole story and the part you played. When he was young, we thought we were truly blessed. Tris was special, our golden boy. He always did well in his exams at school, and he was popular, especially with the girls. So handsome, he was, with that blond hair and blue eyes. Women turned to look at him as he went by, and I used to feel the glow of pride.

'For our sins, we were boastful, our son this and our son that. When friends told us how well their children were doing in nursing or IT or accountancy, we'd smugly tell them Tris had landed his first job on a newspaper. Then he got into radio, then TV – only a backroom job, but he was expecting a break to get in front of the cameras, and who could resist that smile? It was only a matter of time.

'Our children are not to be worshipped. We look at Flora now, and think she'll always be that delightful, sunny girl, but if that were true of all children, where do all the awful people we know come from, the cruel ones and the bad-tempered and the miserable? I don't mean to depress you, Izzy, of course I don't, but I began to get a sense of my son as someone lacking a strong moral compass. That's a hard thing for me to admit, especially since he's not here. Drink was his trigger. He'd get loud and boisterous, argumentative sometimes. I remember once when he came to us for lunch. He brought me flowers, and of course he opened a bottle of wine, and then another. We ate, and he drank, and then he said he was driving back to London. Eamon tried to persuade him to stay the night and sleep it off, but he wouldn't have it. When he found out Eamon had hidden his car keys, he got angry.

'I can't tell you how that felt. Eamon gave him his keys,

and we were glad to see him go. Imagine that, being pleased to see your child leave. I didn't sleep that night, wondering if he'd got home safe, but I thought if the police hadn't been round to tell us there'd been an accident before dawn broke, then he'd got away with it.

'Happily, the police never came. He met Dolly shortly afterwards, and she seemed to calm him down. At least he'd listen to her when she said he shouldn't drive. Work hard, play hard, that became his mantra. They got married, and we thought it was going to be happy ever after, especially when Bailey came along. He was such a delightful child. I still send him a card for his birthday every year, to the last address we have for Dolly, even though I know there's little chance of it reaching him. You never know, maybe he knows we think of him and miss him.

'Time went by, and we began to have an inkling things weren't good in the marriage because we saw them less and less. We didn't know for sure, though, that things were going wrong until we had a call from Tris to say they were living apart for a while. Eamon took the call, and I heard him ask if it was to do with alcohol, and Tris said there'd been an accident.'

'What kind of accident?'

Steph sighs. 'An accident that may not even have been an accident, though he swears it was. Somehow he hit her in the face. He says he was messing about, and maybe he was, but he was drunk, of course, and that muddies the water. Regardless, he put Dolly in hospital, ruined her hearing and her career. They divorced not long after, and that was the last we ever saw of Dolly and little Bailey, who's grown into a man who doesn't know his grandma and grandpa. And do you know what my greatest fear is? That you'll do the same with Flora and remove her from our lives.'

Izzy touches Steph's hand.

'Never.'

Steph gives an appreciative smile. 'Thank you. Now we come to the good part of the story, and that's you. Soon after he first met you . . . Where did you two meet, anyway? I don't think I ever knew.'

Izzy smiles, remembering. 'I was trying on hats, at a vintage stall in Portobello market, and someone behind me said, *Not black, it isn't your colour*. That's the first thing he ever said to me. I turned round and there he was, and I was blown away. Tristan Hart, talking to me! I tried on a couple more hats and then he did the same, and he made me laugh. Then he asked if he could buy me coffee, and coffee became lunch. And that was it.'

'Love at first sight,' says Steph.

'I don't know about that. We both felt we had chemistry, I think.'

'For him it was. Let me tell you how I know. A few days after he met you, he came to see us and said he'd met someone very special. Eamon went to open a bottle of wine, and Tris turned it down. For him that was unheard of, but he said he'd given up, gone cold turkey, just like that. Of course we were delighted, but very dubious. His past history gave us no reason to hope he'd stick with it. We sat in the garden a while, drinking tea, and it was as if our golden boy was back with us, at long last. When Eamon went inside, Tris took my hand. He said how sorry he was for all he'd put us through, and he told me he was never drinking again because he was going to marry you. He knew what alcohol did to him, and he couldn't bear the thought of ever seeing anyone but his best self reflected in your eyes. Isn't that beautiful? Those were his very words. He changed for you, Izzy. You were his saviour, and you brought out everything that was good in him. You made him the son we always hoped he'd be, a son we could be really, truly proud of, not because he was a celebrity but because he was a good, kind, decent human being. You and Flora transformed him and let him shine. For that we are so, so grateful.' She takes Izzy's hands. 'With the refuge he was building, he was trying to make recompense, right his wrongs. He knew how close he'd come to being one of those men he despised, men who terrify the women they should love, men who beat women.'

'There but for the grace of God . . .'

'Exactly. He came to be a big believer in karma, and second chances. He said you were his second chance, and he wasn't going to mess it up.'

'Thank you for telling me,' says Izzy, 'but I wish he had told me himself.'

'I didn't agree with his decision to keep it secret, but he always said that if you knew his past, you would have thought less of him. You would have doubted him.'

'But I did doubt him. I doubted his fidelity, I doubted his love for me and Flora. I thought he was going to leave us.'

'You had every right to doubt him when you found out he was keeping secrets. But he kept them because he wanted nothing from his past to sully your and Flora's lives. Now you know his reasons, what will you do about the refuge?'

'I'll make sure it gets finished. I think that's what he'd want.'

'I know it is. If there's anything we can do to help, please let us know.'

'I will.'

'And please, let's still be family. We've lost one grandchild and a daughter-in-law. We'd be beside ourselves if we lost the pair of you too.'

Eamon is leading a giggling Flora back inside.

'There's no danger of that,' says Izzy. 'Flora loves you both, and she needs you to tell her who her father was. I want you both in our lives, for all our sakes. Especially Tris's.'

'Someone thinks we should have ice cream,' calls Eamon from the kitchen, and Flora calls out, 'Strawberry!'

'What the lady wants, the lady gets, as far as Grandpa's concerned,' says Steph. 'She wraps him round her little finger.'

'Isn't that what grandpas are for?' asks Izzy. 'And anyway, I think strawberry ice cream sounds like a brilliant idea.'

FIFTY-SEVEN

Gemma has been gone five days, and Laura has lost the ability to sleep. Every night, she lies down in the bed, closes her eyes and tries to empty her mind, to open the channels for sleep to take over. But it isn't sleep that fills her brain but images of Gemma: Gemma crying, Gemma being shouted at by people in uniforms, Gemma cold, distressed, unable to protect herself from the vicious acts of unspeakable bullies. Worst of all, she sees Gemma finding something to make a noose, hoisting herself out of harm's way.

When dawn comes and there's been no call to say anything bad has happened, Laura takes it as some kind of reassurance that Gemma might be OK, and falls into fractured sleep. Eventually – not caring about the time – she gets up and sits drinking coffee in an insomniac's haze, debating whether it's too early to add a small whisky to the cup, listening to the hateful silence of the house into which her children used to breathe life, wondering what they're both doing. Josh, at least, is safe with someone who loves him.

But Gemma is at the mercy of strangers.

How did it come to this?

*   *   *

Laura feels inclined to ignore the doorbell, being still in her dressing gown and wholly unfit for company. Aidan has gone to the bank, trying to raise by whatever means he can the funds to repay Tris's loan. If absolutely necessary, they'll borrow more against the house, but whatever route they take, the repayments are going to hurt. She and Aidan have agreed they'll share the pain, that once she's pulled herself together she'll go back to work. What's important is the gesture to Izzy, small recompense for the devastating blow Gemma's inflicted.

Whoever's come calling is persistent, and when the bell rings a second time, Laura wonders if the press have tracked them down. On the third ring, out of curiosity she wanders into the hall and opens the door a crack.

'Laura! I knew you must be here.'

'Hi, Philly.'

'Can I come in? Just for a moment. I'm sure you don't want visitors, but could you make this one exception? Only for a couple of minutes.'

Laura opens the door, and Philly steps into the hall. She's her usual chic self – white jeans, blue linen shirt and those Italian slides Laura used to love, in the now-gone days when she cared about such things – and she's carrying a wicker basket.

Philly closes the door behind herself and touches Laura's arm.

'How are you? I absolutely cannot imagine, I cannot imagine . . . Don't bother putting the kettle on, I shan't stay. Jerry and I just didn't know what to do – I mean, what could we possibly do? But we wanted to make a gesture. It's only a small thing, a silly thing, really, but I thought it couldn't hurt.'

Reaching into the basket, she lifts a cloth to show Laura what's inside.

'I made you a cake. No matter how bad things get, we can always eat cake, and you have to keep your strength up. That girl needs you more now than she's ever done.'

'Oh, Philly.'

Philly puts down her basket and enfolds Laura in her arms, offering the comfort of a motherly embrace.

'No tears,' says Philly. 'I'm not good with tears. But promise me you won't make any hasty decisions. Sterndale is your home, Laura, and we want you to stay. Now's not a time to be running away to be among strangers, is it?'

'Everything's such a mess,' says Laura. She pulls away from Philly and wipes away tears with her dressing gown sleeve. 'Everyone hates us.'

'I know things look black, of course they do. And at a time like this, you'll be needing a drinking companion, and here I am. I don't mind what we drink – tea, or coffee, or my strong preference would be for gin – but whenever you're ready, you know you can give me a ring. We don't all hate you, Laura. I don't hate you. You're my friend.'

That evening, Philly pours gin and tonics with ice and a slice of lime, handing one to Jerry as she sits down next to him on the sofa.

Jerry doesn't like to be interrupted while he's reading, and he's near the end of a Ken Follett novel of 1940s espionage. But Philly's feeling lonely, needing companionship that's more than physical proximity.

'I went to see Laura earlier on.'

Jerry glances up from his book, but his eyes go straight back to the page. 'Mmmm?'

'She was in a terrible state, so distraught, but who wouldn't be? I didn't stay long. I just left her the cake.'

Jerry looks across at her. 'What cake?'

'I made her a coffee and walnut cake. For God's sake, Jerry, you saw me take it out of the oven. We had a conversation about it then.'

'Slipped my mind. Cheers.'

The crystal tumblers ring as they touch them together.

'I hope they stay here. Sterndale can be cruel, but it can be kind, too. I'm afraid what Gemma's done might wreck their lives, and I think it's up to all of us to try and save them.'

Jerry puts down his book and squeezes her hand.

'You can't save everyone, old thing.'

'She'll be in prison a long time, won't she? She'll be an adult woman when she comes out.'

'I suppose she will.'

'It's such a terrible shame, isn't it? Just when she should have been starting out. One rash moment, and it's all finished.'

'People get through things, Philly. They always have done. Wounds heal, and all that. Look at us.'

Philly looks at him. 'Are we healed, Jerry?'

Jerry gives her hand another squeeze. 'We're getting there, old thing. Now, can you stop interrupting while I get on with my book? I've only a few pages left to go.'

FIFTY-EIGHT

On the kind of day when – if life were still normal – the Ridley family would have packed a bag and headed for the nearest beach to dip toes in the sea and eat waffles on the pier, Laura, Aidan and Josh are going against the flow, driving east, inland.

Josh is silent in the back, playing on the new phone he's been bought so they can keep in touch more easily when he's spending time at Grandma's. Fifteen miles in, Laura has given up attempts at bright conversation or proposals for coffee stops and lunchbreaks. The reason for their journey hangs over them like a miasma, and Aidan drives in silence, responding with a shake of the head when she asks whether he's thirsty or wants the radio on. If Josh weren't there, she'd challenge him, because his depression is making the difficult much harder, as if he's punishing her for something she hasn't done.

The satnav counts down the miles, laying out the road to a small Derbyshire town Laura had never heard of, before this. She's expecting somewhere pretty like Sterndale, but when they reach their destination, they find instead an ex-mining town struggling to drag itself from the mire of the post-in-dustrial slump.

They turn into a suburban road of detached houses and bungalows.

'This can't be right, can it?' asks Laura, and she sees from Aidan's frown he's wondering the same.

The road winds, and begins to look as if it's reaching its end. Passing the last of the houses, they make a sharp turn to the left.

The secure unit is there, intimidating and formidable, fenced well above head height in dense green metal.

Whatever Laura was picturing, it wasn't this. The unit's website shows pictures of recreational areas and classrooms, makes promises of education and opportunities and sympathetic rehabilitation.

But this is no school. Unmistakably, this is a prison.

Aidan glances across at Laura, knowing she'll be shocked. He parks the car, and when the engine stops, takes her hand.

Laura's staring through the windscreen at the solid fortress wall.

'Is she really in there?' she whispers. 'Is this where they've been keeping her?'

Aidan nods.

'Is this where they'll always keep her, somewhere like this?'

Aidan nods again, and Laura turns to him, closes her eyes and lowers her head on to his shoulder.

'How will she bear it? How will we bear it?' she asks, and the easy tears begin to fall.

Aidan puts his arm around her shoulder.

'She will. We all will. We don't have any choice.'

'I don't know what to say to her. What can we possibly say?'

'That we still love her and we'll stand by her, that we'll always be there for her. Because we have to be there for her. Time will go by, you know, and she'll survive. We've all got to keep looking forward, to the day that she comes home.'

EPILOGUE

Three weeks before Christmas, Eamon picks up the mail from the mat by the front door, and as he sorts through the bills and the catalogues, finds a card with unknown handwriting and a US postmark.

'Do we know anyone in America?' he asks, as Steph opens the flap.

The note inside the card begins *Dear Grandma and Grandpa.* There's news of a job in Albany, New York and a serious girlfriend, a phone number, an email address and a WhatsApp handle.

> *I'm coming back to the UK for Christmas, and I was wondering if you'd like to meet up. No pressure – I know it's been a long time – but I'd love to see you and for Mallory to meet you.*
>
> *Hope to hear from you.*
> *Love,*
> *Your grandson Bailey*

Steph reads the note twice, and hands it to Eamon.

'We won't recognise him,' she says. 'And he'll think we've got so old.'

'That doesn't matter,' says Eamon. 'He wants to see us, and that's the best Christmas present we could have.'

The party at Fairview – on the first anniversary of Tristan's death – is a modest gathering: no press, no publicity. Izzy and Flora are there, along with Steph and Eamon, Martina, Rachel who will manage the place, a trio of local councillors and four women and their children who will be the first to move in.

The toasts are made in sparkling elderflower cordial, and there are balloons and a bouncy castle for the kids.

The plaque outside the front door is simply engraved with Tristan's name, and the years of his birth and death.

Rachel leads a tour of the facilities: a communal lounge, laundry and kitchen; large, airy family bedrooms; a garden with swings and a climbing frame, and a summer house designated as a quiet space. The garden is surrounded by a high fence, and there are iron gates across the driveway, with keypad entry.

Fairview is safe and secure.

In the breeze, Flora's unicorn balloon bobs above her head as she proudly holds the string. Izzy's getting ready to leave, and Martina comes to say goodbye.

'We couldn't have done it without your help,' she says. 'If you'd pulled the plug, I'd have understood. I know we're not your problem.'

'Tris might have been part of the problem, though, and he knew it.'

'You turned him from that path, Izzy. He wanted to be a

better man for your sake. He loved you and Flora so much, and this is his legacy, a place of healing, a springboard for moving on. You should be very proud of him.'

'I am.'

'You won't be a stranger, will you?'

'We'll come whenever we can. Thanks for all you're doing too.'

'My absolute pleasure,' says Martina, and she gives Izzy a hug.

At home, Izzy finds Flora in the garden, trying to tie a piece of paper to the string of her balloon.

'I drew a picture for Daddy,' says Flora. 'I drew flowers and me and you, so he'll know it's from us. Can you help me tie it on tight?'

Izzy secures the knot, and holds Flora's hand as she leads them to the centre of the lawn.

Flora looks up into the summer-blue sky.

'It's very high up there,' she says. 'Do you think it will find him?'

'I know it will,' says Izzy.

Flora lets go of the string. The unicorn balloon floats up and up, shimmering and turning as it rises over the garden, then beyond the treetops and away.

In silence, Izzy and Flora watch, until the speck the balloon has become vanishes from sight.

Foxcote Lodge is sold.

In the empty bedroom, Izzy's vain hope is that she'll find a last, faint whisper of Tris. Everything that was part of his life with her – his clothes, his razor and cologne, his favourite books, the bed they used to share – is gone, and the van has driven away, taking only Izzy and Flora's things to their new home.

She'll be sad to leave. They had such happy times.

Standing at the window she looks out, remembering the last time that he was here, how he brought her flowers, and kissed her neck. She misses him so badly.

It's time to hand over the keys. Outside, she locks the door for the last time, and rests her hand a moment on the planks of the old door, saying goodbye.

At her feet, the forget-me-nots are blooming. As she bends to pick a sprig for a memento, a white butterfly settles by her hand.

ACKNOWLEDGEMENTS

My grateful thanks to everyone who's played a part in bringing this book into the light: my insightful, inspiring editor, Toby Jones; my always-supportive agent, Christopher Little, alongside Emma and Jules; ex-Det Sgt Terry Parry, who'll answer any police procedural question, even from half-way up a mountain; Ken Fishwick, whose forensic eye for a glitch in the narrative is second to none; my early readers, Lorraine, Phil and Vivienne; and always for Andy's unwavering faith.

Thank you all.

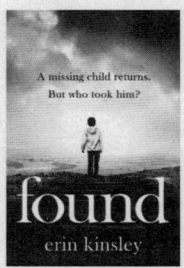